EVERY
LAST
FEAR

EVERY LAST FEAR

ALEX FINLAY

St. Martin's Paperbacks

This is a work of fiction. All of the characters, organizations, and events portrayed in this novel are either products of the author's imagination or are used fictitiously.

Published in the United States by St. Martin's Paperbacks, an imprint of St. Martin's Publishing Group.

EVERY LAST FEAR

Copyright © 2021 by Alex Finlay.
Excerpt from *The Night Shift* copyright © 2021 by Alex Finlay.

All rights reserved.

For information, address St. Martin's Publishing Group, 120 Broadway, New York, NY 10271.

www.stmartins.com

Library of Congress Catalog Card Number: 2020042042

ISBN: 978-1-250-81712-9

Our books may be purchased in bulk for promotional, educational, or business use. Please contact your local bookseller or the Macmillan Corporate and Premium Sales Department at 1-800-221-7945, ext. 5442, or by email at MacmillanSpecialMarkets@macmillan.com.

Printed in the United States of America

Minotaur hardcover edition published 2021
St. Martin's Paperbacks edition / December 2021

10 9 8 7 6 5 4 3 2 1

PROLOGUE

They found the bodies on a Tuesday. Two days after the family had missed their flight home. Six days after all texts and social media had gone dark. The last post was a selfie saying they'd arrived in Mexico: the dad and mom making exaggerated duck faces, the teenage girl pink-cheeked and mortified, the little boy wearing plastic sunglasses and a gap-toothed smile.

The rental wasn't beachfront. It was off the beaten path, a small structure at the end of an unpaved alleyway, carved into a patch of roadside jungle in Tulum. The smell hit the local cop in the face when the property manager opened the front door. The maid hired to clean up after departing guests was sitting on the cement stoop, her hands working a string of rosary beads, her face streaked with tears.

The place was sweltering.

And filled with the buzz of flies.

But for all the decay in the air, there was no blood.

No obvious signs of foul play. That's when the cop knew he needed to get out of there.

Within the hour, men in white hazmat suits trudged through the property, eyes fixed on handheld air sensors. They found the mother lying on the couch, frozen, a paperback tented on her chest. In the bedroom, the girl was on top of the made bed, her cell phone still clutched in her hand. The boy was tucked in tight, peacefully, stuffed bear at his side.

The team inspected the stove and the water heater.

Then they drifted morosely out the patio doors to check the exterior gas line. That's when they found the trail of blood. And the father—at least what was left of him.

CHAPTER 1

MATT PINE

"Rough night? You look like you slept out here with us."

Matt studied the chessboard, ignoring the weathered black man sitting across from him at the battered table in Washington Square Park.

"Ain't you cold? Where's your coat?"

"Shush, Reggie," Matt said, waving the questions away with a hand. "I'm trying to concentrate." He continued to plot his move on the board. A cool morning breeze pushed through the park, and Matt rubbed his hands together from the chill. It was *way* too cold for April.

Reggie made a sound of amusement in his throat. "Take all day. Ain't gonna matter."

In two years Matt hadn't won a single game against the West Village's homeless Bobby Fischer. Matt wondered sometimes what had brought the highly intelligent man to the streets, but he never asked. He moved his bishop, capturing the pawn on g7.

Reggie shook his head, as if disappointed in him.

Eyes on the board, Reggie said, "What, you just getting back from a party or something?"

"Yeah, over at Goddard." Matt directed his head to Goddard Hall, a washed-brown brick tower just off the park.

"Goddard? Hangin' with the freshman girls," Reggie said with a gravelly laugh. He knew more about NYU than most grad students. Maybe that was it; maybe he'd once attended the university.

It was odd because people usually confided in Matt, told them their life stories, their secrets, their problems. He guessed he just had that kind of face. Or maybe it was because he preferred listening, observing, over talking. And boy, could Reggie talk. Yet despite his incessant chatter, Reggie offered no clues about his life before the park. Matt had looked for signs of the backstory. The man kept a green military-looking bag; maybe he'd been a soldier. His hands and nails were always impeccably clean; maybe he'd worked in the medical field. His street talk at times seemed genuine, at times forced. Maybe he was hiding his real identity, on the run, a criminal. Or maybe he was just a guy who'd hit hard times, loved to play chess, and didn't feel the need to justify his life to an annoying college kid.

"My man. Out all night with the coeds." Reggie chuckled again. "How's that pretty redhead of yours feel about that?"

A fair question. But that pretty redhead had broken up with Matt yesterday. Hence too many drinks at Purple Haze. Hence the after-party at Goddard and the frolic upstairs with Deena (or was it Dana?). Hence 7:00 A.M.

in the park with bed head and no way to get back into the dorm—his security card, room key, and phone in the pocket of his missing coat.

Reggie moved his rook to g8, then gave a satisfied yellow smile. "I'm startin' to wonder how you got admitted into that fine institution." Reggie gazed at the admissions building, the purple NYU flag flapping in the wind.

"Now you're starting to sound like my father," Matt said, moving his own rook to e1. His eyes lifted to Reggie's. "Check."

Reggie moved his king to d8, but it was too late.

Queen to g3. Checkmate was inevitable.

"Mother . . ." Reggie said. He called out to a player at one of the other tables. "Yo, Elijah, check this out. Affleck gone and beat me." Reggie always called Matt "Ben Affleck"—his derogatory shorthand for "white boy."

"Beware the quiet man," Reggie said, in a tone like a preacher, quoting from something Matt didn't recognize. "For while others speak, he watches. And while others act, he plans. And when they finally rest, he strikes."

Reggie dropped a wadded bill onto the table.

"I'm not taking your money." Matt stood, cracked his back.

"Hell you ain't," Reggie said, flicking the bill toward Matt. "You're a film student—you're gonna need it." He cackled.

Matt reluctantly scooped up the money. He looked up at the dark clouds rolling into the city. He loved the smell of an imminent rain. "At least let me get you breakfast at the dining hall. I've got some meal swipes left."

"Nah," Reggie said. "They didn't seem so happy last time. . . ."

Reggie was right. Limousine liberalism had its limits, as Matt had learned from his time with the privileged student body of New York University. He was an oddity to most of his classmates, an apolitical Midwesterner.

"Fuck 'em," Matt said, gesturing for Reggie to join him, when he heard a familiar voice from behind.

"There you are. We've been looking everywhere for you."

Matt turned and saw the resident assistant from his dorm. Why would the RA be looking for him? Phillip usually appeared only if the music was too loud or the halls smelled like weed.

"There are federal agents at the dorm," Phillip said, concern in his voice. "They want to talk with you."

"Agents?"

"Yeah, the FBI showed up at six this morning. They said you're not answering your phone."

"What do they want?" Matt asked. It was probably about his older brother. Ever since that fucking documentary, everything was about Danny.

"I don't know. But if you're doing something out of the dorm you shouldn't, I don't—"

"Relax, man. I'm not—" Matt paused, took a breath. "Thanks for letting me know. I'll go see what they want."

Phillip let out an exasperated sigh and sauntered off.

"You in some trouble?" Reggie asked.

"I guess I'd better go find out. Rain check on break-fast?"

Reggie nodded. "Be careful, Affleck. Nothing good ever came of federal agents knocking on your door at six in the mornin'."

A half hour later Matt sat on his small dorm bed, the room spinning.

The lead FBI agent—Matt couldn't remember her name—was talking again, but it was just a jumble of words. When Matt didn't respond, the agent knelt in front of him, a concerned look on her face. Her partner, a lean guy in a dark suit, hovered in the background, shifting on his feet.

"I spoke with the dean," the agent was saying, "and they've arranged for a grief counselor. And you don't have to worry about your classes."

Matt tried to stand, but his legs buckled, blood rush-ing to his head. The agent guided him back to the bed.

"All of them?" Matt said. She'd told him twice al-ready, but he didn't believe it.

"I'm so sorry."

Mom.

Dad.

Maggie.

Tommy.

He stood again, said something, then tripped to the bathroom. He dropped to his knees and emptied his guts into the toilet. He hugged the dirty bowl, unsure how long he was there.

At some point he heard a soft tap on the door.

"I'll be out in a minute," he managed. Gripping the sink, he tugged himself up. He turned on the faucet and splashed water on his face, then glanced at his reflection in the mirror. He looked like he felt.

Back in the room, the female agent was alone, her partner having cleared out.

"How could something like this happen?" Matt asked, the sound of his voice strange to him, hoarse and distant.

"They think it's a freak accident, a gas leak. But that's what we're trying to get to the bottom of. Both the Bureau and State Department are working on it. We've reached out to the Mexican authorities. I know this is the worst possible time, but I need to ask you a few questions."

Matt sat down again, nodded for her to continue.

"We understand they were on vacation."

"Uh-huh, spring break for my little sister and brother." The words caught in his throat. "They decided to go at the last minute. My break didn't match up, so I couldn't . . ." He stopped, fighting back tears.

"When's the last time you heard from them?"

Matt thought about this. "My mom sent a text from the airport the day they left. Maggie sent one a few days ago." He felt a stab of guilt. He hadn't read, much less responded to, his little sister's text.

"How about your father?"

He shook his head, every part of him numb. They hadn't spoken since their fight over Christmas break. His heart sank. The last thing Matt had said to him—

"For the timeline—to help us understand things—

it's important that we see those texts. If you don't mind?"

"Yeah, sure. But my phone, it's in my coat, which I left somewhere last night."

"Do you know where?" the agent asked. She was sympathetic, but Matt could tell she was getting impatient.

"I think it's at the bar." He'd grabbed the tiny mountain of his clothes before slinking out of the girl's dorm, so it had to be the bar.

The agent nodded. "I can take you there."

"I don't think they'll be open this early."

"What's it called?"

"Purple Haze, on East Thirteenth."

The agent pulled out her phone and walked to the far end of the room. She looked out the rain-speckled window, murmuring commands to someone. "I don't care. Just tell them to get somebody there now," she said, making her way back over to Matt.

"You up to going to the bar with me?" The agent took a few steps toward the door.

Trancelike, Matt nodded.

"You want to get a jacket or umbrella? It's raining."

Matt shook his head and followed her out.

A small crowd had gathered in the hallway, gawking students. Matt didn't know if word had spread about his family or if they thought he was being arrested for something.

The agent—he still couldn't conjure her name—pushed ahead to the elevator. Inside, Matt said, "Has the media got this yet?"

The agent gave him a knowing look. "It hit the wire, but they haven't released your last name. They wait a little while to allow time to notify the family."

"You know what's gonna happen when they find out, right?" Matt shook his head in disgust. *That goddamn Netflix documentary.*

The agent nodded.

The elevator doors spread open and they were met by a mob of reporters and blinding camera flashes.

CHAPTER 2

The ride to the bar was a blur. Matt sat in the back seat in the stop-and-go traffic of Greenwich Village feeling punch-drunk from the news and from the paparazzi hurling questions at him: *Why weren't you in Mexico with your family? How do you feel? Do you think it was really an accident? Does your brother know?*

The agent had just plowed through the crowd, grabbing Matt's wrist and dragging him in her wake. When a guy with a camera stepped in front of them on the way to the car, she'd calmly flashed her badge and looked him up and down. He'd cowered away. New York paparazzi weren't timid souls, so the guy must have sensed that she wasn't one to trifle with.

Now, Matt stared out the window, the wet road smeared with red taillights. His thoughts skipped again to the reporters. *Does your brother know?*

Danny had no television, internet, or phone, of course. But Matt's dad always said that news—particularly bad news—had a way of penetrating prison walls at light speed. And with Danny's celebrity status from the documentary, he'd hear soon enough.

The car pulled in front of Purple Haze. The place looked grimier in the daylight, the roll-up metal security doors covered in graffiti. Trash bags puddled with rainwater piled on the sidewalk. A man in a tracksuit was bouncing on his feet under the awning. He peered into the car like he was expecting them, and walked over.

"You with the Feds?" he said, stooping so he could see inside the car. He was heavyset and balding. Sweat beaded on his forehead, even in the chill.

"Special Agent Keller," she said, all business. Matt finally had a name.

"I got a call about a problem at the club," the man said in a Brooklyn accent. "We run a clean operation, so I don't—"

"I don't care what kind of operation you run," Keller said. There were no niceties. No bedside manner. Keller gestured to Matt in the back seat. "He left his coat in there last night. His phone's in the pocket. We need you to let us inside."

The club owner hesitated. Bunched his lips. "Well, you, ah, got a warrant?"

Keller glowered at him. "You really want me to get one? I might have to come back with a team of agents at, say, eleven tonight. Who knows what we'll find."

The owner held up his hands in retreat. "Look, I'd get his stuff if it was there," he said. "But my bouncer, I let him take whatever's left behind after closing."

"Wonderful," Agent Keller said, letting out a breath. "I need his name and address."

"I'm not sure I have—"

"Name and address, or I'm back to us having a problem."

"All right, all right. Give me a minute."

Agent Keller nodded, and the owner disappeared inside. He returned with a Post-it note scrawled with the information. Keller plucked it from his hand, then lurched from the curb.

Twenty minutes later they were in front of a towering glass building in Tribeca. Keller turned into the mouth of a garage and stopped at a checkpoint. A guard examined her credentials then waved her inside.

"The bouncer lives here?" Matt asked as they circled down the basement lot. It was a high-end building in a high-end neighborhood, not somewhere you'd expect club muscle to live.

"No. I sent some agents to track him down."

"So what's here?"

Keller pulled the car into a spot next to a line of identical dark sedans. "Someone needs to tell your brother."

"Wait, what?" Matt said. He tried to unpack what she was saying. Then: "No."

There was a long pause while Keller searched his eyes. "I know this is a lot," she said. "And I can't pretend to know what you're going through. But I spoke to your aunt and she said your parents would've wanted it to come from you."

The hair on Matt's arms rose.

"He's *here*?" Matt asked, knowing that didn't make sense.

"Not quite. We need to head up to the roof."

The first helicopter ride of Matt's life and he couldn't tell if the floating in his gut was from being airborne or the surrealness of the day. The water of the Hudson was choppy, the sky a dreary gray. Agent Keller sat next to him with her back straight, her face expressionless.

She wasn't chatty. And not one to multitask. There was no staring at her phone, no reading the newspaper. Her job was to escort him to Fishkill Correctional upstate, and that's what she did. Matt never understood why Danny, convicted of killing his girlfriend in Nebraska, was incarcerated in New York. It was his third prison in seven years.

When the chopper hit a patch of rough air, Matt thought about Tommy. On family trips, while everyone else was white-knuckled gripping the airplane armrest with even the slightest bit of turbulence, his little brother would giggle with delight. Not an ounce of fear. He would've loved this ride.

Matt swallowed a sob, picturing Tommy on the plane to Mexico with no idea it would be the last flight of his life.

The helicopter touched down at a small airfield in a rural area. Matt removed his seat harness and headset and followed Agent Keller out. The propellers whirled, and he ducked down in a reflexive action he'd seen a million times in the movies. Keller walked upright.

She spoke to a man in a stiff suit next to a black SUV

waiting for them at the edge of the tarmac. It wasn't her partner from earlier, but they looked similar. Dark suit, sunglasses, blank expression. Neo from *The Matrix*. Keller and Matt climbed in back, and the vehicle made its way along country roads until the cement fortress came into view.

By now Matt's palms were sweating, his head pounding. The reality was sinking in.

They're really gone.

And soon he'd have to take away almost everything that his older brother had left in this world.

CHAPTER 3

EVAN PINE

BEFORE

"Evan, I'm so glad you made it." Dr. Silverstein gestured for him to take a seat across from her on the leather couch.

Evan's eyes drifted around the office. The framed diplomas, the neat desk, the grandfather clock that was out of place in the charmless no-frills office complex.

"I'm sorry I didn't call last week," Evan said. "You can charge me for missing our—"

"Don't be silly. I saw the news about your son on TV. I'm so sorry, Evan."

She kept saying his name. A trick of the trade, he presumed. He imagined a much younger Dr. Silverstein diligently taking notes in her psychology class. *Repeat the patient's name often to show you're listening.*

He shouldn't be so hard on her. She was a good therapist. And it must be difficult counseling someone who was attending sessions only because of a spouse's ultimatum.

"So what's next?" she asked. "Legally, I mean. For Danny."

Evan didn't want to talk about it, but there would be no escaping it here. "The lawyers say this is the end of the road. The Supreme Court refused to hear the case, so that's it." He shrugged.

Silverstein gave him a sympathetic look. "And how's Danny? Did you get to talk to him?"

Evan thought of the call when he broke the news. He pictured his son's face pressed to the dirty telephone at Fishkill, knowing he'd probably spend the rest of his life there, or some other godforsaken hole.

"He took it better than I'd anticipated. He actually spent most of our call talking about Linkin Park."

Dr. Silverstein's expression was curious. Evan realized she had no idea what he was talking about.

"They're a band. The day I called Danny about the appeal, the radio said it would've been the singer's birthday. He died a few years ago. Danny and I, we used to . . ." He trailed off. His mind ventured to the two of them driving home from football practice, Danny, smelly and sweaty, cranking up the car stereo, both of them belting out the lyrics to "Numb."

"Something the two of you used to bond over?" Silverstein said. "The music . . ."

Evan smiled in spite of himself. "In high school Danny was obsessed with the band. I never understood why. Their songs are so rage-filled. Songs about teen angst, wrecked father-and-son relationships—the opposite of me and Danny." More fitting for Evan and Matt.

"How's the rest of your family dealing with the news? Olivia?" Before Evan started his solo sessions last year, the Pine clan used to trek out to this very office every other Saturday for family therapy, so Silverstein knew them and their brand of dysfunction well.

"Liv?" Evan said. "I think she's come to terms that Danny isn't getting out."

"And how does that make you feel?"

It used to make him angry. Enraged. But now he was jealous—jealous that his wife didn't spend every waking moment feeling like she'd been thrown into Lake Michigan with cinder blocks anchored to her limbs. Evan had once read about dry drowning, a person slowly dying hours or even days after leaving the water. That's how he'd felt for the past seven years, oxygen slowly being stolen from his damaged insides. "I understand. We all had to find ways to deal with it."

Dr. Silverstein seemed to see right through his forced reasonableness. But she'd prodded enough for now.

"And how about the rest of your kids?"

"Maggie's hanging in there." He smiled, thinking of his daughter. "She's busy wrapping up her senior year, so that helps. But she's always been my trouper—she believes that her big brother will get out, regardless of what the Supreme Court says."

Dr. Silverstein offered a sad smile.

Evan continued. "Tommy, well, he's just too young to understand. And Liv shelters him from it all." Shortly after Danny's arrest, Liv learned she was pregnant—having a baby at "advanced maternal age," as the doctor diplomatically put it. Unplanned and with the worst timing in the world, but somehow the pregnancy and that little boy saved them, especially Liv.

Silverstein waited a long moment. Another psychologist trick. *Let the patient fill the silence.*

When Evan didn't bite, Silverstein finally asked: "And Matthew?"

Evan looked at the floor. "We still haven't talked."

"So it's been what, four months?" Her tone was matter-of-fact, not judgmental.

Evan nodded, folded his arms. He didn't want to elaborate, and was surprised when Dr. Silverstein didn't push it.

She looked at Evan thoughtfully. "Sometimes," she said, "after a traumatic event—and in its own way I think this court decision was its own trauma—it can be good for a family to reset. To spend time away from your usual surroundings. Have fun, even."

"You mean like a vacation?" Evan said, trying to hide the *what the fuck* tone in his voice.

"Maybe. Or just some time away together. As a family."

"I'd love to, but we really can't do it—financially, I mean." He blew out a breath, deciding he might as well get his money's worth for the session. "They let me go."

"Who?" Silverstein said, her voice concerned. "You mean your job?"

"Yep. Twenty-five years, and *poof.*" He made an explosion gesture with his hands.

"What happened?" Dr. Silverstein's eyes flicked to the grandfather clock, like she was worried she'd need more time now.

"The inevitable."

"What do you mean by that, Evan?" She was leaning forward in her chair, fingers laced, full eye contact.

"I mean, I don't blame them. It's a big accounting firm, and my billable hours have been terrible, particularly since I transferred to the Chicago office. I lost my main client six months ago. And let's face it: the show."

"You mean the documentary?"

Evan tried not to lose his patience, but what other show could it possibly be? The reason anyone knew or cared about Danny Pine. The reason the Supreme Court's refusal to review Danny's life sentence made national news. The reason Evan had tricked himself into thinking his son would come home after seven long years. The pop-culture phenom *A Violent Nature.*

"Yeah," Evan said, "you've seen it, right?"

"I've seen it, yes."

"Well, you know then."

"I'm not sure what you mean."

"I came off like a lunatic."

"No."

Evan gave her a disappointed look.

"I think you came off like a father devastated about his son being wrongfully imprisoned for murder."

"And a lunatic."

She didn't answer. But she agreed. He could see it in her eyes.

She mercifully stayed away from the questions that had haunted him for the past week. *What are you going to do for money? How will you pay the mortgage? Maggie's tuition?*

"Are you okay?"

Evan sat back, exhaled loudly. "It's funny, when I got the call that the court denied Danny's appeal, I was listening to a Linkin Park song—one released shortly before the singer died. Over the years, his songs had become less angry, more melancholy." Evan swallowed over the lump in his throat. He could feel Dr. Silverstein scrutinizing him. "The song said something about no one caring if a single star burned out in a sky of a million stars."

Silverstein narrowed her eyes. "The singer of this band," she said, "how did he die?"

"Suicide," Evan said. The word hung in the air.

"Evan," Silverstein finally said, her voice serious, "are you—"

"Of course not."

Dr. Silverstein leaned in closer. "The medications you're on," she said, her tone softer, "in some people they can cause intrusive thoughts."

"Don't forget the fatigue, sexual problems, and insomnia—all really helpful for someone who's already depressed."

Dr. Silverstein bunched up her face. "I appreciate the humor, but I'm being serious. The medications can cause suicidal thoughts. The meds can trick a patient into thinking there's only one solution."

Or maybe they cause the patient to finally see the truth.

"You've got nothing to worry about, Dr. Silverstein," Evan said. "I'm fine."

By her expression, Evan could tell she didn't believe him.

Like he said, she was a good therapist.

Excerpt from
A Violent Nature

Season 1/Episode 1
"A Body at the Creek"

OVER BLACK - 9-1-1 RECORDING

                    OPERATOR
    9-1-1 operator, what's your emergency?

                    CALLER
                (breathing heavily)
    I'm at Stone Creek, walking my dog. And
    there's a body—I, I, I think it's a girl.

A dog barks in the background. It sounds
terrified.

                    CALLER
    You need to get someone here right away.

                    OPERATOR
    Slow down, sir. You say there's a body of
    a girl? Is she breathing?

                    CALLER
    No, her head, there's so much blood . . .
    dear god . . .

INSERT - LOCAL NEWS FOOTAGE

                    ANCHOR
There's been a big break tonight in the
murder of Charlotte Rose. The Adair teenager was last seen at a house party and
found bludgeoned to death at Stone Creek.
Our sources say there's been an arrest
tonight, the victim's boyfriend, Daniel
Pine. . . .

INT. STUDIO
SUPERIMPOSED:

"Louise Lester, Institute for Wrongful
Convictions"

                    LESTER
At first, I was skeptical, I mean, the
Institute gets thousands of requests for
help from prisoners claiming to be innocent. And this one came from the inmate's
twelve-year-old sister. But then we examined the trial record.

Lester shakes her head in disgust.

The prosecution's theory was that Danny
and Charlotte were at a house party and
Charlotte told him she was pregnant and
they had a fight. Danny then got really
drunk and sometime after the party the two
of them got into it again, and he pushed

her and she fell, suffering a fatal head
trauma. Danny then panicked and moved her
body to the creek in a wheelbarrow, and
smashed her skull in with a large rock, a
big bloody mess. But there was no blood on
his clothes, no DNA, no physical evidence
of any kind. Not one trace. Does that
sound like the work of a staggering drunk
teenager? And then we found out that the
prosecutor had withheld exculpatory evidence from the defense. . . .

CHAPTER 4

MATT PINE

The cinder-block room in the prison smelled of bleach. Matt studied Agent Keller, who sat quietly across from him. She was a woman of few words. But she exuded a confidence that was comforting. Even in a maximum-security prison amid murderers, rapists, and the worst society had to offer—with the faint howls of those damned souls just outside the door—she was calm and composed.

"Taking a while," Matt said, just to break the silence. They'd been in the room a good half hour.

Keller nodded.

"I haven't seen him since we were kids," Matt continued, nervous talking. He'd never visited Danny in prison. Dad always said that Danny wanted it that way. His brother refused to let his siblings see him locked up like an animal.

So Danny was frozen in time in Matt's mind. The archetype of a small-town football star. Danny was no Tom Brady, but in Adair, Nebraska—where Friday-night lights were second only to the enclaves of Texas—his brother had been a big deal.

"How old were you when he went away?" Keller asked, as if fighting a disdain for small talk.

"Fourteen."

Another nod. "Were you close? I mean, before . . ."

"Yeah," Matt lied. When they were small, they used to play together for hours, building forts, climbing trees, playing LEGOs, but when Danny made it to high school and became a local celebrity, Matt was no longer part of his universe. Plus, the relationship between his father and Danny sucked out all the air from the room. His father just didn't see Matt.

Then beautiful Charlotte was murdered. Last seen at a high school house party, she'd been bludgeoned to death somewhere unknown, her body dumped by the creek near their house. Police found blood in a wheelbarrow hidden in the overgrown shrubs along the path that crossed the Pines' property. No one ever understood why Charlotte's body had been moved. Or why her skull had been crushed with a huge rock postmortem. They'd been sure of only one thing: the perpetrator was her boyfriend, Danny Pine.

From that point on, nothing was the same. It was Year Zero for the Pines. There was before Charlotte, and after. Now Matt had a new Year Zero.

"So you haven't seen him since . . ." Keller didn't finish the sentence.

"My parents kept us away from the trial. We've talked on the phone, but yeah."

The last time Matt had seen Danny free was the night

Charlotte was killed. That night had otherwise been momentous for Matt. Jessica Wheeler had asked him to sneak out to meet her. It was before he'd had a phone, and she'd slipped him a note in ninth-grade science class, the culmination of weeks of flirting. Jessica had folded the note in a square and tied it with a red string, like a miniature package. Matt remembered pulling at the bow, his heart fluttering as he read the note.

MEET ME AT THE KNOLL AT 3 A.M. TONIGHT?
YES OR NO
CIRCLE ONE

The Knoll was a famous make-out spot at the top of a secluded hill near the creek. A place for stargazing and bad decisions. He of course circled *yes*. And he'd been shocked that she was actually there: holding a flashlight, wearing her pj's and slippers. On their backs in the cold grass, they stared at the stars dotting the ink-black sky, the clouds blowing past the moon.

"This reminds me of the stargazing scene from A Walk to Remember," Matt said. "You ever see that movie?"

She shook her head.

"It's old and not very good. Not many Nicholas Sparks adaptations are. But the scene was solid."

"Have you always loved movies so much? I mean, like, you always compare things to stuff in movies."

Matt smiled. "Sorry. It drives my family crazy."

"I think it's cute."

"I want to make movies one day. NYU has this amazing film school. My grandpa, before he got sick, he said that movies are the poetry of our time."

She turned and faced him.

"Nicholas Sparks . . . You ever see The Notebook*?"*

"Of course. The critics hated it, but it's a cult classic. The kissing in the rain scene is considered—"

Jessica put a finger over his lips. She removed it, and her mouth softly touched his. It put Ryan Gosling and Rachel McAdams to shame.

Matt touched his lips involuntarily, remembering the electricity slicing through every part of him, when the door jutted open.

"Matty?"

Matt stood, taken aback at the prisoner before him. The teenage football star was a grown man. He still had the good looks, the blond hair, the square jaw. But Matt saw a hardness in his brother's once clear blue eyes. And by Danny's steely gaze, he obviously wasn't happy to see Matt.

"What are you doing here?" Danny said. "I told Dad that I didn't want—" Danny stopped, eyed Keller. "Who are you?"

Matt said, "Why don't you sit down."

When Danny didn't take the seat, the guard pulled

out a chair. "Sit down, Dan," he said. It was stern but had an undercurrent of concern, as if the guard knew what was coming.

Danny sat, his eyes locked on Matt's.

Keller said, "Let's give them a moment."

The guard seemed to welcome the opportunity to escape the room. Yeah, he definitely knew what was coming.

"What the hell's going on, Matty?"

Matt swallowed, fighting the welling in his eyes, the fist in his throat. "There's been an accident."

"Accident?" Danny said. "What accident? What are you—"

"Dad and Mom. Maggie and Tommy. They were in Mexico for spring break. They're gone, Danny."

"Gone?" Danny's voice was laced with fear and disbelief.

"They think it was a gas leak. At their vacation rental," Matt continued.

Danny placed his palms flat on the table and leaned back, as if he were distancing himself from Matt's words. The muscle in his brother's jaw pulsed. He started to speak, but it was as if the words had been ripped out of his throat.

For the next ten minutes Matt watched as his older brother shattered into a million pieces, just as Matt had that morning.

Eventually someone knocked on the door. The guard poked his head in.

"We've gotta get you back," the guard said. "Say your goodbyes." The guard was about to shut the door again when he gave Danny a pointed look. "And get yourself straight."

Danny wiped the tears away with his shirt. Matt realized that the guard was telling Danny to collect himself. It wasn't the kind of place to show weakness.

"I'll call you when I know more," Matt said.

Danny made no reply.

Matt sat there, not knowing what else to say. What else could he say? Their parents and siblings were gone. And they barely knew each other.

The guard returned, and ushered Danny to the door.

Before leaving the room, Danny turned to Matt and said, "Don't come back here, Matty." Danny swallowed. "They wasted too much of their lives on me. Don't waste yours."

And then he was gone.

Keller was at the doorway and had witnessed their goodbye. "You okay?" she asked.

Matt didn't respond. He was pissed she'd made him do this.

Another guard arrived to escort them out of the facility. He led them along a yellow line painted on the cement floor. Matt could feel the eyes of prisoners in the rafters above them. Waiting for a security door to buzz them through, Matt surveyed the dreary facility. At the far end, he saw the guard marshaling Danny to his cell.

His brother still walked with the swagger of a small-town football star. Maybe it was a show for the other prisoners. But even after all these years, he still had the same cocksure stride.

Matt's mind went back to that night with Jessica Wheeler. His own skip in his step after he'd walked her home. Nearly four in the morning, and his smile so bright that it was probably visible on the black footpath. The path near the house where he saw the dark silhouette of his brother—in the letterman jacket and with that swagger—pushing a wheelbarrow toward the creek.

CHAPTER 5

Matt rode with his head resting on the back window of the Suburban. Rainwater pulsed along the glass.

Keller sat in the front passenger seat, cell phone pressed to her ear. For whatever reason, they didn't take the chopper back to the city. He wasn't sure how long they'd been driving. An hour? Two?

The SUV veered off I-87 and pulled into a Shell station. The agent driving, wearing sunglasses even though it was drizzling, got out and started filling the tank.

Keller twisted around. "I'm gonna get some coffee," she said, opening her door. "Want anything?"

"A Mountain Dew would be great," Matt said. "I need to wake up."

Keller gave a disapproving frown and headed to the station's small convenience store.

Matt's thoughts returned to Danny. He imagined his brother in his cell, fighting the tears. What a terrible place, where any sign of emotion was taken as weakness, easy prey. He thought of his brother's prison muscles and cold eyes.

Keller returned with a coffee and small plastic bag from the store. Instead of returning to the front seat, she got into the back next to Matt. From the bag she retrieved a bottle of water and an apple and handed them to him.

"They were out of Mountain Dew," she said, clearly lying. "Anyway, at the academy they taught us that water will wake you up more than caffeine."

"Is that so?" Matt said, eyeing the paper cup of coffee in Keller's hand.

She gave him a knowing smile and took a sip. The driver started the engine, but Keller stayed in the back. Matt realized that she wanted to talk about something.

"Look," she said as the SUV merged back onto the interstate, "I know this isn't a great time, but we need your help with something."

Matt straightened himself. Took a big drink of the water. "Sure."

"The Mexicans are being difficult about"—Keller took in a breath—"about releasing your family to come home. They say they need an immediate family member to sign some papers before the bodies can be released."

"Fine. I'll sign whatever they send over."

"That's just it. They won't just send the papers. They need someone there in person."

"Wait, what?"

"We're working our diplomatic channels, but the locals are being a pain. They haven't been particularly forthcoming with information, and they're saying we need a family member there in person."

"Why would they do that?" Matt asked.

"It could be they're worried about tourism. What happened isn't the best PR in the world. Or it could be some bureaucrat on a power trip. Or"—she looked Matt in the eyes—"or they could be hiding something."

Matt pondered this. "If you think it's necessary," he said, "then, sure, yeah. When do you need me to go?"

"We've booked you a flight out tomorrow morning."

Matt let out a breath. Could this fucking week get any better? He gave a noncommittal nod, then continued gazing out the window. He wasn't particularly travel ready. He had less than one hundred dollars in his bank account. And he'd stubbornly refused any money from his parents after the fight with his father.

They sat in silence for a long time as the SUV made its way to the Henry Hudson Parkway and into Manhattan.

The rain had subsided and there was a sudden part in the clouds, the sun beaming through the gloom. The gold tinge on the buildings brought Matt back to one of their family traditions. Every July, his father's accounting firm held its annual meeting in New York and they'd all come along. The event overlapped with "Manhattanhenge," one of two days a year when the setting sun aligned perfectly with the New York City street grid. When the fiery ball of the sun was framed in by skyscrapers as it dipped below the horizon. Matt thought back to the last Manhattanhenge before Year

Zero—the family sitting at a café on Fourteenth Street, Dad and Mom holding hands, tipsy on wine and being in the city. Danny checking out the girls strutting by in movie-starlet sunglasses and short skirts. Maggie's nose in a guidebook, spouting out facts about the rare solar event.

Matt flashed to the same café last year: everyone in their assigned seats, Dad next to Maggie, who was across from Mom. Next to Mom, Tommy, who'd taken Danny's old seat. And Matt on the outside, trying to squeeze in at the small table. Everyone going through the motions, pretending the ritual still had meaning. *The new but not improved Pines.* And now he had an ache on his insides that both versions of his family were dead. After all of the bitterness, the anger, the longing for the original Pines, he'd give anything to have his bizarro post–Year Zero family back. Give anything to tell his father he was sorry for the things he'd said. Tell his mom what she meant to him. Tell Maggie what a light she was in his life. Tell Tommy that he was their savior. But that life, whatever his grievances, was over. The devastation, the fragility of what they'd had, was almost more than he could take.

"Where would you like us to drop you?" Keller asked. "The dorm?"

"Do you think they're gone yet?"

"Who? The reporters?"

"Yeah."

Keller frowned. "I doubt it. Do you have a friend we can—"

"You can take me to East Seventh, if you wouldn't mind."

The driver looked at Keller in the rearview, and she gave him a nod. The SUV jerked around other cars until traffic was at a standstill. The driver flipped on the strobe mounted to the dash, and the vehicles ahead splayed, creating a narrow path.

Matt watched out the window again as the end-of-the-day crowd headed on foot to happy hours, commuter trains, and cramped apartments.

Finally the SUV drew to the curb on Seventh.

"Here?" Keller said, glancing at the run-down barbershop and dry cleaner next door.

"My friend lives upstairs." Matt looked up at the four-story building in need of a paint job.

Keller nodded. "I just got a text that we have your phone," she said. "I can bring it to you before your flight tomorrow, if that works?"

"Okay."

"We'll also have an agent fly to Mexico with you."

"I don't need a babysitter," Matt said.

"It will just help make sure you're—"

"I'd prefer to go alone."

Keller frowned. "All right. But at least let us have our consular officer pick you up at the airport. He'll take you to Tulum."

When Matt didn't object, Keller retrieved a sheet of paper from her handbag, and handed it to him. "This has your flight information."

Matt remained silent.

"Does your friend have a number so we can reach you?"

"I don't know it. It's in my phone." The art of remembering a ten-digit number extinguished by Apple.

"Okay. Here are my numbers." She handed him a business card.

Matt glanced at the card. SARAH KELLER, FINANCIAL CRIMES SECTION. He wondered for a moment how a financial crimes agent had gotten stuck babysitting him. He'd assumed that the FBI was involved either because of Danny and the documentary or because of the death of Americans abroad. Whatever.

He opened the back door and stepped onto the sidewalk. The clouds had returned, the sun buried behind them again.

"And, Matt," Keller said before he shut the door, "I'm really sorry for your loss."

Matt looked at the federal agent, and he believed her.

CHAPTER 6

Matt stabbed the buzzer on the dilapidated apartment building again. Still no answer. He looked up and down the street. It was lined with dented cars and walk-ups with window-unit air conditioners jutting over the sidewalk. He glanced inside the darkened windows of the barbershop. Just the outline of four chairs facing mirrors. Matt rang the buzzer one more time, and when it went ignored, he walked down an alley to the back of the place. A rickety fire escape clung to the structure. It was rusty and looked like an accident waiting to happen. Matt jumped up, clasped the bottom rung, and tugged. The ladder skated down with a loud clank.

Matt clambered up to the fourth floor. On the narrow metal ledge at the top he peered into the window. And there was Ganesh. Passed out, enough weed paraphernalia on the coffee table to stock a head shop. The window was open a crack, and noise from the blaring television seeped outside. Matt tapped on the glass.

When Ganesh didn't stir, Matt wedged his fingers

under the window frame and lifted. The window was warped from rot and age, and it jammed halfway up. He crawled through the hole.

"Ganesh," Matt said, but his friend didn't move. He was out cold, mouth wide open, still wearing his plastic-framed glasses, a bag of potato chips on his lap.

"Ganesh," he said again, louder, over the din of Fox News blasting from the television mounted on the wall.

Ganesh shot up, startled. He looked around, then seemed to relax when he registered that it was Matt.

"Dude, you scared the shit out of me," Ganesh said. He spoke with a slight Indian accent, barely detectable, and sounded more British than Indian.

"Sorry, you weren't answering the door, so I—" Matt pointed his chin at the window. They'd made the same climb once before when Ganesh had forgotten his keys. Matt was sober this time, at least.

"No worries." Ganesh's curly hair was a mess. He dusted potato chip crumbs from his shirt, then gave Matt a long sad look. "I heard . . . Did you get my texts? I don't know what to say."

Matt nodded. Nothing Ganesh would say—nothing anyone *could* say—would make one bit of difference.

Ganesh leaned forward and lifted a tall cylindrical bong from the coffee table. Lighter in one hand, bong in the other, he gestured to Matt, offering the first hit.

Matt held up a hand to decline. He was never one for weed. And he always found it strange how Ganesh, a law-and-order Republican, used the drug as a crutch. But he supposed that was the enigma of his roommate from freshman year. Ganesh was finishing his four-year degree in three, and had already been accepted to med school to specialize in neuroscience. Fitting—Ganesh's own brain could provide years of study. He was a conservative who chose to attend liberal NYU. He was an immigrant who loved to chant "Build the wall." He was sophisticated, yet highly susceptible to cable news conspiracy theories. He grew up in a ten-million-dollar penthouse in Mumbai, yet chose to live in a shithole apartment on the outskirts of the East Village.

Ganesh blew out a lungful of smoke and aimed the remote at the television. "That douche RA was on TV talking about you. So was your girl."

"Ex-girl," Matt corrected.

"I DVR'd it," Ganesh said. He scrolled through the recordings displayed on the screen, and clicked on one for the local news. Up popped Phillip's preppy face.

"We're all heartbroken," Phillip said.

"You and Matt Pine are close?" said the blond reporter holding the microphone.

"Oh yeah. I'm not just the dorm's RA. We're like family."

Ganesh barked out a cough of smoke at that.

Next up was Jane, her long hair flowing like she'd just had a blowout, her eyes wet and glistening.

"Mr. and Mrs. Pine were so wonderful. They treated me like one of the family. And Matthew's sister, Margaret, was such a special girl—she was the family rock, and was going to MIT in the fall. And Tommy"—Jane's voice cracked—"he was just a sweet little boy."

The emotion was real. Just yesterday, Jane had told Matt that she loved him but he couldn't give her what she needed. Whatever that was. Jane dumping him shouldn't have come as a surprise. Yet for such a supposedly observant guy, he sure hadn't seen it coming. She was from old money, raised in a breathtaking apartment on the Upper West Side, destined to marry one of those guys from Stern who wore business suits and carried briefcases to class. Matt sometimes suspected that Jane dated him—a film student and scholarship kid—just to piss off her parents.

The screen jumped to an image of Danny from the documentary. Matt reached for the remote and turned off the set.

He and Ganesh sat quietly for a long while, Matt lost in his head, Ganesh stoned, chomping on more salt-and-vinegar potato chips, not cluttering up the conversation with platitudes. This was one of the things Matt liked most about Ganesh. He never littered conversations. When the documentary had come out during Matt's freshman year, Ganesh kept him sane during the chaos. "Don't stress, bro," he'd said. "Let's make lemonade out of it, and use the show to get some girls." It hadn't been the worst advice.

Now Ganesh said, "There's a party in Brooklyn I was gonna hit up if you wanna come?"

"I think I'll just hang out. You mind if I stay here tonight?"

"Of course, man, as long as you need. It'll be like the old days," Ganesh said, as if their freshman year had been a lifetime ago. In many ways, it was.

"I can skip the party," Ganesh said. "If you want some company, I can—"

"No, you should go. It's been a long day. I'm just gonna get some sleep."

"Cool, cool, cool," Ganesh said. He disappeared into the bedroom and came out wearing a hoodie and smelling of Axe body spray.

"Your ex keeps texting me looking for you. So is everybody else. You want me to—"

"Hold off telling them where I am. I wanna be alone for a bit. I'll reach out to everyone in the morning."

Ganesh nodded. "You sure you don't wanna come? Take your mind off things?"

Matt shook his head. This wasn't one where he could just make lemonade out of it. "You go, have fun."

Ganesh stuffed his hoodie pocket with what was left of the bag of weed on the coffee table and headed out.

Finally alone, Matt balled up on Ganesh's sofa, and he wept.

CHAPTER 7

SARAH KELLER

Agent Keller slid the key into the door of the small ranch-style house, moths circling the porch light above her. Readington, New Jersey, wasn't a fancy neighborhood, which was just as well. That would've been cost prohibitive, given her FBI salary. But it was safe, filled with working-class families and young couples in starter homes.

In the entryway, she stopped at the sound coming from the kitchen. She dropped her keys softly in the bowl on the front table and crept down the hall, walking carefully, avoiding the creaky patch of wood floor.

Outside the kitchen, the noise was louder. A shaking sound like maracas.

And giggling.

Staying quiet, Keller peeked inside.

At the stove was Bob, making one of those old-fashioned popcorns, the kind you shake on the stovetop, creating a dome of foil. Two feet away the twins watched him in action. Michael wore dinosaur pj's and Heather the cotton nightgown with Belle on it.

Bob grasped the thin metal handle, rattling the foil pan quickly, and the two wiggled their bodies at the same speed as the jostling. He stopped suddenly, and the twins froze in place—Michael's hands in the air like a scarecrow, Heather trying to hold in her laugh. Bob then made wide figure eights with the pan as the grease sizzled, and the kids made circular movements with their hips, spinning invisible Hula-Hoops.

Keller felt warmth run through her. Bob was bald, and not in the slick stylish way of the young agents at the Bureau. He had an old-school doughnut of thick black hair. His stomach hugged his frayed concert T-shirt. But he evoked the awe of a movie star in the eyes of their children. And to Keller.

Some girls wanted to marry their fathers. It was the reason why so many couples were unhappy, Keller surmised: women seeking idealized versions of the first man in their lives. But Keller had no illusions about her dad. Whereas her father was a hard-charging lawyer who spent too much time worrying about appearances, Bob was a stay-at-home dad who—well, look at him. Whereas her father thought showing emotion was for the weak, Bob wore his heart on his sleeve, crying during movies and at the kids' school performances. Whereas her father had engaged in an affair with his secretary in the oldest of clichés, Bob was as loyal as a Labrador. Most of all, he was kind.

"Mommy!" the twins said in unison when they finally saw her spying in the doorway.

Keller knelt down and accepted the squeeze and she felt that sensation she loved.

Bob moved the popcorn pan to an unlit burner, and came over and gave her a kiss.

"We're going to watch *Frozen*!" Heather said.

"Again," Keller said, eyeing her husband. "But isn't it past bedtime?"

"Pleasssse, Mom, please," Michael said.

"Daddy said we could," Heather chimed in.

"Give Mommy a minute to relax," Bob said. "She's had a long day." He looked at Keller. "Can I make you something to eat?"

"I picked up a sandwich," Keller said.

"How about some wine?" he said as he cut into the tinfoil dome and poured popcorn into a plastic bowl.

"*That* I could do."

He looked at the twins. "You two go get the movie started," he said. "We'll be right there."

Michael took the bowl of popcorn and padded off to the living room, his sister at his heels.

"Small bites!" Bob yelled after them. "Popcorn's a choking food."

Keller sat at the small kitchen table as Bob pulled a wineglass from the cupboard and placed it in front of her. He displayed the bottle and, in a fake French accent, said, "Only the finest from the Trader Joe's collection." He filled the glass.

Keller swirled the wine, then put her nose in the glass before taking a taste and swishing it in her mouth. "It's no Whole Foods 2019, but it will do."

He sat beside her. "Long day, huh?"

Keller exhaled heavily. "I took him upstate to Fishkill prison so he could tell his brother."

"How's he doing?"

Keller took a drink of the wine. "He's twenty-one. His parents and little brother and sister are dead, and his older brother's in prison. And let's not forget the media circus."

Bob listened as Keller told him about her very long day.

"I just kept thinking of his family," Keller said. "The little boy was the same age as the twins."

Bob put his hand on his wife's. "Speaking of, it's a bit too quiet in there. I'll be right back." He left the kitchen to check on the kids. He returned carrying Heather in one arm, Michael in the other, both fast asleep.

"Ahh, I wanted to cuddle them," Keller said.

"Look on the bright side. Were you really up for *Frozen* again?"

Bob carried the twins to their bedrooms. When he made it back to the kitchen, Keller said, "I'm sorry I've been working so much lately."

"Don't you apologize."

Keller drained the rest of her glass.

"Do you think there's a connection with the father's accounting firm?" Bob asked as he poured her a refill.

Keller's money-laundering investigation into Marconi LLP was the only reason she'd been dragged into this mess with the Pines.

"I doubt it. Evan Pine wasn't a big player at the firm. He was only on my interview list because he'd been fired," Keller said. Fired employees were always the most willing to dish dirt.

"It's a big coincidence, though," Bob said. "The firm is in bed with the cartel, and the family dies in Mexico."

"That's what Fisher said, but it's a stretch. He's just using the connection to get us involved with a high-profile case, curry favor with State and headquarters."

"So you think it was just an accident?"

"I didn't say that."

Excerpt From
A Violent Nature

Season 1/Episode 3
"You Fucking Idiots"

BLACK SCREEN

The sound of a murmuring crowd is broken by
THE JUDGE'S voice announcing the jury has
reached a verdict. FADE IN ON:

INT. COURTROOM VIDEO FOOTAGE

The judge reads the verdict, and the specta-
tor section is a mix of cheers and sobbing.
The judge calls for order, when a man rises.
He's pointing angrily at the judge, then the
prosecutor, the defense lawyer, his finger
landing on the jury box.

                    EVAN PINE
    You fucking idiots! Shame on you, shame on
    all of you.

                    JUDGE
    Order! I will not have outbursts in this
    courtroom.

                    EVAN
    He's innocent. You fools. You fucking
    idiots!

TWO SECURITY OFFICERS confront Evan Pine,
a struggle ensues, and he's dragged from
the courtroom.

                    EVAN
  He's innocent. My son is innocent!

CHAPTER 8

EVAN PINE

BEFORE

Evan examined the wild-eyed man with curiosity. With the wrinkled shirt and unruly hair, the man looked like one of those homeless street preachers who hold Mass outside the subway. Or an angry cable news pundit on a bender.

"With the advent of DNA," the man ranted, "we learned something that people still just don't seem to get: we lock up a shocking number of innocents. And you know what? About a quarter of them confessed. So when people say innocent people don't confess to crimes they didn't commit, well, it's horseshit. And teenagers falsely confess at rates much higher than adults. They just tell the police what they want to hear. One study of people exonerated through DNA found that forty percent were kids who falsely confessed. . . ."

Evan clicked the mouse on his laptop and paused Netflix. *Horseshit*. It wasn't a word he'd normally use. But there Evan was, for twenty million viewers to see.

He'd once made the mistake of reading the comments section on one of the forums for the documentary.

The father has lost his shit.
He's so devastated, he can't see straight.
Free Danny Pine!
Boo fucking hoo, I hope his son rots for what he did to that poor girl.

Off-camera, the documentary filmmakers, Judy and Ira Adler, were quietly stoking Evan's flame. They meant well, the Adlers. They believed Danny was innocent. But in the aftermath, Evan couldn't help being angry with them. For exploiting their private lives for public entertainment. For getting his hopes up. He clicked the mouse, and his face was animated again.

A voice spoke from off-screen—Judy's. "But if Danny wasn't involved, how did he know that Charlotte's head had been crushed with a rock?"

"He didn't *know* anything," Evan replied, angry at the question. "Those two cops, they fed him all the details. Watch the tape, for Christ's sake."

The screen jumped to the now infamous interrogation video. It showed Danny with his head down on the table in the windowless interview room. The cops had picked him up at the house early that morning. Evan had been out of town for work. Liv had been running errands, and had missed the calls from Maggie.

The burly cop, Detective Ron Sampson, slammed his open hand on the table, making a loud smack. Danny jolted up, his face puffy and tear-soaked.

The other cop, Wendy White, with her frizzy hair and circa-1985 bangs, said, "Just tell us what you did, and we'll work this out. You can go home."

"I didn't do anything."

"Stop lying!" Sampson said, his voice showing the frustration of several hours of interrogation. Evan felt a sting of guilt that no one—not Evan, not Liv, not a lawyer—had been there to help his son. Danny had turned eighteen just two weeks before. Technically an adult, so the cops didn't need to notify his parents. Still, if Evan had caught a different flight and not been in the air, or if Liv had just been home and . . . Evan stopped himself, deciding not to go down that road again.

Sampson continued playing bad cop: "We have your prints on the rock." A lie.

White: "Just tell us the truth and we can get you home. We can talk to your mom and dad and get this sorted out. I'm sure it wasn't something you planned."

Danny shook his head.

Sampson: "Let's just lock him up now. I'm sure his cellies will have a good ol' time with a firm young man like him."

White: "No, not yet," she said in a soft tone. "Just tell us the truth, Danny, and we'll get you home."

Exhausted and tearful, Danny finally said it: "Okay."

"Okay, what?" White said.

"I did it."

"Did what?" Sampson said. He put a reassuring hand on Danny's shoulder. "Tell us what you did to Charlotte."

"I hurt her with a rock."

"Good job," White said. "What'd you do with the rock?"

"I, ah, threw it at her." It came out more like a question.

"You know you couldn't throw a rock that big, Danny," Sampson said, yanking his hand from Danny's shoulder. "I'm done," the cop said, standing, the chair scraping loudly against the linoleum floor. He made a show of pulling out handcuffs.

"What'd you do with the heavy rock?" White continued, her voice urgent, like she was trying to head off her partner.

Danny shook his head, said something indiscernible.

"You already told us you did it, and we have the proof. The only thing that'll help is if you tell us what you did to her head."

Danny swallowed. "I hit her with the rock."

"Where did you hit her?" Sampson said, sitting down again.

"Her head."

"Good boy," White said. "You're doing great."

"How many times did you hit her with the rock?" Sampson continued.

"Once."

"Stop lying, Danny," Sampson said, "we have the proof."

"Just tell the truth and we'll work this out, we can get you out of here," White said. "One hit wouldn't cause her head to smash in like that."

Danny gulped down a sob.

"Just tell the truth," White said.

"Two times."

"No," Sampson said.

"Three," Danny replied.

"Okay, good job Danny, you're doing great," White said. "Now why did you do it? Was it because you'd had a fight at the party?"

He nodded, his eyes on the floor.

"Great job, Danny."

"And you then used the wheelbarrow and took her to the creek."

Danny put his head on the table. "Okay."

The two cops looked at each other, and Sampson gave White a tiny nod. They had what they needed.

Danny lifted his head and looked at both of the detectives. In a quiet voice, he said, "Can I go home now?"

Evan stabbed the laptop keyboard with his finger, shutting down Netflix. No matter how many times he watched the video, his blood always flowed hot, his fists clenched. He remembered Danny crying when Evan finally got to the station house. No sound was more heartbreaking than your child sobbing. Danny was shell-shocked, asking when he could go home, worried because he had a school project due on Monday.

Evan clutched the bottle on the counter and poured himself a large glass of Scotch. It worked as well as—no, better than—his therapy session earlier that day.

The house was quiet. Liv and Tommy were in Nebraska, seeing to Liv's father. He'd been causing problems at the nursing home again, and Liv needed to convince them not to kick him out. Maggie was staying the night with a friend. If there was ever a good time, it was now.

At the kitchen counter, the lights dimmed and shades drawn, he clicked the mouse again and opened the banking site to the savings account. Less than two thousand dollars. The checking was no better. And the mortgage was due in a week. He'd managed to conceal his deception—the tens of thousands he'd spent on lawyers and investigators for Danny. But the reckoning was coming. He imagined Liv seeing the statement for the first time. Evan telling her he'd been fired, that he'd been pretending to go to work.

He imagined his wife's face. The anguish, which would turn to fury when she would inevitably insist on examining the rest of their accounts. She'd find Maggie's college fund down to $12,332, not enough to cover even the cost of the dorm room at MIT.

He closed the site and set up an automatic email timed to send to Liv tomorrow morning. It told her to call the police and make sure Maggie stayed at Harper's until they removed his body. It told her where to find the files on his computer with notes to each of the kids. And it told her where to find the information on his life insurance, which he'd confirmed would pay out even after a suicide. A cool ten million.

He thought of Dr. Silverstein's warning. *The meds can trick a patient into thinking there's only one solution.*

But he wasn't being tricked. It had started as a whisper in his ear. The voice of reason, snaking into his subconscious, confirming his every last fear: "They'll be better off without you." He was doing this for them. To spare them financial ruin. To spare them living with someone who was broken. That's what the voice kept saying. But deep down he knew it wasn't for them at all.

It was for him.

To turn off the faucet of despair.

He slammed the fistful of pills into his mouth, then chased them with the Scotch. They went down hard, and he had to suppress the gag reflex. He poured another glass and downed it quickly as he waited for the pills to take effect.

Evan wasn't a religious man. But he liked the idea of organized religion, with an emphasis on the *organized* part. As an accountant, he found virtue in organization and order. And something about the rituals and traditions of religions—rules largely aimed at making you a better person—was appealing. Back in Nebraska, Liv had insisted that they attend church every Sunday. Faith had helped her through her mother's death when she was ten. After Danny was convicted and they moved to Naperville, Illinois, Evan had no patience for it all. Still, while he was waiting for the pills to do their thing, he said the words nonetheless: "God, please forgive me. And take care of them."

As if answering, his iPhone chimed. Not the usual ring.

He looked at the screen. It was a FaceTime call. He didn't ordinarily use FaceTime, and he didn't recognize the number. He was going to ignore it, but if this was divine intervention, he'd better answer.

He swiped the phone. The screen was dark, but he heard music and the din of a crowd, like a nightclub or a bar. His own image floated in the small box in the upper right corner. He looked much like he did in the documentary. The camera jostled about, then a woman's face appeared. It was shadowed, but he could somehow tell she was scared. She was walking quickly, bumping into people, her heavy breathing and muffled music pounding through the phone's tinny speakers. Finally she came under some grim lighting and stopped.

Evan's heart stopped as well. He couldn't breathe. Couldn't think. He moved his own face closer to the screen.

She said something into the camera, but he couldn't make it out. But it was the face—the freckles, the strawberry-blond hair, the small scar on her forehead—that caused every nerve in his body to tingle. Evan rubbed his eyes with his balled fists. It just couldn't be.

He fumbled for the volume, turning it up.

She said the words again, and this time they were clear.

"Help me."

A hand grabbed the woman by the hair and the phone jerked violently and went black.

Evan blinked several times, trying to process. He ran to the sink and jammed two fingers down his throat. Vomit projected out of his mouth. Brown liquid and pill capsules. Many were still intact.

His legs felt weak and his thoughts muddled. He didn't know if it was from the shock or if some of the pills had made it to his bloodstream. He needed to stay awake. Needed to understand what he'd just witnessed.

Gripping the iPhone, he pulled up the number. The caller ID said MOLOKO BAR and gave a place of origin: Tulum, Mexico. Light-headed, he clicked on the number. His own face projected on the screen as it rang. But no one answered.

Answer, he thought.

Please answer, Charlotte.

CHAPTER 9

MATT PINE

Matt tried to sleep, but his mind was turning too quickly, the springs on Ganesh's sofa doing the rest. Staring at the cracked ceiling of Ganesh's apartment, he listened to the sounds of New York. A cat howling (at least he thought it was a cat). Sirens in the distance. Garbage trucks banging around. He struggled to pinpoint what he was feeling. It was more than grief, a stew of guilt and remorse and sorrow and pain—but also something more familiar: deep, unflinching loneliness.

Since Danny's arrest, loneliness had been a steady companion. It started the summer they'd moved from Nebraska to Illinois after getting run out of their hometown. Nothing was more lonely to a kid than a summer move. Friends were hard to find. School was out, the neighborhood kids away for camp or vacations or jobs.

Movies had been Matt's refuge. He'd spent the first half of the summer watching Scorsese and Hitchcock and Kubrick and Coppola and Nolan. Concerned, his mother pushed him to go outside, get some fresh air. She'd goad him out of his room, and when Tommy was napping, they'd quietly play board games or talk in whispers, and pretend things were normal. One of the guys at his father's new office belonged to a country club and secured Matt a job as a golf caddie for the second half of that summer.

Matt loved the job. It was where he'd met Chad, the caddy manager. Chad was a former pro golfer who'd gotten throug : life on his smile (and trust fund). The caddies spent much of the day sitting in the caddy shack, waiting out the rain or the lulls on the green, listening to Chad dispense his wisdom, watching him flirt with Angela, the big-chested college girl who drove around in a golf cart selling beer from a cooler.

Chad would give Matt and the other teenagers advice. About bringing girls home ("Have a Glade PlugIn air freshener near the door; they'll think the apartment is really clean"). About their customers ("Don't bother sucking up; they give the standard tip unless they're trying to impress a business client or a girl"). About higher education ("College is a snowflake factory for woke morons; the only reason to go is for the chicks"). About life ("My dad was rich, a CEO with a room full of award: and no one gave one shit when he died"). Matt four 1 himself jumping out of bed, eager to make his shift. Not for his love of the game—carrying golf bags in th : sticky Chicago heat was hard work. But because he was part of the gang.

Then the morning came when someone had whispered in the country club manager's ear that Matt's brother was in prison. For murder. And Chad, his eyes downcast, asked Matt to turn in his hat and smock. Matt never saw Chad again, but imagined he was still there, doing what he loved, lusting after golf cart girls, giving advice to sad fourteen-year-olds.

Over time, Matt's loneliness mutated into a medley of anger and resentment, and he started getting into fights. He had a pang of guilt remembering that it was a fight—on the schoolyard after his brother's conviction—that was the inciting incident for their family's move to Illinois, his parents deciding it was time to get out of Dodge. For the most part, Matt had managed to keep the beast caged since high school, that side of himself hidden from everyone—well, nearly everyone. After returning from winter break and a massive blow-out with his father, a frat boy had made the mistake of saying something disgusting to Jane at a party. Matt pictured the kid's bloody face, Jane crying for Matt to stop, yanking him away.

Matt sat up, clicked on the television. At four thirty, it was channel after channel of infomercials and lawyers asking, "Have you been injured in an accident?"

When he couldn't take it anymore, he decided to go for a run. Exercise always helped him focus. It slowed down his thoughts, burned off nervous energy. Kept the beast at bay. This early it would also allow him to slip into his dorm before the paparazzi arrived for the morning shift.

He went into Ganesh's room. His friend wouldn't mind if he borrowed some workout clothes. Inside the messy dresser, he fished out a wrinkled Under Armour

shirt and pair of shorts. Ganesh was a big guy—he'd
gained thirty pounds since freshman year, a by-product
of the munchies from all the weed—so Matt was swimming in the clothes. But he didn't plan on seeing anyone, so they'd do.

He took the filthy stairwell to the ground floor and
jogged under pools of lamplight along Seventh. The
pavement felt good under his feet. The clouds had rolled
away and the air smelled fresh.

He picked up his pace when he hit Cooper Square,
running on the cracked sidewalks, crossing the street
speckled with orange construction cones from the never-
ending roadwork. By the time he saw the arch of Washington Square Park, he was saturated in sweat and his
thoughts were clearer. He started formulating a plan.

He'd use the credit card, the one his parents had given
him for emergencies—*real* emergencies, his mother had
joked, not pizza emergencies—for the trip to Mexico.
Keller said the authorities just needed his signature, and
he'd get his family home. He'd call his aunt to discuss
the arrangements. Aunt Cindy was a strong personality
and would have views. He needed to call her anyway,
to check on her and his grandfather. When he got back
from Mexico, he'd figure out the house, the cars, the finances, returning to school, Danny.

He was starting to feel overwhelmed again.

As he ran, he heard his father's voice. Before the con-
stant tension, Dad could always talk Matt off the ledge.
His father would say, "How do you eat an elephant?"
Dad would cup Matt's chin in his hand, look Matt in

the eyes, and answer his own question: "One bite at a time."

When Matt was younger, the message got lost in his wandering thoughts. He'd say to his dad, "What kind of person would eat an elephant? How would you cook it? And aren't elephants an endangered species?"

His dad would smile, tousle Matt's hair. "One bite at a time, Matty."

Matt jogged through the park. In the dark section, the one students knew to avoid, figures lurked near the shrubs. At this hour, you could find yourself in a scene from *28 Days Later,* running from vibrating tweakers or lethargic opioid zombies. He made his way past the chess area, his thoughts jumping to his last game with Reggie. The momentary thrill of winning that game had been stolen from him like everything else.

In his peripheral vision, he saw a figure. The silhouette of a tall guy in a ball cap. Probably a married guy trolling for an anonymous same-sex liaison, another charming feature of twilight in the park.

He ran until he saw the light burning in the lobby of his dorm tower. Catching his breath at the crosswalk, he scanned the area and didn't see any news vans or photographers. Traffic hurtled along, the city awakening.

"Got a light?" a voice said from behind him.

Matt turned around. It was the guy in the ball cap. It was pulled down low, shadowing his features. All that was visible was the bottom half of the man's face. He had a scar that ran from his nostril to his lip, like from cleft lip surgery. He held a cigarette between his fingers.

"Sorry, I don't." Matt said it firmly in the polite *don't fuck with me* tone you needed to take with the more aggressive creatures of the park. Matt turned back to the street, waiting for the light as cars flew by.

That's when he felt the shove from behind, and plunged into traffic.

CHAPTER 10

Matt hit the asphalt hard, hot pain shooting up his hip. But the sensation was dulled by the fear seizing him as he watched the blinding headlights race toward him. Matt's body went stiff as he braced for impact. The lights went dark, the vehicle swerving and then screeching to a stop. Matt could see only starbursts now, but felt someone clawing at his clothes, roughly patting him down, jabbing a hand in the pocket of his shorts. He started swatting at the blurry figure, and by the time his vision was clear, the man was gone. The door of the cab that had barely missed him flew open and the driver ran over.

"Are you stupid, boy?" the cabbie said. "I could've killed you."

Matt apologized, though he wasn't sure why, since he'd been shoved into traffic. Mugged right in front of the guy, though the assailant had picked the worst victim possible, a college student in borrowed clothes with no wallet, money, or phone. Matt's eyes darted around, looking for the man in the ball cap. An obese guy scuttled over and offered him a hand up.

Matt yanked himself to his feet, and the two made their way to the sidewalk. Matt's side ached from the fall. He watched as the cabbie stormed back to his car amid the cacophony of honking horns.

Matt turned to thank the man who'd helped him up, when he was assaulted with camera flashes.

"You mind?" Matt said, realizing the guy was one of the paparazzi.

"You said you were okay." He said it like it gave him permission to invade Matt's space.

"Did you see who pushed me?" Matt asked.

"Pushed you?" The paparazzo said it almost with glee. Like the value of the photos had just increased. "I was just gettin' here. I didn't see nothing until I heard the commotion. I thought you tripped." The guy looked up and down the street. "You're Matt Pine, right?"

Matt didn't answer. He started walking toward the lobby of the dorm tower.

"Someone pushed you?" the guy said, keeping pace. "Who'd wanna do that?"

Matt kept walking, the pain in his hip and leg from hitting the asphalt intensifying.

"How are you feeling? Did the Mexicans tell you what happened to your family? Have you spoken with your brother? Do you think this will help with getting Danny a pardon?" the man asked while simultaneously taking shots with his camera.

Matt wanted to tell the guy off. Punch him in the face. But he just limped to the dorm entrance. Turning his head from the camera, Matt pushed the red intercom button. At last, a guard appeared and buzzed him inside.

Normally, the guards were unfriendly and sent you to the student center to get a new security card before letting you in. But today the guard just put a hand on Matt's shoulder.

"Let's get you to your room, Matt."

The guard must have heard the news. The man quietly escorted Matt to the tenth floor and unlocked the door to his room. Jane was in the entryway. She was bleary-eyed and uncharacteristically disheveled. She flung her arms around him. Matt noticed that the communal area, the small prison cell that passed as the living room, was crowded with friends. The gang from freshman year was on the IKEA couch and beanbag chairs and spots on the floor. Empty beer and wine bottles from the vigil were piled in the recycling bin in the corner.

Matt had read somewhere that there were no friends like the ones from freshman year, and it was true. They'd all resided in Rubin Hall, known unofficially as the "poor kids' dorm." It was a converted hotel from the 1960s. Famous for its squalor and lack of air-conditioning. You only put Rubin on your dorm-selection list if you had to. It was the lowest-cost option for housing, and the university concentrated its scholarship kids there. During the first week of freshman year there was a heat wave, so Matt and the other tenants on his floor had a slumber party in the common area, the only space with air-conditioning. It was there he'd met what became his college family. He cast his eyes around the room.

Kala stood, looking gorgeous and fashionable even after staying up all night. She was in the Tisch drama school and had come a long way since that first year at Rubin. Back then her hair had been several shades too blond and her trailer park drawl too thick. They'd been fast friends—a point of contention with Jane— partly because of their love of old television shows and movies, partly because Matt never judged Kala's rural Oklahoma roots. After all, his family had been run out of small-town Nebraska.

Kala had been the first to approach Matt after the documentary broke and everyone learned about his secret—his incarcerated brother and disgraced family. Kala confided that her father was in prison. At the time, she hadn't said for what. But as they became closer, Matt learned it was for abusing Kala's mother. And Matt sensed the abuse hadn't stopped with mom.

Kala hugged him, holding him a long while. She whispered in his ear, "You've always been there for me, and I'll always be there for you. I love you."

He felt his eyes filling with tears.

Woo-jin was there as well. At six seven, he was hard to miss. He crouched over for an awkward hug. Woo-jin was from South Korea and on a basketball scholarship. He was a quiet kid, embarrassed by his heavy accent. When Woo-jin was struggling with classes, Matt had tutored him.

He next saw Sofia. She was wearing her green military jacket, which suited her militant personality. No cause was too trivial for Sofia. She approached relationships with the same fire and passion. She'd been in love no less than six times freshman year, with Matt talking her down from every breakup. Unsurprisingly, she looked like she'd taken the news the hardest. Her eye makeup was raccooned from tears, her long auburn hair a mess. Sofia's body shuddered when she hugged him. It caused Matt's to shudder as well.

Curtis was next. He was the brains of the group. He'd won the National Spelling Bee at nine, the second Black kid to ever win the competition, the first from the atrocious Mississippi public school system. He had a near perfect SAT score and been offered scholarships from every Ivy. He'd accepted NYU not for academic reasons, but because it was the only school that had a congregation of his small, obscure religious sect nearby. After classes all day, he attended services two hours every other night. He didn't use alcohol, didn't take drugs, didn't swear, and didn't even drink caffeine. And he'd struggled with the loose ways of NYU. He and Matt had long talks late at night about religion and Curtis's battles with temptation. Matt had told him that he needed to have faith in his faith.

"I'm praying for you, my friend," Curtis said as he pulled him into a hug.

"I know you are," Matt said, his voice breaking. "I think I need it."

The only one missing was Ganesh. He was always the loner of the group. In his contradictory way, he loved a crowd but kept everyone at a distance.

Matt surveyed this group of people he loved. On the exterior, each was objectively attractive. He could almost imagine them in a remake of *Felicity* (a reference only

Kala would get), good-looking NYU students out to take on the world. But like life, each was more complicated. Ganesh called their group the "Island of Misfit Toys." Sofia chided him, since the reference was from *Rudolph the Red-Nosed Reindeer,* which she thought was racist and homophobic for reasons Matt couldn't comprehend.

At last, Matt said to the group, "Thank you for coming. It means a lot."

There was a chorus of *we're here for you, whatever you need,* and the like.

"If you don't mind, I'd love to get a shower and some rest. . . ."

The group fumbled around, collecting their things. They had another procession of hugs at the door.

Jane hung back. After the last mourner departed, she said, "Where have you been? I was worried. I called everywhere, and you weren't answering your phone and Ganesh ignored my texts and—"

"I'll tell you all about it. But I could use a little time to myself."

Jane's face crumpled. "Matt, I would've never— If I knew, I wouldn't have—"

"I know. It's okay." He waited by the door, signaling that she should go. He didn't want to do this now.

"It was a mistake," she said.

Matt gave a fleeting smile. "No, it wasn't."

"Let's talk." It was plain she wasn't leaving.

Just a day ago he'd been mildly devastated that they were through. But after what had happened, he saw things as they were. Matt and Jane were never going to make it. His Rubin friends were surprised it had lasted a year. Shit, Matt was surprised it had taken Jane so long to realize he was a much bigger project than she'd anticipated. And she'd said some mean things in the end: that he was a mess. That he'd never be anything if he didn't start focusing. On school. On her. That he needed to see someone about his anger at his father. At his brother. That after he'd pummeled that frat boy, she was afraid of him.

The worst part was that she'd been right about all of it, and now none of it mattered.

"Matthew, please, talk to me."

She followed him as he went to the bathroom and turned on the shower. She watched as he removed Ganesh's ridiculously large clothes. He'd seen Jane twice stop herself from asking about the getup. He stepped into the stall and let the hot water beat down on his face. Through the foggy shower door, he saw Jane's silhouette disappear.

After toweling himself off, he returned to the room. Jane was sitting on the bed, her mouth downturned.

"Are you going to talk to me?" she said, watching him throw on some jeans and a T-shirt.

"I'm not sure what there is to say."

He pulled a duffel from under the bed, and began stuffing clothes into the bag. He searched the dresser for the small document pouch, the one his mother had made for him. It held things grown-ups needed—his social security card, passport, birth certificate. It was also where Mom had tucked away the emergency credit card. When the pouch wasn't in plain view, Matt yanked the drawer from the frame and dumped it on the floor. And there it was, the letter-size, expandable pouch. He scooped it up.

"What are you— Where are you going?" Jane asked as he stalked to the door.

"To get my family."

CHAPTER 11

Matt stormed out of the building, Jane calling after him. He pushed past the photographers and hailed a cab to La-Guardia. In the back, he bumped around on the cracked vinyl seat for a long while, staring out at nothing. The closing scene from *Michael Clayton*. The cab slammed the brakes hard, then swerved around a car that had cut them off, the cabbie cursing out the window.

If they crashed, Matt realized, few people would really care. Jane would make a show of how upset she was, and sure, the gang from Rubin Hall would get together, tell a few stories, give some toasts to Matt Pine. But he'd soon become an afterthought. Talked about in the larger context of bad luck or family curses or famous tragedies. One Pine wrongfully locked up for murder, four Pines killed in a freak accident while on vacation, and the other one—what was his name?—dead in a car wreck on the way to the airport to claim the bodies of his deceased family members. They'd say *seize the day* lest you suffer the fate of the Pines.

Not today, he thought as the cab yanked to a stop outside the airport terminal. Inside, he gave the dour-faced airline worker the confirmation number the FBI agent had given him, and retrieved his ticket. He then found an ATM and breathed a sigh of relief when, after several tries, he remembered the PIN for the emergency credit card: 1010. His parents' default passcode, October 10, the month and day they'd met in college. Another surge of grief consumed him. Pocketing the five hundred dollars, he then submitted to the torture of modern air travel—long lines, shoes off, no liquids—and soon he was at his gate, the duffel draped over his shoulder.

Matt sat in the chair of molded plastic for a long while, staring blankly out the large windows onto the tarmac. The planes lifted off and landed in the morning sun. Thousands and thousands of strangers who would never cross paths again, intersecting at this one point in time. Grains of sand at the beach. Ants on a hill. He needed to shake the morbid thoughts.

By nine thirty, the gate was getting crowded. It was then Matt had the feeling that someone was watching him. He scanned the crowd—the businessmen yacking on cell phones, the college kids with neck pillows, the rare traveler dressed to the nines amid the sloppy masses—but he didn't see the culprit. But he had no doubt he was being watched. He knew the feeling.

He'd refused to participate in the documentary, but he couldn't escape the family photos and old news footage sprinkled over ten dramatic episodes set against a haunting score heavy on cello and violin. After it aired,

people would often give him the *Do I know you from
somewhere?* look. The true believers, the Danny Pine
faithful, made the connection, and Matt would have
to turn down selfies or apologize that he wasn't really
a hugger. He'd unwillingly become part of a national
mystery, a game of Clue where journalists—and internet detectives—came up with elaborate theories and
spent an unbelievable amount of time trying to prove
whodunit.

The show had struck a chord. A beautiful young girl
disfigured in the most gruesome way. The all-American
boy wrongfully accused. A small town painted in the
worst kind of light—and, of course, the suspects overlooked.

The documentary pointed to one in particular, Bobby
Ray Hayes. He was in prison for killing several young
women. He'd sexually assaulted and murdered the girls,
then smashed in their skulls with large rocks. The
media uncreatively called him "the Smasher." Depending on where you were from, you'd call the Hayes clan
white trash or hillbillies or rednecks. After the documentary, they were called that and then some. And the
youngest in the brood—a shark-eyed menace named
Bobby Ray—was straight out of central casting as a
creepy killer of women.

Matt spotted a man in an expensive-looking suit pretending not to look at him. The guy fit the profile. Danny
Pine's "fans" were a decidedly well-heeled crowd, people
who couldn't wrap their heads around a wrongful
conviction, oblivious to how often it happened to the
poor. Spend a few minutes with Matt's father, and he'd

give you an earful about the 2,852 individuals on the National Registry of Exonerations who'd collectively spent 23,540 years in prison for crimes they did not commit.

"Matthew," a voice said from behind him. It was the FBI agent. Keller.

"Hey," he said.

"I heard you had some excitement this morning," Agent Keller said.

Matt didn't understand. He hadn't reported the guy who'd shoved him into the street. It was just a few hours ago.

She held up her phone, displaying a story from some web news rag. The headline read: SURVIVOR OF "A VIOLENT NATURE" FAMILY ATTACKED.

Matt groaned.

"There's also a feature story about your family in this morning's edition of the *Times*." She said it like a warning. "Are you okay? What happened? Were you really attacked?"

Matt told her about the man with the cleft lip scar.

"Why didn't you call me? Or report what happened to the NYPD? What if—"

"I'm fine, just some bruises. I didn't get a good look at the guy and he didn't get anything, so there wasn't anything to report."

Keller didn't seem thrilled by his response, but she couldn't do much about it. She retrieved a sheet of paper from her handbag. "This has the name of the consular officer who will meet you at the airport. He'll know where to go, but just in case, I also included the address of the police station and the name of the local officer in charge of the investigation."

Matt glanced at the paper, then folded it up and tucked it into his front pocket with his passport.

"Hopefully it will be pro forma," Keller said. "You'll sign some papers and they'll release the bod—release your family. The consulate will help with the paperwork for their flight home."

Matt nodded.

Keller handed him a folded copy of the *Times*. He glanced at the front page. The photo was a punch in the gut. It was a selfie of his family in front of a sign for the Cancún airport. They were hamming it up for the camera. Where the hell had the *Times* gotten the shot? He realized that his mom had probably posted it on Facebook, the place where she pretended that their family was doing just fine, thank you very much. Under the photo, a caption:

EVAN PINE (51), OLIVIA PINE (51),
MARGARET PINE (17), THOMAS PINE (6).

Under the selfie were separate shots of Matt and Danny. The one of Matt was another Facebook grab of him last summer. Danny's was his mug shot.

"I don't want to read this."

"I'm not asking you to," Keller said. "But this Mexican squad doesn't seem like the most sophisticated bunch, so if they question whether you're with the family, the photo may help. It also may remind them that the world is watching how they handle the case."

A distorted voice blared from the overhead speakers. It was hard to understand, but travelers started lining up to board.

"All right," he said. "I'd better get going."

"This will probably help." Keller gave Matt his wallet and smartphone.

"Thanks."

"You have no idea what a pain it was. The bouncer has a business on the side selling phones. There's no money in your wallet."

There never had been.

Matt looked at the face of the iPhone, cracked from the hundreds of times he'd dropped it. The phone was fully charged—thanks to Keller, no doubt. The device's wallpaper was a photo of Jane, one she'd uploaded herself. She looked particularly regal in the shot.

"You find anything helpful on it?"

"We haven't looked. We needed your password. And your permission." Keller looked at him. "You mind?"

Matt thumbed the sensor, unlocking the device. He took a deep breath before checking his text messages. There were hundreds of them. Many from unfamiliar numbers, but dozens from friends. There were no new messages from his father. One text from his mother, saying they were getting on the plane and that she loved him. Something she did out of habit whenever she flew. The fatalistic precaution in case the plane went down.

But then he saw it. The unread text from Maggie.

Excerpt from
A Violent Nature

Season 1/Episode 4
"Holmes and Watson"

INT. PINE FAMILY HOME - HOME OFFICE

Twelve-year-old MAGGIE PINE sits behind a
cluttered desk. File boxes and mountains
of papers fill the space. In the background
stands a homemade crime wall, complete with
red string zigzagging from newspaper clip-
pings to photographs to other clues mounted
on the board by pushpins. Maggie wears a
T-shirt with the picture of a horse on it,
metallic braces on her teeth.

                    MAGGIE
  My brother Matt loves movies and watches,
  like, a trillion. So one night my best
  friend was sleeping over and we were spying
  on him, like we always do, and I saw part
  of this movie, I don't remember the name
  of it, where these lawyers, like, saved the
  day by digging through boxes at the clerk's
  office. So it gave me the idea.

C.U. on Maggie's hands digging through
a box. She retrieves a sheaf of papers.
She's beaming, proud of the find.

                    MAGGIE
So when we went back to Nebraska to visit
my grandpa one time, I went to the county
clerk and told her I was doing a school
project—it wasn't a lie; Mrs. Melhoose
said I could—and the clerk let me dig
through the old case files. And I found
this.

INT. STUDIO

EVAN PINE sits on a stool, the background
dark.

                    EVAN
Maggie brings me copies of notes from a
couple of police interviews. One about a
suspicious man at the house party that
night, the last place Charlotte was seen
alive. The other, a tip from an anonymous caller who said Charlotte's murder
looked a lot like two others in Kansas.
After Danny went to prison, several other
girls in Kansas, Nebraska, and Missouri
were killed in the same way: their heads
smashed in with large rocks.

INSERT - NEWSPAPER HEADLINE

"Break in the Smasher Case: Plainville Man
Arrested for String of Grisly Murders."

                    EVAN

The prosecution failed to turn over the
reports. If we could've looked into
the Smasher back then, we might not be
here right now. The failure to give
Danny's lawyer the reports broke the law;
they're required to turn over exculpatory
evidence. And we got our first big break
for seeking post-conviction relief.

INT. PINE FAMILY HOME - HOME OFFICE

Evan and Maggie sit at the desk together
studying the case file.

                    EVAN (V.O.)

From then on it's been Magpie and me.
Holmes and Watson, though I'm not sure
who's Holmes and who's Watson.

CHAPTER 12

MAGGIE PINE

BEFORE

"Your boyfriend's here." Harper moved her eyebrows up and down.

Maggie had already seen Eric at the doorway to the high school's tutoring center. She rolled her eyes. "Cut it out."

"Seriously, he's into you. He only comes on the days you're here. Like, he's literally, almost, like, stalking you."

As with most of their generation, Harper overused *like* and misused *literally*. Maggie looked across the Center. It was filled with the usual cast: jocks who were trying to pull their grades up to a C so they could take the field, stoners who'd been given the choice between the Center or detention, and the nerds who tutored them. Well, except Harper, who was what some would call a hot nerd. Eric strutted through the room— that was the word, *strutted,* high-fiving other boys as he made it over to the check-in table.

Standing before them now, he grabbed the pen to sign the log, then offered a rakish smile.

"Any chance you can help me with algebra?" he asked Maggie.

Her face reddened as she felt Harper's sideways glance. "Sure."

Eric smiled again and directed his blue eyes at an empty desk in the corner. He gestured for Maggie to follow.

Maggie tried not to get wooed by his charm. Eric was royalty at their school, *literally,* as Harper would say, and for once with proper usage. Homecoming king. Maggie's older brother Matt would call Eric the archetype from an eighties John Hughes movie. She had to admit he was dreamy. *Dreamy*—what an old-fashioned word. She was starting to sound like her mother.

She sat next to Eric, who flopped open his textbook. "I don't get rational expressions."

Maggie tried not to look surprised.

"I know, I know, you were doing this stuff in fifth grade." His face flushed as if he were actually embarrassed. He was adorable even when he was uncomfortable. The world was not fair.

"No, rational expressions are super hard," she said, lying. "And they're pointless. When in life are you ever going to use them?"

"Right?" he said. "But I bet you will at MIT."

Maggie's heart fluttered: he knew where she was going to college. She scooched closer, and for the next half hour tried to stay professional while helping him work through some problems. He smelled of cheap cologne and masculinity. But she needed to keep her thoughts in check. Guys like Eric Hutchinson were trouble. And they usually didn't appreciate girls like her. They would someday, her mom assured her, but it took longer for the male brain to develop.

"I like your shirt," he said.

Maggie looked down at the vintage AC/DC T-shirt, one of her dad's favorite bands. "You know tutoring is free, right? You don't have to flatter."

"I'm not. It's cool."

"All right, focus . . ." She smiled.

They continued with the problems. Then Eric said, "How's your brother's case going?"

This wasn't as surprising as Eric knowing where she was going to college. Maggie had been a major character in the documentary. The faithful daughter and sister helping chase down leads. It had given her a moment of celebrity at school, but it was more of the pitying variety. Though some of the internet trolls speculated that when she got older—she'd been only twelve when the documentary was filmed—she'd be quite the beauty, like her mother. Or her "hottie" brothers.

Ugh. It was all the world seemed to care about. And in pure hypocrite mode, here she was fawning over handsome Eric.

"We've had some setbacks with the case, but I got a great tip the other day," Maggie said. "Setbacks" was an understatement. The United States Supreme Court wasn't a setback; it was the end of the road. But Eric likely wouldn't care about the intricacies of the legal system. Or was she underestimating him?

"A tip? You mean like evidence or something?"

"Yeah, wanna see?"

He nodded as she pulled out her phone.

"I run social media for the case. We get a lot of weirdos and trolls, but also some legit people. And we get tips now and then." She tapped and swiped as she spoke. "Usually it's nothing, but then this came in."

It was a jostling cell phone video, the first two seconds a blur of bodies, music blaring in the background.

"What is it?" Eric said, leaning in closer.

"It's the party." She was assuming that Eric, like everyone else, understood the shorthand from the documentary. The night her brother's girlfriend, Charlotte, was killed, she'd attended a house party. Danny had been there too, like all the seniors. The local police had raided the festivities, and Danny and Charlotte had been separated in the melee. Witnesses reported seeing a very intoxicated Danny later that night at an after-party in a cornfield; Charlotte was never seen alive again.

"It could be him, the U.P.," Maggie said, pointing at the screen.

"You mean, like, the Unknown Partygoer?"

He'd definitely watched the documentary. The Unknown Partygoer had become a thing—Facebook memes, late-night talk-show bits, even shirts. The filmmakers focused on the fact that the police had identified everyone at the party that night except for one guest. A white male who a witness had aged anywhere from his early to late twenties and who no one seemed to know. The person the documentary suggested was the real killer. Who many believed was a loser named Bobby Ray Hayes, the Smasher. Maggie put the video in slow motion.

Eric looked on, seeming fascinated.

"The date stamp shows it was the night of the party. Phones weren't as sophisticated then, but we can tell that much." Maggie directed a finger at the screen. "There's Danny." On the tiny screen, her brother was laughing before downing the contents of a red Solo cup. He wore a tank top, showing off his bulging biceps and looking like a bro with a group of boys in letterman jackets. Right before the video turned black, they saw the silhouette of a face.

"There," Maggie said, freezing the video.

"You think it's him? Like, the real Unknown Partygoer?" Eric asked.

"I'm not sure. But it raises more questions than it answers, because *that* is not Bobby Ray Hayes." Her father had never believed the Hayes narrative. The pieces didn't fit as perfectly as the documentary had suggested.

"Holy shit. Who sent it to you?"

"I don't know. It was an anonymous tip."

"What do the cops say?"

Maggie sighed. The cops couldn't care less, particularly the Nebraska cops in charge of the investigation. As far as they were concerned, Danny Pine's case had brought them nothing but public scorn and even death threats. One of the cops who'd interrogated Danny had committed suicide after the Netflix series aired.

"They didn't return my calls. They never do—they say the case is closed."

"Well, that's"—Eric searched for the word—"it's bullshit."

Maggie smiled. She liked him.

"So, tonight," Eric said, "some of us are getting together. At Flaherty's house."

Mike Flaherty. Another member of senior class royalty.

"You mean like a party?" Maggie asked.

"Not really," Eric said. "Well, sorta. But maybe you could stop by. It's the last blowout before everyone leaves for spring break."

In the Pine home—after what happened to Charlotte—few dangers were greater than a high school house party. Maggie wasn't sure whether it was because her father thought there was real peril or if it was just the memories it conjured.

"Maybe," she said, surprised it had escaped her lips. The Center's bell rang.

"Maybe," he repeated, drawing out the word, flirtatious. He gave her a crooked smile. "If you come, we can work more on algebra."

"Really? You do a lot of math at parties?"

"You wouldn't want me to fail out, would you? I'd lose my scholarship," Eric said earnestly. She'd heard that he'd been admitted to the University of Michigan on a lacrosse scholarship. The school was normally well out of reach for a C student, again proving that life was not fair.

"Maybe," she said again, butterflies floating in her stomach.

"I'll text you the address." Eric grabbed his book, then strutted out.

Why was it that they all strutted?

Maggie returned to the check-in desk to help Harper close the Center. They had to finish the log and lock up the room.

"What was that about?" Harper asked.

"What do you mean?"

Her best friend gave her a look.

"He invited me to a party."

"At Flaherty's?" Harper said, her mouth agape. Of course she'd already been invited. They were best friends, both bookish young women, but Harper had a wild side, and drifted seamlessly between social groups. One day it was a movie and pizza at Maggie's, the next hiking with the nature club, the next a rager with the jocks.

"Yeah. He said it was more of a get-together than a party, though."

Harper shook her head, like Maggie was being naive. "And . . . ?"

"And I don't know. You know how my dad feels about parties."

"Mags, we're graduating and you haven't been to a single party. You haven't had one drink. And don't get me started about sex. Do you really want to go to college so, like, pathetic?"

Maggie swatted her friend with a sheath of papers.

"Come on, let's go tonight," Harper said.

"Let me think about it."

"What's to think about? You're sleeping over at my house anyway, so you don't have to ask your dad. And if the party sucks, we leave."

Maggie wanted to go. Wanted to see Eric. But she

didn't like sneaking around. Didn't like the betrayal of a house party, of all things. "I'll think about it."

And think about it she did.

By ten that night Maggie and Harper were pulling up to Mike Flaherty's house in the back of an Uber.

"I don't think this is a good idea." Maggie watched as the group on the front porch cleared a path for two boys carrying a keg of beer up the steps and through the large front doors. Flaherty's dad owned a chain of car dealerships, and the place was a sprawling McMansion. The Uber driver honked at some kids who were blocking the half-circle driveway.

"Relax," Harper said. "It's gonna be fun. And you look *amazing*."

Maggie tugged up her top. She'd borrowed it from Harper, and it showed *way* too much cleavage. She'd also made the mistake of letting Harper do her makeup. And she'd nixed her glasses for contacts. They felt like grains of sand under her eyelids every time she blinked.

Inside, Maggie's stomach churned at the scene: a throng of kids bouncing to the beat of pounding dance music, the smell of beer, sweat, and weed.

"Where are his parents?" Maggie asked. It was her first ever high school party. She hadn't expected it to be so, well, cliché.

Harper shrugged. She led Maggie through the great room, which was now a dance floor filled with kids twerking and grinding. There was even a cheesy DJ bobbing behind a sound system.

They wound through the crowd to the dining room, a

formal number with a chandelier, and the site of an epic beer pong game on the long table. Mike Flaherty was at the head of the table wearing no shirt, and some type of headband tied around his forehead. Muscles rippling, Mike stood on tiptoes and took a shot like a basketball player at the free-throw line. The small white ball flew in the air, bounced, hit the lip of a red cup but missed, prompting a *so close* groan from the crowd.

"You need to relax," Harper said out of the side of her mouth, sensing Maggie's stiffness. "I'm going to get us drinks," she said. "I'll be right back."

"Wait," Maggie called, but Harper was already weaving through the horde. Maggie tucked a strand of hair behind her ear, trying not to look nervous. It wasn't that she didn't like to have fun, or was a prude. And Harper was wrong: she'd had a drink before, and even made out with Reeves Anderson after the science fair. But for her entire high school career, she'd been living with the aftermath of a party just like this one.

She felt a pit in her stomach about lying to her father. *But she hadn't really lied, had she?* She'd said she was staying the night at Harper's, which was true. Dad didn't ask about their plans. And she couldn't spend her life avoiding parties, right? She was headed to college soon. Matt told her that he went to parties all the time at NYU, though she couldn't imagine Matt's uptight girlfriend going to a gathering like this one.

The crowd roared again at a ball plopping into the cup, and Maggie thought about the cell phone video—the anonymous tip she'd received from that night. The last hours before Charlotte's murder. The six seconds of video had the decadent feel of this party—as if something could veer out of control at any moment, which made tonight both scary and exciting.

She'd spent many nights thinking about the infamous house party seven years ago. What had happened? Had Danny and Charlotte really gotten into an argument? Why did they separate when the cops busted up the party? And why couldn't Danny remember anything? Maggie hadn't been allowed to attend Danny's trial, she was only ten years old at the time, but she'd since read all the transcripts.

PROSECUTOR: You attended a party?

DEFENDANT: Yes.

PROSECUTOR: At Kyle Brawn's house?

DEFENDANT: Yeah.

PROSECUTOR: What time did you leave?

DEFENDANT: I don't remember. I drank too much. I blacked out.

PROSECUTOR: You ran out when the police arrived?

DEFENDANT: I don't remember, but I must have.

PROSECUTOR: You fought with Charlotte at the party.

DEFENDANT: No.

PROSECUTOR: She told you she was pregnant and you had a fight.

DEFENDANT: No!

PROSECUTOR: If you don't remember anything, how do you know that?

Someone touched her shoulder, and Maggie turned around, thinking Harper had returned. But it was him.

"Hey," Eric said. "You made it." He'd obviously been at the party awhile. His eyes were glassy, speech slurred.

She smiled, not sure what to say.

"Come with me," he said, dragging her by the hand.

Soon she found herself in a laundry room making out with him. He reeked of pot and stale beer, and her eyes kept going to the dirty laundry piled in the basket on top of the dryer. She pulled away.

"What's wrong?" Eric slurred.

"Nothing, but this isn't how I—"

He grabbed her by the arms, pushing her against the wall. He jammed his tongue into her mouth. With one hand, he managed to hold both of her wrists above her head. With the other hand, he started groping her breasts.

"Stop," Maggie said, yanking back.

But he didn't. He kept her arms pinned. The fingers of his large hand squeezed her wrists together, both arms against the wall. It hurt and she was scared. And his other hand managed to slide down, unbutton her pants. Panic enveloped her.

She looked him in the eyes. They were nothing like earlier at the Center.

They were dark.

Wolfish.

"I said, *stop!*"

Another wave of terror coursed through her. Of all the horror stories her father had warned her about— exaggerated fears of a man who couldn't bear another loss—here she was. He would be so disappointed in her. And she was in herself.

But there was one positive that had derived from all of Dad's fears: he'd made sure his children were prepared if they ever encountered a monster. Self-defense classes, role-playing, emergency planning.

Maggie steeled herself. "Slow down," she said, softer. "I'll let you, but what's the rush? Take off your shirt."

He released her arms, yanked his hand from the waistband of her pants, then clumsily tugged off his shirt and threw it on the floor. Unexpectedly, he unbuttoned his pants and they dropped to the floor around his ankles.

"Touch it," he said. His rank breath wafted over her.

Maggie tried to remain calm. She put her hands on the balls of his muscular shoulders now. She stared seductively into his eyes, trying not to show the panic in hers. "If that's what you want." She drew back slightly like she was going to lower to her knees, and Eric's body shuddered.

She squeezed his shoulders tightly, using them as an anchor as she rammed her knee into his balls.

Eric doubled over and howled. Maggie pushed him hard. With his pants still around his ankles, he toppled to the laundry room floor.

He started yelling at her as she heaved open the door and ran.

CHAPTER 13

In the car ride home, tears spilled from Maggie's eyes. She felt emotionally hungover, adrenaline ripping through her. Anger at Eric. At herself for being such a fool.

"Talk to me," Harper said. She was in the back seat with Maggie. One of Harper's friends Maggie didn't know was driving.

Maggie wiped her eyes. Her chest convulsed in a flutter of tight breaths.

"What did he do?" Harper said. "I swear to God, I'll—"

"I don't want to talk about it."

"That motherfucker."

"It's okay. *I'm* okay. I just want to go home."

"You're not gonna stay over?"

"I just want to go home."

Harper told the girl driving where to go. They made their way down the suburban roads, Maggie staring out at nothing, tuning out Harper ranting about Eric. Finally they pulled up to Maggie's house.

"Text me later," Harper said as Maggie unbuckled her seat belt.

"Can you tell I've been crying?" Maggie asked, worried her dad would ask questions if he was awake.

Harper wiped Maggie's eye with her thumb. "I'm so sorry."

"It's not your fault," Maggie said, slipping out of the car. "It's mine," she added quietly to herself.

She unlocked the front door, surprised that the lights in the entryway and down the hall in the kitchen were still burning bright. It was late. Dad was usually in bed by now, and he was a stickler about saving electricity.

She thought of just heading up to bed. But if he was awake, he'd wonder why she was home and not staying over at Harper's. She tried to look composed as she walked quietly down the hallway.

That's when she saw her father on the kitchen floor.

CHAPTER 14

"Dad! Oh my god!" Maggie ran over to her father. He was out cold, a pool of vomit on the kitchen floor near his head.

She crouched down and shook his shoulders, fumbling for her phone to call 9-1-1.

But her dad jerked awake. He sat up quickly. His pupils were dilated, and he seemed off balance.

"Dad, what happened?" Maggie said in between ragged breaths. "Are you okay?"

Her father looked around, confused. He wiped his mouth with the back of his hand. Then he seemed to have a flash of lucidity.

"I'm fine, honey," he said, grabbing the counter with one hand and pulling himself up. His movements were slow, labored, like an elderly person with arthritis. "I'm sorry I scared you."

Maggie stared at him, trying to process the scene. "What happened? Did you slip and bump your head?" Her eyes went to the vomit. When Maggie was little, her mother seemed obsessed with concussions, the plight of a football mom, and Maggie remembered that throwing up could be a sign of a serious head injury.

"No. I think I may have gotten food poisoning. After dinner, I got this intense heat in my face and I threw up." Her dad went to the sink and ran water from the faucet, cleaning whatever was in the basin. "I must've passed out. But I'm okay, I'm fine."

What would make you so sick you'd pass out? Maggie's eyes were drawn to the bottle of Scotch on the counter. It was nearly empty, less than a finger of brown liquid settled at the bottom. Her dad wasn't much of a drinker—well, until lately. She started to put things together. He was passed-out drunk. Embarrassed to tell her.

"You're home," her dad said, more upbeat. He grabbed for the paper towel dispenser, unraveled a handful, and cleaned up the mess on the floor, casually, as if it weren't strange at all.

"I thought you were staying at Harper's?"

Maggie considered telling him about the party. About what had happened with Eric. She was still shaken up. But she, too, was embarrassed. Weirdly ashamed. But most of all, she worried that her dad might go off half-cocked. Call Eric's parents. Or confront him, even.

"I wasn't feeling well myself," Maggie said. "I wanted to sleep in my own bed."

"Can I get you something?" Her father opened the cupboard where they kept Advil and over-the-counter medicine.

"I'm fine," she said.

He seemed to believe her. And he didn't notice that she was dressed for a party, not a lazy sleepover. Just as well. Her dad didn't need more to worry about.

Her father had a glint in his eyes, like he'd just realized something. Maggie felt a jolt, worried that he knew she was lying. But he rushed to his smartphone on the counter and gestured for her to come over.

"You're not going to believe this," he said. His tone was excited, eyes manic.

He started thumbing the phone. "I got a video call. Right before I got sick."

Maggie just watched him.

"It was her, Magpie."

"Who?"

He looked at her intently: "Charlotte."

Okay, he must've bumped his head. "What are you talking about?"

"She called. She seemed scared. I saw her. She was alive. . . ."

"I think maybe you weren't feeling well"—she eyed the bottle—"and you just thought you—"

"No," her father said. "She was older, but there was no mistaking it. I've looked at hundreds of photos of her. It was Charlotte."

"Then it's a prank," Maggie said. "Somebody found a girl who looks like Charlotte. Or they did some CGI. A sick joke." It wouldn't be the first time someone had played a cruel prank on their family.

"She said *help me,* Magpie." Her dad looked like he was going to tear up.

"Charlotte's dead, Dad. They found her body. She's—"

"No, think about it. The girl's head was smashed in, face completely disfigured."

"But DNA—they must've—"

"I don't think they ever ran Charlotte's DNA. And why would they? No one questioned that it was Charlotte."

"But, Dad . . ." Maggie trailed off. She'd seen him like this before. Going down the rabbit hole. Yesterday it was the video of the party—the image of the Unknown Partygoer. Today, a FaceTime call showing a dead girl alive and kicking. In truth, she kind of liked it. The light in his eyes—the rare optimism, the enthusiasm— spending time together working the case. What strange daddy issues she must have, bonding over her imprisoned brother and his murdered girlfriend.

She decided to humor him. Let him sleep it off. Maggie gestured for him to give her the phone. "You said it was FaceTime?"

"Yeah. I tried calling back, but it just rings." He handed her the device.

She held the phone, still studying her father.

"The call, it said it was from a town in Mexico."

Maggie examined the call log. The phone said it was from Tulum, a place called Moloko Bar.

"There are services that can generate fake caller IDs," Maggie said. "It could be a scam."

"Or not," her father said.

Maggie pulled up a travel site on the phone. It

described Tulum as "a stylish vacation spot along Mexico's eastern coast, with amazing beaches, historic ruins, and a cooler, more laid-back vibe than the mega-resorts of Cancún and Riviera Maya."

Her father stared over Maggie's shoulder at the photograph on the travel site: a beautiful young woman on a beach sitting on a swing set made of carved wood, paper-white sand under her feet, the neon-blue ocean behind her.

Maggie googled Moloko Bar. It was a nightclub, images of young women in glittery attire getting bottle service, apparently having the time of their lives.

She looked at her dad again. It was as if a lightbulb had gone off over his head.

"Next week," he said, "for spring break, how'd you like to go on a trip?"

Maggie tipped her head to one side. "Where? You mean there?" She pointed at the screen.

Her dad nodded slowly, his eyes alight.

"I thought we couldn't go anywhere this year—that money was—"

"Let me worry about that."

"But Mom is—"

"They get back from Nebraska on Sunday. We can leave later that day or the next morning."

"I don't think Mom will like—"

"Let me handle your mother."

He was acting impulsively. No, obsessed, crazy. Maybe he did have a concussion. But Maggie didn't have the heart to pop this balloon tonight. He'd come around.

"Get some sleep," he said. "We've got a lot of planning and packing to do tomorrow."

She wanted to tell him what had happened earlier. That she'd lied to him and was sorry. That she'd been terrified. That she'd used what he'd taught her and gotten away. But instead she kissed him on the cheek and said, "Good night, Dad."

Sitting on her bed in her sleep shirt, Maggie hugged her knees as her mind returned to the party. Her heart thrummed looking at the fingerprint bruises on her wrists. She'd been a fool. Believing Eric was interested in her. Believing he was a sweet boy, like her brothers. She tried to suppress the tears, but that look in his eyes. If she hadn't tricked him into letting his guard down, he would've . . . She didn't want to think about that. She wanted to forget about tonight. She wanted this stupid year to end so she could leave for college and start over. Someplace where it mattered how intelligent you were, and not just how you looked or how well you threw a ball. Someplace where she wasn't just Danny Pine's sister.

She wished her mom was home. She could call her, of course. But she didn't want to call this late, worry Mom while she was out of town. Mom had enough going on, dealing with Grandpa. And returning to that town where everyone hated them.

She thought about Eric again, pretending to care about Danny's case. Faking interest in the video. She reached for her laptop, which was at the foot of the bed. She wanted to check for any comments or tips about the video. If there was one thing the Pines were good at, it was using Danny's case to avoid their problems. Excitement flickered in her chest. The page was filled with dozens of new comments, potential tips. But then she read them:

> Slut
> You should KYS
> No one invited a loser to the party
> Your brother's a killer and you're a whore
> Skank!!!!!!!

A sob escaped her mouth. It was Eric or his friends, it had to be. And *KYS*? Kill yourself? Because she'd rejected him? Or was all this to deter her from saying what had really happened in that laundry room? She snapped the laptop shut. She pinched her eyes closed and cried herself to sleep.

CHAPTER 15

MATT PINE

The consular officer who was supposed to pick up Matt at the airport was a no-show. Matt texted Agent Keller, then made his way past the luggage turnstiles crowded with travelers waiting anxiously for their bags. He stopped at the rental car counter, but they had no vehicles available. The rental agent told him that Tulum was about two hours away, and cabs and shuttles were just outside the main exit.

He careened around the frazzled masses and through the surprisingly small doors that led outside. Bright sunshine assailed him.

Near a cluster of vans, a rotund man holding a clipboard approached him. "Welcome to Mexico," he said in accented English. "Do you have a reservation?"

"I don't. I need to get to Tulum," Matt said.

The man grimaced. "We're booked solid, my friend. This is our busy season."

Matt let out a breath. "There's nothing? I'll take anything you have. It doesn't have to be nice."

The man paused, like he was thinking. He unclipped a walkie-talkie from his belt and said something into it in Spanish. A distorted voice responded.

"It won't be very comfortable," the man said, "but we can probably fit you in. Three thousand pesos."

"Will you take US?" Matt asked, showing the man a twenty-dollar bill.

"Yes, one hundred sixty dollars."

Matt had five hundred dollars in cash, the ATM's daily maximum. "I'll take it."

"Bus *cinco*," the man said, pointing to a line of vans. They were larger than standard vans, but smaller than buses.

Matt didn't speak Spanish, but *cinco* was easy enough. What college kid hadn't been to a Cinco de Mayo party? Matt paid the fare and hesitantly tipped the man a twenty—he didn't have smaller bills—leaving Matt enough for a shuttle back to the airport and dinner. He found the van with a sign displaying the number five.

The driver was leaning against the vehicle smoking a cigarette. He was a thick man with a thick mustache.

"I understand you have room for one more to Tulum," Matt said, looking back toward the man with the clipboard.

The driver crushed out his cigarette on the sidewalk. Without saying a word, he led Matt to the back of the van. Matt could see the outline of travelers through the tinted windows. The shuttle looked packed. The driver then opened the back hatch and gestured for Matt's duffel bag.

Matt threw it inside, and the driver started rearranging the other bags. He was piling them to one side in a very particular way.

"Oh," Matt said, realizing that the man was making room for *him*. He climbed inside and sat in the cramped space surrounded by luggage. It wasn't as bad as he'd expected. At least he could stretch out his legs. That was more than he could say for the Spirit Airlines flight.

"Are you okay back there?" a woman said from the main compartment. She had a sweet Southern accent.

Matt pulled himself up on the seat back so he could see into the crowded cabin.

"It's great. Thank you for letting me hitch a ride."

"You let us know if you need anything, hon." Her voice held a motherly hint of concern.

Matt spent the next two hours bouncing around in the back, watching out the rear window as they cruised south on Highway 307. It could've been any nondescript road in the US, except for all the litter: bags of garbage, old refrigerators, bottles and cans bordering the highway. Also, every ten miles or so Matt noticed wooden structures like guard towers or hunting platforms, many with men holding large automatic weapons.

It was nearly five o'clock. They'd arrive soon. He'd have just enough time to get to the police station, sign the papers, and make it back to the Cancún airport for his nine o'clock return flight to New York. Agent Keller said they could extend the stay if needed. But he had no interest in seeing the beaches, ruins, or other sites. In and out.

The seat back blocked Matt's view of the cabin, but he could make out some of the travelers up front in the reflection of the van's window. He spied three kids, under ten by the looks of them, draped all over their parents. Even in the distorted reflection, the mom and dad looked bone tired. He thought of his family in a van like this one: Tommy with his face pressed to the window; Dad lost in his thoughts, pondering some Danny conspiracy; Maggie making an agenda for the trip; Mom with her nose in a book.

Matt pulled up that last text Maggie had sent him, the one Keller had taken an interest in. It was a photo of Matt's father. It was zoomed in on his face, with a road behind him and what looked like the entrance to a business—a nightclub, maybe. Nothing out of the ordinary.

Scratch that. It was slightly unusual that Maggie would send Matt a shot of their father, given tensions of late.

In a sociology class at NYU, Matt had read about a study finding that by the time kids are eighteen, they've had an average of 4,200 arguments with their parents. Matt and his father had probably shattered that mean. It hadn't always been like that. Before Danny's arrest, Dad had been the one to encourage Matt's interest in filmmaking, buying him moviemaking software, researching old Super 8 cameras, setting up screening parties for Matt's short films. It wasn't football, but Dad—and Mom, too—seemed genuinely impressed with his work. By the time he'd won his first film contest senior year, it barely went noticed in the Pine home. Dad had Danny, Maggie had Dad, Mom had Tommy.

Matt stared at the photo of his father, stomach acid crawling up his throat at the thought of their last words:

> "It would be great if you could appear with us on the show."
>
> "I'm not going on the Today show, Dad."
>
> "The lawyers say public attention on the case could make a difference at the Supreme Court. The justices don't accept many cases, so anything we can do to—"
>
> "What part of no don't you get?"
>
> "You're being selfish."
>
> "Oh, that's just rich, coming from you."
>
> "What's that supposed to— Never mind. Fine. Do nothing, go back to school, and enjoy your carefree college life while your brother sits in a filthy prison cell."
>
> Matt stomped to the front door, grabbed his coat, yanked it on. "I will. You know why, Dad?" Matt paused a beat. "Because that's where Danny fucking belongs."

He had charged outside into the cold night, snowflakes floating peacefully in the sky, the strange quiet of a recent snow. He recalled how alone he'd felt that night. How alone he'd felt carrying around the truth about his brother, watching his father and sister spin their wheels trying to prove Danny's innocence. But it was nothing compared to what he was feeling right now.

The shuttle finally jerked to a stop in front of a blocky cement building. No one would know it was a police station save for the black-and-white Dodge Charger fitted with sirens parked out front. The van's back door swung open and Matt pulled himself out, tipped the driver, and raised a hand to the kids waving at him until the van disappeared down the road. He took a deep breath. It was time to claim the remains of his family.

One bite at a time, Matty. One bite at a time.

CHAPTER 16

SARAH KELLER

After her trip to the airport, Keller sat in her small windowless office in the FBI's New York field office, poring over a report. It was the initial data set analyzing the Pine family's digital footprint. Without their laptop computers or smartphones, the report was lighter than usual—limited to internet searches, social media posts, GPS locations—but the file was still three inches thick. There was no known crime, the word so far was freak accident, but something was gnawing at her.

Many agents scoffed at the notion of cop intuition, arguing that it was the kind of magical thinking that led to tunnel vision and convicting innocents. But Keller always followed her gut. And here it told her two words: *foul play*. So under the pretext of her money-laundering investigation of Marconi LLP, she'd had the IT nerds work their relationships with the internet companies and get the data. Once the Mexicans delivered the phones and laptops, she'd have a more complete picture.

Keller flipped through the stack, brushing through the

pages and pages of unintelligible code until she found the search engine report. It contained every search made through the family's internet service in the past three months. Searches about takeout food ("menu for Thai Garden"), the weather ("is it going to rain today"), education ("best MIT dorms"), leisure ("what's on TV tonight"), health ("why can't I sleep"), arts and crafts ("how to make slime"), and the other infinite queries of an ordinary American family.

In the Financial Crimes Section, where agents had to analyze mountains of data, she'd learned to separate the wheat from the chaff. For search engine reports, Keller's go-to trick was to jump to what users had purposefully deleted from their search history. Typically, it was what you'd expect: lots and lots of pornography.

But the Pine deleted searches included no porn-related inquiries. Someone, however, had erased some troubling searches from the history:

```
Does life insurance pay if you kill your-
self
How to make sure insurance pays if sui-
cide
How many Zoloft needed to overdose
Effects of parent suicide on kids
```

The sound of Keller's office phone interrupted her. She plucked the receiver from its cradle. "Keller," she said, in her official voice.

"Judy and Ira Adler are here to see you," the receptionist said.

"Who?" Keller clicked on her calendar to see if she'd forgotten an appointment. "I don't see anyone on my schedule."

"They say they're here about the Pine investigation."

Keller thought about this. Officially, there was no investigation. And certainly not one anyone would associate with Keller. She was effectively a babysitter, assigned because of Bureau politics and the strained connection to the Marconi case. While the receptionist waited with an annoyed breath through the receiver, Keller tapped "Judy Adler" into her computer's search engine. A Wikipedia page appeared: "Judy Adler is an Emmy Award–winning filmmaker and producer. She rose to prominence with her documentary series *A Violent Nature,* which she codirected with her husband, Ira."

Keller released her own annoyed breath. "I'll be right out." She made her way down the hallway. Through the glass security doors she got a look at her visitors.

Judy Adler was probably in her late fifties. She wore black, and had dark hair with severe bangs. With her was a man of a similar age, who wore slightly tinted eyeglasses and had disorderly gray hair.

In the reception area, Judy approached with a confident stride, sticking out her hand.

"Special Agent Keller, thanks for meeting with us. I'm Judy Adler. This is my husband, Ira."

Keller was tempted to say that she knew who they were, but just shook both their hands, nodded politely. "What can I do for you?"

"We hoped we could talk"—Judy looked around the

empty reception area as if to confirm no one was listening—"about the Pine investigation."

"I don't know what you're referring to."

Judy Adler gave Keller a knowing smile. "There're photos of you with Matthew Pine all over the internet. It took our people about five minutes to identify you. . . ."

The damn paparazzi from the dorm.

Before Keller responded, Judy Adler said, "We're filmmakers. We made a documentary about the Pines. Maybe you've seen it—*A Violent Nature*?"

"Some of it," Keller said, not offering a compliment. She actually thought it was well done—the Adlers were good storytellers. The old family photos of the Pines, the eerie string music, the interviews and news clips expertly interspersed for dramatic effect. Keller realized that Judy Adler was the interviewer, the faceless voice off-screen who'd probed subjects about Charlotte's death.

"We had our investigator go down to Mexico," Judy said. "He found something, and our lawyer said we should talk to the FBI."

She had Keller's attention now. By the look on Judy Adler's face, she knew it.

"Why don't you come back to my office."

The Adlers signed in and secured guest badges, then followed Keller to her office. Keller gestured to the visitor chairs and took her seat behind the desk. She subtly closed the computer research file on the Pine family.

Keller said, "Just so we're clear, whatever we discuss is off the record."

Judy frowned but gave a resigned nod. Her husband

still hadn't said anything. They struck Keller as one of those couples where the husband needed to be the strong, silent type.

"You sent an investigator to Mexico?" Keller asked.

"We stuck him on the first plane out after we heard. We're making a sequel to the documentary. And obviously, what happened is relevant to the story."

"What's the sequel about?" Keller asked.

"Today?" Ira Adler said, speaking for the first time. He had a husky, breathy voice, friendly, nonthreatening. "We started off focusing on Danny's appeal," Ira said. "There were some famous appellate lawyers working the case, and we had lots of public support."

Judy spoke now. "But it turns out *famous* appellate lawyers"—she put the word in air quotes—"are about as interesting as Nebraska. Do you know the state's official slogan?"

Keller shook her head.

"I swear I'm not making this up." Judy raised her hand like she was taking an oath. "Nebraska's slogan is 'Honestly, it's not for everyone.'" She coughed out a laugh, then said, "I've spent months there and they aren't lying. We're going back tonight."

Keller suppressed a grin.

"Anyway," Judy continued, "our big climax—the Supreme Court's decision—went to shit when those nine idiots denied Danny's appeal, so we almost scrapped the whole project."

"But then we decided to focus on the girl," Ira said. They had the rhythm of a couple who had been married a long time.

"You mean Charlotte?" Keller said.

"Right," Judy continued. "I mean, one of the criticisms we got over *A Violent Nature*—and it wasn't totally unfair—was that Charlotte seemed to get lost in it all. We were so focused on that awful interrogation of Danny Pine and the Unknown Partygoer and Bobby Ray Hayes that we never really gave the victim her due."

"So what does the accident in Mexico have to do with Charlotte?" Keller asked.

"Well, what if it wasn't an accident?" Judy said, holding Keller's gaze.

Keller felt a flutter in her chest. *Always trust your gut.* "The Mexican authorities haven't said anything about foul play," Keller said.

Judy said, "Maybe our guy knows how to ask a little more persuasively."

"By paying someone off," Keller replied.

Judy didn't flinch. "I wouldn't call it that. And I can assure you, we broke no Mexican laws." She snapped her fingers while simultaneously pointing at her oversize handbag, which was just out of reach. Ira passed her the bag, and Judy fished out a tablet. "But things work differently down there." Judy swiped at the tablet. "They're more free with investigative materials. . . ."

"You have their investigation file?" Keller asked. This was important because Keller had received diddly-squat from the Mexican authorities. The local cops in Tulum had snubbed the FBI's Mexico legal attaché, and the consular officer had been astonishingly unhelpful.

"If you can call it that," Judy said. "They're not

exactly skilled investigators. I doubt they get training about much of anything, let alone how to manage a crime scene or investigate homicide."

Homicide.

"So what's in the file?"

"Photos of the scene—they at least did that much."

Keller swallowed. The Adlers had postmortem photographs of the Pine family. Keller didn't want to look at them, but she had to. She eyed the tablet and nodded for Judy to pull them up.

A few swipes later and Keller's breath was stripped from her lungs. Mrs. Pine, even more beautiful than in the photos Keller had seen, was lying on the couch, a book resting on her chest. She looked like she was taking a nap.

"I don't see any signs of foul play," Keller said. "It looks consistent with a gas leak."

"Look again," Judy said.

Keller moved her face closer to the tablet, studying the screen. Olivia Pine's face was peaceful. Her long legs—she was a runner, by the looks of them—stretched out on the sofa. There was no blood or obvious signs of trauma. Next to the sofa was an end table. On it, a lamp and coaster. Nothing seemed disturbed or as if there'd been a struggle.

Keller could feel Judy staring at her, waiting for her to see. Then she did.

"The book," Keller said, touching the novel on Olivia Pine's chest with her finger. "It's upside down."

Judy gave an exaggerated nod.

Keller thought it over. If Olivia Pine had passed out from the gas while she was reading, the book would have fallen in place. It wouldn't be upside down.

"It's staged," Keller said.

More nodding from Judy.

"That doesn't mean she was murdered," Keller said. "The cops could've bungled the scene and put the book back on her chest to cover themselves."

Judy didn't respond. Instead she reached for the tablet, swiped, and handed it back to Keller.

Keller's heart sank at the sight of the girl, Margaret. Matt called her Maggie. She was on her stomach on top of the bed.

This time Judy didn't wait for Keller to see it. She pointed her index finger at the screen. On Maggie's wrists there were tiny bruises, like fingerprints, as if she'd been held down.

"What about the father and little boy?" Keller asked.

"No signs of struggle with the boy. But the father, his body was found outside on the back porch. I've gotta warn you," Judy said, swiping the tablet, "the photos aren't for the faint of heart."

Keller tried not to gasp. Evan Pine was little more than a bloody stump. An image fit for a horror movie. "What the hell . . ."

"Tulum has a lot of wild dogs," Ira Adler chimed in.

Dear God. Keller needed to warn Matt in case the Mexicans required him to personally ID the bodies. Keller looked away from the image, thinking. That Evan Pine was outside supported the Adlers' foul play theory. He confronted someone trying to get in from the back of the property, they killed him, and the dogs got to the body. The intruder then subdued the rest of the family and cut the gas line. At the same time, Evan could've realized there was a gas leak and stumbled outside before succumbing to the toxic air. But there was an alternative theory. Keller's mind jumped back to the suicide searches on the family's computer. Was this a botched suicide? Or worse, a murder-suicide? She kept those thoughts to herself.

"I'm going to need copies of the photos," Keller said.

"Our lawyer says we don't *have* to give them to you, not without a warrant anyway," Judy said.

Keller let her stare show her displeasure.

"But maybe we can help one another," Judy said.

"How so?" Keller asked, after a long moment.

"Our investigator found something the local cops overlooked." Judy reached into her handbag again. She retrieved an overnight delivery envelope. Slipping her hand inside the cardboard sleeve, she carefully removed a small Ziploc bag.

"What's that?" Keller asked. Inside the bag was a leaf or part of a plant.

"The police let our guy view the crime scene."

Keller opened her mouth to say something, to castigate them for potentially contaminating the scene, but Judy waved her quiet.

"I know, I know," Judy said. She was a hand talker. "But they'd already closed the case, designated the deaths accidental."

"What did he find?" Keller asked, deciding a lecture on crime scene protocol wouldn't get her anywhere.

And she wanted to know what was in the bag sitting on her desk.

"The scene was immaculate," Judy said. "Wiped down from top to bottom, the kitchen and bathroom trash cans all empty, even though there was nothing in the cans outside."

It was suspicious. Unusual. But there were plausible explanations. "Maybe the local police let the maid clean the place," Keller said. "Or maybe the Pines cleaned up before . . ."

Judy offered a resigned nod. "The Tulum cops certainly didn't think there was anything to it. But our investigator said it had the earmarks of a professional. And when he examined the scene outside—where they found Evan Pine's body—he found this." Judy handed Keller the plastic bag. "The patio of the rental is surrounded by a tall fence, which is why no one saw the body sooner. The gate was unlatched. Our investigator spotted this near the gate."

Holding the bag at eye level with her thumb and index finger, Keller saw it. A drop of red, about a millimeter in diameter, staining the green leaf.

"Couldn't it just be Evan Pine's blood?" Keller said.

"Maybe. But he was pretty far away from the gate and the plant was at shoulder height, higher than you'd expect if it was cross-contamination from the dogs tearing out of there. But that's what we hoped you could tell us."

Keller narrowed her eyes.

"You could run the DNA, see if you get any hits," Judy continued.

"The FBI isn't a private DNA testing service. And we can't disclose confidential investigation materials," Keller said.

Judy frowned. "Look, our lawyer says you don't have jurisdiction and we have no obligation to give you the sample. And we can hire DNA experts and genealogists and have them run it through public and consumer DNA databases. But let's save us both some time, help one another out here."

Keller wasn't so sure that the Adlers' lawyer was correct. Federal racketeering statutes gave the US jurisdiction over murders committed abroad if the crimes facilitated a domestic criminal enterprise, and the Marconi case gave her a hook. Still, a good lawyer could tie things up for months or even years.

"What is it exactly that you want?" Keller asked.

"Simple. Run the sample through CODIS, and let us know the results." CODIS was a series of databases that stored millions of DNA profiles collected by federal, state, and local law enforcement. If the sample came from someone who'd been convicted or arrested—or had a family member who'd been convicted or arrested—CODIS would likely get a hit. And if the Feds didn't get a hit in CODIS, they had relationships with private ancestry companies people used to test and analyze their DNA.

Judy added, "That's all we need. And if you get a hit, we'll commit not to disclose anything without your prior approval. If it turns out to be nothing—Evan Pine's blood or an animal's or whatever—then we'll know."

Keller thought about the photos of the family, thought

about the pain in Matt Pine's eyes that morning. Keller wasn't sure she would get authorization to disclose information to the Adlers, but there was no way she was letting them walk out of there with the evidence.

"Okay," Keller said, "you've got a deal."

CHAPTER 17

After the filmmakers ambled out of the field office, Keller arranged for the red droplet on the leaf to be analyzed and run through CODIS. She then turned back to her computer forensics file on the Pine family. She was having a hard time concentrating, questions firing through her head: Was the crime scene staged? If so, then who would want to kill the Pines? Was it an accident, Evan Pine inadvertently gassing his family while killing himself? Or was it an intruder? A third party making it look like a tragic accident. But who and why? Could it be related to her money-laundering investigation of Marconi? And if it was a third party, a contract killer, as the Adlers' investigator speculated, how could the perp be so careful to wipe the scene clean but leave DNA behind? And why would the perp be bleeding? Did Evan and the intruder have an altercation, and the killer was injured?

She needed to stop, slow down. She wasn't making a

movie, like the Adlers. She needed to take things slowly, methodically, objectively. She would get the results from the DNA tests, she would have the bodies autopsied, she would conduct interviews. And until then, she'd review the digital forensics and documents.

She thumbed absently through pages of data until something caught her eye. Two days before the family left for Mexico, the teenage girl, Maggie, had deactivated all Danny Pine social media. Keller soon thought she knew why: the girl was being cyberbullied. At 2:00 A.M. there had been an onslaught of messages—hurtful, vile messages. Teenage girls were the worst kind of mean. But what had precipitated them? Keller examined the feed on the Free Danny Pine Facebook page. The last post was a video that Maggie called "tip."

Keller was about to watch the clip when her office phone buzzed. She glanced at the display on the old desk phone. It was her boss, Stan Webb.

"Special Agent Keller," she said in her official voice. Stan was a formal man, so as a rule Keller kept things formal.

"I need you to come with me to D.C.," Stan said, without pleasantries. Stan had never asked her to accompany him to headquarters, so this was unusual.

"Sure. When do you—"

"Right away," Stan said, like it was the last thing in the world he wanted to do.

"Today?" Keller felt a sinking in her gut. Being beckoned to HQ—with the boss—couldn't be good. And it was more time away from Bob and the twins. "Is everything okay?"

"You know how they are. The field offices don't exist until a reporter calls asking about one of our cases."

"It's about the Pines?"

"Appears so. I could kill Fisher for getting us involved." Fisher was Stan's boss in Washington, a politico who looked over the East Coast field offices and who'd wormed them into the Pine case. "You'll need to be prepared to brief the deputy director on the status. And on the Marconi investigation."

"Of course. When do we need to leave?"

"Ten minutes ago. We're taking the jet. Wheels lift at fourteen hundred hours."

Stan always spoke in military time and Keller had to do the conversion in her head: 2:00 P.M. She looked at her watch. She had an hour to get things in order. She wouldn't have time to go home, but she kept a travel bag at the office. She traveled some for her job, but she'd never flown on a Bureau jet. Someone was taking the Pine situation seriously.

And that was without knowing the family could've been murdered.

At just before two, Keller mounted the narrow stairs of the Gulfstream. She was embarrassed that she was excited for the flight, her first ever on a private plane. Working for the Bureau wasn't like those television shows—*Criminal Minds* or *CSI*—where agents jetted around hunting serial killers. In Financial Crimes she was largely a desk jockey, analyzing documents, writing reports, occasionally meeting with financial institutions to wrench bank records out of their grubby hands.

She looked around the cabin. It didn't live up to expectations. The jet was better than flying commercial for sure. No waiting in lines or middle seat hell. She had a single seat and her own worktable. But it was hardly glamorous. The plane had the feel of an aging Greyhound bus: dated decor and worn plastic. The flight attendant was a plump woman in a polyester uniform.

Stan sat in his own single seat, a comfortable distance across the cabin. He wore a stiff suit and a sharp part in his hair and glasses with no frames. If you didn't know he was a Fed, you'd think he was a tech executive or a German banker.

They weren't exactly what you would call friends. It was something better, in Keller's estimation: a boss who valued results, not face time. One who didn't steal credit, didn't play favorites, and didn't micromanage. He was direct and played it straight. If you fucked up, he'd tell you. But you knew he'd always have your back. His only vice, if you'd call it that, was his fear of Fisher and HQ. No, it wasn't fear. It was self-preservation. In her time at the Bureau, Keller had observed that the Washington types wouldn't just throw you under the bus if it suited their needs. They'd get behind the wheel, run you down, then slam the bus in reverse and make sure the job was done. It helped to jump when they called, to show the politicos the respect they thought they were due.

After the plane took off—a steep and bumpy climb—Keller briefed Stan on what she knew about the death of the Pines. He seemed surprised about the fuss over the case.

"You haven't seen the documentary?" Keller asked.

He shook his head. Not a surprise. She suspected that Stan was one of those people who didn't own a TV.

"I read the piece in the *Times* this morning," he said. "The deputy director said the president has taken an interest because his daughter is obsessed with the case."

Keller contemplated her boss, unclear if Stan was kidding. He had a dry sense of humor.

"Have you heard from the kid yet?" Stan asked.

"He texted and said the consular officer who was supposed to pick him up from the airport didn't show, so he's just heading to the police station on his own."

"Keystone fucking Cops. We need those bodies. An accident is spectacle enough, but if autopsies show they were murdered . . ."

"I had only one call with the consular officer assigned to the case. He called me *sweetheart* and told me I didn't understand how things worked down there, and that he'd take care of everything. I've texted him to see what the hell is going on."

Stan shook his head. "Fucking bureaucrats. And that's coming from a career bureaucrat. Hopefully the kid handles it. If the locals give him trouble, I'll call the embassy and see if our people in Mexico City can help."

An hour later Keller was in the back of a cab crammed next to her boss, gazing out the window. Unlike gloomy Manhattan, it was a beautiful spring day in D.C., the marble government buildings gleaming, the Washington Monument jutting into the blue sky. The cabdriver groused about the traffic, explaining that it was peak cherry blossom season. "I'll never understand all the excitement over some damn pink flowers," he said, laying on the horn as they inched along Twelfth Street.

Keller thought about her family. They should take the train down to D.C. soon. The twins loved the museums, walking along the gravel perimeter of the National Mall, getting ice cream and riding the carousel. That was about all that Keller knew or wanted to know about the District of Columbia.

They finally arrived at the FBI building, a brutalist structure that had seen better days. They'd been talking about moving HQ for years, but politics (what else?) always got in the way. The cab dropped them on Ninth and Keller paid the driver. It was Bureau etiquette: the junior agent, no matter his or her rank, paid for cabs. She imagined Stan, a G-man to his core, traveling with Fisher and suffering the same indignity.

Several layers of security later—multiple ID checks, mantraps, key card swipes—and they were in the office waiting area for Deputy Director DeMartini. The puffy-faced man burst from the back offices. He gave Stan and Keller a curt nod and said, "Walk with me."

It was hard to keep stride. The deputy director was a tall man, at least six two, which seemed to be a prerequisite to making it to the top in testosterone-laden federal law enforcement.

"I've got to brief the director on the dead family in seven minutes. What do we know?"

Stan started, his report as precise as a Swiss watch. "It was a spring break trip for their younger kids. The tickets were booked at the last minute, just a day before they left. They likely died on the third day, Wednesday. Phone and social media activity went dark then. They missed their flight home a few days later, and the property management company's maid found them when she came to clean up the place for the next guests. The Mexicans say it was an accident."

DeMartini shook his head. "Your email said something about foul play?"

"I'll let Agent Keller brief you."

Keller tried to steady her breath from the brisk walk. She gave the report in clipped cop-speak, mimicking Stan. *Just the facts, ma'am.*

"Initial reports are that cause of death was a gas leak. But the locals have been uncooperative. We don't have the bodies yet, but there are photos suggesting the scene was staged."

DeMartini stopped, narrowed his eyes, waiting for her to elaborate.

Keller told him about the visit from the Adlers, described the photo of the mother's paperback upside down, the marks on the girl's wrists, the father's bloody remains. The unusually clean crime scene. But most important, the drop of blood.

"Why don't *we* have our *own* forensics—or the bodies, for that matter?" DeMartini said, his question plainly rhetorical, but his tone indicating that he didn't like the Federal Bureau of Investigation getting bested by filmmakers, of all people.

"The locals. They wouldn't talk to our Legats and

won't release the remains without a family member claiming them in person. We sent the surviving son there today."

"Couldn't our people at State cut through the bullshit?"

"I'm not sure how hard they've tried," Keller said.

Stan gave her a look: perhaps she shouldn't have said it.

"Fuck that," DeMartini said. He fished out his phone, clicking on it with his big thumbs. "Get me Brian Cook at State," he said into the device. "I know. Tell him it's important." He waited a long moment. "B.C., how the fuck are ya?" The deputy director started walking again, and Keller and Stan trailed after him. "Look, I'm sending over two agents who need your help with something. Any chance you can fit them in? Yeah, within the hour."

He listened for a moment, barked a laugh at something, then said, "I owe you one. Let's hit some balls at Chevy soon. I'll have Nadine get you on my calendar." DeMartini pocketed the phone. He stopped again, this time in front of the director's office suite. "Fisher said something about the father having a connection to an ongoing case?"

"The father worked at Marconi LLP. He was fired a couple weeks before the family left for Mexico," Stan said.

DeMartini shook his head like he hadn't the foggiest.

"Marconi's been a target for two years. Money laundering and the usual. The firm's the Sinaloa Cartel's bank."

"You rousted them yet?"

Keller was about to speak—to note that approaching Marconi would jeopardize two years' work—but Stan beat her to it.

"Tomorrow morning, first thing."

"Keep me posted. The *administration*"—DeMartini said the word with an exasperated sigh—"is very interested in this case. I do not want to get my updates from the *Post*."

"Understood," Stan said.

"Cook at State should be able to get you what you need in Mexico. Go to the C Street lobby. And send me a report after you shake the tree at Marconi."

Stan and Keller nodded, and DeMartini turned and pushed through the mahogany door of the director's suite without saying goodbye.

Keller looked at Stan. "Two hundred miles for six minutes."

"You wanted a long meeting?" Stan replied.

They took the elevator to the ground floor.

"I was surprised about Marconi," Keller said. "I mean, we haven't done any prep and it could mess up a lot of work. If they think we're onto them, they'll start destroying documents. And it could all be for nothing. We don't have one shred of evidence that the Pine deaths are related to Marconi or the cartel."

Stan looked at Keller and in that droll way of his said, "You wouldn't want to disappoint the president's daughter, would you?"

CHAPTER 18

MATT PINE

Matt approached the front desk of the small station house. The place had all the charm of Danny's prison in upstate New York—a dilapidated single-story structure with low ceilings and mangy carpeting.

"Hello," Matt said to the woman at the counter.

She flicked him a glance. She was middle-aged and wore glasses pinched to her nose.

"I'm here to see Señor Gutierrez," Matt said, looking at the paper Agent Keller had given him with the investigator's name.

The woman responded rapidly in Spanish. Matt didn't catch a word of it, but she seemed to be scolding him.

"I'm Matt Pine," he said loudly and slowly, as if that would help. He showed the receptionist his passport, but she just gave him a bewildered expression.

From his duffel, he pulled out the newspaper Keller had given him. He laid it flat on the counter. He pointed to the photo. "My family," he said.

The woman looked at the newspaper and lifted her eyes, peering over her glasses. She started back with the fast-talking Spanish. If it all wasn't so morbid, it would be almost comical. A scene from *Lost in Translation*.

Matt said the only phrase he remembered from high school Spanish. *"No hablo español."*

The woman stopped. Let out an exasperated breath. She pondered Matt at length, and finally pointed to the detective's name on the sheet of paper. Then she gestured out the door.

"Ah. Señor Gutierrez is out." Matt paused. "When will he—" Matt stopped again. He pointed to a clock on the wall behind the woman. It was one of those old-fashioned clocks you'd see in elementary schools, round with a white face and black numbers.

"What time will Señor Gutierrez return?" Matt pointed to the officer's name then the clock again.

The woman seemed to get it. She stood and pointed to the 9 on the clock. He'd be there at nine tonight. No, the woman made a gesture like she was sleeping, then made a circular motion around the clock past the nine and around once until she stopped at the nine again. Tomorrow morning: 9:00 A.M. So much for getting out of there tonight. He considered asking to speak to another officer, but there didn't seem to be anyone else at the station house.

Outside, the sun was disappearing on the horizon. Matt started walking toward the main road ahead in the distance. He passed a run-down auto repair shop, a convenience store with no windows, and a chicken place, by the looks of the hand-painted rooster on the sign. He felt as he did in certain parts of New York— safe enough, but on alert.

A scruffy dog ran up to him. "Hey there, buddy." Matt risked giving the stray a rub behind the ears. His fur was matted, and he had scars, but he was friendly. His face looked like he was smiling. Matt couldn't help but smile back at him. The dog made a sound like he was trying to talk.

"You hungry?"

The dog looked up at him. Matt unzipped his duffel and found a bag of pretzels, the snack from the airplane. The dog started dancing in circles.

"Not the healthiest, but here you go." Matt emptied the bag on the ground. "See you later, Smiley."

Matt made it to the main road, the dog trailing behind him, hoping for more food. Highway 307 was a long row of shops, bars, restaurants, and currency exchange stations. Tourists were drifting in and out of stores, buying trinkets, and shopkeepers sat on stools out front.

Matt's stomach growled. Like Smiley, who'd wandered into one of the shops, he was hungry. He realized it had been more than twenty-four hours since he'd eaten anything. His appetite was gone. Eating, like other ordinary things, seemed so trivial now. But he couldn't keep running on only despair. Spotting a cantina, he decided he'd get some food, then find a place to stay. The establishment was seat-yourself, so he took a stool at a tall bar table. A waitress appeared, and she mercifully spoke English. He ordered a Mexican beer and two tacos. *When in Rome*.

He glanced around the place. In the far corner was a group of young women, loud and rowdy and the epitome of Ugly Americans. A few tables over was a foursome—they looked like tourists from Japan—sitting politely with their neat polo shirts and hands folded. At the bar were a mix of locals and vacationers.

He wondered why his parents had picked Tulum. They'd never talked about going to Mexico. The internet said Tulum was a hot spot for celebrities, cool and off the beaten path. That didn't sound like Evan Pine's scene at all. Maybe one of those celebrities—wherever they were, Matt sure as shit didn't see any—had offered to help with Danny's case. That seemed a lot more plausible than his father deciding to have an impromptu spring break getaway. Especially since his mother had been in Nebraska. It didn't make sense.

Matt tapped on his phone, searching travel sites for a place to stay. After several searches, he hadn't found a single vacancy, not even in the cheap motels. Maybe he could try a walk-in, since the travel websites might not have up-to-date vacancies. Or there might be some dumps too low-end for Expedia. He texted Agent Keller to see if the FBI could arrange accommodations, though he wasn't holding his breath, since the consular officer hadn't even bothered to show up at the airport. Worst case, he'd stay out all night. It wouldn't be the first time.

He started to pull up another site, but a young woman interrupted him.

"Hi," she said, staring at him with doe eyes as she slipped onto the stool across from him. She had glossy dark hair and high cheekbones and wore a bikini with jean shorts.

"Hi," he replied, curious. He glanced over toward the group of obnoxious American women, since he assumed she was part of their group, but they were gone.

"I'm so sorry, but would you mind if I sat with you for a few minutes?" Before Matt could respond, she said, "Behind me, those two guys at the bar. I don't want them to know I'm here alone."

Matt shot a quick glance toward the bar. He saw two hard-looking men with leathery skin and crude tattoos hunched over their beers.

"I promise, I'm not a stalker." She had full lips, and her face lit up when she smiled.

"It's no problem. They were bothering you?"

She nodded, twisted a strand of her hair. "Once they go, I'll leave you alone. I promise."

He didn't say so, but he actually liked the company. It had been a long, lonely day.

"I'm Hank, by the way," she said.

"Hank," he repeated.

"My dad wanted a boy," she explained with the practice of someone with an unusual name. She had an accent. It wasn't Southern, more Midwestern, a rural lilt. It reminded Matt of his friend Kala's twang when they'd first met, before she started hiding it.

Hank laughed hard at nothing, then reached over and placed her hand on Matt's. "Sorry," she said. "Just in case they're watching."

The waitress brought over his beer and the tacos.

Matt asked if Hank wanted anything, but she ordered just a glass of water.

"I thought you weren't supposed to drink the water?" Matt said.

"I'm an Oklahoma girl; I can handle it."

"I knew it, a Midwesterner. I'm one too. I used to live in Nebraska."

"You're a Cornhusker? I think I'd better take my chances with the creeps," she said, smiling. "Where in Nebraska?"

"I moved a long time ago, and you wouldn't have heard of it anyway."

"Where do you live now?"

"New York, I go to NYU. But my home is just outside Chicago." Matt looked down at the table. Was Naperville his home anymore? Was there anything left for him there? When he raised his eyes, Hank was studying him.

"So, you waitin' on someone, friends?" she asked.

Matt shook his head. "I'm here on my own."

She tilted her head to the side, gave him a curious look. But she didn't ask.

"How about you? You're here by yourself?" Matt asked, his eyes sliding back to the men at the bar who'd been bothering her.

She frowned. "I'm here for a bachelorette party." Lowering her voice, she said, "I can't stand the bride or her friends."

"No?" It was a long way to come for someone she didn't like.

"My brother's fiancée," she explained.

"Ah," Matt said.

"The things we do for family, right?"

Matt took a swig of his beer, felt a sting in his chest.

"They're all her friends and super drunk and annoying," she continued, "so I hung back when they hopped to the next bar. But she makes my brother happy, so what can you do?"

"The elusive hunt for happiness," Matt said. God knows Matt had been on that pursuit for some time. Even before, he wouldn't say he'd been depressed or even sad. Despite the friction, he always knew his family loved him. He had close friends he cared about and who cared about him. He had, for all intents and purposes, a privileged life. But there was always this hollowed-out feeling in his chest he hadn't been able to shake since Year Zero. "I took a class on happiness at school," he said.

Hank stared at him, openmouthed. "Wait, you're telling me that your college, which probably cost more than a house in Arkoma, has classes on *happiness*?" She said it like she was really dumbfounded.

Matt smiled, realizing how it must sound. "The class is called 'The Science of Happiness.' And it wasn't so much about how to be happy, but about dealing with mental health wellness. But they did teach us an exercise that can make you happier."

"Having rich parents," Hank said, with a smile.

"No, it's not money or status or even a fiancée that makes people happy."

She leaned in, excited to learn the secret.

"It's kindness," Matt said. "Studies prove that doing five random acts of kindness a day leads to more happiness. But it has to be five, for some reason. I forget why."

Hank narrowed her eyes. "So is that why you let me sit here, to meet your daily quota or something?" She smiled again.

The waitress came over with the water. Matt looked at Hank. "You sure you don't want anything?"

"You know what, why not?" she said. "I'll have a margarita."

"Make that two," Matt said.

CHAPTER 19

Matt peered over at the bar and noticed that the guys who'd been bothering Hank were gone. He was almost disappointed, since he was enjoying her company. He learned that she was an avid football fan and wasn't kidding about her disdain for Nebraska, even though the Cornhusker–Sooner rivalry had died down in recent years. He also learned that she'd dropped out of community college, but planned to go back. That she was a hairstylist. That she loved dogs. He avoided telling her why he was there. It was all mindless small talk, precisely what he needed.

"They're gone," Matt said, directing his gaze to the bar.

She looked over her shoulder, and let out an exaggerated sigh of relief.

"Want me to walk you out to get a cab in case they're still hanging around outside?"

"I have a rental car. But if you wouldn't mind walking with me . . . ?"

It was dark outside, late. The men were nowhere to

be seen, which was a good thing. Matt could hold his own, but there were two of them and they looked like they'd been in their share of fights. And after he'd lost control on that frat boy, he'd pledged to stop with the fisticuffs.

A dog ran up to them. It was Smiley from earlier.

"Speaking of stalkers, this guy's been following me since I got here."

Hank crouched down and cupped Smiley's face in her hand. "Oh my god. He's so cute. Look at this face!"

The dog followed them down the main drag. Hank said, "He's so friendly. I heard that you've got to be careful. There're packs of wild dogs around here that are dangerous." She looked at Smiley again. "But not this sweet boy."

"You staying nearby?" Matt asked.

"No, we're right on the beach. They wanted to be adventurous and explore the bars here in town. How about you?"

"I actually need to find a place. I was supposed to be in for just the day, but got delayed."

"You came all the way here with nowhere to stay?" She seemed amused by that.

"Long story."

"I'll bet."

"I'll find somewhere."

She gave him a sideways look like she knew better during the busy season. She stopped at a beat-up Toyota parked haphazardly on a side street.

"It was great to meet you," Matt said. "Have a great time at the wedding."

"You obviously haven't seen the bridesmaid dresses." She paused as if she were pondering something. "Hey, I won't be surprised if our hotel has an opening. My brother booked a block of rooms and a couple people canceled last minute. I can drive you."

"I don't want to put you out."

"You won't be. Let's call it a random act of kindness," Hank said. "But I'll warn you, it's an eco hotel. My brother's fiancée is an earthy type—vegan, environmentalist, self-righteous."

Matt thought about his friend Sofia. "I *love* that type. And you know the first rule of Vegan Club, right?"

Hank shook her head.

"Tell *everyone* about Vegan Club."

She laughed.

Matt dropped into the passenger seat. Hank drove down the gravel road, veering around people on old bicycles, past storefronts covered in graffiti and open-air food stands. After a while, the road turned desolate—the only light the weak beams from the rental car, thick forest on either side of them.

"You weren't kidding about this place being in the middle of nowhere," Matt said, breaking the quiet.

Hank gave him a quick smile.

Matt reached for his phone. She seemed to know where she was going, but he thought he'd look up the hotel. She said it was on the beach, but they seemed to be heading into a rural area away from the ocean.

"Shit," he said.

"What is it?" Hank looked at him, but turned her eyes quickly back to the dark road.

"My phone, I must've left it at the bar." Matt searched his pockets, then dug through the duffel, yanking out his clothes and the newspaper Keller had given him. Without a phone, he'd be screwed.

He started looking around the car somewhat frantically. "Would you mind pulling over?"

Hank hesitated. "We're almost there," she said.

"Please," he said.

Hank slowed the car and parked on the gravel shoulder.

She turned on the car's interior lights as Matt opened the passenger door, stepped outside, and crouched low, looking on the floorboards and under the seat. Why was he such an idiot with phones?

He climbed back inside and sat next to Hank, defeated. He was about to ask her to take him back to the bar when he noticed she was staring intently at the *New York Times* story, studying the photos of Matt and his family.

Hank looked at him. "This is—wait—this is why you're here? This is your family?"

Matt gave a tiny shrug.

She looked at the newspaper again and back at Matt. "Oh my god." She had a faraway look in her eyes.

"Sorry," Matt said. "I would've told you—I just didn't want to put a damper on the night."

She looked out at the lights approaching from down the long strip of road.

Something was different. It wasn't pity or sadness.

It was panic.

She reached under her seat, then shoved something in his hand. A phone.

His phone.

"You took my . . . I don't understand."

"I didn't sign up for this." She looked up the road. The headlights were getting closer. "You need to get out," she said.

"Here?" Matt said, totally confused. He looked out into the gloom.

She leaned over, tugged at the door handle, and shoved open his door.

"Run," she said, the other car getting closer. Then louder: *"Run!"*

So that's what he did.

Excerpt from
A Violent Nature

Season 1/Episode 6
"What Was Lost"

EXT. DAY - RURAL ROAD

A mail truck plods down the road. It stops
at a circular patch of land with mailboxes
lining the perimeter. CINDY FORD gets out of
the truck and stuffs mail into a box.

> CINDY
>
> After Danny's trial, my sister and her
> family moved to Chicago. Liv and Evan lost
> most of their friends, and they had to
> sell the house to pay for the lawyer. But
> I think they probably would've stuck it
> out if it weren't for their kids getting
> teased at school. Matt got into a fight one
> day and that was it—they packed up and
> moved.

Cindy points to several dirt roads that
jut out of the circular patch of land.

> CINDY
>
> They call this area "the Hub." One of the
> roads leads to the creek, where they found
> Charlotte. Another leads to my sister's

old house, which is why they thought Danny
was involved, I suppose. But there's a
bunch of other roads, one that leads to
the highway, others take you to about a
dozen houses. And if you cut around those
bushes, there's an opening called "the
Knoll," a make-out spot for teenagers. If
someone was looking to go after a teenage girl, all they'd have to do is lie in
wait.

A run-down muscle car tears out from one
of the roads, music blaring, dust flying.
Teenagers scream out the window, and an
empty beer can hits the side of the mail
truck.

                    CINDY
Why didn't I leave too? Someone needed to
stay to take care of our dad. And it's not
usually like this. The kids have just been
showin' off since you all arrived with
your cameras. Maybe you could do me a favor and turn off your camera for a minute.

In the distance, the muscle car has doubled back and is racing toward the Hub.
Cindy leans inside the mail truck and
retrieves what looks like a jar full of
nails. She walks to the road and empties
the jar.

CINDY

You deliver people's mail, you learn a lot about them, and I'll tell you, most of the people round here have no room to judge anybody. And if you try to run me outta *my* own town, it's gonna cost you, and it'll be a helluva lot more than four new tires.

CHAPTER 20

OLIVIA PINE

BEFORE

"Please, Mommy, I've gotta go."

Liv looked in the rearview of the rental car. Tommy was wiggling around in the car seat, making a show of grabbing himself to let her know he was serious.

"We're almost to Aunt Cindy's house. Do you think you can make it, buddy?"

Liv had just hit Main Street in Adair, Nebraska. It hadn't changed. As promised, it was a main strip with a hardware store, a diner, an old-time movie theater, a drugstore. Adair wasn't a depressed farming community like many in the Heartland. Most of the town worked at Adair Irrigation, the country's largest manufacturer of water management systems. A factory town surrounded by cornfields.

They'd left Adair under the cloud of Danny's conviction. It had been a quiet ostracism, fueled more by whispers than overt scorn. But then Netflix released the documentary, and the whole country seemed to turn on Adair, revitalizing and intensifying the town's contempt for the Pines. The last thing Liv wanted was to stop anywhere she'd be recognized. But based on Tommy's red face and squirming, she had no choice. She knew Parker's Grocery had a public restroom, so she veered into the lot.

"I'm stopping, jelly bean. Hang on." The store had a new sign but was otherwise the same as when Liv was a girl. Her father would take her to Parker's every Saturday to buy candy, at least until the cavities sprouted and her mom put an end to it.

Holding Tommy's hand, she walked quickly inside. Liv's stomach clenched when she saw the woman behind the register. Danielle Parker hadn't changed much either. Still heavyset with eyes that were too close together, and a perpetual scowl. Liv walked head down to the back of the store to the public restrooms, Tommy trying to keep up with her long strides. She clasped the restroom door handle, but it was locked. Of course it was.

"Wait here, sweetie. I need to get the key."

"Quickly, pleaasssse," he said, nearly bursting.

Liv went back to the counter. "Hello," she said, forcing a smile. "Could we have the key to the restroom, please? My son is about to have an—"

"Bathroom is for payin' customers only."

Liv paused a beat. She looked Danielle in those narrow eyes. With no time for a standoff, Liv jammed her hand into a large plastic container near the register, removed a fistful of hard candy, and dropped the colorful assortment on the counter.

"Five-dollar minimum," Danielle said.

Liv was about to lose it, but she looked back and saw Tommy doing a pee dance. "How much is the whole container?" Liv asked, gesturing to the plastic jug of candy.

Danielle made a face like she was doing a complicated math problem in her head. "Twenty bucks," she said.

Liv dug into her handbag and smacked a twenty down. "Can I have the key please?"

Taking her sweet time, the clerk retrieved a key that was connected by a string to a large plastic slab, and slid it across the counter.

Liv snatched it up and rushed to the bathroom. She unlocked the door, and Tommy ran inside, yanking down the front of his pants and squirting indiscriminately until making it to the bowl.

When he was done, he let out an audible sigh of relief.

"Feel better?"

He gave a wide-eyed nod.

Liv considered the urine all over the toilet seat and floor. She should leave it for the witch out front. But that was all she needed, Danielle telling everyone she'd vandalized Parker's. She cleaned up the mess and dropped the key on the counter on their way out. But before reaching the door, Liv stopped. She marched back to the counter and scooped up the giant container of candy. She could feel Danielle's glare burning into her as she and Tommy left the store.

"Welcome home," she whispered to herself.

CHAPTER 21

Liv pulled the rental car into the driveway and frowned at the scene. The house, her childhood home, was in a state of disrepair. The hedges were in desperate need of trimming. Shutters crooked, paint peeling.

Cindy met them at the door. She, too, showed signs of neglect. Her hair had a two-inch band of gray at the part. She wore polyester pants with a threadbare cardigan.

Liv's older sister had never been one to primp, and when they were kids, many wondered aloud how the two could be related. In high school Liv had been the town beauty, voted Irrigation Queen three times in the sexist pageant held every summer. She'd inherited their late mother's delicate, faintly aristocratic features. Cindy was their father's daughter. Big boned. A wide face and nose.

"Is this Tommy? I can't believe it," Cindy said in that raspy voice of hers. "You were just a baby the last time I saw you." This was directed more at Liv than Tommy.

"It's me," Tommy said earnestly.

"Well, come on in and give your auntie a hug."

Tommy hesitated, but sauntered over and gave her a sideways hug.

"I'm sorry we're late," Liv said. "Flight delays, then—"

"Visiting hours are over soon," Cindy cut in, "so we probably should get over there if you want to see him today."

They took Liv's rental since Cindy's vehicle didn't have a car seat. Her sister glanced at the giant container of candy wedged between the front seats, but didn't ask. It wasn't long before they were on another lonely highway headed to the nursing home. On either side of them were vast fields, punctuated with telephone poles, birds balancing on the lines.

"They say we have a week to find him somewhere," Cindy said, matter-of-fact.

"Or what?" Liv replied. "They'll throw an elderly man with Alzheimer's out on the street?"

"No, they'll just hire an overpriced caregiver, put him in the most expensive room, and charge us an arm and a leg until we relent."

"Have you looked into other places?"

Cindy nodded. "Most won't take wanderers, much less disruptive residents. And they're pricey."

"How pricey?"

"Four times what we're paying."

Liv guffawed. They could barely afford Twilight Meadows. "We can't swing any more money. With Maggie leaving for college, we're going to struggle just to cover our mortgage." It was even worse than that, she believed. But after their last fight, she'd relinquished the monthly bills to Evan. For now she was staying blissfully ignorant. A reckoning was coming, she knew.

Cindy just stared ahead at the miles of flatland.

Liv didn't want to say it, but she had to. "The house. Have you considered selling—"

"Where would I go?" Cindy said, her tone indignant.

"I don't know. It's a big place. Maybe you could—"

"What, rent a room above Pipe Layers?"

Liv frowned. "Of course not." Then again, Cindy might fit in with the toughs who rented the flophouse rooms above the town's only bar. Before taking her job running the local post office, Cindy had been employed by Adair Irrigation like their father. Working alongside the lifers on the line hadn't exactly softened her rough edges.

Liv scolded herself—she was being too harsh. Like the candy from Parker's, her sister might have a hard exterior, but there was a soft center in there. Though you might spit out the sour candy before ever finding it.

Cindy said, "I get that this town hasn't been good to your family, but this is my life." Cindy had stubbornly stayed in Adair. Most of the citizens hadn't held her relation to the Pines against her, probably for fear she'd throw away their mail.

The hum of tires on the road filled the silence.

"Is there any way we can convince them to let him stay?" Liv said at last.

Cindy frowned.

"It can't be that bad," Liv said.

"He's wandered off four times. And last week Dad

threw a bedpan against the wall and called the nurse a"—Cindy lowered her voice because of Tommy—"a effing *c*-word."

Liv put her fingers on her temples and massaged them. She'd been there only an hour and already her head was pounding.

"Trust me," Cindy said, "I got into it with the staff. They threatened to ban *me* from the home if you can believe that."

Liv could believe it.

"But I got a call yesterday from the director," Cindy said. "He said there may be something *you* can do to help."

Liv looked at her sister. "What is it?"

"I'll let him tell you," Cindy said.

Liv sat quietly again, annoyed that Cindy was keeping her in suspense.

Purposefully changing the subject, Cindy said, "You hear about Noah?"

"Hear what?"

"Your old boyfriend's getting promoted from lieutenant governor to the big boy job. Governor Turner's gotten himself caught up in some mess with young girls. Turner's expected to resign any day now; they say he may be indicted. By law, the lieutenant governor fills the rest of the term."

Liv thought about this. A rush of excitement flooded through her. Noah had been an outspoken supporter of Danny, and as governor he would head the Nebraska pardon board. Just when she'd given up on Danny ever being let out, something she'd never say out loud, a glimmer of hope. Then again, that was the cruelest thing about Danny's case. Matt always said it was like the scene from an old mafia movie: *Just when I thought I was out, they pull me back in.* It had nearly destroyed Evan. And their marriage.

After checking in at the front desk, they walked past a communal area that was filled with elderly people sitting at tables playing board games or watching television. Two frail-looking men, both in wheelchairs, sat across from each other in the far corner, studying a chessboard. Liv's thoughts drifted again to Matt. He loved the game. She made a mental note to call him. Matt was still angry at Evan, at Liv as well, she supposed, but he had a sweet heart and he'd come around.

In the residential section, Cindy stopped in front of a closed door. Underneath a medical chart there was a sign that read, I'M CHARLIE FORD. I HAVE TWO DAUGH-TERS AND FOUR GRANDCHILDREN. I WAS IN THE ARMY THEN SPENT MY CAREER WORKING AS A WELDER AT ADAIR IRRIGATION. It was a cue card for the staff, to give them conversation starters and to remind them that her father was a real person before the monster had stolen him.

"You think it's okay for . . ." Liv directed her glance at Tommy.

"It should be fine. If not, I can take him into the courtyard. The shelter brings over dogs to play with residents, so maybe there'll be some puppies."

"Puppies?" Tommy said, perking up.

Cindy knocked loudly, waited a beat, then opened the door slowly when no response came.

Their father was sitting in his old lounge chair from home, staring blankly at a television that had the volume muted. The room was spacious, at least—a hospital bed lodged in the corner and a small round table for meals.

Liv's heart sank at the sight of him. He was too thin, the skin on his neck loose, his hands bony around the arms of the chair.

"Hi, Dad," Cindy said in a loud voice.

Their father didn't turn his head.

Cindy stepped in front of the television and crouched at eye level. "I have a surprise for you." She stretched out her arm for Liv to come within their father's field of vision.

Liv walked over. Tommy stayed by the door, a puzzled look on his face.

"Hi, Daddy," Liv said.

Her father's eyes lifted to Liv's face. Then his own face brightened.

"Olive Oyl?"

Liv broke into a smile. He'd called her that since she was a little girl. They'd watched *Popeye* cartoons together, and he'd show her his tattoo and flex his biceps and laugh like the sailor. Though he hid it from the outside world, he was a tender man, her father.

She knelt down and put her hand on his, trying not to tear up.

Tommy strolled over to his mother. "Hi, Grandpa."

"Danny boy!" her father said.

"I'm Tommy," he said, offended.

His grandfather appeared confused.

"How about we give your mommy some time to catch up with Grandpa?" Cindy said, taking Tommy by the hand. He hesitated until Cindy added, "Was that a puppy I heard barking?"

Liv mouthed *thank you* as they left the room. It was then she saw the sadness in her sister's eyes. Cindy had their father's face, but Liv had his heart. She pulled a chair from the dining table and positioned it next to the recliner. They watched the muted television, a sports channel, for a long while. Her father held her hand, intermittently turning to her and smiling.

Unexpectedly, he blurted, "Where's Eddie Haskell?"

It was her father's nickname for Noah Brawn, Liv's high school boyfriend and the soon-to-be governor. Haskell was a character from an old television show known for his insincere flattery and sneakiness. The nickname wasn't meant as an insult. Just a recognition that Noah—with his politician's charm, even as a teenager—wasn't fooling her dad.

Liv was about to explain that she was married to Evan, but her father's thousand-yard stare had returned. He was like a time traveler, jumping from year to year, place to place, the timeline scrambled along the way.

Liv's mind did its own time travel. She was home on a break from Northwestern and had a dilemma. There was a boy, someone new—a decision to be made. She'd dated Noah throughout high school, but they attended different colleges. At first they'd stayed close—speaking every night on the phone, spending breaks together. But predictably, they started drifting.

And then Liv met Evan.

"What should I do, Daddy?"

"Who treats you better?"

"They both treat me well."

"What do your heart and mind tell you?"

"Mind says Noah. He's driven, wants to be governor someday, maybe even run for president. I know with him I'll have a bigger life."

"And your heart?"

Liv smiled, thinking of Evan. "I can't explain it, but when he's near me, I feel more at ease than anytime in my life. And he's willing to come back to Adair like I want. He said he doesn't care about Chicago or his career; he just wants to be with me. Have a family, make a life."

Her father rubbed his chin. "I can't make this decision for you, Olive Oyl."

"What would Mom tell me to do?"

Her father gave a fleeting smile. "She'd probably tell you to go for the boy who wants to be part of your story, not just you being part of his."

The grunt of a snore interrupted her thoughts. Her father's head drooped to his chest.

Cindy popped her head in. "Tommy's playing with the dogs. The staff said they could watch him for a few while we talk to the director."

Liv softly removed her hand from her father's and stood. She kissed him on his head. "Let's get this over with."

CHAPTER 22

The director of Twilight Meadows smiled at Liv and gestured for her to take a seat. Dennis Chang wore khakis and a Mister Rogers sweater. His desk was paperless, the office spotless, the domain of a perfectionist. Cindy didn't say anything, just plopped down in the seat next to Liv's.

"Mrs. Pine, thank you for meeting with me."

"Call me Liv," she said, trying to build rapport. If she couldn't convince this man to let her father remain at the home, it would be a disaster.

"Liv," Chang said. He took a breath. "I'm sorry to meet under these circumstances."

Liv nodded. She didn't recall any Asian families back when she was in school. Nebraska wasn't a cultural melting pot. But Adair was more diverse than most areas. Adair Irrigation attracted people from all over the country, luring executives with high pay and a cheap cost of living, the promise of an idyllic Mayberry existence for their kids. Even after moving away, the company was a mainstay in the Pines' lives—Evan's main client at his accounting firm was Adair Irrigation. Her father's best friend from high school had been a vice president and had stuck by Evan even after he'd transferred to the Chicago office.

"I really hope we can work something out," Liv said. "My father was a pillar of this community. He raised a family here, like his father. He worked at the plant for forty years, coached high school football. And he's a kind, sweet man. He just—"

Chang held up a hand, not aggressively. Just an assuring gesture that she didn't have to go on. That he knew all this. "No one is questioning your father's character or the many, many contributions he's made to this community. It's just that, given his condition, I'm not sure we have the ability to give him the care he needs and deserves."

Liv felt her eyes welling up. Perhaps it was seeing her father, being back in this town, but her emotions were raw. "Is there *anything* we can do? Maybe we could arrange to have an extra caregiver check on him periodically. Or maybe we can talk to his doctor about his meds. I saw him today. He was a bit confused, but—"

She turned to Cindy for backup. But her sister just sat silently, something resembling a scowl on her face.

Liv added, "He's lived in Adair his whole life. And the other facilities are so far away, and . . ." She didn't finish the sentence, noticing that Chang was about to say something.

"As your sister may have mentioned to you, we've been talking about possible solutions," Chang said.

Liv looked at Cindy, who remained quiet.

"Here's the thing," Chang said, leaning forward. "My company has been trying to open several other facilities around the state, and we've been having licensing issues. One of our competitors has been raising baseless complaints. Not about resident care," he added quickly. "But that we're unfairly undercutting on price and trying to run other facilities out of business."

Liv wasn't sure where this was heading.

"Governor Turner wasn't receptive, but the lieutenant governor—an Adair native, as you know—was always willing to at least hear us out. But his hands were tied." Chang shifted in his chair. "You may have heard that—"

"That Noah Brawn will take over for Turner," Liv said, finishing his sentence. And there was the rub.

Chang nodded. "I understand you were high school friends, and you may hold some sway with Brawn. . . ."

Liv's hard stare returned to her sister, who didn't look back at her. Then, against her better judgment, Liv said, "Tell me what you need me to do."

CHAPTER 23

SARAH KELLER

Even in the late afternoon, the State Department lobby was bustling. Men and women in business suits stood in line to check in at the long security desk stationed at the center of the atrium. Flags from around the world lined the perimeter. Keller thought she saw a national news correspondent, blond hair and big sunglasses, walking out of the building with an entourage.

After checking in, Keller and Stan were whisked up to the fifth floor. Unlike the modern glass-and-steel lobby, it had the feel of an old-time country club. Lots of portraits, heavy rugs, dark wood. Before they entered the back offices, a woman at yet another reception desk gave them a small key with a plastic fob engraved with a number. The receptionist directed them to a wooden cabinet that had tiny numbered drawers with keyholes. "Please store your phones in there," the receptionist said. They didn't need to check their firearms. Just the real security threat: their cell phones.

Brian Cook was another tall man. *Sweet mother,*

Keller thought. But unlike the beefy FBI deputy director, Cook was thin and athletic, with a Midwesterner's affability.

Following quick introductions, Stan said, "Thanks for fitting us in on short notice."

"No worries," Cook said, directing them to a worktable. His office was small for someone so high up at the State Department, Keller thought.

"DeMartini says you need help with one of our consulates?"

Keller briefed him on the death of the Pines.

"I haven't watched the documentary," Cook said, "but I saw the piece in the *Times*. What a tragedy. Such a handsome family. I understand our people aren't giving you what you need?"

"I'm sure they have heavy caseloads, but we're having issues with the consulate assigned to that area," Keller said, charitably. "Matt Pine, the surviving son, is in Mexico. A consular officer was supposed to meet him at the airport to take him to Tulum to get the bodies released, but the consulate rep never showed. And he's not returning my messages."

"What consulate office is Tulum?" Cook said, more to himself than to Keller and Stan. Still sitting, he wheeled his chair to his desk and tapped on his computer. He squinted at the monitor. "It's in Mérida. That's a pretty cush gig. Cancún, Cozumel, Playa del Carmen, Tulum. What's the consular officer's name?"

"Gilbert Foster," Keller said, feeling almost guilty— almost—that Mr. Foster was about to have a very bad day.

"Let me make some calls. This shouldn't be a problem."

"You need us to step out?" Stan said, gesturing to the door.

"No need. I'll be right back."

For the next fifteen minutes, Keller and Stan talked about Keller's meeting tomorrow morning with Marconi LLP. She wasn't thrilled about making the first approach without adequate prep. Strong investigations and interrogations required planning. It was not a seat-of-the-pants endeavor.

Stan listened patiently, nodded sympathetically, and said, "I get it. But it is what it is," one of his favorite expressions.

"Just scheduling the meeting may spook them," Keller said. "And then they'll start destroying evidence."

"Not if you make it about Evan Pine. A routine interview about the death of one of their former employees who died abroad. And don't tell them you're coming—just show up."

That all sounded right.

"And I thought you said we already had the goods on Marconi?" Stan added.

"We do, but—"

"But what? We can't afford to get analysis paralysis on this one." It was another Stan-ism. *Analysis paralysis,* the problem of agents not wanting to make an arrest until every single conceivable piece of evidence—the records, the wiretaps, the witnesses—were tied up in a neat bow. Was she being too timid? Too cautious? She had Marconi dead to rights on the records. But money-laundering prosecutions were complicated. The targets hired expensive defense lawyers who hired fancy financial experts who either explained everything away or made it so damn complex that a jury couldn't possibly understand the case. These prosecutions had no CSI or DNA evidence, which juries had come to expect from watching television. It all typically came down to a terabyte of bloodless records. In Keller's experience, you needed a live person—an employee or another insider—to convey the story to the jury. She had the records, but no flesh-and-blood witness.

"Tell you what," Stan said. "I'll ask the Chicago office to back you up. If things go south, you can give them the signal and they'll grab up all the computers and servers. I know the SAC, Cal Buchanan. He's a BSD, but effective." *BSD* was Bureau shorthand for the most aggressive agents, the ones who didn't hesitate to put the government's heavy foot on someone's neck. The charming acronym stood for *Big Swinging Dick*.

Keller nodded. There was no point in debating it.

Cook finally returned to the office. "The bodies will be released today. They're at a funeral home in Tulum that has experience with expedited shipping of HR. The HR and personal effects will be sent to a funeral home in Nebraska, and the Bureau can decide how it wants to take things from there."

HR, Keller thought. Human remains. What an impersonal way to refer to someone's family.

"You have a new contact," Cook continued. "Carlita

Escobar." Cook said her name with the hint of a Spanish accent. "I'm told she's no relation to Pablo Escobar—she'll apparently tell you that every time you talk to her. But Pablo used to have a compound in Tulum, so, just sayin'. Anyway, she's well connected and takes no shit, so you shouldn't have any more problems."

"I hope she wasn't too hard on Mr. Foster," Keller said facetiously.

"I think he'll enjoy his new post in Acapulco," Cook said. "We have an advisory against US travel there, so it should be pretty, ah, *exciting* for him. Best of luck with your case."

CHAPTER 24

"I'm really sorry," Keller said into the phone.

"How many times do I have to tell you to stop apologizing?" Bob said. "Didn't you read that article I sent you?"

Keller could picture the smirk on his face. He'd sent her one of those top ten lists for professional women that make the rounds on Facebook. Career advice written by world-weary twenty-two-year-olds.

"*Don't Apologize* was tip number one," Bob said.

"I'm traveling so much lately. You're taking on more than your share."

"Um, though my modeling career is about to take off, I think you're forgetting how we have food." Bob paused a beat. "And besides, I like being a kept man. No, a Stepford Husband."

She felt her heart rate slowing, her blood pressure leveling. She could swear she actually felt it. Bob always had that effect on her.

"Whose phone are you on?" he asked, changing the

subject. "The caller ID was blank and the reception is terrible."

"I'm on the plane."

"*Whaaat?* And you're just *now* telling me that?" he said. "You're like Clarice Starling. Or is it more like *The Wolf of Wall Street*? Tell me Stan's there coked out of his mind with a bunch of hookers."

"Stop it," she said, smiling in spite of herself, the image of her buttoned-up boss getting wild with prostitutes unfortunately shooting through her mind. "Stan had to get back to the office."

Her boss had left her to handle the meeting at the Marconi accounting firm on her own. Given the interest HQ had taken in the Pine case, Keller didn't know whether to be flattered or concerned. Stan either had great confidence in her or was distancing himself from a potential shit show. Stan was a stand-up guy, so Keller decided to believe the former.

"So what's in Chicago?" Bob asked.

"Probably blowing up two years of work on my cartel case." Keller had the Marconi file spread out on the worktable in front of her.

"Wow, they really want to know what happened to the Pines," Bob said. "The power of television, I guess."

"And the president's daughter, a law student and fangirl of *A Violent Nature*."

"I hope you're kidding."

Keller didn't reply.

"When do you think you'll be home?"

"I'm not sure. I'm going to hit the accounting firm in the morning and, if I have time, try to talk to some of the girl's classmates. I doubt it will go anywhere, but might as well while I'm there." She hesitated, then added, "I won't be surprised if they want me to go to Nebraska. That's where they're sending the bodies." She'd tried calling Matt Pine, but it went right to voicemail. She'd texted him as well, but he'd ignored her. Or his phone was dead.

There was a beat of silence on the line. She almost apologized again, but then Bob said, "I'm proud of you, you know?"

Tears welled in Keller's eyes. "I love you," she said.

"Right back at you, G-woman. Give 'em hell tomorrow," he said. And in an exaggerated tone of urgency he added, "And eat some deep dish. It's Chicago, for Christ's sake."

CHAPTER 25

MATT PINE

Matt watched from the cover of the woods as a car jerked to a stop in front of Hank's Toyota. A car door slammed and a figure stalked to Hank's driver's side. In the darkness, all Matt could make out was the form of a man. He must've worn heavy shoes, boots perhaps, because they crunched loudly in the gravel shoulder of the country road.

The man stopped, said something Matt couldn't make out, then did something that caused Matt's heart to free-fall. He started sprinting toward the precise spot where Matt was hiding.

Instincts took over, and Matt turned and hauled ass. He darted through the brush, branches lashing his face, thorny bushes snagging his shirt. A light, the beam from a powerful flashlight, locked on to Matt's back, a long shadow before him. Matt hurdled over a downed tree, then cut sharply to the right, then left, then right again, trying to evade the spotlight.

He lunged behind some thick brush, the flashlight

beam disappearing for a moment. Matt darted deeper into the woods, not looking back. He kept going, his lungs on fire. When he found pitch blackness again, he stopped behind a large tree to catch his breath. He took in the humid air, trying not to make a sound. His heart was beating so hard, it felt like an alien trying to rip through his chest.

He thought he'd lost whoever was chasing him, but the forest grew suddenly quiet. The flashlight beam re-appeared. It swept through the mist, like a searchlight from prison movies, back and forth across the grid. The light grew brighter and Matt stayed deathly still. Then the light went out. Darkness, the only sound blood whirling in his ears.

Matt stood ramrod straight, his back against the rough tree bark. Listening for the man's footsteps. He should call for help, but who? Did Mexico even have 9-1-1? And what did it matter? He had no idea where he was. And even if his phone pinged his coordinates, it would be too late. But shouldn't he try? He quietly pulled the phone from his pocket. It was dead. Of course it was. His mind tripped back to Hank shoving it in his hand. Who was she? What did they want from him? There were much easier ways to roll someone. And surely there were more promising targets than a college kid with a cracked iPhone and a few hundred bucks. His mind jumped to the man with the cleft lip scar patting him down in the middle of the street.

A small eternity passed, but the quiet finally gave way to the hum of the jungle. Night creatures. Leaves rus-tling in the treetops. Wild dogs barking in the distance.

At long last, when he thought his pursuer had moved on, Matt took a step. The snap of twigs under his foot seemed to echo in the night. Or was that only in his head? He took another step, half expecting his stalker to materialize from the darkness.

The monster never appeared. But Matt took no chances. He walked slowly, stealthily, one soft foot after the other, navigating through the thicket of trees. It went on like this for a long while until he saw another light. Not the flashlight, thankfully. Headlamps of a car winking through the trees. He wouldn't be lost in the jungle all night, at least. It was a road, however desolate.

When he made it to the tree line, he had a difficult decision to make: risk walking along the roadside, or travel in the shadows until he reached civilization. The road had the obvious benefit that someone might take pity on him and give him a ride. But that someone could end up being the person who was hunting him. Also, who in their right mind would pick up a stranger at this hour? He decided to use caution. Stalk in the shadows and assess each vehicle as it approached.

So he walked. About an hour passed and only two vehicles appeared. The first, a dump truck that barreled by before Matt could even try to wave it down. The second, a motorcycle, its driver fueled by testosterone and Red Bull given the speed of it.

Fatigue was setting in. He was tempted to find some soft ground and cover and get some sleep. But he feared what might lurk in the jungle. Coyotes or dogs or who knew what else. And the bugs. His mind wandered as he kicked along. He actually thought about the movie *The Road,* inevitable given his predicament. A father and son traveling a postapocalyptic highway, exhausted and in search of shelter and food. Matt didn't care much for the film, but his dad, in a clumsy effort to bond, had invited him to see it. Evan Pine wasn't a movie guy, but he was a reader, and the film was based on one of his favorite novels. Matt remembered Dad trying to conceal the tear that rolled down his cheek at the pivotal scene, the dying father's words to his son. *You have my whole heart. You always did.* Sitting in that dark theater, Matt knew that his father was thinking of Danny.

Headlights burned behind him. Matt turned, and down the long stretch of road he saw what looked like a pickup truck. He considered hiding in the brush, but he was so damn tired. The truck drew closer, the sound of its rattling muffler filling the air. He fast-walked to the side of the road, stretched out his arm, and stuck out his thumb. Is that how you hitchhiked in Mexico? As the truck puttered by, Matt met eyes with a kid, about ten or so, who watched him out the passenger window. Matt dropped his arm, defeated. But then red taillights lit up the night, and the truck pulled to a stop.

Matt jogged over. He peered inside the cabin. Next to the boy was an old man, the kid's dad—no, grandfather probably. The gray-haired man looked warily at Matt.

Where should he have them take him? "Ah, hotel," Matt said, too slowly and too loudly, as if that would break through the language barrier.

The old man looked to the kid, and the boy said something to the man in Spanish. The only words Matt could make out were *zona hotelera*. The old man replied to the kid in Spanish.

The kid then turned back to Matt, nodded, and gestured for Matt to get in the back.

"Gracias," Matt said, and climbed into the bed of the pickup. It was empty except for a rucksack and piles of rakes with what looked like seaweed strung through their teeth.

Matt felt the cool metal on his back as he stared up at the sky. The truck accelerated and wind whooshed overhead. The white noise, staring at the incandescent stars and the treetops blurring by, was hypnotic.

Matt decided to close his eyes for just a moment. The next time they opened, the sky was purple, the boy standing at the back of the truck. Matt sat up quickly. They were parked at a beachside lot. The old man and kid removed the rakes and the rucksack.

Matt jumped out of the truck bed. "Thank you," he said.

The boy turned. With a smudge of dirt on his face, bare feet, and rake over his shoulder, the kid looked like a 1950s hobo.

"Hotel," the boy said, his arm extended, index finger pointed down the beach. There were torches burning and hut-like structures. The boy and the old man walked in the other direction, headed toward a group of figures forking rakes at small mountains of seaweed.

Matt walked toward the lights, his sneakers sinking and filling with sand. He passed a group of huts and a wooden platform that had a tiki bar on top of it. A sign read MI AMOR. He pushed along, passing fenced-in cottages and villas. He came upon a cluster of beach chairs and tables. A path led to a hotel, which was dark and quiet. No one would be there until sunrise.

He sat on the canvas chair, gazing out at the ocean. He suddenly felt the sting of the scrapes on his arms and face, the grime of his travels. Looking around at the deserted beach, he stood, stretched his back, then stripped down to his boxers. He ran toward the ocean and dove in, surprised that he didn't feel the usual jolt from the cold. It was like a warm bath. And there he floated, lost in the sound of the waves, numb from the crushing grief, until a thin line of orange appeared at the horizon. Today, he hoped, would be a better day. And really, could it possibly get worse? He'd go to the police station, meet with Señor Gutierrez, sign the papers, and be on his way. What a shit show. He thought of Hank, the fear in her pretty face. He felt hollowed out, his thoughts fuzzy, like the whole thing was just a bad dream.

A very bad dream.

CHAPTER 26

MAGGIE PINE

BEFORE

Maggie awoke to a feeling of dread and a loud thunk. She swung her legs out of her bed and went to investigate the noise. In the hallway she found two suitcases strewn haphazardly on the floor. Another fell from the hole in the ceiling.

Then her father's feet appeared on the folding ladder attached to the attic door. Her dad's eyes flashed when he saw her as he descended.

"Morning, Magpie," he said. "Hope I didn't wake you. I'm just getting the bags for our trip."

"I can see that," Maggie said. This was really happening. A good night's sleep hadn't made him think more clearly. Cooler heads hadn't prevailed. Maggie should call her mom. She was the best at talking her father down.

"Dad, you're not serious about Mexico? I don't think—"

"Why wouldn't I be serious?"

"It's just kind of, I don't know, *sudden*."

"It's your senior year, you're leaving us soon, and you deserve a trip. Besides, my doctor said a vacation would be good for me. While we're there, we'll check things out from the call."

He said it so casually that it all almost started to make sense. But Maggie knew better.

"I think you need to consider that it was a prank. I mean, putting aside that, like, Charlotte is, um, *dead,* why would her cell phone have the name of the night-club? It's weird, and it's super easy to spoof a caller ID."

"Well, that's why I have you, sweetie."

Maggie furrowed her brow.

"You're gonna trace the call, see if it really came from the club."

Maggie let out a cough of a laugh. "I am, am I? And how will I be doing that?"

Her father clutched the handle of one of the suitcases.

"You'll figure it out. You always do."

With that, he grabbed the other suitcase and directed his chin to the third that had skittered down the hall to the landing of the stairwell.

"Pack beach clothes," he said. "And I'll need your help packing stuff for Mom." His eyes flared again and he disappeared into his bedroom.

Maggie lugged the suitcase to her room, then plopped down on the bed. She was definitely calling Mom. At the same time, she liked the idea of sitting on a beach in Mexico. Away from her computer and her phone and her problems. Time to clear her head. And if she was honest, she liked the confidence her father had in her. He really believed she could track an anonymous call made from Mexico. Not a doubt in his mind. Still, she needed to get Mom involved. She tapped out a text:

> *You might want to call Dad and ask him about Mexico. . . .*

She considered telling her mom to call her, that they needed to talk about something important, but she tossed her phone on the bed. She reached for the laptop on the nightstand. She didn't want to look, but she needed to. She pulled up the Danny Pine site. More cruel comments. She read a few of them, then slammed the laptop shut. She felt the tears coming again.

No, she decided, screw them. She had nothing to be ashamed of. She'd done nothing wrong. She wouldn't be intimidated. Eric was a piece of garbage, and she wouldn't let last night define her. She opened the laptop and started tapping out responses to the vitriol. But she stopped suddenly—trolls fed on hate and drama and engagement. Instead she'd simply take away their platform. She clicked on the keys until the Danny Pine sites were all deactivated, temporarily anyway. Her brother had enough problems without her drama. She'd give things time to calm down. Her classmates' attention span was limited. Things blew over quickly.

Now she'd distract herself with a project. She thought of her father, the feverish look in his eyes. His unwavering confidence in her. *You'll figure it out. You always do.*

She reached for her phone again and scrolled through her contacts. She clicked on the number for the call. A phone call. When was the last time she'd made one of those to someone other than her parents? Such an antiquated method of communication. But it's what you did if you didn't want to write something down—if you didn't want a written record—if you were going to do something illegal.

CHAPTER 27

Maggie banged on the door to the garage. Toby peeked out from the sheet covering the window, saw it was her, and opened the door.

"Hey," Toby said. "You got here fast."

Maggie couldn't remember the last time she'd been to Toby's poor man's Batcave. She looked around. Toby's fortress had expanded. He had a large L-shaped desk with six monitors. Computer hardware was stacked in four-foot cabinets, a tangle of cords and flashing lights. To complete the cliché, crushed energy drink cans and grease-stained pizza boxes were piled in a trash can. Steve Jobs in training.

They'd been friends since the sixth-grade science club. In middle school they'd been inseparable, prompting jokes about them being a couple. But it was never like that. Toby showed no interest in her—or any girls, for that matter. Some speculated that he was gay, but that wasn't it. The truth was that the older Toby got, the less use he had for humans. By the time they'd reached high school, he'd retreated into his computers and his mission to create the next Big Thing. Not some silly app. The next PC or iPhone or idea that would change the world. Though they'd grown apart, Toby answered her call on the first ring, and didn't hesitate when she'd asked to come over.

"Welcome to my lair," Toby said with his infectious smile. He still had the same hairstyle that looked like his mom cut it, the same skinny torso and pasty complexion.

"Wow." Maggie made an exaggerated show of scanning the room. "This has gotten . . ."

"Out of hand? Unabomber-like?" Toby deadpanned.

"What are you working on?" Maggie said.

Toby smiled. "I can't talk about it. You could be a corporate spy from MIT."

Maggie punched him in the arm.

"Ow," he said, rubbing the red spot on his bony upper arm. He stared at her for several seconds. "Are you, like, okay?"

Why would he ask her that? Because she hadn't been to the Batcave in so long? Or had he heard gossip about the party?

"I mean, on Snapchat some kids were saying—"

"I'm fine," Maggie said, not making eye contact. She composed herself, forced her eyes to look up at his. "I need your help with something."

"I figured," he said, collapsing into a worn couch that was pushed against the garage wall.

"It may require you talking to some of your sketchy web friends," Maggie said.

"Hey, they're not sketchy. Unkempt. And weird. But not sketchy."

"Whatever you say."

He shrugged. "What do you need?"

"I need to know how to track someone through their cell phone."

Toby kicked his feet up on the coffee table, which was just some boards on top of cinder blocks. "Easy, get the phone and download a tracking app. Don't you watch TV?"

"But I don't know whose phone it is. All I have is the number."

Toby scratched his chin, then stood and moved to the computer workstation. He put on a headset mic. Maggie tried not to smirk. He started typing, then said something into the mic. He laughed, pecked at the keys some more. Then: "Thanks, bro."

Unlike when she'd see him in the hallway at school—stoop-shouldered, fast-walking, eyes on the floor—here Toby was the most confident man alive.

He yanked off the headset. "Well, that was easy."

"What do you mean?"

"You got two hundred bucks?"

Maggie narrowed her eyes. "What for?"

"You want the location of the phone or not?"

"You want me to send someone two hundred bucks? Is he a Nigerian prince?"

"You want to track the phone? Then yeah. Two hundred and they can give you the coordinates for any phone for the past month. My friend said it's legit. Bounty hunters use this service all the time."

"It doesn't sound legit."

Toby threw up his hands.

Maggie thought about her options. Two hundred dollars was *a lot* of money. She'd been tutoring and babysitting like crazy to earn enough for a new laptop for college. But she didn't want to disappoint her father. "You sure?"

"He sent me a brochure. It's, like, a real company."

Toby pulled up the link and Maggie read over his shoulder. It was called location aggregation. The cell phone companies sold massive amounts of cellular location data to other companies that resold it to still other companies, which packaged the service to banks and others who used the data to verify what people put down on forms. The brochure said that banks could quickly cross-check an applicant's address by looking at the cellular records.

"What's to stop a stalker or abusive spouse from tracking their victims?" Maggie said.

Toby let out a sigh. "You wanna change the world, or you wanna track the phone?"

"They'll take Venmo?"

Toby nodded. "I need the phone number."

Maggie gave it to him.

Toby made the transaction. Just a few keystrokes. "They'll email the results within the next twenty-four hours," Toby said. "Now, you wanna tell me what this is about?"

"No."

"Okay, then you wanna tell me what happened last night?"

"No," Maggie said. "But I could use your help with something else." She batted her eyelashes. Toby let out a groan. He nodded for her to continue.

"Is it possible to call someone using FaceTime or Skype but doctor it so it looks like someone else?"

"You mean, like, I'd call you but could make it look like I was a different person?"

"Yeah."

"I don't know, you're going to MIT," Toby said. "You tell me."

Maggie swatted him. "Don't be a dick."

Toby thought about it. "Sounds like a deepfake."

Maggie shook her head. She'd heard of deepfakes, but didn't know much about them.

"The Russians developed it to fuck around with our elections," Toby said, tapping on his keyboard, his eyes trained on the giant monitor in front of him. "It's software that can make images come to life. They use it to make politicians appear drunk or say or do things that make them look bad. They basically just put one person's face on another's body and can make it look super realistic." Toby held up his iPhone and started videoing her. "I'll show you."

Maggie suddenly felt self-conscious. Her face reddened. "I don't want to be filmed. I haven't—"

"Shut up, and say something outrageous." He continued to point the phone at her. "Say, 'Toby is a super-sexy stud.'"

"I'm *not* saying that."

He looked at her over the phone. "All right, just say anything."

"Okay," Maggie said, "Eric Hutchinson is an asshole. A total asshole!"

Toby lowered the phone. He nodded as if he agreed with that. How much he knew from the online rumor mill was hard to tell, and he mercifully didn't probe.

"There's open-source code these porn freaks developed based on the Russian technology," Toby said as he uploaded the video from his phone.

Maggie made a face like he was messing with her.

"Really. They developed it so they could put the faces of A-list actresses on existing porn clips. I can show you if—"

"I'll take your word for it."

He gave a *suit yourself* shrug and turned back to the computer. "Okay," he said, "now, who's your favorite actress? Or singer, or whatever."

Maggie was at a loss for a few seconds. She wasn't a big pop-culture person. "Try RBG," Maggie said.

Toby frowned, shook his head. "How about someone who isn't, like, seventy years older than you."

"You said the software was good. . . ."

Toby sighed, then pulled up images of Justice Ruth Bader Ginsburg. Maggie then saw the video clip he'd just recorded of her on the screen. No makeup, bags under her eyes, unbrushed hair. At the same time, she thought she looked more grown-up, tougher. Her mind skipped to her kneeing Eric in the balls. She was a badass, she told herself. And that prick wasn't going to get the best of her.

On another monitor, hundreds of RBG images flicked by.

Toby said, "This is gonna take about twenty minutes. I can make some pizza rolls if you wanna hang?"

"I'd *love* some pizza rolls," Maggie said. She had a memory of the two of them in middle school, watching TV and eating a pile of the roof-of-the-mouth-burning snacks.

Toby disappeared, then returned with a plate full of pizza rolls. While they ate, Toby told her his plans. He was taking a gap year to work on his secret project. His parents agreed on a one-year plan—if he wasn't supporting himself by then, he was off to Cambridge.

"Are you excited for MIT?" he asked.

"Yeah, a little nervous leaving my dad behind."

He started to say something, but stopped himself. "How's your brother's case going? Does all this"—he pointed his chin to the computer monitor that was still flashing images of RBG at rapid speed—"have something to do with it?"

Maggie was spared the explanation when Toby noticed that the program was complete.

"Ready?" he asked.

Maggie nodded.

Toby wiped his hands on his pants and went back to the workstation. On the screen was a frozen image of Ruth Bader Ginsburg. But she was wearing Maggie's clothes. Toby clicked the mouse and the video began. It was both amazing and troubling. The late RBG stood in Toby's garage and said, "Eric Hutchinson is an asshole. A total asshole!"

"How in the hell . . . ?" Maggie said, impressed.

Toby beamed, proud of himself. "Give me an hour to

adjust the lighting and minimize the blurriness around the head"—he pointed at the screen—"and it would take an expert to tell it's a fake."

Maggie shook her head. "Play it again."

He did. This time Maggie studied it closely. RBG's mouth moved in sync to Maggie's words. Her head was proportional to Maggie's body. "You can do this for anyone if you have an image?"

"Yep, though the more images of the person, the better the quality. But these porn dudes spent a lot of time on this, so the tech is solid."

Never underestimate the power of a creep with too much time on his hands.

"You made a video. Could someone do this from a live call?"

"Probably," Toby said. "But if the caller didn't talk much, they could also just make it look live and pump in a video feed."

"Can you make me one more?" Maggie asked.

"Sure," Toby said, biting into a pizza roll, red goo dripping down his chin.

Maggie leaned over his shoulder and tapped on his computer, pulling up Netflix.

"Whose image are you looking for?" Toby asked.

Maggie didn't reply. She just clicked the mouse, fast-forwarding until she found what she needed. She paused on the image. Charlotte's pretty face looked back at the two of them.

Maggie stood up tall, adjusted her hair. "I need you to film me again."

Excerpt from
A Violent Nature

Season 1/Episode 8
"The Unknown Partygoer"

INT. CAR – SUNRISE

Lieutenant Governor NOAH BRAWN looks ahead
at the sun casting highlights on cornfields
lining the two-lane highway.

                    NOAH
  I've known Detective Ron Sampson for
  years. I don't believe he intended to co-
  erce a false confession. The Adair force
  had never handled a homicide case, never
  had sophisticated interrogation training.
  And even good people, dedicated profes-
  sionals in the system, make mistakes. It's
  one of the awful truths of our supposedly
  foolproof justice system: innocent people
  aren't just locked up because of odious
  wrongdoing, but also because of devastat-
  ing human error.

                  INTERVIEWER (O.S.)
  Interrogation experts we've talked to
  haven't been so charitable to Detective
  Sampson or his partner.

NOAH

I understand. The interrogation is hard
to watch. But I believe Ron had his
doubts himself and wanted to keep investigating, but was shut down by the county
prosecutor.

INTERVIEWER (O.S.)

You're no fan of Rusty Halford?

NOAH

Don't get me started.

INTERVIEWER (O.S.)

Did Danny's case inspire all the work
you've been doing for criminal justice
reform?

NOAH

Absolutely. Fifteen percent of cases
recorded in the National Registry of Exonerations included false confessions. Almost
a third involve eyewitness identification,
which we've learned is notoriously unreliable. Jailhouse informant testimony makes
up another fifteen percent. We're trying to
fix that in Nebraska and nationwide.

INTERVIEWER (O.S.)

This sounds really personal to you.

NOAH

You're damn right—forgive my language.
I've known Danny's mother since high
school. And I knew Charlotte. After my
wife passed, I used to eat at the diner a
few times a week where she worked. My son
went to school with all these kids. And
it offends me that the prosecutor had a
report about an unknown man at the party
that night, and a separate report about
eerily similar crimes in a neighboring
state, and he doesn't give this stuff to
the defense. That's not how a fair system
operates.

INTERVIEWER (O.S.)

You believe the Unknown Partygoer and the
Smasher are the same person?

NOAH

To paraphrase my son: "Duh."

CHAPTER 28

OLIVIA PINE

BEFORE

Liv forced down another sip of the awful convenience store coffee as she parked at the lot next to the city center in Lincoln.

She made her way up the steps to the State Capitol building, through security, and to the elevators leading to the interior offices of the ornate structure. She recalled making this same journey two years ago, just after the documentary came out. Back then she'd come to see if Noah could convince Governor Turner—a toad-faced sycophant who'd been in office for three decades—to support Danny's petition for a pardon. A long shot, yes. But Noah had played an important role in *A Violent Nature*: the crusading politician out for justice. His handsome face was interspersed throughout the ten episodes. The documentarians were particularly fond of filming Noah driving from his home in Adair to the capital as he waxed poetic about criminal justice reform. His defense of Danny and condemnation of the system that convicted him were eloquent.

It didn't hurt that Noah was from Adair. He'd been the mayor before his election to lieutenant governor. His son was a classmate of Danny's. But most of all, he had a very personal connection to that ugly night: Noah's son had thrown the house party where Charlotte was last seen alive. Most politicians would have tried to distance themselves from the case, but Noah owned it. Liv never knew if it was out of loyalty to her, or guilt about the party where Danny had consumed so much alcohol that he couldn't remember anything about that night.

The documentary made Noah an internet heartthrob, the dashing widower-politician trying to free an innocent man. Women of a certain age made suggestive comments about him on Facebook. He'd participated in a speaking tour about the problem of wrongful convictions. He was even invited on *Bill Maher* and some of the political shows, a rarity for the lieutenant governor of a flyover state.

Liv walked into Noah's office. The receptionist, a pretty woman in her twenties, greeted her with a plastic smile.

"Hi," Liv said, "I'm Olivia Pine. I'm hoping to get a moment with Lieutenant Governor Brawn."

The young woman pecked at her computer. Her eyes searching the monitor, she said, "I don't see an appointment."

"I don't have one. We're old friends. I'm visiting from out of town. Can you tell him Liv is here?"

The receptionist smiled, not as friendly as before. "Please have a seat."

A few minutes later a young man came out from the interior offices, and Liv was taken aback.

"Mrs. Pine?"

He wore shirtsleeves rolled to the elbow, and had his father's gray-blue eyes.

"Oh my goodness, Kyle. You're so grown-up."

Liv felt a sudden ache in her chest. Seeing Noah's son, a former classmate of Danny's, flooded her thoughts with the what-ifs and what-could-have-beens.

"How are you?" Kyle said as they exchanged an awkward hug. Noah had once told her that Kyle suffered a lot of guilt about throwing that party. Liv never held it against the boy; he was a kid. The class president engaging in his first act of rebellion, if only to impress the jocks. And the truth was that if Danny and Charlotte hadn't been partying there, they would've been partying somewhere else. Liv and Evan had a recurring fight, blaming each other about the lax oversight of their son.

"I'm well," Liv said. "And you? You're working for your father?"

"Part-time. I'm in law school at UNL."

"That's great, Kyle, just terrific." Liv felt the ache again.

Kyle didn't ask why she was there, just led her through the door to the back of the suite and into his father's office.

Noah came around from behind his desk. "What a surprise."

"Not an unpleasant one, I hope."

"Are you kidding me?" He gave her a hug. They both made a point of patting the other's back.

"I see you've met the office whipping boy," Noah said. He put a hand on Kyle's shoulder.

"I did. I thought I was looking at a photo of you from college."

"But without the mullet," Kyle added with a small laugh.

"Hey, that was totally the style. Tell him how cool I was, Livie."

Hearing the old nickname threw her off balance. "He certainly *thought* he was cool," Liv said, giving Kyle a knowing smile.

"I'll let you two catch up," Kyle said.

"Great to see you, Kyle," Liv called after him.

Noah directed her to the sitting area. She took a wing chair opposite him on the settee. The office was tastefully decorated, except for the vanity wall. Dozens of framed photos of Noah with politicians and famous people. Her eyes landed on one of him and George Clooney sitting at a long table, like it was a panel discussion, looking suitably serious. *A Violent Nature* hadn't thrust just Liv's family into the spotlight.

"I hear you're getting a promotion," Liv said.

He gave a knowing half smile. "If I'd known you were coming to town," Noah said, "I would've taken you to lunch. Or—"

"It was last minute," Liv said. "My dad . . ."

"Oh no, I hope he's okay."

"He's fine. About to be evicted from his retirement home, but fine."

"Oh yeah?"

"He's been giving the staff hell."

Noah chuckled. "I'd expect nothing less from Charlie. He gave me my share of hell back in the day."

Liv smiled.

"I'm really glad you stopped by," Noah said. "I thought after last time . . ." He trailed off.

"I'm sorry about that. I was in a bad place."

"No, I should apologize."

"How about we both just start again?"

"I'd like that," Noah said. After a moment he added, "I saw the Supreme Court denied the appeal."

Liv nodded.

"And you heard I may be appointed governor, and want to see if I can help with the pardon process. . . ."

"Oh, Noah, no," Liv said. "Well, strike that—yes, of course I'd want help, but that's not why I came."

"No?"

"I came for a *different* favor."

Noah smiled. His teeth seemed whiter, straighter than before. Porcelain veneers, she thought. Whatever it was, he had improved with age. Time unfairly favored those with the Y chromosome.

"My sister and the director of the nursing home hatched something up. Thought the soon-to-be governor may be able to cut through some red tape on some of the company's licensing problems, and they'd be willing to look past some of my father's, um, behavior problems."

"Ah, Dennis Chang put you up to this."

"I normally wouldn't ask, but they're going to kick my dad out. We don't have any other options. And—"

"Okay," he said. "Done."

Liv didn't understand. "What do you mean? You think you can help?"

"No, I mean it's done," Noah said. "After he struck out with Turner, Chang has been on me for months about the licensing issues. They want to open more facilities, and they've been in limbo."

"So, really? That's it?"

"Really. Go back. Tell him he'll get good news by the end of next week. But only if he guarantees your father has life tenure."

"But what if— Are you sure this is legal? I don't want to get you in any trouble."

"Trust me. Just tell him life tenure for your dad and he'll get good news by the end of next week. If he says no, you'll have to figure it out, since he's getting the good news either way. The license thing was cleared two days ago." He flashed a smile.

"This is amazing. You don't know what a relief—I can't thank you enough for letting me know."

"Yes, you can."

Liv gave him a look.

"I'm meeting Kyle and his partner at Vincenzo's tomorrow night for dinner. Join us," he said.

"I don't know," she said. "I've got Tommy with me, and I haven't spent any time with Cindy, and we leave on Sunday and—"

"Bring them," he said.

"I'll need to talk to Cindy."

"Tell you what, Livie," Noah said, walking to his desk. He picked up a pen and wrote something on a piece of paper. "Here's my cell number. Talk to Cindy and if you can make it, just let me know. I'd love to catch up."

"I have your number," Liv said.

"I had to change it after the documentary came out," he said.

"Your adoring fans," Liv replied.

"They're not all fans," he said.

Liv examined the paper. It was his official stationery: thick stock with Noah's name and the state seal at the top. It hadn't changed in seven years. Not since that morning he'd left her the note on the hotel room pillow, saying that he had to get home early to deal with the fall-out from his son's house party—the one that eventually sent her son to prison.

CHAPTER 29

MATT PINE

Matt awoke to a tap on his shoulder. He sat up quickly, squinting at the bright sun, confused for a second, but then remembering he'd slept on the beach. Before him was a young Mexican man wearing a white polo shirt and tan shorts. Other similarly dressed men were setting up umbrellas, unfolding chairs, and raking the sand. Matt looked toward the ocean. It was early and only a few people were on the beach. A couple with two young kids walked the shore, searching for shells, running from the waves.

"I'm sorry, sir, but this area is for guests only," the man said.

"I am a guest." Matt stood, brushed himself off, and walked toward the footpath that led to the hotel, hoping the guy wouldn't call his bluff. He continued through the back door of the lobby, his damp sneakers squeaking as he made his way to the entrance of the facility. Out front, a bellhop hailed him a cab to the police station.

It took fifteen minutes to reach the station house. Matt took a deep breath before walking through the front door, which was propped open with a brick.

The lobby was a sweat lodge. He didn't remember it being so hot yesterday. Behind the front desk was the same receptionist. She had an old metal fan on the desk, blowing around hot air. She gave Matt a sympathetic look and he worried he was in for a repeat of yesterday.

But this time she picked up the phone, murmured something, then put down the receiver. She showed Matt to a small room, this one even more sweltering than the reception area. Without saying a word, she motioned for Matt to take a seat, and then slipped out.

It was a long wait. The room had white walls smudged with fingerprints, and was furnished with only a marred table and three chairs. It was quiet, save for the hum of the lights above. Matt thought of Danny sitting in a room like this one. The setting—isolated and windowless, the air hot and thick—was intimidating. Add some overly aggressive cops, and it was no wonder why so many people falsely confessed. They just wanted to get out of the situation, out of the room. He almost felt bad for his brother.

The door opened, and in walked a stern-looking man wearing a black military-style uniform and combat boots that didn't suit the climate.

"Señor Gutierrez?" Matt said, rising and extending a hand.

Gutierrez didn't shake Matt's hand. Instead he pulled out the chair roughly and took a seat across from Matt.

Matt sat back down, the cop still glaring at him.

One would think that losing your family might warrant some sympathy, or at least civility. But Gutierrez seemed put out by Matt's presence.

"I was told you needed me to sign some papers to release my family so they can come home," Matt said.

"Who told you this?" Gutierrez said in accented English. His tone was clipped, accusatory.

Matt looked at him for a moment, taken aback. "FBI Special Agent Sarah Keller. She said the consulate would be—"

"*Pfft.*" Gutierrez glowered at Matt. "We released the bodies yesterday."

Matt felt his jaw pulse. "So you already—"

"The investigation is closed."

Matt digested that. This entire trip had been for nothing. And the investigation was closed? It had been only a few days. Given the guy's demeanor, Matt doubted they'd done any meaningful investigation. Matt looked at Gutierrez and said, "And . . ."

"And what?"

"And what did your investigation find?"

Gutierrez's eyes turned dark. "Ask your friends at the FBI and consulate."

"Look, this may not be important to you, and you may not be equipped for this type of investigation, but my family's dead. So I'd appreciate it if—"

"You want to sass me, boy?" The man pulled out a nightstick from a ring on his belt and smacked it on the table.

Matt swallowed hard. "I'm not sassing. I'm— Never

mind." Fuck this. He wasn't going to get anywhere with this guy. Matt stood to leave.

"I didn't say you could go. Sit down." When Matt didn't oblige, Gutierrez stood, gripped the nightstick with his right hand.

"Sit!"

Matt held up his hands, palms in retreat, and slowly lowered to his chair.

"I meant no offense," Matt said. That wasn't true. If Matt had learned one thing from his father, however, it was to never underestimate the power of an angry cop. When his dad gave talks about Danny's case, he always warned parents to teach their children to treat police officers like a big dog they didn't know. Most dogs were friendly, but you still wouldn't just rush up to pet the creature; you'd use caution, make sure it didn't bite. And you'd certainly never poke it with a stick. The same was true with cops. Most were hardworking, decent people. But the profession also attracted a certain breed. Like a rabid dog, you might not know the good from the bad until it was too late.

"So tell your children no matter how angry they are, no matter how unjust the situation," Dad would say, "that they should be overly respectful, overly cautious, and not make any sudden moves—it could save their lives."

Matt followed the advice. "It's been a hard time," Matt said. "I meant no disrespect. I've been up all night."

"I know. Fraternizing with prostitutes."

"What are you—"

Just then a woman burst into the room, the reception-ist trailing after her. The woman wore a business suit, her face twisted in anger. In Spanish she started casti-gating Gutierrez.

Gutierrez said something in an equally harsh tone. Matt's eyes went from one of them to the other, a tennis match of insults he couldn't understand.

The woman finally pointed a stern finger at Gutier-rez. She said something as if it were a dire warning.

To Matt's surprise, Gutierrez, so amped up just mo-ments ago, retreated.

The woman looked at Matt now. "Let's go, Mr. Pine."

Gutierrez didn't try to stop them.

Outside, the woman handed Matt a business card. "I'm Carlita Escobar—no relation—from the consulate."

"I thought Mr. Foster was assigned to—"

"He's been reassigned. I'm taking care of your case."

Matt didn't know what was going on, but he didn't much care. He just wanted to get the fuck out of there. "The officer said my parents were released last night."

"That's right. Senior State Department officials in-sisted, and I had to go over Gutierrez's head. You have some important friends, Mr. Pine."

Matt didn't know what she meant by that, but again he didn't really care. The last twenty-four hours had been what his friend Ganesh would call "a dog's breakfast."

"Where did they send my family?"

Escobar retrieved her phone from her handbag, then tapped on it as if she were looking for the details.

"Nebraska," she said. She pronounced the word

Knee-Baraska, like she'd never heard of the place. "They went out on a flight last night."

It made sense. The family plot was in Adair. Someone must've talked to his aunt.

"We have a car to take you to the airport." She gestured to a town car parked nearby. "You'll want to go now," Escobar said, and glanced at the station house. "You should get out of Tulum."

CHAPTER 30

SARAH KELLER

The bright morning sun reflected off the skyscrapers lining Michigan Avenue. Sarah Keller walked into the lobby of the office tower, her first visit to the Chicago branch of Marconi LLP. She'd analyzed the company for two years—talked to former employees, scrutinized bank records, studied bios of the executives—so it was strange to visit the place in person. Headquartered in New York with offices in nine other states, the entire firm wasn't dirty—at least, Keller didn't think so. Just the Chicago office.

A line had formed at the main reception desk of 875 North Michigan Avenue, men and women in stiff suits checking in for meetings at the law firms, telecom, and other companies housed in the impressive one-hundred-floor tower. Keller waited patiently, then displayed her badge to the security guard working the desk. Without hesitation or questions, the guard gave her a key card. He didn't work for Marconi, and his job was just to make sure no one unauthorized made it to the elevator banks. He wasn't about to give the FBI a hard time. No analysis paralysis for this guy.

Keller rode the elevator up with a throng of smartphone-staring executives. She smiled at the twentysomething in wrinkled slacks who held a card-board tray filled with four coffees. Keller's ears popped from the elevation.

She'd just spent two hours with a team from the Chicago field office, getting them up to speed. As Stan had warned, the Chicago SAC was a bit of a bull in a china shop, and more than willing to bust into Marconi swinging his dick. She'd convinced them to exercise restraint. She'd send a signal—the single click of a pen that was actually a transmitter—if they should storm the offices. She didn't want to do that. She'd prefer to continue building the case. But she supposed they already had the goods. Payments from various cartel-controlled accounts. The intricate web of investments and shell companies to wash the funds. The return of the money, less a hefty commission. But they didn't have a single witness who could put the story together for a jury. R. Stanton Jones, their original inside man and the tipster who'd gotten them started with the investigation, had vanished. It was possible he'd been rammed through a wood chipper or dissolved in a barrel of acid, favorites of the Sinaloa Cartel. Or maybe he'd just decided to change his identity and start anew. The taps on Marconi phones revealed no clues about what had happened to the middle-aged accountant. The Marconi executives seemed as baffled as everyone else at Jones's disappearance.

Keller's team had approached other former employees and gotten some good intel, but no one who knew the nitty-gritty, as Keller did after spending nearly two years tracking and analyzing the records. She'd intended to talk to Evan Pine because fired employees were always the most prone to turn on their companies, but he'd died before she got to it. Was he murdered, as the filmmakers speculated? Or was it a murder-suicide? Based on an analysis of internet history artifacts, the Bureau's computer forensics team believed that Evan, not Liv, had made the searches suggesting he was planning to off himself. Maybe he was. But murder his wife and kids? Everything she'd learned about the man said he wouldn't kill his family. Most of his internet searches related to caring for them when he was gone.

She stepped off the elevator and into the Marconi complex. It was as she'd expected: not too sleek, not too extravagant. Understated elegance. No one wanted someone flashy handling their money.

Correct that, the receptionist was showy—strikingly pretty, with a model's symmetrical features. Keller watched the woman closely as she approached. Much could be learned in these initial encounters. The receptionists of companies—particularly smaller branch offices like Marconi Chicago—usually knew where the bodies were buried. They saw who came and went, were tapped into the secretarial gossip circles, and needed *something* to make the boring job bearable. Would the woman look worried? Scared? Nonchalant? Or excited at the break in her routine?

"Hi," Keller said, friendly enough. "I'm Special

Agent Keller. I'm here to see Devin Milbank." Keller showed her badge, watched the woman's face.

"One moment, please," she said. The woman smiled, but Keller saw a twitch. A barely discernible flash in the eyes.

The receptionist tapped on the keyboard, and in her headset mic said, "Sheryl, I have a Special Agent Keller from the FBI here to see Mr. Milbank." A long silence followed as she listened on the other end. "No, she didn't say." The woman's glance returned to Keller. "If you'd like to have a seat, Agent Keller, someone will be right with you."

"I prefer to stand," Keller said, if only to see the woman's reaction. Another smile, a nervous twist of her hair.

Keller waited patiently, gazing out at the spectacular view, the tops of other skyscrapers and the green water of Lake Michigan spanning out to the horizon. It was nearly ten minutes before another woman, pretty again, appeared in the lobby. The delay meant the executives were having a pre-meeting. Probably a panicked one. The woman escorted Keller to the door of a glass-walled conference room. The glass was frosted so Keller couldn't see inside.

The woman held the door open. Two men stood when Keller entered.

The first man was taller than she'd expected. She'd seen him only in photos and media appearances. The head of Marconi Chicago, Devin Milbank. If the office was dirty—and it was—so was he.

"Special Agent Keller," he said in his deep baritone.

He shook her hand, a tight squeeze with lots of eye contact. He motioned to the other man, who was almost a foot shorter than Milbank, rotund in a pinstripe suit. "This is Mel Bradford, our general counsel." The man stuck out his sausage-finger hands and gave Keller a vise of a shake.

"Are we waiting on anyone else?" Milbank said.

"Just me," Keller said.

He nodded as if he were impressed by that. Or maybe relieved: the meeting couldn't be anything serious if they'd sent a woman all by her lonesome.

They sat near the end of the long glossy table.

Milbank began. "It's not every day we get a visit from the FBI. How can we help you, Agent Keller?"

"I'm here about Evan Pine."

The lawyer next to Milbank seemed to relax immediately. He sat more naturally, less stiff in the leather chair.

Milbank said, "We couldn't believe it. What a tragedy."

Keller nodded. "It looks like an accident," she said, "but when an American dies abroad under unusual circumstances, we need to look into it."

"I get it," Milbank said. "We've received several calls from reporters. After that TV show, Evan was something of a celebrity."

"How long did Mr. Pine work here?" Keller already knew this, but needed to begin somewhere, get him talking.

"In this office, about seven years. Before that, he was with the Omaha branch for nearly twenty years. The firm let him transfer because of that business with his son. The family needed a fresh start." He didn't mention firing Pine.

"Could you tell me who Mr. Pine's closest friends were in the office?"

Milbank let out a breath. "Evan wasn't really close with anyone here. That was sort of the problem."

"What do you mean?"

"Evan never really engaged with the office. He was always distracted, preoccupied. The first couple of years we just thought it was the transition. But it didn't change. Until the documentary aired, we didn't understand the extent of his struggles."

"But you kept him on for several years." Keller said this as an observation, not a question.

"He had a major account," Milbank explained. "Adair Irrigation was pretty loyal to him. Stuck by him for nearly all of that time, even after the Netflix show. An executive there apparently was an old friend of Evan's father-in-law."

"I gather something changed? I mean, I understand you let him go recently."

Milbank shifted in his chair. "Evan's contact at Adair retired and the new person shuffled the deck chairs and a different team took over finance. Evan had delegated nearly all the day-to-day work to others at our firm, and when the new Adair team came in . . ."

"Did the documentary have anything to do with it?" Keller asked. She didn't have to say why. Evan Pine came off like a man obsessed, a little unhinged, even. Not someone you'd want handling your finances.

"It didn't help," Milbank said.

Keller considered Milbank. His gray suit complemented his thick gray hair. He wasn't trying to rush her, wasn't impolite or arrogant. But Milbank was still on edge, she could sense it.

"When was the last time you spoke to Evan?"

Milbank thought about this. "It's been probably a year."

Keller gave an expression of surprise.

"His direct supervisor told him he was being let go," Milbank said, anticipating the question.

How gracious, after more than two decades with the company. Keller felt a surge of anger. Evan had a family, four kids, and they'd unceremoniously shown him the door.

Keller examined her notes. She could go on asking all her questions, but it would be a waste of time. She'd conducted hundreds of interviews during her career. Continuing down this path would just be spinning her wheels.

Devin Milbank was smiling again, playing the cooperative corporate executive. Keller thought about Evan Pine's internet searches again. His plan to kill himself to save his family from financial ruin. And she thought of this man not even showing the courtesy of firing Evan to his face. Keller decided to take Stan's advice: no more analysis paralysis. She glanced at the lawyer, who wasn't paying attention, eyes on his phone.

"Just a couple more questions, and I'll let you get back to your day," Keller said.

"Of course," Milbank said. "Anything to help."

"How long has the Sinaloa been a client at the firm?" Keller held Milbank's gaze.

The man was still for a long beat, as if forcing himself to show no reaction. The lawyer wasn't staring at his phone anymore.

"I thought we were here to talk about Evan Pine," the lawyer said. "As I understand it, Mr. Pine had only one major account, so I don't—"

"It relates to Mr. Pine," Keller said. It wasn't a lie. She had intended to talk to Pine about whether he knew anything incriminating against the firm that had fired him. But it didn't matter whether it was true. What a lot of people didn't know was that law enforcement can lie with impunity to suspects.

Milbank spoke: "I'm not familiar with that name, but in any event we keep our clients' affairs in confidence. I'm not sure I understand why—"

"It's a simple question."

Milbank's eyes moved to the lawyer.

"Agent Keller, we'd be more than happy to set up an appointment and discuss anything the FBI would like, but I'm going to advise Mr. Milbank not to answer any more questions."

"Need to call Mexico first?" Keller said. She clicked her pen one time.

The lawyer stood. "I'm afraid this interview is over."

Another thing people usually didn't know about the system: a suspect who isn't under arrest can walk out of an interrogation and even be outright rude to law enforcement.

Keller shook her head. "And we were getting along so well." She didn't leave her seat.

The lawyer and Milbank were both standing. "I'd like to know the name of your supervising agent," the lawyer said. "I don't think he'd appreciate how you're—"

Keller held up a hand to silence him as she casually glanced at her phone. She just scrolled her feed, finally looking up at them.

The two men stared at Keller, not clear what to make of her. She wasn't getting up to leave. She just sat there like she didn't have a care in the world.

The lawyer started to speak again, but Keller held up a finger, shushing him a second time.

"Hold on." She tilted her head, cupped a hand around her ear as if she were trying to hear something. After a long moment she said, "There it is."

Milbank and the lawyer looked baffled.

Then came the sound of heavy footsteps. The door burst open, the glass walls vibrating, and in charged a tall man in a suit and cowboy boots, followed by half a dozen men and women in blue windbreakers.

Keller tried not to gloat as Cal Buchanan handed the lawyer a search warrant. The lawyer read the document and turned as white as the papers.

"Call everyone to the conference room," Buchanan barked at the head of Marconi Chicago and its general counsel. *"Now!"*

Stan was right about Cal: BSD.

Standing at last, Keller held out her hand, gesturing to Milbank. "Please give me your phone."

The lawyer moved his heavyset frame between Keller and Milbank, his face red with anger.

"Please step aside," Keller said calmly.

The lawyer held his ground.

"Have it your way," Keller said. She whirled the lawyer around and cuffed him.

She'd likely hear about this later. Pinstriped lawyers didn't take kindly to being physically restrained. Out of the corner of her eye she caught an admiring look from Cal Buchanan. *Who's the BSD now?* Keller thought.

Keller left the agents to do their thing. The files, she hoped, would reveal dirt on the lower-level people, who would turn on their bosses, provide the human factor her case against Marconi was lacking. If not, they'd have to go with just the documents.

Keller navigated around the employees shuffling to the conference room, and made her way to the elevator. On the ride down, she thought about the interview, how the temperature in the room had changed when she'd switched the topic from Evan Pine to the cartel.

Her instincts told her two things: First, the Chicago office of Marconi LLP would be shuttered within the year. Second, the firm had nothing to do with the death of the Pines.

CHAPTER 31

OLIVIA PINE

BEFORE

Liv drove home from Lincoln feeling excited, giddy almost. Her father would be allowed to stay in the nursing home. She'd come to Adair to solve a problem and she did it. She couldn't remember the last time that had happened. She felt a sense of accomplishment. She called Cindy to give her the news and check in on Tommy, and even her morose sister sounded impressed.

Liv's thoughts meandered as she cruised the interstate. She opened both front windows, and flashed to an image of herself as a teenager, driving too fast in her father's station wagon, the wind blasting through the cabin, her hair dancing in the tornado. She didn't crank up the music—that was Evan and Danny's thing. Instead she listened to the howl of the wind.

She thought about Noah. As a boy, his master plan had been to move up the ranks in local politics, become governor, then make a run for the big leagues—the Senate, or even president of the United States. He looked the part. More handsome now than when he was

younger, with the perfectly symmetrical face and Clark
Kent curl in his hair. The slow movements and gait
of confidence. As if he'd grown into the part. He'd become mayor of Adair in his early thirties, and everyone thought he'd be on the national political scene by
now. But life got in the way. Having a child, his wife's
cancer. But he'd scrapped his way through farm-belt
politics to become the number two man in the state.
And now he'd be governor.

The elevation had personal significance for Liv—not
the nostalgia of seeing her old boyfriend achieving his
dreams, but the fact that Noah would lead the pardon
board. In Nebraska, the governor didn't have the uni-
lateral power to pardon. There was a pardon board made
up of the governor, the attorney general, and the secretary of state. Governor Turner had shut down any pros-
pect of a pardon, but Noah could make it happen. He just
needed the courage to do so. Would he have it? Liv felt a
pang of doubt. Noah was a born politician. He'd test the
winds, see what the polling said about it. Would voters
expect him to use his newfound power to correct the in-
justice he'd rallied against on-screen? One would hope.
All she could do was try.

If Noah convinced the board to pardon Danny, maybe,
just maybe, life could go back to something resembling
the days from *Before*. It wasn't perfect back then, of
course. And even before Danny's arrest, she and Evan
had grown apart. She'd betrayed her husband. And her
children. Guilt engulfed her, but she decided to shake
it off.

Not today.

She took the ramp into Adair and cruised through town until she hit the familiar country road that led to her childhood home. Her mind went again to herself as a teenager. The curve leading to the property was coming up and she planned to accelerate right at the arc, as she had done since she was sixteen, when she'd come home with a shiny laminated driver's license.

Before she reached it, she tried Evan's cell again. She was excited to tell him the news. But it went straight to voicemail. She listened to his recorded greeting amid the sound of the wind. Evan hadn't changed his voice message in years. He sounded upbeat, friendly. Like the man she'd fallen in love with.

After the beep she said, "Hey, it's me. Give me a call when you get time. I have news." She paused. "Good news."

Good news. It had been so long since she'd had any of that. She pushed down on the accelerator, and the rental car picked up speed. The wind blew more fiercely as she hit the famous curve, her hair lashing around the car.

That was when she saw the red cherries in her rear-view mirror.

CHAPTER 32

"Seriously?" Liv said aloud as she pulled the car to the shoulder. There wasn't another vehicle on the road, probably not one for miles, yet the small-town cop had pulled her over for going a little above the speed limit. What was the cop even doing here? In her entire childhood Liv couldn't recall a police car ever patrolling the desolate winding road.

She started digging through the glove box, looking for the rental car's registration papers, when there was a loud tap on the glass.

Lifting her gaze, she was blinded by a flashlight beam directly in her face. It made no sense. It wasn't even dark outside. The ray finally swung away and all she saw for a moment was the afterglow. Finally her vision cleared enough to make out the officer's face.

Liv's blood went cold.

It was her.

There was no mistaking it. She still had the same frizzy eighties hair with the bangs. The same tomboy demeanor. One of the stars of Danny's interrogation video, Officer Wendy White.

"You know why I pulled you over?" the officer asked.

Liv took a deep breath. She needed to hold her anger. She'd heard enough of her husband's talks to know that little good came from lipping off to a cop. But with this woman, this foul creature, Liv wasn't so sure she could bite her tongue.

"I have no idea."

"Speeding."

"Well, I'm glad the deer and squirrels are safe now."

Officer White's expression turned dark. "Step out of the car, ma'am."

"Pardon?"

"I said step out of the vehicle."

"I don't understand—"

"I'm not gonna ask again, ma'am."

Liv let out a loud, exasperated breath, and slowly climbed out of the car. "This is harassment," she said.

The officer—she was a good six inches shorter than Liv—made a sour face. "Harassment? You don't have a clue what real harassment is."

Something about the way the officer said it sent another jolt through Liv. She looked around. Just the winding road and grassland.

"Look," Liv said, her tone conciliatory. "We got off on the wrong—"

"Shut up," the cop said. "Turn around and put your hands on the vehicle."

"You can't be serious. You're not actually going to—"

Liv's breath was taken from her as the officer spun her around and shoved her against the hood.

"Hands on the car!"

Liv complied. The officer's hands ran up and down her body, roughly frisking her.

"Hands behind your back."

She wasn't really going to handcuff her? Liv was breathing heavily, thoughts reeling. She put her hands behind her back and flinched when the hard metal hit her wrists.

"Ow, you're hurting me," she said as the officer clicked the cuffs too tight.

"Turn around."

Liv turned slowly. The two women's eyes met. Was she really going to arrest Liv? She couldn't possibly. It would be all over the news: COP WHO COERCED WRONG-FUL CONFESSION FROM DANNY PINE ARRESTS MOTHER WITHOUT CAUSE. Liv felt acid rise from her stomach. It wasn't happenstance that the officer was on this road. She must have heard Liv was in town.

Lying in wait.

If that was the case, maybe she had no intention of arresting Liv. She felt a trickle of sweat roll down her side.

Then, a sign of hope. Up the road, an old Humvee, one of those weird military trucks, headed toward them. Liv recognized it—her father's friend and neighbor, Glen Elmore. A quirky vehicle for a quirky man. Liv's dad was always a sucker for people who bucked convention.

The cop looked over her shoulder at the Humvee,

which was taking the curve fast. Something about that section of asphalt inspired a heavy foot.

Turning back to Liv, the cop said, "When an officer asks you to do something, you best do it." She had deep wrinkles around her mouth and lining her forehead, too many for a woman her age.

"That hasn't worked out so well for my family." Liv felt anger in her chest. She shouldn't have said it, but Glen's truck was getting close. He'd surely recognize Liv, stop to see what was going on.

Officer White stepped into Liv's personal space. She smelled of cigarettes and sour coffee. "At least you still have a family. Sampson's wife and kids aren't so lucky."

Sampson. This wasn't just about how the documentary had skewered White's reputation; it was about the death—the suicide—of her partner, Ron Sampson. The news speculated that it was the pressure from being villainized in the documentary. The calls and threats to the station house. The public shaming.

Mercifully, Glen's Humvee pulled behind Liv's rental.

"Get back in your vehicle," White called to Glen as he climbed out of the tanklike cabin.

"Olivia, I heard you were in town. It's good to see you, dear," Glen said, ignoring White. "How's your dad?"

Liv smiled. "He's okay. Getting himself into some trouble at the home."

Glen smiled back. "As I'd expect. I need to get over to see him. It's been too long." He turned to the cop. "Wendy White, what in the Sam Hill are you doin'?"

"I said get back in your vehicle, Glen."

"Young lady, I knew your daddy when you were a glint in his eye, so don't you tell me what to do."

White's mouth turned to a slit. "This is police business."

"Like hell. Uncuff her before you ruin what's left of your career. For Pete's sake." Glen shook his head. "I'd hate to call Sheriff Graham."

White drew in a breath, bunched her face. She yanked the keys from her belt and unlocked the handcuffs.

Liv massaged her wrists, which were red from the shackles.

The officer walked angrily to her patrol car without saying a word. She revved the engine, then tore off, throwing dirt in the air.

Liv hugged Glen hello.

"I'm sorry about that," Glen said. "She's been a mess since that TV show. Whole town's been outta sorts."

"I'm sorry about all that," Liv said, unsure why she was apologizing for holding this shithole town accountable for what it had done to her family.

"To hell with 'em all."

She smiled at that. "How are you, Glen?"

"I could complain, but I won't."

"Doris?"

"She passed."

"I'm so sorry," Liv said. "I didn't know. No one told—"

"Well, all right then," he said. As when she was a girl, Glen was a man of few words, and even fewer emotions.

"All right then," she replied.

CHAPTER 33

SARAH KELLER

"It's been just awful. Maggie, she was"—the school principal looked at the ceiling, searching for the right word—"she was *decent*. A kind girl whose family had been through so much but she still was positive, a bright light. She was admitted to MIT, and was so excited. . . ."

Keller nodded. Mrs. Flowers wore a flowing blouse with a chunky wood necklace. Her office at Naperville High School was filled with photos of her with students. Knickknacks from travel, a lot from African countries by the looks of them. Keller could imagine her greeting the students every morning. The kind of woman who saw promise in everyone, underpaid and overworked, but delighted to be there. The twins were years away from high school, but they should be so lucky.

"I'd like to talk with some of Maggie's friends," Keller said.

Flowers's expression tightened while she considered whether to allow her students to talk to the FBI without notifying their parents. But she picked up a phone and asked someone to call Harper Bennett to the office.

A few minutes later a pretty young woman appeared in the doorway. Eyes wide, she approached apprehensively, as if concerned she was in trouble for something.

"Harper, please come in," the principal said.

Harper Bennett had green eyes and stylish brown hair with chestnut highlights. Keller was surprised at her outfit. She wore what looked like flannel pajama bottoms, white tube socks with sports sandals, and a sweatshirt that said BOULDER.

"This is Agent Keller with the FBI."

Harper's eyes got even wider.

"She has questions about Maggie. I know this is a hard time, but we hoped you could help."

Harper nodded, and took a seat next to Keller's in front of the principal's desk.

When Principal Flowers showed no intention of leaving, Keller said, "Is there a conference room or somewhere Harper and I could—"

"Oh," the principal said. She paused, then said, "Harper, you're okay with me stepping out?"

Harper nodded again, and the principal hesitantly left the office.

Keller gave the young woman a sympathetic smile. "First off," Keller said, "I'm really sorry about your friend."

Harper's face reddened, and she tucked her legs under her.

"I have some questions, if you don't mind?"

"Sure, but, like, I don't understand. They said it was,

like, a freak accident. And you're the FBI, and I don't get—"

"I know you must have a lot of questions. The FBI often gets involved when an American dies in a foreign country. Even for accidents." Not totally true, but no need to get into it. Keller still didn't have confirmation that there'd been foul play. And it didn't matter. The deputy director, and the president himself, wanted to get to the bottom of the death of the Pines—so murder, accident, or whatever—that was what Keller needed to do.

Harper looked at her skeptically, but nodded for Keller to continue.

"You and Maggie were close friends?"

"Best friends," Harper corrected, swallowing hard. "Since she moved here in sixth grade."

"When's the last time you saw her?"

"Like, in person? Or online or—"

"Let's start with in person," Keller said. The kids were different now. When Keller was a girl, it was the landline telephone, meeting at the mall or roller rink. Now they stayed connected through tiny screens.

Harper looked at the floor. "We went to a party a couple days before she went on her trip."

"Was this a birthday party or a school party—or a *party* party?"

"Party party," Harper said. "A kid from school, his parents were out of town."

Keller's smile said, *No big deal, I was a teenager once.* "How was Maggie? I mean, did she seem like herself?"

"She didn't want to go." Harper's voice broke and

tears spilled from her eyes. "I made her and then she was, like, nearly assaulted and it's all my fault and, like, the last time she saw me, she was upset and I should've—"

"It's okay," Keller broke in, reaching for Harper's hand. The girl was gulping for air, her face blotchy. "It's all right," Keller continued. "You did nothing wrong." She moved closer, giving Harper time to collect herself.

Harper dragged the sleeve of her sweatshirt across her face, wiping the tears.

"I know it's hard," Keller said, finally, "but can you tell me what happened the night of the party? Just tell it from the beginning, leave nothing out."

And Harper told her. That Maggie's mom was out of town. That she'd lied to her dad, who had a thing against parties. That Maggie was going there to see a boy. That she and the boy slipped away, and Maggie ran out of the party crying and upset. That Harper and a friend drove Maggie home.

And then came the cyberbullying. That explained the messages.

"Did you see her after that night?"

Harper shook her head. "She shut down the sites about her brother and said she needed a break from social media, from her phone."

"Was that unusual?"

"She wasn't a big phone person. But she lived for the sites about her brother. You saw the show, right?"

Keller nodded. Her chest tightened with the idea of the girl from the documentary—the pugnacious investigator helping her father—escaping the party after God knows what happened with the boy.

"When you saw the messages and that she'd shut down the sites, did you reach out to her?"

"Of course. She was my best friend. And there was no fucking way I was going to let those fucking—" Harper stopped herself. "Sorry."

"It's okay."

"I told her I was there for her."

"And what did Maggie say?"

"She said they were going to Mexico for spring break. That she was okay and just needed to get away."

"Did you know her family was planning to go on a trip?"

"Not until after the party. She said her dad decided at the last minute."

"Did she text you from Mexico?"

Harper shook her head.

Keller decided that Harper had calmed down enough to return to questions about the party. "Did you tell anyone—your parents or a teacher or anyone—about what had happened at the party?"

"She didn't want her dad to know. She said he didn't . . . She made me promise."

"Who's the boy?" Keller asked. She wanted to shake the name out of Harper, but she needed to be patient.

"Eric Hutchinson," Harper said. "He's telling people he didn't do anything, that she just freaked out and kicked him in the balls for no reason, but that's not Mags."

All the kids knew something had happened, but not one had talked to an adult.

"Anything else you can remember about the party?

Or anything unusual about Maggie before she left for Mexico?"

Harper chewed on her lower lip. "There is one thing."

"What's that?"

"After we heard about the accident, Toby Lee came to find me. He said Mags had asked him for help before she left for Mexico."

"Toby's a classmate?"

"Yeah. He said she was trying to track down someone's phone. Toby's a computer guy."

Tracking a phone? That was unusual. "Did he help her?"

"I think so. He can give you the details. But he thought it was weird."

Keller wanted to shout, *So why didn't either of you tell anyone?* But such was the teenage brain.

Keller thanked Harper for her help, asked her not to tell anyone what they'd discussed, and sent her back to class.

Alone for a moment, Keller felt her jaw clench as she realized that one of the last experiences a seventeen-year-old girl had on this planet was an upsetting incident with a boy. Harper said his name was Eric Hutchinson. Keller checked her watch. She needed to talk to Toby Lee about this phone-tracking business. But there was no way she was going to let what happened at that party die with Maggie Pine.

The principal returned to the office.

"I'd like to speak with Toby Lee," Keller said. "But first, bring me Eric Hutchinson."

CHAPTER 34

Eric sat up straight, arms folded, a scowl on his handsome face. He wore a shirt that had a picture of crossing lacrosse sticks and read EAST COAST DYES. His father—a ruddy-faced man with the build of a former athlete—sat next to him in a similar pose, chewing gum and glowering at Keller.

When Eric had been called down to the office, he'd refused to speak to Keller without his father there. A wise move, all things considered. It was always the affluent, the well-educated, who lawyered up—or in this case, parented up. They'd been exposed to lawyers, or studied Miranda in their AP Government classes, or had been schooled by America's biggest educator on police procedure and the Bill of Rights, *Law & Order*.

Though not every kid. Danny Pine hadn't been so worldly-wise. If he had just asked to speak to a lawyer, he'd probably be a free man. Keller had watched the video of his interrogation several times, and it turned her stomach. That didn't mean the interrogating officers were corrupt. They were small-town Nebraska cops with little training. And the scant interrogation instruction they'd received—a method known as the Reid Technique—had one critical flaw: it often resulted in false confessions. The great strides in DNA had not only freed many innocents, but had proven, contrary to conventional wisdom, that people did in fact confess to crimes they did not commit, especially juveniles.

A couple years ago, Keller had attended an interrogation best practices workshop and she'd been shocked at the number of false confessions. Keller remembered her instructor, a renowned expert in interrogation techniques, saying, "We used to teach you to look for signs of lying, like bad eye contact, fidgeting, but that's just what kids do when they're uncomfortable. We used to teach you to prod the suspect with a few details of the crime, but we found out that kids just parrot the words back. And we used to teach you to employ minimization techniques and tell kids that if they told the truth they could go home, but we found out that kids often jumped at the chance and confessed, believing that their innocence would be straightened out later." The instructor closed the session by saying, "I interrogated a fifteen-year-old who falsely confessed and spent eleven years in prison for a crime he didn't commit. It's my goal in life that it never happens again."

That didn't mean Danny Pine was innocent. He was an obvious suspect. He'd dated Charlotte, and the truth of the matter was that it was rarely a stranger who killed you; it was usually someone you held dear. As Keller knew too well, the sheep spends its life worried about the wolf, only to be eaten by the farmer.

Keller looked at the wolf—no, wolves—sitting across from her.

"What's this about?" Eric's father said to Keller. "And I do *not* appreciate the school letting our kids being grilled by a federal agent without a parent present." His glare landed on Principal Flowers, who insisted on being present at the meeting.

Keller didn't flinch. She never had trouble with alpha males. She'd grown up with one, and understood that the alpha-ness was born of their own insecurities. These men who loved to tell women to stop being so emotional were in fact the ones who let their emotions control them. She handed the kid's father a printout of some of the messages that had been sent to Maggie Pine.

"What's this?" Mr. Hutchinson said.

"That's what we wanted to ask your son."

Mr. Hutchinson looked at Eric. His son's face showed the first break in the facade.

"Why were you and your friends sending these messages?" Keller asked.

Eric was about to say something when his father extended an arm across his son's chest like a shield.

"Whoa, hold on, lady. I don't see my son's name on any of these messages. And if I need to get our lawyer here, I—"

The principal spoke, trying to take things down a notch. "Agent Keller is here about the Pine family. She didn't fly across the country about teen cyberbullying. But as part of her work"—the principal nodded at the printouts—"the FBI uncovered these messages targeting Maggie Pine just before her death."

Keller chimed in now. "That's right. Cyberbullying is usually a school matter. But sexual assault . . ."

"Sexual assault?" the father spit out the words.

"Witnesses say your son had been alone with Maggie Pine at a house party, and that she ran out, upset. The anonymous messages appear to be trying to intimidate her to be quiet about whatever happened."

Keller looked at the boy's father, who pulled at the collar of his dress shirt. His jaw was set. It was the boy's face thirty years from now, puffier but just as arrogant. She wished the mother had come. If the messages to Maggie Pine wouldn't faze the mom, there was no hope for this kid.

"You've got nothing," Eric's father said, aggressively working the gum in his mouth.

It was a day of doing things the hard way, it seemed. "That's your response? That's what you want to teach him?"

"What I teach my son is none of your goddamn business." Mr. Hutchinson glared at the principal. "This is unacceptable, Barbara."

Keller released a breath. "You're right. I've got no basis to arrest your son. No basis even to hold him. But I do have enough to contact his college. I understand he's been accepted to Michigan for lacrosse." The principal had briefed Keller on Eric before his father arrived.

The color drained from Mr. Hutchinson's face. He

looked to the principal, but he'd get no support from her now.

Keller threw out a lifeline. "All I want is for Eric to answer some questions. And to know that you're taking this situation seriously."

The man thought about this, then nodded for Keller to continue.

Keller looked at Eric. "Did Maggie say anything to you about her trip, or anything that stands out in your mind?"

Eric shook his head. "I didn't know her that well. I'd see her in the Center."

"The Center?"

"The tutoring center after school. I'd flirt with her, you know, and stuff like that."

"So before spring break you saw her?"

"Yeah. I went to the Center. I asked her to go to the party and stuff like that. I didn't do anything, and I—"

Keller put up her hand. She feared losing her temper if she let him lie.

"I saw her at the Center before break. She was, like, talking about her brother's case."

"Anything in particular?"

"She showed me a video someone had sent her. A tip and stuff like that."

Keller nodded. If he said "and stuff like that" one more time, she might have to arrest him.

"What did she say?" Keller had watched the video several times, but nothing had caught her eye. She made a mental note to watch it again, and to check on the status of the computer team's enhancement of the footage.

Eric said, "Maggie was excited. She thought it showed the U.P., you know, from the show."

"What else did she say?"

"That was it. I asked her to go to the party. I didn't talk to her again until then."

"That's it?"

He nodded.

"And what happened at the party?"

The boy's father tensed.

"Nothing," Eric said. "She said she wanted to talk alone and I figured, you know. So we were, like, just kissing and stuff, and then she just got freaked out, kneed me, then took off. I didn't do anything, I swear. I told some people, and they said she was saying I tried to force her, which isn't true. If they sent her messages telling her not to lie, it wasn't my fault. I didn't tell them to."

It was a convincing performance. Untrue, but convincing.

"Young man," Keller said. "Do you know how easy it will be for the FBI to trace who sent the anonymous messages to Maggie Pine? And if just one of those messages was from you—or if any of the kids who sent them say you asked them to do it—then you've just lied to me. Do you know the penalty for lying to a federal agent?"

The boy swallowed.

"Five years in federal prison."

The boy's father spoke up. "But you said—"

She held up her hand to silence him. "The statute of limitation is five years." Keller took in their pathetic expressions. "My office has a good relationship with the

University of Michigan's police force. If they get a report—so much as a rumor—that you've been anything but a perfect gentleman, I'm going to pay you a visit. And you *will* find out the consequences of lying to me today."

The boy started to speak.

"Don't," she said. "If I get wind that you were even rude to a girl . . . Do you understand?"

The boy nodded.

She looked at the father. "He dodged a bullet today. That happens once."

"Understood," the father said, looking like a beaten man.

"A perfect gentleman," Keller said sternly.

"A perfect gentleman," the father repeated.

It wasn't justice for Maggie Pine, but maybe it would save the next girl. With no witnesses and a dead victim, Keller decided it would have to do.

CHAPTER 35

MATT PINE

Matt slept nearly the entire flight. He'd spent several hours at the Cancún airport, killing time by dispatching texts to his friends, and eating terrible Americanized Mexican food at an overcrowded chain restaurant in the center of the departure gates. The margaritas were good, though, and the waitress packed him a giant slushy tequilaed mess in a Styrofoam to-go cup for the plane. That ensured that he was out cold until he hit the Dallas/Fort Worth airport, and again on his connection to Omaha.

He cracked his neck as the plane taxied to the gate.

As he waited for the passengers to deplane, the usual jackasses had marched from the rear of the plane and stood in the aisle out of turn. He imagined for a moment his mother saying *Rude!* under her breath. After helping the old woman in the seat in front of him pull down her carry-on, Matt sauntered out.

Adair, Nebraska, was about an hour and a half's drive from Omaha. His aunt had offered to pick him up, but he declined. Aunt Cindy meant well, but she was a bit much. It'd be expensive, but he'd take an Uber (they had Ubers in Nebraska, right?) and maybe Cindy could lend him his grandfather's old station wagon.

At eight o'clock the Eppley Airfield terminal was quiet. It was a haze of fluorescent lights and tired-looking TSA workers. He followed the signs to ground transport, plodding past the kiosk for Omaha Steaks and down the escalator with the rest of the herd. Some familiar faces from the plane—the guy with the bad tattoos, the old lady he helped with the bag, the pretty young woman who kept stealing looks at him—were standing by the luggage turnstile. And then he saw it. The curly-haired man with bloodshot eyes. Matt ambled over to him.

"You look like shit," Ganesh said after the two man-hugged.

"What are you doing here?"

"Your texts from Cancún were pathetic, so I thought you could use some company."

He was right about that.

"You got a bag?" Ganesh said, looking at the luggage conveyer belt.

Matt shook his head. He'd left his duffel in Hank's car on that rural road in Tulum.

"Then let's get the fuck out of here."

They proceeded to the parking garage, where Ganesh clicked the key fob on his rental. The lights on a massive Escalade flashed.

"Trying to blend in, I see." Adair, Nebraska, wasn't known for its luxury vehicles.

"What's the problem? It's American made." The sum total of Ganesh's understanding of rural America was

from the movies. Matt had introduced him to a favorite, *My Cousin Vinny,* which was set in Alabama, but it
was all the same to Ganesh.

The SUV smelled of cheap air freshener.

Soon they were heading out of the garage, through
downtown Omaha and its tiny skyline, and onto the
interstate, which turned to a dark highway and an ex-
panse of flatland. They flew by errant farmhouses, stray
windmills, and pretty much nothing else for miles.

"There's so much space," Ganesh said, scanning the
emptiness. "In Mumbai there's no land left. The only
way to go is up."

"Are the rural areas of India any better?"

"Haven't seen much of the country, to be honest."

Matt filled him in on his trip to Mexico. The bizarre
encounter with Hank. The scare in the woods. The hos-
tile Mexican cop. The imposing consular officer, Carlita Escobar.

"You, my friend," Ganesh said, his Indian accent
more prominent than usual, "had one fucked-up week."

"You can say that again."

"You, my friend, had one fucked-up week," Ganesh
said with a big grin.

It was another hour before the water tower for Adair
appeared on the horizon. Ganesh said, "It's like from
the documentary."

Matt recalled the opening credits from *A Violent
Nature,* which included an aerial shot of the town. The
voice on the GPS said to take the next exit, and Ganesh
took it too fast, the Escalade nearly careening off the
ramp.

"You're going to kill me on the way to a funeral," Matt said.

As they made their way into town, Matt didn't look out the window. He didn't want to face the memories or the nostalgia or whatever would flood through him at the sight of his childhood hometown. He just closed his eyes and waited for Ganesh to take them to the Adair Motel.

The establishment's name fit the town: no frills, straightforward, matter-of-fact. It was one of the few places that wasn't named after the proprietor who'd started the business. Places like Parker's Grocery, Sullivan's Ice Cream, Anne's Diner, and so on. Matt supposed no one wanted their legacy to be a low-end motel.

It wasn't long before the vehicle came to a stop.

Matt opened his eyes, gazed out the window. "What are you doing?" he said. They were parked in the gravel lot of Pipe Layers, Adair's only bar. Before Charlotte's murder, Matt's parents would go there once in a while, usually for a friend's birthday or a fundraiser for the football team. On a Friday night, the lot was full, the place still the only game in town.

"You look like you could use a drink," Ganesh said.

"I could use a shower."

"Come on, just one."

It was never just one with Ganesh. But Matt liked the company, and the Adair Motel wasn't exactly the Four Seasons.

"One," Matt said.

"Sure, sure, sure," Ganesh said. "I can add this to my list of bars."

Some people wanted to visit each of the fifty states, some to camp at every national park, some to dine at every Michelin-starred restaurant. But Ganesh strived to have a drink at the weirdest bars in the world. He bragged that he'd been to a bar made completely of ice in Sweden, a bar shaped like a casket in Ukraine, a bar in the trunk of a six-thousand-year-old tree in South Africa, a vampire bar in Tokyo, a bar decorated entirely with women's undergarments in Florence, and the list went on. He was about to be sorely disappointed.

Pipe Layers looked like Hollywood's idea of a small-town tavern. It had a long, over-varnished bar with several locals drooping on stools, staring at themselves in the tarnished mirror: weathered farmers, line-workers from the irrigation plant, some saggy-faced old-timers, a barfly. But at the high-top tables and booths, the crowd was younger. Stylish couples—carpetbaggers who worked in white-collar jobs at Adair Irrigation—and casually dressed men and women in their twenties, playing darts and pool.

All of them seemed to stop and stare when Matt entered the establishment. It reminded him of Mexico when the jungle went suddenly quiet: creatures going still from the presence of something that didn't belong. A threat. The silence lasted only a beat, and the din of the bar returned.

"I have a surprise for you," Ganesh said.

Matt narrowed his eyes.

From the back of the place came a procession of familiar faces. Kala led the group, looking glamorous as always. Next, Woo-jin towering over her, followed by

Sofia in her green military jacket. Curtis, probably the only black guy in the entire bar, was last in line. An inconspicuous group they were not. Ganesh had mobilized the Island of Misfit Toys from Rubin Hall. And they'd dropped everything to be here for Matt. He tried to contain the emotion swelling his chest.

"You didn't need to come," Matt said as he hugged Kala, then Sofia. He bumped fists with Woo-jin, who wasn't one for hugs, and pulled Curtis into a shoulder embrace.

The group convened at two tall high-top tables. Ganesh and Woo-jin headed to the bar to get some pitchers.

As usual, all male eyes were on Kala. She was used to it, Matt supposed. The subtle and not so subtle glances, leering from older men who knew better.

"Look, an old jukebox," Sofia said. She grabbed Kala by the arm. "We'll be right back."

The girls walked confidently through the crowd and leaned over the smudged glass of the jukebox, pointing and giggling. The crunchy opening riff to "Highway to Hell" by AC/DC soon filled the bar. Matt got a lump in his throat listening to one of his father's favorite bands.

"You okay?" Curtis asked.

"It's surreal. Being back here." He looked over at the jukebox again. Two men were talking with the girls. Sofia laughed at something one of them said. Kala paid them no mind, her standard MO.

"When did you all get here?" Matt said. "I mean, how'd you beat me here?"

"Ganesh sent a group text this morning," Curtis said.

"He'd bought everyone tickets and booked a block of rooms."

Some say the rich are different. In many ways Ganesh was not. He was actually pretty normal by NYU standards: a bright kid living in a crappy apartment, who spent a lot of time smoking weed and trying to hook up with girls. But he was different. Beyond his eccentricities, Ganesh was uncompromising. A concert they all wanted to see sold out? He'd hire the musician to play at a private party. His friends couldn't afford spring break? He'd charter a plane and rent a beach house. *Hamilton* tickets? Easy. Reservations at the Polo Bar? No problem. Ganesh didn't care about material things. He valued experiences and friendship. Money was always available, an afterthought, a means to an end. The rich were indeed different.

Curtis pondered Matt at length. "Are you sure you're okay? If you want to talk, want to get out of here, we can—"

"No," Matt said. "Seeing you, having us all together like normal, it's exactly what I needed."

The girls found their way back. "Where the fuck are those drinks?" Kala said. She looked over to the bar.

"Were those guys bothering you?" Matt asked.

"We live in New York. I think we'll be fine, Dad," she replied.

Matt smiled. He preferred edge to pity any day of the week.

Laughing, Sofia said, "Their names were Stormy and Lightning. They told me their brother's name is Thunder. I shit you not."

Ganesh and Woo-jin finally arrived, each carrying a pitcher. Woo-jin also held a glass of water for Curtis.

And it wasn't long before Sofia was nattering on about politics and the latest Twitter outrage, the guys talking sports, and, of course, Matt and Kala launching into a fierce debate about the best film directors. It was like they were at Purple Haze on a typical Friday night.

"M. Night Shyamalan doesn't hold a candle to Jordan Peele," Kala said.

Matt grunted. "I'll give you that Peele revitalized the horror genre. Made it smart, weaving in social commentary. But I've got three words for you: *The Sixth Sense*."

"I've got three for you: *The Last Airbender*. Horrible. And Peele doesn't arrogantly give himself cameos in his own films."

"It's just fashionable to hate on M. Night."

"You saying my views are just fashionable?" Kala held his stare as she took a gulp of beer. Her pretty eyes twinkled when she was angry.

"Yo, lighten up," Ganesh said. "I want this stupid debate settled by the time I get back with another round." He headed to the bar.

Kala seemed to realize she was, well, being Kala. Matt could've hugged her for it.

"I'm sorry," she said. "I should've—"

He reached across the table and put his hand on hers. "If your views are ever fashionable, it's because you started the fashion."

Her eyes glistened as if she was going to say something about his family, something that was going to make them both cry. But she shook it off, realizing it was the last thing she should do.

"I just don't get how you can like Shyamalan so much."

Matt smiled again. She had a point, since most of the NYU film school snobs looked down on M. Night Shyamalan. But Matt loved Shyamalan's movies because they were grounded in destiny—the protagonists unaware that everything in their lives had led up to a moment; that everything suddenly made sense; that they had a purpose in the universe.

Matt's thoughts were interrupted by a commotion at the bar. He didn't have a clear line of sight, but he saw the mop of curly hair bobbing around, and he knew.

"Shit," he said, jumping from the stool and threading through the crowd. At the bar, he found Ganesh in a stare-down with three young men. Other patrons had stepped back, sensing trouble.

Matt put a hand on Ganesh's shoulder, not acknowledging the other men. "Hey, what's up?"

Ganesh's jaw was jutted, hands balled into fists. Woojin and Curtis suddenly materialized next to Matt.

"Let's go sit down," Curtis said. "It's not worth it."

Eyeing Matt and his friends, one of the locals—he had cropped hair with a C-shaped scar on the side of his skull—said loudly to his own friends, "You hear the one about the black, the Chinaman, and the terrorist who walked into a bar?"

The three men burst into laughter.

Kala sidled up to Matt, whispered in his ear, "Ignore them."

He should listen to her, he knew. But instead Matt said, "Korean." He held the guy's stare.

"What?"

"He's from Korea, not China," Matt said, looking up at Woo-jin.

The man pushed closer to Matt, his shoulders thrown back.

Woo-jin tried to defuse the situation. "We don't want any trouble," he said.

The man repeated the words in a mock Asian accent. "Oh, you no want no trouble. You love him long time."

More laughter.

"Why don't you and I go outside?" Ganesh said, nudging his way in front of Matt. "Or are you too scared to go without Semen Breath and Muffin Top?" Ganesh looked at the two men flanking the leader. It was a line from the movie *The Judge*. Matt knew because they'd watched it together, but the men were clueless.

The heavier man Ganesh had called Muffin Top hitched up his pants.

"Nobody asked you, Osama bin Fuckface," the leader said.

Matt grabbed Ganesh just in time, holding him back from jumping on the guy.

The man's legs were spread, a fighting stance. His friends seemed less enthusiastic.

That was when Matt realized that he recognized them, the friends. He looked at Semen Breath. "It's been a long time, Steve. How's your sister doing?"

Steven Ellison's eyes immediately hit the floor. They'd been in Cub Scouts together. Gone on camping trips. Had playdates. Steve's older sister had a severe disability and was in a wheelchair, unable even to feed herself.

"She's good," Steve said, his eyes sheepishly lifting to Matt's.

"And, Nate, you still playing baseball?" The man Ganesh had called Muffin Top had been the star of their Little League team.

Nate, too, looked down, embarrassed.

But the leader, he was familiar, though Matt couldn't quite place him, said, "You pussies can get all nostalgic, but this motherfucker"—he poked a finger in Matt's chest—"thinks he and those Jew filmmakers can drag us all through the mud, and then just show up in *our* bar like nothing's happened."

"I had no part in the documentary," Matt said.

"The fuck you and your shit family didn't."

Now Matt felt his blood turn hot. The rage he'd worked so hard to bury all these years coming to the surface again. "Say one more thing about my family, and Steve and Nate are gonna have to carry you out of here." Matt meant it.

The crowd that had formed around them parted, and a blur of dark hair whooshed by. It was a young woman. She walked right up to the leader and put herself between the man and Matt.

"Ricky, what the hell are you doing? I'm gonna tell Mom that you're—" She stopped, spun around, and stared intensely at Matt and his friends. "If you put one finger on him, you'll be charged with murder. He's got a plate in his head. One tap could kill him." She looked at Matt.

"You should know better."

Matt couldn't believe it. After all the years thinking about that night at the Knoll—his electrifying first kiss—and it was her. Jessica Wheeler. As Matt stood staring, the crowd dispersed. Jessica shepherded Ricky, Steve, and Nate back to their table, wagging her finger at them. In just a few seconds, she'd ended the standoff. Shamed them all.

Back at their table, Matt watched Jessica as she continued to scold the three, then led her brother to a back office. She must work at the place. Matt had a vague recollection of Ricky Wheeler now. Ricky had been on the football team with Danny, but they hadn't been close friends. Ricky looked much different these days. Not just older and heavier; there was a slackness in his face. The slurred speech Matt had attributed to drinking too much might be from a brain injury. Matt watched the door to the office, waiting for Jessica to come back out.

"Hell-o," Kala said, snapping her fingers in front of Matt's face.

Matt was about to explain when his cell phone chimed. Agent Keller's number. He swiped the device.

"Matt, it's Sarah Keller." She said something else he couldn't make out. The connection was fuzzy, and the bar was loud again.

"I'm having a hard time hearing you. Hold on one second." Matt plugged an ear with his finger and pushed through the crowd.

"Can you hear me?" Keller asked.

Matt stepped outside the bar. He made his way past two men smoking near the front door, and to the parking lot, which was lit by a single streetlight. It was good to be out of the stale air of the bar. "Yeah, sorry about that."

"No worries. I heard you had some problems in Mexico," Keller said.

"You can say that."

"Carlita Escobar said you had a run-in with the local police. Are you okay?"

"I'm fine. Just a long-ass day."

"I can imagine." She paused. "I hoped we could catch up tomorrow. You have time to meet?"

"Yeah, but I'm not in New York. I changed my flight and came to Nebraska."

"I know, so did I. Could we meet in the morning? I saw a diner on the main road, so maybe we could get some breakfast?"

"Sure, but I don't understand why you came all the way here to—"

"I'll fill you in on everything tomorrow. But right now I have a question for you, and it's not something I want to ask."

Matt waited.

"We'd like to conduct autopsies."

"Autopsies?" Matt processed this. "I thought—the gas leak—the Mexican cop said they closed their investigation. I don't under—"

"I promise you, Matt, I'll explain everything tomorrow, but I have to tell the Lincoln field office if they need to have someone available."

"I don't understand." Matt's mind was racing. "It doesn't make sense. Why would—"

"Matt, there's no easy way to say this, but there's evidence of possible foul play."

Matt felt his knees buckle a little, the air stripped from his lungs.

"Are you there?" Keller said. "Matt?"

"Yes. Okay, you have my consent."

"Thank you. We understand your aunt plans to have the funeral on Sunday. So the medical team will be done by tomorrow. It's been given top priority."

Matt just held the phone, still trying to process. Trying not to think of his family dissected on cold stainless-steel tables.

"And, Matt," Keller said.

Matt still didn't reply.

"I'm really sorry."

Matt severed the connection. He stood there outside the old bar, the sound of music leaking from cracks in the walls. For whatever reason, his thoughts drifted to Kala and Jordan Peele and M. Night Shyamalan and destiny.

And then it hit him. Maybe that was it. Maybe this was why he'd survived.

To find out what really happened to his family.

CHAPTER 36

OLIVIA PINE

BEFORE

"Do you miss your mommy?" Tommy asked.

Liv gave a fleeting smile. She looked at her mother's white marble headstone in the back half of the cemetery, remembering the day when she was ten years old—a cold winter morning, the wind biting her wet cheeks as she watched them lower the casket into the ground. Today the sun was shining and the family plot didn't look so dreary. Old trees gave plenty of shade, tiny American flags and flowers adorned graves, and the grounds were well maintained. Were it not for the hundreds of dead underfoot, it would be a nice spot for a picnic. Her great-great-grandparents had purchased this serene family plot more than one hundred years ago.

"I miss her every day." Liv eyed the vacant spot next to her mother's grave. Sadness flitted through her chest as Liv realized that it wouldn't be long before Dad joined her.

"I'd miss you if you died," Tommy said.

Liv crouched down. She looked at him with those beautiful gray-blue eyes. "You don't have to worry about me dying."

"Promise?"

Liv hesitated. Visiting her mother's grave had obviously scared Tommy, and she wanted to comfort him. But she couldn't promise him she would never die.

"I'll be an old gray-haired woman"—she stood and stooped her back and feigned a stagger—"and you'll have to help me walk."

Tommy giggled. "I almost died once, right, Mommy?"

Ugh, more with the death. It served her right for bringing him here. "Nope. Your silly appendix just decided it was time to come out." She tickled his tummy.

In truth, the pediatrician had missed the signs, mistaking Tommy's stomachache for constipation. When his appendix ruptured, it was life-threatening, compounded by the hospital not having enough of Tommy's rare blood type on hand. She remembered the terror—Evan running into the hospital, panicked—and them both thinking, but not saying, *Why us?*

Tommy rubbed the scar on the lower right side of his abdomen. Then came the barrage of questions. *Where do you go when you die? Why do we bury dead people? Do worms eat your body? When would I die? How about Daddy or Maggie or Matt?* Liv noticed he didn't ask about Danny. It shouldn't have surprised her. After all, he'd never met Danny in person. Her oldest son had forbidden any of his siblings from visiting him in prison. Tommy had seen photos of Danny, and knew he was in jail for something he didn't do. But his big brother was like a storybook character, a fable, a super-hero, a legend fueled by Evan Pine.

"You want to get some ice cream?" Liv asked, try-ing to change the subject.

Her son's questions stayed with Liv as she watched ice cream drip down Tommy's arm at Sullivan's Ice Cream. She'd been thinking a lot about death herself lately, but she supposed it was her age, her father's con-dition, perhaps. Maybe it was Evan's blowout fight with Matt over the holidays, the two still not speaking to each other. Maybe it was the Supreme Court denying Danny's appeal. Maybe it was Maggie graduating and soon leaving them for college. Maybe it was knowing this town, her childhood community, hated her.

She scanned the ice cream shop. Only a few custom-ers sat at the small circular tables, and no one seemed to be paying them any mind. The girl behind the coun-ter was about fifteen, so maybe she didn't know or care about the documentary.

A Violent Nature had been a blessing and a curse. A blessing, since it had rallied the public—not to men-tion some top lawyers offering pro bono assistance—to help Danny. A curse, because it subjected her family to the ugly in the world, the haters, mostly disappointed middle-aged men sitting behind computer screens and spewing venom.

She thought of Officer White's face yesterday. The hatred in her eyes. What would've happened if Glen Elmore hadn't shown up? Liv was being silly. The cop was just trying to scare her. Liv was fourth-generation Adair, so one would think they'd cut her a break. But the town was unforgiving. It was a wonder that her sister chose to stay behind. And she hoped her father would never understand the dreadful turn of events. He'd loved this place, as had she, and it would devastate him.

She thought again about the empty plots next to her mother's grave. Would she someday be buried there? That was what her will instructed. So did Evan's. But they'd made those choices when the kids were little. Before Danny's arrest and imprisonment, before *A Violent Nature*.

The world was divided into before and after those events.

Liv's world had been secretly divided even further. Before the affair with Noah, and after. In the wake of Danny's arrest, she'd vowed to leave Noah in the past. To never be alone with him, and avoid even talking to him if possible. It had been a mistake fueled by too much wine and, for lack of a better excuse, a midlife crisis. Liv had chosen this life, giving up a career to raise a family in a small town. But as the children grew older and needed her less—and as she and Evan had lost themselves to parenting—she started entertaining fantasies about where life could've taken her. She was still an attractive woman, but she wasn't getting any younger. And the heads she turned these days were typically topped with gray. She didn't want to admit it, but her looks had always been a big part of her identity. What would she be when they were gone? When the kids were gone? Then she'd run into Noah at the supermarket, of all places.

One thing led to another, as they say. It lasted exactly one month. She'd visit him at his office and he'd bend her over his mahogany desk. She'd straddle him in the front seat of the car parked in a cornfield they'd frequented as teenagers. She'd slink to his hotel when he stayed the night in Lincoln for work. The sneaking around—the risk—was part of the thrill, if she was honest about it. Noah had been a single man since his wife died, but the lieutenant governor sleeping with a married woman would still be a scandal in conservative Nebraska. And she of course could lose everything.

In a way she did.

The night Charlotte was killed, Evan had been out of town for work. Liv met Noah at the hotel and told him it was over. They talked until three in the morning— much of it him trying to convince her to leave her husband—but she held her ground. The affair was an illusion, Noah lonely and isolated after Vicki's death, Liv lonely and isolated in the throes of domestic life. She loved her family, loved Evan.

That night she'd fallen asleep, and when she awoke he was gone—left to tend to the house party that changed her life. On her drive home, trying to beat Evan's return from his business trip, she ignored calls from home. When she arrived, Maggie ran outside and told her that the police had taken Danny.

She'd planned on telling Evan about the affair. Planned on telling the police, if they ever asked. But she decided the weight of her betrayal was more than Evan—more than her family—could bear. As it happened, the investigators never asked where she was that night. Why would they? They had their man the moment Danny walked into that station house alone.

She would never forgive herself. So she'd vowed she was done with Noah Brawn. She would never speak with him again. She certainly would never be alone with him. Promised God that if he would just set Danny free, she would never, ever . . .

But here she was. Planning to go to dinner with him tonight at the same Italian restaurant they'd gone to before senior prom. But why shouldn't she go? Her fucking vow hadn't freed her son. Hadn't brought Evan back to her.

She nearly jumped when her phone rang and her husband's name appeared on the screen.

"Hey there," Evan said. "How's our favorite town?" Evan sounded like he was in good spirits, upbeat. It was so infrequent lately that it was notable.

"It's been a bizarre trip so far," Liv said, looking around the ice cream store.

"Yeah? Sorry I missed your call. Your text said you worked things out for your dad. Everything else okay?"

"It's fine. I'll fill you in on everything later," she said. "We're at Sullivan's."

"I don't miss much about Adair, but I do miss their rocky road," Evan said.

Liv didn't respond. She was in no mood for nostalgia.

"Sure you're okay?" Evan asked.

She decided to swallow her medicine. "I saw Noah."

"Yeah?" Evan said flatly.

Liv explained how he'd fixed the problem with the nursing home.

"That was good of him."

"But that's not the good part. He's being appointed governor."

"What do you mean? How—"

"Toad Face Turner is likely going to be indicted. Some tawdry mess with underage girls. I'm surprised you haven't heard. It's all over the news here."

"Karma's a bitch," Evan said. "Do you think Noah will do it? Do you think he—" Evan didn't finish the sentence, as if saying the word *pardon* would jinx it.

"I don't know. He's invited me to dinner tonight—with his son, and Cindy and Tommy," she added quickly.

"If anyone can convince him," Evan said, "it's you."

She didn't know how to respond to that. Changing the subject, she said, "So Maggie said I need to ask you about Mexico?"

"That little sneak. I'll tell you all about it tomorrow when you're back. Hey, can I talk to the little man?"

"Sure." Liv handed Tommy the phone. "It's Daddy."

Tommy clutched the phone and said, "Hello." He listened, a look of wonder sprouting on his face. "Really? The beach? Another airplane?"

Liv realized that Evan must have booked a spring break trip, one they couldn't afford. She actually liked the idea of a getaway. It had been so long. And Mags worked so hard in high school, she deserved it.

"Awesome! I love you too." Tommy held out the phone for Liv to take from him.

"What was that about?"

"You'll see."

Liv was going to press him but she noticed a middle-aged woman, a beady-eyed mess with smeared makeup and disheveled hair, staring at her.

"I need to get going," she said. "But is Mags okay? I had some missed calls from her."

"Magpie is great. I have her helping me with a project."

Always a project. She wanted to tell him to just hang out with her. Watch a movie. Get dinner. Anything that wasn't a "project" relating to Danny's case.

"Hey, Liv," Evan said. His tone was more serious now.

"Yes?"

"I'm sorry."

"For what?"

"For everything."

What the hell was going on at home? "Are you okay?"

"Never better," he said.

She left the ice cream shop holding Tommy's hand, which was sticky and gross but she didn't mind. It was something people without kids would never understand. It wasn't gross to her.

They walked down Main Street, her thoughts returning to when she was a girl. In those days they spent more time outside—running the fields, fishing at the creek, riding bikes. The rental car was parked at the curb in front of the pharmacy. Tommy was playing a game of avoid-the-sidewalk-cracks, using her arm to swing over offending crevices. He didn't want to break anyone's back, after all. Never mind the shoulder surgery she might need.

At the car, Liv dug through her handbag for the keys.

She was still holding Tommy's hand, and had to contort her body so her other hand could rifle through the bag. She finally felt the key fob for the rental and pulled it out.

When she looked up, she was startled by the sight of a woman—the crazy lady from the ice cream store. She was standing too close, her pupils saucers.

"They said you were here," she said in a raspy voice. The woman blinked several times.

Still clutching Tommy's hand, Liv put her body between the woman and her son.

"I'm sorry?" she said, trying to sound polite.

"My Ronnie was a good cop, and he didn't kill himself," she said.

Oh God, Liv thought. It was the cop's wife. She clicked the key fob, turned, and picked up Tommy. "I'm sorry, we really need to go," she said, avoiding eye contact.

Liv opened the door with one hand, ushered Tommy safely inside, and shut the door and locked it. The fear she'd felt for her son's safety turned to rage. First Danielle Parker at the convenience store, then the cop yesterday, now this. She'd had enough of this goddamned town and its lunatic residents. Liv gave the woman a harsh stare.

Examining the woman more closely, though, Liv's anger dissipated. Detective Sampson's wife was frail and sad-looking and a mess.

"I'm sorry for your loss," Liv said. She was ashamed that she wasn't sure she meant it. Ron Sampson had railroaded her son.

The woman didn't reply, just dug through her bag.

"They say I'm nuts. They won't listen to me." Liv could smell alcohol on the woman's breath. But this was more than booze. Pills, painkillers, maybe.

"But my Ronnie didn't kill himself."

"I really need to go." Liv started to walk around the car to the driver's side. Tommy had his nose to the window. He waved to her, oblivious.

The woman started bawling.

"I'm sorry," was all Liv could manage.

"Ron was sorry too," the woman said. "About what he did, about what happened to your boy. He said he was gonna fix it."

This grabbed Liv's attention. What on earth was she talking about? Ron Sampson had bullied Danny into confessing.

"He scheduled a meeting with those movie people," the woman continued. "Was gonna tell them everything, and then . . ." She started crying again. "He wouldn't do it. He wouldn't leave me."

The woman started digging in the bag again, and Liv feared for a second that she'd produce a weapon. But Mrs. Sampson pulled out a wrinkled manila folder.

"Ronnie told me that this proves everything." She shoved the file into Liv's hands. "I'm sorry about your boy," Mrs. Sampson said.

And then she ran off.

CHAPTER 37

EVAN PINE

BEFORE

Evan tried not to get bent out of shape about Liv having dinner with *him*. She was trying to help. So was Noah, Evan supposed. Though Noah's altruism always tended to benefit himself. Granted, he'd been a strong advocate for Danny. But doing so had elevated his political stature and brought him heartthrob status. And it distracted from the fact that it was his son who'd thrown the party that night. At Noah's house, no less.

Before Danny's arrest, Evan had never been jealous of Noah Brawn. He thought Liv saw Noah for who he really was: a glad-handing politician. But Evan and Liv had drifted apart before Evan had even realized it, and Noah was undeniably handsome and charismatic. And if Evan were being honest, he had let himself go. Now Evan couldn't help but envy the man. He wanted to call Liv back and say, *Hell no, you're not going.* Something in Liv's voice said that she hoped he'd tell her not to go. That she wanted him to fight for her. Put *her* above everything else, even the hope of a pardon. It was one of those moments where he realized how much he'd failed her.

He picked up his cell. *Do it. Call her.*

But then he heard the jangle of keys at the door and Maggie strolled into the kitchen. She seemed excited, a sparkle in her eyes.

"Hey, Magpie. You just missed Mom's call."

"How's Grandpa?" Maggie asked.

"He's still having trouble, but at least they'll let him stay at the home."

"Did you tell her about the trip?"

"No, but apparently *someone* did."

Maggie's face reddened and she gave a timid smile. "I didn't tell her. I just mentioned that she might want to talk to you about Mexico. What'd she say?"

"Not much. I didn't get into it. Said it was a surprise. Don't worry, it will be fine."

"Will it, Dad?" Maggie took a stool next to her father at the kitchen counter.

"Will it what?"

"Be fine. I mean, it's kind of crazy."

Evan grinned. "I've got to live up to my reputation."

Maggie didn't laugh. The documentary's portrayal of Evan as unhinged was a sore spot for his daughter.

He gazed at her, marveling that he'd helped produce such an amazing person. He'd always known she was special. From the time Maggie was a baby, Liv would say that their little girl had a "special edition" heart. It filled his own heart with pride to see that she'd never changed. It was the great mystery of parenting: Who would these little people become?

Would the predictions you made when they were babies come true? Were their personalities forged by the age of seven, as he'd read somewhere? Would the morals you tried to instill stick? Or would there be a twist in the story? One fitting of those crime novels Liv loved so much.

"You're not crazy," Maggie said, intruding on his thoughts.

He had another surge of emotion. He loved this girl so much. He thought of the pills he'd jammed into his mouth. How could he have considered . . .

"Before we go on the trip," Maggie said, "I need you to watch something." She drew her laptop from her bag and placed it on the counter. "And if after you see it, you still think we should go, I won't say another word."

Evan was intrigued. "Of course, sweetie. What is it?"

Maggie tapped on her laptop. A video came up. She clicked play and Evan's heart was in his throat at the image on the screen.

Charlotte. Alive. Standing in front of a cluster of computer monitors. Her outfit was familiar. Then it hit him. She was wearing the same sweatshirt as Maggie.

Then Charlotte spoke: "Dad, it's me. I know it looks like Charlotte, but it's me. And if I can do this in Toby's garage, whoever called you could too."

Excerpt from
A Violent Nature

Season 1/Episode 9
"The Smasher"

INSERT – LOCAL NEWS FOOTAGE

A reporter stands in front of razor-wire
fencing surrounding a prison.

> REPORTER
> Bobby Ray Hayes pled guilty to killing
> seven women, a deal prosecutors took to
> give the families closure. But questions
> remain about whether the Smasher had more
> victims. The prison wouldn't allow me to
> meet with Hayes in person, but they per-
> mitted us to talk by phone. Viewers are
> warned that what you're about to hear is
> highly disturbing and not suitable for
> younger viewers.

CUT TO the reporter sitting in an office
in front of a speakerphone.

> HAYES (O.S.)
> You want to know what I did to them?

> REPORTER
> No, I wanted to talk about whether there
> are other victims.

                    HAYES

When I was ten, my mom's boyfriend would
take me up to the old warehouse by the
train tracks in Plainsville. Mom was real
happy 'bout it, like I finally had a father, you know?

                   REPORTER

Was this Travis Fegin?

                    HAYES

Travis would bring some pot and beer and
a bag full of melons. I was like, what in
the hell he doin' with the melons? But
then we'd go up five stories, and drop the
melons and bottles from the roof. Travis
got the idea from some old late-night talk
show. We'd have a good ol' time laughing
and watching stuff splatter on the cement.
But then Travis would want to play another
game. . . .

                   REPORTER

Travis Fegin disappeared when you were
twelve.

Hayes snickers through the phone.

                    HAYES

Did he now?

                          REPORTER

Did you—

                          HAYES

So the first girl, the one ridin' her bike
home from school. I took her up there.
You wanna know what I did to her before I
chucked her off the roof?

                          REPORTER

I'm here to talk about whether there were
any other victims. To give you a chance
to—

                          HAYES

She was so young, so smooth, she didn't
understand. . . .

A GUARD's voice bellows in the background.

                      GUARD (O.S.)
Get your [bleep] pants on!

There's more yelling and then the sound
of a dial tone.

CHAPTER 38

MATT PINE

The bed at the Adair Motel was as hard as he'd expected. Matt wrestled with the sheets, his thoughts jumping from his call with Keller, to the scuffle at the bar, to Jessica Wheeler. He shifted his eyes to the plastic alarm clock: 2:34 A.M.

Maybe he should go for a run. No, he should try to go back to sleep, but he was too wired. *Possible foul play,* Agent Keller had said. It was hard to get his head around that. Who'd want to kill his family? They wouldn't have brought much money to Mexico. And who would kill a little boy? Maybe Keller would have some answers. They'd agreed to meet at the diner in the morning.

From there, he'd go visit his grandpa. Spend some time with his aunt.

Matt startled at a tap on the door. He sat up. Had he really heard that, or was it just his imagination? He clicked on the lamp, listened.

He padded in bare feet to the door and put an eye to

the peephole, but no one was there. He stepped over to the heavy curtains and opened them a crack. The parking lot was dimly lit, but he didn't see anyone. Maybe it was Ganesh or Kala or one of his other friends.

That was when he noticed something on the floor. Someone had slipped a folded sheet of paper under the door. A note wrapped in red string.

He scooped it up, pulled at the string, and felt a flutter of excitement in his chest:

> MEET ME AT THE KNOLL AT 3 A.M. TONIGHT?
> YES OR NO
> CIRCLE ONE

Matt remembered circling yes on an identical note seven years ago in science class. He checked the time again: 2:39 A.M. He could borrow the Escalade from Ganesh, but he'd been drinking. He could wake up Curtis to drive him. Or, if he went on foot, he could probably make it. He examined the note again. Then he threw on his shirt and jeans and reached for his sneakers.

Matt made it to the Knoll with five minutes to spare. He was sweaty, worried that he smelled from the run, but he was cooling off in the breeze. It was warmer tonight, but otherwise a lot like that night when he was in ninth grade: the leaves rustling overhead, the only light from the moon, which was intermittently covered by clouds. The same pounding in his chest. He wasn't an innocent boy anymore, of course. He'd kissed his share of girls since then. But none had sent fire through him like Jessica Wheeler. He was glamorizing it all, he was sure. Why was it, he wondered, that we do that? Rosy up memories and make them idealized versions of what really happened.

He stood at the center of the opening in the trees, imagining Jessica all those years ago appearing from the forest, holding a flashlight, wearing pajama bottoms and a tight sleep shirt. He reminded himself that he knew nothing of this girl—this woman—now. They were likely very different people. He'd spent his formative years in Chicago, college in New York. She'd stayed in Adair, apparently working at Pipe Layers. It had been only seven years, but that was a full third of their lives. But something about the way she'd pushed through the crowd at the bar, fearlessly taken charge and broken up the altercation, gave him the same rush he'd had in ninth grade.

Matt scanned the area and didn't see her. Maybe she'd thought better of it. Or it was a prank. Or worse, someone luring him up there to get some payback for the documentary's hit job on the town. But he'd never told anyone of that night, and only Jessica knew about the note.

A light appeared from the woods.

Jessica ambled over to him. "You came."

She clicked the flashlight off and they stood there. In the silver haze he saw the girl from science class. The delicate heart-shaped face. She was older, her hair longer, more stylish. She was still about an inch shorter than Matt. They'd grown at the same pace. And those lips . . . Matt needed to snap out of it.

The words were caught in his throat for some reason, so he just nodded.

"Sorry for the sneaking around," Jessica said. "You're not the most popular guy in the world after that TV show. And I have a business to run. . . ."

That explained it. She didn't want to be seen with him. Wonderful. "You run the bar? I thought you just—"

". . . worked there as a dumb cocktail waitress?"

"I didn't mean—"

"I'm just playing with you," she said. "After my brother's accident, I had to put college on hold. Ricky couldn't take over the place when my uncle got sick. Stanford let me defer for a while, but I think that ship has sailed. The bar does pretty well, though. There's not much to do in Adair. But, as you can see, the hours suck."

"Stanford, wow."

"I wanted to get as far away as possible. See how that worked out?"

"For both of us."

"Come on," she said, "you can walk me home."

Matt followed her down the hill and to the worn path until they reached the large circular patch of grass and dirt everyone called the Hub. From there they took a dirt road that led to her childhood home. He was going to ask if she could still possibly live in the same house, but he thought better of it. He knew the answer and did not want to make her say it. They walked shoulder to shoulder along the narrow road.

"I didn't think you'd come," Jessica said.

"Why's that?"

"Well, you haven't exactly received a warm reception."

Matt released a noise of agreement.

"I'm sorry about my brother," she said. "He hasn't been the same since the accident. He gets confused. And he doesn't have many friends, so he shows off for those assholes who only hang out with him for the free drinks he sneaks them when I'm not looking."

Matt nodded. "What happened to him?"

"Car wreck. Mangled more than his body. Traumatic brain injury. You wouldn't notice the TBI at first, but if you talk to him for a while . . ."

Matt gave her a sympathetic look. As a girl she'd been sweet, empathetic. It was what had attracted him. And by the sound of it, putting her life on hold to care for her brother, taking over the family business, she hadn't changed.

"So why'd you call me out here?" Matt asked, examining her profile in the pale light.

This time it was Jessica who blushed. "I don't know."

"Sure you do."

"To say I'm sorry, I guess."

"Sorry for what?"

"I wasn't exactly a good friend after what happened with your brother."

Matt thought about this. For the first time, he remembered that Jessica had ghosted him after Danny's arrest. Avoided him at school. Not returned his calls. How was it possible he'd forgotten? He had such vivid memories of that night. The itchiness of the grass on his back as they lay watching the stars. The feel of her hand holding his as they walked this very path. The way she tucked her hair behind her ear in the prelude to the kiss.

After Danny's arrest it was a montage of misery, with lots of gaps in the timeline: his parents fighting. The sound of his father sobbing behind the closed bathroom door. The reporters outside the house. The receiver of the landline phone in the kitchen dangling off the hook. The whispers and stares whenever they went into town. The moving van. Maybe forgetting was a defense mechanism. Blocking out the unpleasantness.

Matt had a troubling thought: maybe that was why Danny couldn't remember anything about the night Charlotte was killed. Blocking out what he did.

Jessica looked down at the grass. "If I could go back in time, I'd tell my mom I could be friends with whoever I wanted. I'd be stronger, a better friend. I saw the pain you were in, and I should've—"

"You don't need to apologize."

"But I do."

"Okay, you just did." He smiled. "And I can honestly say I've never given it another thought."

They continued down the road, the sound of their footfalls filling the silence. "I'm so sorry about your family," Jessica finally said.

Matt nodded, still not sure how to respond to the condolences. As if acknowledging the tragedy made it real.

"How long are you in town?" she asked, trying to evade the awkward moment.

"I'm not sure. The funeral is Sunday. I'll probably

leave soon after that, depending on whether my aunt needs anything."

"Cindy is a character. I was surprised you weren't staying with her."

"I'm deathly allergic to cats. All my friends from New York are staying at the Adair Motel, so it made sense." The truth was that his aunt was best taken in small doses, so the cats were a convenient excuse.

Jessica nodded as if she remembered his severe cat allergy, but he suspected she didn't. Matt flashed to a memory of himself as a young boy, visiting a family friend, gasping for air, wheezing, his mother running the shower, rubbing his back, telling him to breathe in the steam.

"A bunch of reporters were at the bar last night, complaining about the motel. I heard them talking, saying even more are on the way. The national newspeople."

"Not surprising. They *love* the Danny Pine show." The never-ending fascination was an ongoing curiosity to Matt.

"You aren't kidding. They asked me a bunch of questions, but I said I didn't know anything."

"Like what?"

"You know, stuff about all the conspiracy theories."

Matt looked at her, gave a small shake of the head. He was probably the only person in the country who hadn't kept up with the case. The vast conspiracies from the talking heads and internet detectives, grown men and women with too much time on their hands.

"They asked if I'd ever seen any of the Hayes family in town, if I thought they'd have a reason to hurt your family." The Smasher's family. Matt had watched the documentary—just once, which was enough—but he'd never forget that sinister brood.

Jessica went on, "One of the reporters had super-weird questions. Asked if I'd heard rumors that Charlotte was still alive, that she faked her death to get away from her dad. Or was taken by sex traffickers."

Matt snorted. "The tabloids . . ."

"He said he was with the *Chicago Tribune*."

Matt shook his head in disgust.

"They wanted to talk with Ricky, but I wouldn't let them."

"Why would they want to talk to your brother?"

"Didn't you watch the documentary? Ricky was the one who identified the Unknown Partygoer."

Matt had no recollection of that. More memory gaps. "If he identified the U.P., which helps my brother's case, then why did he say those things tonight about—"

"I told you, he gets confused."

When he saw the yellow glow of her house's porchlight in the distance, Matt experienced a moment of déjà vu.

Jessica must've felt it too. "You remember that night we met here?" she asked.

"A little," Matt said. *Just the softness of your lips, the volcano erupting inside me, the feeling I've been chasing since I was fourteen years old, before loneliness settled into my bones.*

"You?" Matt asked.

"A little," Jessica said in a playful tone that acknowledged they both were lying.

Without thinking it through, Matt asked, "Did you see anything that night? Anything unusual?"

She considered him. "Like, what do you mean?"

He made no reply.

"All I remember is you and me, right here." She seemed to blush, since they were standing near the spot of the famous kiss. "And then later hearing Ricky's truck pull up. He was drunk and had no business driving. He and his date were fighting."

She looked up at him now, as she had that night. Matt had the urge to pull her close, to kiss her. She had a similar look in her eyes.

"It was great to see you, Jessica," Matt said, breaking the spell. He held out his hand for a shake.

The corner of her mouth turned upward. "It was good to see you too, Matthew. Let's not make it another seven years." She turned and vanished into the darkness, just like she'd done that night.

Matt ambled back along the road to the Hub. He stopped in the grass at the center, the moon peeking out from the clouds, providing a sliver of light. He half expected to see the back of his brother's letterman jacket—PINE in yellow letters above the shoulder blades—pushing a wheelbarrow toward the creek. All at once, he had another memory that had eluded him: the figure stopping in shadows, head pivoting toward Matt. The darkness concealed his face. Yet there was no question: he was staring directly at Matt.

CHAPTER 39

OLIVIA PINE

BEFORE

Liv tipped the bottle so the rest of the pinot noir dripped into her glass. She'd already dispatched a text to Noah, apologizing that she couldn't make it to dinner. After the encounter with Detective Ron Sampson's former partner *and* widow, she'd had her fill of the past. Of this town. She'd have time to lobby Noah to grant the pardon after he was appointed governor. So she'd resorted to every parent's secret weapon to get out of an engagement: *Tommy's not feeling well.*

The truth was that Cindy took Tommy out to dinner. Liv didn't know if it was because her sister really wanted auntie time with Tommy before they left tomorrow, like she'd said, or if she'd sensed that Liv needed some alone time. Cindy had left not one but two bottles of pinot on the counter, so Liv thought it was the latter. Liv was twisting the corkscrew into the second bottle when her cell phone chimed.

She was going to ignore it, but ever since that morning with Danny when she'd let her calls go to voicemail on her race home from the hotel, she never ignored calls.

Certain things made her superstitious, irrationally so. She'd been taking a nap in the middle of the day when her mom died, and she never napped during the day again. It brought bad things. It had been a lazy winter afternoon when she'd snuggled up with the family dog and gone to sleep, then awoken to Cindy shaking her shoulders, bawling, the last time she'd seen her big sister cry. So no matter how tired she was, she never napped. Even in college, and even when the kids were babies and she was dead on her feet, she never, ever took a midday snooze. Similarly, after she missed Maggie's call saying the police had taken Danny—correction, after she'd *ignored* Maggie's call—she never let a phone go unanswered.

"Hello," she said expecting a telemarketer or robo-call.

"Mrs. Pine, this is Alvita from Twilight Meadows," the woman said in a Jamaican accent. "I'm afraid your father is missing."

It was bad enough she had to deal with her father sneaking out of the home on her last night in town, but even worse was having to ask Noah for help. She'd had too much wine to drive. And she didn't want to ruin Cindy's evening with Tommy or put her son through the ordeal. She had little choice but to call him. Besides, she told herself, Noah would be better with the nursing home staff. And he liked playing the white knight; he always had.

"He's gonna be fine," Noah said, his hand on the steering wheel. He was one of those people who never lost their cool. She couldn't recall a single instance when Noah Brawn had lost his shit. When she'd broken it off in college, he was as cool as a cucumber. It wasn't that he lacked passion. His speeches on false confessions were the stuff of a brimstone preacher. Even his stump speech for mayor back in the day had some fire in it. It was just that his steady-as-they-go demeanor also revealed an emotional distance.

"I know," Liv said. "I'm just so pissed. I mean, how hard is it to keep an eye on an elderly man with dementia?"

Noah just nodded as he navigated the dark roads to the rural highway. After a time he said, "So, I'm waiting."

Liv looked at him quizzically.

"For you to say the magic word—*pardon*."

Liv regarded him. He looked straight ahead, the profile of his strong jaw and his serious expression reminded her of segments from *A Violent Nature*. Maybe it was all the wine, but she decided not to insult his intelligence and deny that she wanted his help.

"Can you—help, I mean?"

"I'd like to."

"But . . ."

He turned his head to her, then looked back at the road. "But assuming Turner resigns, which is probably a safe bet, I'll be the new guy. I wasn't elected into the office, so I need to tread carefully. It's not just my decision.

I've got to convince the pardon board, and two of the three members are Turner lackeys."

"I understand," she said, deflated.

"I didn't say no. It's just we've gotta be smart about it. I'm gonna need you to follow the usual procedures."

"Easy enough. We've filled out the pardon paperwork twice, though I don't think Turner ever looked at our submissions."

"You can count on that," Noah said. "But I will. Still, we need something new. Something that doesn't look like I'm biased or that I'm just trying to stick it to Turner, who still has friends I need. Is there any new evidence?"

"Nothing concrete."

"What about the video your daughter posted? Of the party."

He'd obviously been keeping up with the online chatter about the case. Noah must've sensed her surprise. "Kyle told me about it," he said. "Apparently he's in the video."

"Some think it shows the Unknown Partygoer, but who knows. The quality is terrible and all the armchair detectives haven't come up with anything new."

"Anything else?"

Liv exhaled. "Not unless Ron Sampson's wife isn't crazy."

Noah narrowed his eyes. "What do you mean?"

"I mean she accosted me. Gave me a file. Said Sampson knew something, was going to talk to the filmmakers."

Noah looked at Liv, his gaze skeptical.

"I know . . ."

"What's in the file?"

"Nothing, as far as I can tell. It's a page from some type of log and some blood tests."

Noah veered into the lot of the nursing home. "Sampson's wife, Susan, has had a hard time with his death. Even before, she was known to have a few drinks"—Noah raised his brows—"with her breakfast."

"She did seem pretty out of it, though who am I to talk given my wine consumption tonight?"

Noah laughed. "Ron wasn't a particularly good husband. Logan County actually scooped him up once when they did a sweep of one of the massage parlors. . . ."

Liv grimaced. "I'm surprised the internet mob never picked up on that."

Noah shrugged. "They didn't book him. You know cops."

Yes, she did. They protected their own. The thought of a massage parlor with happy endings made her skin crawl. Sampson's poor wife. No wonder she turned to the bottle or pills or whatever she was on. "She thinks Sampson was murdered," Liv said.

Noah shook his head. "Everything's the Kennedy assassination now."

It was an ironic statement, since Noah himself had been on a speaking tour suggesting Danny had been railroaded, that the Smasher had killed Charlotte.

"But who knows," Noah said. "If you want me to look at the papers she gave you, I'd be happy to. I know the file pretty well, so please send me a copy."

"Definitely. But if there's anything there, Evan will know."

"You've got that right," Noah said. He stopped the sedan in front of the entrance, not bothering to park in one of the spaces in the lot. At the front doors Liv saw Dennis Chang, shifting on his feet, looking irritated.

"You're, ah, angry," Noah said, politely not mentioning the lilt in her voice, what Maggie jokingly called her "wine voice." "Why don't you let me handle this?"

Liv didn't argue.

Noah stepped out of the sedan and shook hands with Chang. They exchanged a few words. Noah patted him on the shoulder. Liv could see Chang's demeanor shift from annoyed to accommodating.

Liv was sobering up, but she still wasn't totally clearheaded. She lowered the car's visor and looked at herself in the mirror. She smacked her own cheek lightly.

Noah returned to the car. "They've searched the grounds," he said. "They think he must have slipped out after dinner, since the nurse saw him then."

Liv shook her head.

"Chang said the last few times he wandered off, he went to your mom's grave at the cemetery. They sent someone to check, but he wasn't there. You have any ideas where he might go?"

Liv cataloged places of significance to her father: the cemetery, the house, maybe the plant.

"Apparently your dad was talking about your mom when they delivered his dinner. He said your mother had spent the last few days with him."

Liv swallowed, realizing that her father had mistaken

Liv for her mom. Everyone always said they looked so much alike.

"Charlie told the nurse that they were going on a date tonight," Noah continued, "and they had to be careful since her father didn't like him. Any idea where he used to take your mom?"

Liv gave him a fleeting smile. "I do."

CHAPTER 40

It was another ten minutes before they made it to the overgrown lot. The landscape was bleak: a cement field in the middle of nowhere, the old-fashioned drive-in movie screen covered in graffiti, the speaker poles rusted and in disrepair, jutting from the ground. All shrouded in darkness save for the headlights of Noah's Mercedes.

Noah eased into one of the spaces. The lot was eerie, apocalyptic.

"We had some days here, huh?" Noah said, breaking the quiet.

Liv didn't respond, but felt her face redden. They'd had sex in the back of her dad's station wagon at this very drive-in. During a Molly Ringwald movie. The theater had gone out of business soon thereafter. She didn't think there was a connection.

She surveyed the area, looking for her father.

"Can you pull to the back?" She twisted around,

looking behind them. "My dad said they used to park near the concession stand so her father wouldn't see him."

Noah slowly turned the car around. "Why'd your grandfather hate Charlie so much?"

Liv continued to look out the window. Weeds surrounded the lot, sprouting through cracks in the asphalt. "My dad always said her father correctly thought she was too good for him." She smiled.

Then she saw something move in the distance. "There," Liv said, pointing to a figure near the shuttered concession building.

Noah stopped the car, and Liv jumped out. Her father approached, his hand shielding his eyes from the headlamps.

"Dad!" Liv threw her arms around him.

She pulled back and looked at him, making sure he was all right. Her father squinted, blinked as if confused. He stared at her face for a long time, not saying anything.

"We were worried about you."

Noah walked over.

Her father's expression brightened with a burst of lucidity. "Eddie Haskell," he said. In a surly tone, half playful, he added, "What in the hell are you doing out here in the middle of the night with my daughter?"

"I'm sorry, Charlie. How about we both get her home?" Noah walked to the vehicle and opened the back door.

Her father sauntered over. "All right. But I don't want to see you out here again. She's too good for you."

After getting her father settled at the nursing home, Noah drove Liv back to Cindy's house.

Before getting out of the car, Liv looked at him. "Thank you, again."

"It's nothing."

"No, it means a lot. Especially after what I said to you the last time I was in Nebraska."

"I deserved it." He paused. "I was just going through a bad time. I thought Tommy looked so much like Kyle when he was little."

"It's okay. They're both handsome boys." She recalled the anger—the fear—when he'd asked her to do the test. She'd been back in Adair, dealing with another episode with her father. The documentary had just come out, and the town was riled up. The governor had refused to support Danny's pardon, and Noah wanted a goddamned paternity test.

So she'd taken the test—told him she'd sent strands of Evan's and Tommy's hair off to an internet paternity testing company under a false name. It felt vile, like she was a guest on one of those awful talk shows where couples revealed the results of paternity tests on live television. When the results came back showing that Evan was the father, she emailed them to Noah. He'd asked that it be sent to a particular email address, one he'd likely made to keep any record of the discussion untraceable. Always the politician.

Noah looked at her as if he were going in for a kiss.

The thought repelled her. She opened the car door, keeping her distance. Making it clear that wasn't going to happen.

"Good night, Noah."

He nodded, his expression defeated. "Send me those papers Sampson's wife gave you," he said. "Maybe there'll be something we can use for the pardon."

Inside Cindy's house, Liv went to Tommy's bedside and watched him sleeping. She leaned over and kissed him on the cheek, praying he would never learn that the strands of hair she'd sent along with the paternity test weren't Evan's. They were Noah's.

Excerpt from
A Violent Nature

Season 1/Episode 2
"They Just Got in My Head"

INSERT - A school photo of DANNY PINE in
his football uniform.

INSERT - PRISON TELEPHONE RECORDING

> EVAN PINE
> I don't understand. They said you confessed
> to hurting Charlotte. Why would you say
> that, Danny? It doesn't make sense.

> DANNY
> (sobbing)
> I don't know why. I don't remember, but
> I'd never hurt her. I, I, I—

> EVAN
> I know, son. I just don't understand why—

> DANNY
> It's horrible in here.

> EVAN
> I need you to stay strong, buddy. I'm
> getting you a lawyer. We'll get this
> straightened out. But I need to know: Did

those cops threaten you? Did they hurt
you?

DANNY

I can't explain why I said it. They just
got in my head.

CHAPTER 41

DANNY PINE

Some people remember vividly where they were when Kennedy was assassinated. Or when the space shuttle *Challenger* blew up. Or when Princess Diana's car crashed. Or when the planes struck the Twin Towers. Memories formed under intense emotions are seared into our thoughts, branded by the hot iron of trauma. Danny Pine had thought a lot about memory over the past seven years.

Everyone always wanted to know *Why can't you remember?* At first it had been the police, though they thought he was lying. Then his parents. Then Dave, his ponytailed criminal defense lawyer. Then those filmmakers. Hell, even the generally uncurious felons at Fishkill. One of them, a psychiatrist convicted of manipulating patients into blowing him, even offered to hypnotize Danny. *Ah, no thanks.*

Nearly everyone was convinced that the truth—what *really* happened to Charlotte—was packed away in the deep recesses of his brain, and if they could just unlock the memories . . .

It wasn't like his mind was a complete blank. Initially all Danny remembered were flashes of the party at what's-his-name's house. Fragments. Running out the back door when someone yelled *Cops!* A bonfire in a cornfield. The dented metal kegs of beer. Then waking up in his bed, a jackhammer pounding his skull, his little sister standing there with a concerned look on her face. *The police are at the door. Where's Mommy?*

But slowly other things came back to him. The ponytailed lawyer said those memories—Charlotte at the party, her face twisted in anguish, *I need to talk to you*—weren't helpful, so he might best keep them to himself.

One thing Danny Pine wished he could forget was his first day inside after his conviction. Them stripping him down, delousing him, shoving a folded stack of prison blues into his arms. Entering the gallery. The rapists and murderers and other scum in the rafters calling down to him and the parade of newbies.

Fresh meat! Fresh meat! Fresh meat!

The sound of his cell door clanging shut on the sweltering top floor, where all the horrid smells of the prison found a home. Looking back, as traumatic as it was, the experience was hardly unique. Every month Danny saw it play out again and again.

He was a different person now. Not a better person, different. When he was transferred to Fishkill last year, he held his head up defiantly as he made the walk that first day. This time the hard cases chanted, *Fresh Fish!*

Fresh Fish! Fresh Fish! Not the most original people in the world, prisoners. The young guy in front of him was crying. Danny didn't even warn him to stop.

By now Danny felt like a hardened lifer, and what passed for famous behind these walls. He'd never seen the documentary. But he understood it had been a big deal. The prison library had newspapers. He also received letters, "fan mail," and had visits from high-priced attorneys. His father said that the new lawyers were the real thing, not in over their heads, like Ponytail. More like Louise Lester, his post-verdict lawyer from the Institute for Wrongful Convictions. Celebrities were tweeting about his case, and virtually the entire country had turned against his hometown, particularly those two cops who'd interrogated him. Even the president's daughter—that's right, the president of the United States—announced she was on Team Danny. But slowly, the attention, like his hope, faded.

Now things had turned dangerous for him. Word spread that his parents had left him a fortune in life insurance. You did *not* want to be known as someone with a fortune in this place. Worse, he'd heard that Damian Wallace had a beef with him. He didn't know why. But in here it could be anything.

The stretch of hall he was walking that morning was the most dangerous—narrow halls, crowded, only two cameras at each end, none in the middle—so he was on high alert. He walked the line, his eyes hunting for threats. Looking for Wally. The downtrodden line of blue shirts flowed past, no shoulder bumps, no hard looks, no scuffles to create a diversion for the guards.

After surviving the hall without a sharpened toothbrush in his ribs, he exhaled with relief. *This place. This fucking place!* Fishkill had once been a hospital for the criminally insane and Danny swore he was going mad. Would he ever roam outside its bleak walls?

His aunt was trying to get him approved to go to the funeral. *Good luck with that.* The warden wasn't the most compassionate guy around. He'd once told Danny he'd started watching the documentary but had to shut it off. "I know bullshit when I see it," he'd said.

As Danny clambered up the metal stairs, he wondered if he'd ever see the man again, the one who'd held his last hope of getting out. Of looking at the moon. Of sleeping in. Of getting a juicy fast-food burger.

The man had arrived at the prison unannounced, lied and said he was one of Danny's lawyers. It was the same day the Supreme Court had denied review of Danny's case. Danny suspected the timing wasn't a coincidence.

His name was Neal Flanagan, a greasy man in an expensive suit.

Flanagan said he worked for the governor, and for a cool mil Danny could be a free man. He didn't actually *say* any of it, of course, probably scared that the prison recorded visits. No, he produced a sheet of paper with the offer written up. After Danny read it, Flanagan placed the paper in a folder and locked it in his briefcase.

"So do you think you can afford my rates?" Flanagan asked, pretending to be a potential new lawyer for

Danny, a ruse for recording devices that probably didn't exist.

"Where in the hell would I get that kind of money?"

"You're famous."

"I didn't get any money from the TV show."

"What about all those celebrities and do-gooders? They've got money."

Danny rolled his eyes. But he couldn't escape the feeling that something about the man, something about the whole thing, seemed legit. Well, not *legit,* but authentic. It didn't seem like a setup.

"Look, when I get out, I'll get plenty of offers. I can pay then and—"

"No work on credit, Mr. Pine. Talk to your father. Talk to your benefactors. And do it soon. This offer has an expiration date."

"I make fifty-two cents an hour. And, even if I could borrow the money, how do I know you're for real? What if I give you the 'retainer' and you just disappear?"

"We'd provide assurances."

"What kind?"

"Get the money and you'll find out."

"Why? Why would he pardon me now, after everything . . ."

"Retirement planning."

A week later Danny read that the governor was under investigation, and his attorney fixer—Neal Flanagan—had been indicted. And now the governor had resigned.

Retirement planning.

Danny had racked his brain about how to get that

money. But he'd never told his father about the man, the offer, any of it.

He reached his cell and went inside. That was odd: his fat cellmate—who got off his ass only for food and to slug the three feet to the toilet—wasn't on the bottom bunk.

That was when the hair on the back of Danny's neck rose. And his cell darkened with the shadow of a man charging inside.

CHAPTER 42

MATT PINE

Matt walked into the diner, the familiar ring of the bell on the door bringing him back to when he was a kid and they'd go to Anne's for breakfast on Sunday mornings. He had a vision of Danny sitting in front of a giant stack of pancakes, his mother stealing a bite with her fork. It was strange, the things you remembered.

Like the bar last night, the place seemed to go quiet at his presence. A beat of silence followed by murmurs. Today the looks weren't so subtle, heads following him as he passed, necks craning. He threaded through the tables to a booth in the back. Special Agent Keller sat with a cup of coffee in front of her, steam wafting from the mug.

Matt slid into the booth across from her. The diner's patrons were still giving him looks.

"Good morning," Keller said.

"Morning."

She regarded him. "You look . . . tired," she said.

She was right about that. After meeting Jessica, he'd

gotten two hours of sleep at most. He suppressed a yawn.

The waitress came over, topped off Keller's coffee, asked if she needed anything. Matt could swear it was the same woman from when he was a kid. The same beehive hairstyle. She treated Matt like he was invisible.

Keller flicked Matt a glance, frowned. He wasn't imagining it. The waitress was purposefully ignoring him.

"I'll have a cup of coffee, please," Matt said. He wasn't a huge fan of coffee, but he wasn't sure he'd get through the day without it.

The waitress made a noise in her throat. She hesitated as if she were going to refuse, but filled the mug without saying a word.

"Sure you wanna be seen with me?" Matt said to Keller after the waitress had left. "They are making your food, you know?"

Keller gave a close-lipped smile.

"I suppose they think no Pine should ever set foot in here—the diner where Charlotte worked," Matt said.

"I'm not sure that's it," Keller said.

Matt gave her a look.

Keller laid a newspaper on the table. On the front page of the *Lincoln Journal Star* was a photo of Matt next to one of Danny. Matt looked tired, dark circles under his eyes, hair tousled. Maybe even worse than he looked today. It was the photo from his college ID. He remembered taking it after a night of partying that first week of school freshman year when everyone went crazy from the lack of parental supervision. How did the newspaper get it? Next to Matt was Danny's mug shot. Together the photos made them look like criminals. Half true, but still.

Worse, the headline: "A VIOLENT NATURE" BROTHERS SUSPECTS IN MURDER OF FAMILY.

"What the——" Matt looked around the room, appreciating the hostility now. "They think I had something to do with——" Matt felt his throat constrict. His mouth was bone-dry. "I was in New York. Danny's in prison, for fuck's sake. How could they say—I'm going to fucking sue them."

Keller waited patiently, letting him get it all out. Finally Matt just sat staring at his coffee mug, trying to process it all.

"I'm really sorry," Keller said.

Matt's emotions were raging. He tried to read the story, but he couldn't focus on the words. The world was tilting.

"I'm sorry," the agent said again.

"Why would they say this?"

"I don't know. Someone leaked that the crime scene may have been staged, the work of a professional, and that your father had an unusually large insurance policy. That's probably all it took."

Matt swallowed again, his mouth a desert.

"It's not right," Matt said, his voice laced with emotion.

"I know, Matthew," Keller said.

"Is it true, that the scene was staged?"

Keller hesitated. "We're still investigating," she said. "But maybe."

"The funeral is tomorrow. And everybody's gonna think—" Matt repressed a sob. He needed to get it together.

"Here, have some water." Keller slid Matt her glass and he downed it.

"There's more, Matt. When the Mexicans returned your family, they included their effects. All of the phones and laptops had been wiped clean. And it wasn't some mistake by the local cops taking the devices into inventory. They'd been scrubbed in a way that there was zero chance of retrieving any data; not even the most skilled computer forensics agents at the Bureau could recover anything. Whoever wiped them down knew what they were doing."

"But who—why?" Matt's voice was still quavering.

"I don't know."

"Do you think it's related to Danny's case?"

"I honestly don't know."

Matt wanted to scream, *Then what the fuck do you know?* But it wasn't the agent's fault.

As if reading his thoughts, Keller said, "Here's what I do know: After your sister posted the video of the party on social media, she and your dad planned the Mexico trip to chase a lead."

"What are you talking about?"

"A friend of Maggie's from school is a computer whiz. Right before your family left for Mexico, she asked him to track down the location of a phone that called your dad's phone. The kid traced it to Tulum, Mexico. And your father also made several Google searches about Tulum."

"That's why they went to Mexico? Tracking down some clue about my brother's case?" It explained the spur-of-the-moment trip. And it smacked of Dad and Maggie.

"Also, Maggie asked her friend if it was possible to make a video call but digitally make it look like someone else was calling. The kid made her a video putting someone else's face on your sister's. I watched it and it looked real."

"And let me guess," Matt said. "It was Charlotte's face."

"How'd you know?" Keller asked.

"Apparently there are rumors that she's still alive. That it wasn't Charlotte's body at the creek."

Keller frowned.

Matt continued, "So if someone wanted to lure my sister—or, more likely, my father—somewhere, they might do it by pretending Charlotte was still alive."

"It's possible," Keller said.

"But why get them to go all the way to Mexico? And who? Why?"

"I don't know. I'm waiting on test results for some evidence found at the scene."

"What evidence? What—"

"I'll tell you more when I get the results; it could be nothing. But I've also got Carlita Escobar, the consular officer you met in Tulum, checking some things out."

Matt would never forget Escobar, the tough woman who'd caused the Mexican cop to nearly piss himself. He felt an ache in his chest. It was so Maggie to be on the hunt for evidence.

Keller slid a computer tablet across the table.

Matt looked at the screen. It was the photo Maggie had sent him from Mexico.

"We enhanced the photo," Keller said.

Matt stared at his father standing on a road in Tulum, the shadow of a bicycle, a sweat ring at his neck, like he'd been out for a ride. Keller put her index finger and thumb together on the screen and opened them, zooming in on the photo. Behind his father, a couple was standing in front of a building. And for the first time, Matt saw it.

"Oh my god," Matt said, his pulse quickening. A shot of adrenaline galloped through him.

Maggie hadn't really been taking a photo of her father, but using him as the pretext to shoot the couple. The woman was pretty, wore a bikini and shorts. And Matt suspected she had an Oklahoma accent. Right before she died, Maggie had sent Matt a photo of Hank.

But that wasn't the thing that caused Matt's heart to pound. No, it was the tall man next to Hank. He had a hand on his face, like he was going to wipe his brow. Or perhaps was trying to hide his face, only part of which was visible.

Enough to show a scar from a cleft lip.

CHAPTER 43

SARAH KELLER

After breakfast, Keller stood outside the diner with Matt. Her mind was racing. The woman in the photo Maggie Pine had sent to Matt was the same woman who'd lured him to the woods, taken his phone. And the man with the cleft lip fit the description of the guy who'd shoved Matt into the street, tried to steal his belongings. Who were they? What did they want? And why had Maggie Pine sent her brother the photograph on her last day alive?

Keller turned to Matt. "You need a ride to the nursing home?" She gestured her chin at her maroon Nissan rental, parked at the curb near the diner.

"Nah, my aunt is picking me up." Matt glanced down the street. "Shit," he said.

Keller was going to ask what was wrong when she saw Judy and Ira Adler, the directors of *A Violent Nature,* walking toward them.

Judy Adler nodded hello to Keller, then turned to Matt. Her husband hung back, as if conflicted.

"Matthew," Judy said, "I'm so sorry for your loss."

Matt offered a dismissive nod.

"I know this is a terrible time—and I know you wanted nothing to do with us on the last film—but we're doing a follow-up to the documentary, and we'd love to talk to you. We think it could really help your brother, and—"

"Not interested," Matt said. He gazed down the road as if looking for his aunt's car.

"Matthew, you're a filmmaker. You have to understand we're just doing our jobs. And you may not have cared for it, but *A Violent Nature* got your brother's case on the map. No one cared until we—"

"Until you what?" Matt said. "Until you got everyone's hopes up? Made my father look crazy? Pulled my little sister into this mess? Made my family the most hated people in this town? And for what?"

"Matthew, I'm—"

"I said, *not interested.*"

Keller was surprised at the emotion—the hurt—in Matt's voice.

"My brother's still in jail," Matt continued. "And my family went to Mexico on some hunt for clues. If it weren't for this fucking quest—your *film*—they'd at least be alive. My sister would be leaving for college. My little brother would be finishing first grade."

Keller saw the glint in Judy Adler's eyes. Matt had unintentionally given them some new information: the reason his family had gone to Mexico.

Matt seemed to realize it too. He turned to Keller, his eyes apologizing.

Keller gave a look back that said, *It's okay.*

"I'm just asking you to hear us out," Judy said. "We've uncovered new evidence. It could really help. I think your dad would want you to just hear what we have to say."

Keller was about to intercede when Matt's aunt pulled up. She idled the car in front of the diner.

Matt turned to Keller. "Thanks for the coffee. Keep me posted on things," he said.

His aunt Cindy gave the Adlers the stink eye out the car window. When they looked over at her, she held out her middle finger.

Keller and the Adlers watched the car disappear, along with the filmmakers' hopes of interviewing Matt Pine for their sequel to *A Violent Nature.*

"New evidence, eh?" Keller said pointedly to the couple.

Judy said, "Newer than that CODIS and DNA analysis you promised us . . ."

"I'm calling in every favor I have to get us moved to the front of the line," Keller said.

Judy frowned.

"I'm supposed to hear tonight. The moment I get the results, I promise, I'll call. Until then, what's this new evidence?"

Judy looked at her husband, who gave a tiny shrug as if to say, *Why not?*

Keller gestured for the diner's door. Somewhere they could sit and talk.

"No, not in there," Judy said. "You think they don't like the Pines? Well, they *really* don't like us. We've set up base at a farmhouse about ten minutes from here."

"I'll follow you there."

The farmhouse had seen better days. The paint peeling, porch sagging. Several dogs scattered as the Adlers parked the van on a patch of dirt that passed for a drive-way. Keller pulled the Nissan beside them.

Judy got out of the van, a dented Ford. Ira trailed be-hind his wife, something Keller suspected he'd been doing for as long as the Adlers had been married. Judy waved to Keller to follow them inside.

Keller climbed out of her car and looked around. A barn was about thirty yards away, the door falling off its hinges. Beyond that, just fields, not another soul for miles. She stepped around the mud and muck and mounted the porch steps. The wood was soft from rot. She stopped at the door and looked inside the place. Two men in their twenties sat in front of laptops at a long kitchen table. Stacks of papers and empty soda cans cluttered the work space. Dishes were piled in the sink.

A woman, heavyset and wearing sneakers and sweats, was also at the far end of the kitchen table, talking on her cell phone.

Judy called to Keller from inside. "Come on in. We don't bite."

The interior was just as run-down. Cracked linoleum floors, faded wallpaper with bare patches as if some-one had started trying to remove it and given up. An avocado-green refrigerator matched the green laminate countertops.

Ira cleared away some of the trash and clutter from the table, making a space for their guest. "Please, have a seat."

Judy introduced Keller to the others—the production team, who all seemed more attentive when they learned that Keller was with the Federal Bureau of Investigation.

"Sorry about the mess," Ira said, sitting next to his wife, across from Keller. "We've had a lot of late nights around here. Get you some coffee or something to drink?"

"I'm fine. Already hit my caffeine quota. But thank you." Keller looked at the monitors and equipment. "How's the sequel coming?"

"Slow. How's your investigation into the death of the Pines going?"

"Same," Keller said.

Judy Adler gave a slight chuckle, as if amused at Keller's evasive response. She said, "We've been looking into Charlotte and what we've found is, um, *surprising*." Judy looked at a member of the production team. He had a man bun and wore flip-flops with jeans. "Show her."

Keller caught the faint whiff of weed as the guy set a laptop in front of her. He tapped on a few keys, then went back to his seat.

The screen showed a woman, mid-twenties, her hair a dull shade of purple.

"Charlotte wasn't just my cousin, she was my best friend," the woman said.

"You were a close family?" Judy Adler asked from off camera.

The woman made a noise that said *fat chance*. "My mom and Charlotte's dad had major issues. They haven't talked in years."

"Why's that?"

"Uncle John abused my mom when they was kids. Sexually, I mean."

A chill crawled up Keller's back. The woman said it so matter-of-fact. And from what Keller knew about sexual abusers, they didn't tend to stop as they got older. The victims just changed. She continued to watch the video.

"But you and Charlotte were close?"

"Oh yeah. My mom was worried, you know. She told Charlotte she could come to Kansas, stay with us, anytime."

"Did you think Charlotte was being abused by your uncle?"

The woman nodded.

"Did she tell you that?"

"Not in so many words."

"But you thought so?"

She nodded again. "Long as I can remember, she was always talking about getting out of Adair, moving to a big city, changing her name, starting over."

"Did you ever talk to her about it—what was happening at home, I mean?"

"We didn't need to. It was just understood."

"Did you know her boyfriend?"

"Who, Danny? I talked to him a few times when me and Charlotte were Skyping."

"Were you surprised when you heard he'd been arrested?"

"Oh yeah. I mean, we was in shock. It was funny, 'cause that show made a big thing about Danny and Charlotte, like they were high school sweethearts on their way to the altar or somethin'. But he saw other people, and so did she."

"You're saying they weren't serious?"

"Not from what Charlotte told me. She always said Danny Pine was a sweet dumb jock. They had a good time, but it wasn't like they was getting married."

"She saw other boys?"

"I think. Though she thought all the kids at school were immature."

"Did she mention anyone in particular?"

"She said there was someone, an older boy, but wouldn't tell me who."

"Why not?"

The woman shrugged.

"Did you know she was pregnant?"

"I don't think she was."

"But they ran tests and—"

"If that was her." She said this with a roll of her neck, almost like a challenge.

"I don't understand."

"About a week before it happened, she said she couldn't take it anymore. She was gonna take off."

"Couldn't take what anymore?"

The woman looked off camera like it was a stupid question. "She didn't say. But it was obvious. Her dad . . ."

"So you're saying— Then who was at the creek? And why didn't the police—"

"I don't know. But Charlotte said she had friends, important people who could help her get away."

"Who were these friends?"

Judy Adler reached over and stopped the video. "We talked to some of Charlotte's friends. Charlotte had a bit of a secret life. Older boys, drugs. She'd told one friend she'd been assaulted, and she was afraid."

Keller gave Judy a skeptical glance. "There was a trial, blood work. Her body was positively identified."

Ira Adler snapped his fingers and pointed at Keller. "Exactly. And guess who contacted us saying he had something that would blow up what everybody thought about the case. Involving the blood work."

Keller shook her head.

"Ron Sampson."

"The cop who interrogated Danny Pine?"

"We were scheduled to meet, and then . . ."

"He killed himself," Keller said.

Ira tilted his head to the side, held Keller's stare like maybe Sampson *hadn't* killed himself.

It was all too much. Too many conspiracies. Too many leaps. And Keller was starting to think the Adlers had been drinking the Kool-Aid.

"Charlotte's father moved to North Dakota," Ira added. "We've asked him for access to her things, to let us exhume the body for a DNA test, but he's refused to speak with us."

What a surprise. The guy they were accusing of being a child molester didn't want to cooperate. Keller glanced at the computer screen again. In one of the windows she saw a familiar face: Noah Brawn.

Judy Adler followed Keller's gaze, and said, "We interviewed him again. We're hoping that the climax of our film will be a pardon, but we'll see."

Keller gestured to the computer. "May I?" she asked.

Judy nodded, and Keller clicked on the window with Brawn's handsome face.

The interview started with Judy's voice off-screen: "Do you think with all the attention on Danny Pine, Charlotte got forgotten?"

"Absolutely not. I certainly never forgot her. But we won't get justice for her if the wrong man is in prison. We won't get justice until the truth comes out. . . ."

Judy stopped the video. "You get the idea. More of the same from last time: the Smasher, the U.P., blah, blah, blah. We'll see if he puts his money where his mouth is on the pardon."

"You don't think he'll pardon Danny now that he's governor?"

"*Acting* governor," Judy said. "He only got the job because the former governor was a crook and had a taste for young girls. I suspect Brawn will tread lightly until he's actually voted into the office. Have you been following the scandal?"

"Loosely."

"The former governor is a real sleaze. And his henchman, what's his name, Ira?"

"Flanagan. Neal Flanagan," her husband replied.

"That's right. This Flanagan is straight out of a movie. Who knows, it may be our next documentary—right, Ira?"

Her husband shrugged.

"Anyway, Nebraska is unusual since the governor doesn't hold the power to pardon on his own. Brawn's part of a pardon board. And he may be waiting to see who else the governor's henchman snitches on before he starts associating himself with the former governor's people on the board. That administration was *dir-ty*."

Politics. It didn't matter how big or small, it usually was dirty.

"Okay, we've shown you ours," Judy said. "How about you show us yours?"

"I told you, I'll call as soon as I get the CODIS and DNA analysis."

"You've gotta have more than that," Judy said. "Just talk to us, deep background. No one will ever know. The family—they were murdered, right? And what Matthew said, were they really in Mexico chasing a lead? That sounds like Evan. He just couldn't let go."

"I'm sorry," Keller said. "I can't comment."

Judy Adler's mouth was a tight seam.

"But I'll tell you what," Keller added, "I'll talk to Matt, encourage him to speak with you." It was a lie, but no reason to piss off the Adlers. Keep your enemies closer and all that. If they found a lead, she wouldn't want them holding a grudge.

"That would be terrific," Ira Adler said. He'd probably spent their entire marriage playing Good Cop.

Judy added, "We really do want to help his brother."

Keep telling yourself that, Keller thought.

CHAPTER 44

MAGGIE PINE

BEFORE

Maggie looked across the aisle of the cramped flight. Mom and Dad were talking about something, smiling. It had been a while since she'd seen that. And it took a little of the sting out of the past few days. She glanced at Tommy, next to her with all the essentials spread out on the tray table: coloring books, Goldfish crackers, juice box, and his favorite stuffed animal, Sweet Bear. He was watching a movie—one with those creepy blue creatures, the Smurfs—on the tiny screen of Mom's phone.

Maggie wanted to get her mother alone. They hadn't had a moment since they'd whisked Mom away from one airport gate to another. Mom and Tommy stepped off the plane from Omaha, and three hours later were boarding the flight to Mexico. Maggie had expected her mother to be annoyed that it was all so unplanned. She hadn't even gotten to pack her own bag for the beach. But Mom was either putting on a face or she was excited to go. Energized by the spontaneity. Or maybe it was seeing Dad so upbeat.

Ever since Maggie had found him on the floor when he'd passed out (drunk or food poisoned, she still couldn't decide), he'd been different. Make no mistake, Danny's case was still the giant hippo in the room—or was it elephant, she could never remember, whatever—but her father seemed more available, more present. Maggie wondered if her mother would be so carefree about the trip if she knew why they were going. Um, she certainly wouldn't be smiling and ordering another wine right now. Watching her mother drain the plastic cup, laugh at something her father said, Maggie didn't care why they were going.

Maybe she'd hold off telling Mom about what had happened with Eric. *Why ruin the trip, right?* Maggie could handle it. *Just don't think about it.* But it wasn't so easy. She felt a prickling down her spine remembering how he'd pinned her arms against the wall. She still had fingerprint bruises on her wrists. She was being melodramatic. It wasn't like he'd raped her. But she'd felt so powerless, so scared, so ashamed. But if she told Mom, then Mom would tell Dad and then he'd . . . Well, the trip would be wrecked. Maggie also didn't think her father could take another instance where he hadn't been there to protect one of his kids.

The plane hit a patch of turbulence and Maggie clutched the armrest. Tommy gazed up at her, smiling, the headphones giant on his head. When was the last time she'd felt that safe and secure, that invincible? Had she ever? She thought so. Before a young girl was found murdered at Stone Creek. The boogeyman could still be out there, her dad reminded her and anyone who'd listen. Maggie had been on the hunt for him ever since.

Sure, she'd had doubts over the years. She didn't really *know* Danny. She'd been only ten when he went away. He'd been larger than life. The boy who playfully called her *dork,* mussed her hair whenever he walked by, gave her piggyback rides. She remembered him playing tea party with her and her dolls. Remembered going to the football games, feeling special that she was Danny Pine's sister. She didn't remember Danny being home much. Back then their parents didn't believe in monsters, and let the kids come and go. Maggie knew Danny was no saint. He drank too much, wasn't particularly kind to the unpopular kids, and wasn't a great boyfriend, at least from what Maggie had learned working his case over the years. But he also wasn't a murderer. She believed that. Needed to believe that.

Maggie chewed the inside of her cheek, examining the purple spots on her wrists again, wondering if Mom would notice them. She then caught her father gazing at her from across the aisle. He did that a lot. She'd catch him stealing looks at her. He smiled, then put his head back, closed his eyes. Mom rested her head on his shoulder.

That was it, she decided. Maggie would wait to tell Mom about what had happened at the party until they got home. She could suck it up. She had one more decision to make: when to tell her father about the email she'd received right before they boarded the flight. From the cell phone aggregation service—the company Toby had hooked her up with. She thought she'd thrown away two hundred bucks, but the report arrived as promised, a one-page map showing blue pins at two locations in Tulum.

The first was the Moloko Bar, where Charlotte—or someone pretending to be Charlotte—had made the call. It verified the caller ID. But more interesting was the second blue dot. It pinged for only one day at an address a few blocks away from the bar. Maybe that was where the caller lived or was staying. If Maggie showed the report to her dad—who at that moment was ordering another beer and beaming—he wouldn't be able to focus on anything else. Whatever fun they were going to squeeze in before going to the Moloko Bar would vanish. She was going tell him, just not right away. Maybe if she waited, the trip would be about *them*.

She looked across the cabin at her father again. Yeah, who was she kidding?

CHAPTER 45

MATT PINE

"Is he always like this?" Matt looked over at his grandfather, who sat catatonic in his old armchair in the nursing home suite. Matt and his aunt were at the small bistro-style dining table. The room was larger than the one his grandfather had occupied when Matt was a boy. And it was cozy, decorated with framed family photos, houseplants, and furniture Matt remembered from his grandfather's house. Whatever you could say about his gruff aunt, she'd taken good care of her dad.

"He's gotten much worse this year," Cindy said. "But when your mom visited, he came alive. She always had that effect on him."

"Does he know?"

Cindy shook her head. She didn't say so, but Matt could tell she thought there was no point in telling his grandfather about the tragedy. Matt didn't push it. But didn't his grandfather have a right to know that his daughter was dead? That his son-in-law had perished? That two of his grandchildren were gone?

There was a tap on the door and a nurse came into the room. She had a smile on her face—until she noticed Cindy.

"I'm sorry, Ms. Ford, I didn't know you were still here. I can come back."

"Where's Alvita?" Cindy said. "I told Chang that my father didn't need a series of strangers tromping in and out of here. He likes Alvita. *I* like Alvita."

"I'm sorry, Ms. Ford. She's off today."

Cindy frowned.

"I'll come back," the nurse said, retreating as fast as she could out of the room. Matt didn't blame the woman.

Cindy turned back to Matt. "I need to talk to you about something."

"Sure. What is it?"

"It's about the services."

Matt had already fielded dozens of texts from Cindy about the funeral, and wondered how there could possibly be *more* questions—more decisions about the flowers, the photos to display, the program, the obituary, and the other things Matt cared nothing about. He supposed immersing herself in the details was how Cindy was coping with the grief.

"Noah Brawn would like to have the wake at his home," Cindy said.

Matt thought about this. "Mom's high school boyfriend? The guy from the documentary? Won't it be weird to—"

"Look, it's not ideal. I frankly never liked Noah when we were growing up. But he's the governor of the state now. The reason your grandpa has this big room. And I think your parents would want this."

"Are you sure about that? Because I'm not so sure that my—"

"We need Noah for Danny's pardon."

And there it was. His brother's case had dominated his family in life, so of course it would dominate in death. There was no use fighting about it.

"Okay."

"And I know you haven't wanted to talk about it, but we need to take care of your parents' affairs. The house, their credit cards, the will, the life insurance, the—"

"You're right, I don't want to talk about it," Matt said. It came out more sharply than he'd intended, reminded him of the outrageous newspaper story from that morning suggesting he and Danny had killed their family for insurance money. He needed to shake it off. In a softer tone, he said, "After the funeral, I promise."

Cindy looked like she was going to protest, but stopped herself. Purposefully changing the subject, she said, "So what did those assholes the Adlers want?"

She'd asked him the same thing on the car ride over, but he'd shrugged it off. "I guess they're making a sequel," Matt said.

Cindy's expression turned to disgust. "I'll never forgive myself for letting them interview me. The way they treated your father. And now they want to put everyone through it all again? It makes me sick."

Cindy's eyes were misty. The first sign of emotion other than irritation or anger Matt had seen in his aunt since he'd arrived in Adair. He reached across the table and put his hand on hers.

Cindy gave a sardonic smile. "We're a pair, aren't we?"

Matt didn't know what she meant by that.

"All we've got is a guy who doesn't recognize us, and another guy in prison for life." There was dark humor in her voice, masking the pain.

"No," Matt said. "We've got each other."

It was the right thing to say, the kind thing to say. But the truth was, Matt felt alone. And he wondered if he would always feel this way. Wondered if the loss and pain would always consume him. Wondered if he'd ever recover from the magnitude of it all. Eyeing his frail grandfather staring out at nothing in his beat-up La-Z-Boy, Matt decided that Cindy was right. Grandpa was lucky he'd never know the truth.

CHAPTER 46

SARAH KELLER

Since watching the video at the Adlers' farmhouse, Keller had thought a lot about Charlotte's cousin and the theory that Charlotte was alive. It just didn't ring true. For one, if it wasn't Charlotte who was murdered, who was the young woman with her skull crushed in at the creek? And how did the police and prosecutors screw *that* up? Charlotte's father might have been abusing her. And she might not be the innocent cheerleader portrayed in *A Violent Nature*. But that didn't mean she was alive. Even if she was, what would it have to do with the death of the Pines?

Still, Keller wasn't drowning in leads. She was playing the waiting game now. Waiting for the report on the DNA sample, waiting for the report on the facial rec of the man and woman in the photo Maggie Pine had sent her brother, waiting on a report from Carlita Escobar. So, Keller decided, she might as well confirm that it was Charlotte buried at that cemetery.

Short of digging up the body, Keller thought the best

place to test the theory was with those who'd lived the case. Ordinarily, she'd confer with the local prosecutors and detectives. But they'd been under attack since the documentary aired, and had circled the wagons. That left Danny's lawyers. Not his hippie lawyer at the trial, whom the documentary painted as borderline incompetent, notwithstanding the fortune the Pine family had paid him. And not the new white-shoe appellate lawyers the Adlers found too boring to carry the documentary's sequel. Keller wanted to talk to Louise Lester, the passionate attorney who'd taken Danny's case before the cameras were rolling. Who by all accounts was a skilled advocate.

Keller pulled her rental car into the strip mall in North Omaha. It had a payday loan company, a Dollar Store, and a nail salon. She scanned the address on her phone to make sure it was the right place. This was it, all right. Then she saw it, at the far end, a plain storefront with a small sign that read THE INSTITUTE FOR WRONGFUL CONVICTIONS.

Keller found Louise Lester at a cluttered desk hemmed in by piles of paperwork. The place had no walls, no separate offices or even cubicles. Just a large room with about ten workstations, the hum of chatter and clicking keyboards filling the air. It reminded Keller of an old-time pressroom.

These weren't reporters, though. The Institute for Wrongful Convictions was staffed by volunteers—law students, retirees, social justice warriors—which was why Keller had assumed it was open on a Saturday. She felt an electricity in the room.

"Thank you for seeing me on short notice," Keller said. She'd been saying that a lot lately.

Lester gave her a fleeting smile. She wore no makeup, and wore a threadbare suit that was too large for her frame. Keller suspected there was an attractive woman hiding in the boxy attire. Her look screamed, *There are more important things than looking pretty.*

"Just when you think it couldn't get worse for the Pines," Lester said, her tone melancholy. Like the loss wasn't just professional.

"Did you know them well?"

"Mostly Evan. He was a real advocate for us. A wonderful man."

"I saw him in the documentary. He was really passionate."

Lester nodded. "Those fucking filmmakers made him seem unbalanced. I would've never participated if I'd known what they'd do to him. They had the nerve to ask me to help with the sequel, and I told them where they could stick their movie." Lester took a cleansing breath, as if she were stopping herself from getting worked up. As if it were something she'd learned to do as a child to temper the fire naturally blazing through her veins. "I'm sorry," she said. "The Adlers just aren't my favorite people. Evan was one of the finest humans you'd ever hope to meet. He didn't deserve what they did to him. And Judy and Ira, they used him in the worst kind of way. They couldn't care less about him or Danny or the thousands of other wrongfully convicted." She waved her arm around the room. "They just wanted the ratings. To hell with the truth. They just wanted to tell a good story."

"You think the documentary was just a story?"

"Absolutely."

"But you represented Danny Pine."

"Of course. But not because of the half-assed theories in the documentary. Because his confession was laughably unreliable. I've got two dozen other cases that are even worse. But those kids weren't white hometown football stars, the victims not pretty white girls. . . ."

Lester's eyes flared. They had a vibrant intensity. Keller usually didn't care for true believers. She thought they often suffered from tunnel vision, saw conspiracies that didn't exist. Exhibit A was the Adlers back at the farmhouse. But as she eyed the woman across from her, Keller could only hope her twins would live life with such zeal.

Lester continued, "So do I think the Unknown Partygoer or Bobby Ray Hayes or the boogeyman killed Charlotte? No."

"Why do you say that?"

"The Unknown Partygoer is based on the hazy recollection of one kid at the party. He'd been drinking, and he's since had a car accident that left him with a brain injury, so there's no way to test his recollection. Also, someone else would've noticed if some guy in his late twenties was at a high school house party. And eyewitness testimony is notoriously unreliable. You're in the FBI, you know."

"I know a lot of DNA exonerations involved mistaken eyewitness testimony," Keller said, trying to find common ground.

"Try seventy percent. Seven in ten of people freed by

DNA had been convicted based on bad eyewitnesses. Most of the rest, were . . ."

"False confessions," Keller said, finishing Lester's sentence and trying to regain control of the conversation. Keller's eyes couldn't help but lock onto the poster behind Lester's desk. It was a disturbing black-and-white photograph of an African American boy strapped into the electric chair, his round cheeks streaked with tears as someone tightened the chin strap of the metal helmet that was too large for his head. Under the photo it read:

GEORGE STINNEY JR.

EXECUTED IN 1944 AT THE AGE 14 FOR KILLING TWO WHITE GIRLS

EXONERATED IN 2014

Keller ripped her eyes from the image. She needed to focus. "So who do *you* think killed Charlotte?"

Lester coughed a laugh. "I'm not going down that rabbit hole anymore. Trust me, it will consume your life." The case had taken its toll on Lester. Keller remembered a critical scene in the documentary, Lester at the lectern, arguing Danny's case to a panel of appellate judges, her plea both measured and impassioned.

"Charlotte's head was crushed like Hayes's known victims," Keller said.

"Yeah, precisely. But the Smasher's MO was reported in Kansas newspapers before Charlotte was murdered," Lester said. "And the Kansas police had put out a notice to law enforcement in Nebraska and other neighboring states hoping that they might identify more victims, which is ultimately how they caught Hayes.

The prosecutor in Danny's case should've turned over the notes about the anonymous tip identifying the similarities to Charlotte's murder, but the fact that there was a killer crushing young women's skulls was in the public domain."

"So why didn't Danny's trial lawyer look into it?"

Lester shrugged. "The guy had never handled a murder case and was in over his head. But the lawyer says he *did* look into it. Says he got an anonymous tip, too. And that's what the state relied on in our post-conviction fight. I think he was just covering his ass, but the lawyer said he didn't pursue the lead because the forensics didn't match. Hayes sexually assaulted the girls. Then killed them by crushing their skulls, probably during the act. But Charlotte wasn't sexually assaulted. And the medical examiner concluded she suffered a separate skull fracture, likely sometime before her head was caved in."

Keller felt a combination of sickness and anger in her gut.

"So, what, you think someone was trying to make it look like Hayes was the killer?" That suggested some planning, which was inconsistent with a drunk teenager killing his girlfriend in a rage.

Lester said, "Hayes confessed to the other murders to get the death penalty off the table, but still denied killing Charlotte. Why bother?"

"What about Detective Sampson? The Adlers say that before he died he had some explosive information. About the blood work."

"*Pfft.* How convenient. Even if it's true that he'd go to the Adlers—and I find that questionable, since they basically ruined the man's life—he was hardly credible. If he approached them, it was probably just trying to clear his own name. And before you say it, I've seen the Reddit threads that speculate that he was murdered."

Keller wasn't sure whether Lester was a breath of fresh air or whether her years working the case had hardened her, closed her off to any theory that might explain Charlotte's murder. It was for that reason that Keller didn't want to ask the next question.

"Speaking of conspiracy theories, there's one that is building steam, at least with the Adlers—"

"That Charlotte's alive," Lester said before Keller could get the words out. Lester sighed, as if to add, *Tell me you're not taking that seriously?*

"Right. Look, I know how it sounds, but I've gotta ask."

Lester shook her head. "I'd love it if she were alive, but Charlotte's dead. The Adlers don't know this, and it wasn't discussed at the trial, but Charlotte had a distinguishing mark. A tiny tattoo of a heart on her bottom. It was her."

Keller exhaled. She knew it was crazy, knew it would end this way, but she was still crestfallen.

"A piece of advice, Agent Keller?" Lester said, her phone buzzing on her desk.

Keller nodded.

"Don't make Charlotte's killer your one-armed man. I've been down that road, and it nearly destroyed me."

"But what if knowing what really happened to Charlotte is the only way to know what happened to the Pines?" Keller asked.

Lester put her elbows on the desk, laced her fingers. "Then you're fucked, Agent Keller. You're absolutely fucked."

CHAPTER 47

EVAN PINE

BEFORE

"Come on, get in on this, Magpie," Evan said. He held the phone in front of him for an airport selfie. Evan didn't know if it was the bright sunshine, the smell of salt in the air, or being on their first family vacation in years, but he felt great. Revitalized.

"Daaad," Maggie said, shaking her head.

Liv joined in, pressing her face against Evan's. She waved Maggie over.

Maggie was turning red. A group of teenage boys was nearby. They weren't watching, but their presence seemed to be enough to mortify his daughter.

Tommy said, "Can I be in the picture?"

Evan scooped him up. "Of course. But where are your cool shades?" Evan had bought them at an airport kiosk.

Tommy pulled the plastic sunglasses from his pocket and put them on.

"We're going to keep it up until you join," Evan said to Maggie.

Evan and Liv started doing exaggerated poses—sucking in their cheeks, squinting sexy eyes, making peace signs with their fingers.

"Fine," Maggie said, marching over. She moved her face into the shot. "Take it!"

"Say cheese."

"Seriously, Dad."

Evan and Liv laughed, and he took the shot. Maggie quickly distanced herself from them, but Evan swore he saw the faintest trace of a smile on her lips.

Examining the photo, he felt a warmth in his chest followed by a beat of sadness that the rest of the family, his boys, weren't there.

None of that, he told himself. He wanted to keep up the mood, the vibe. He was still buzzed from the warm beer on the plane and the kiss Liv had given him when the kids had dozed off. One that had sent an inferno through him. If she had invited him to the plane's bathroom, he would've risked it and joined the Mile High Club.

So, no dwelling on Danny or Matt. Or that he had no job. Or that they couldn't afford the trip. Or that he'd come chasing another likely dead-end lead. *Stop.*

Liv looked at the photo. "Ooh, I'm going to post that one later."

She had given up on social media months ago, turned inward, and Evan felt another wave of something that suggested things were different. For Evan, it had come with a handful of pills regurgitated into the sink. What had caused the change in Liv? Evan had another thought:

Who. Fucking. Cares. He reached for his wife's hand and she took it quickly, lacing her fingers through his.

"Are we going to the beach, Daddy?" Tommy asked.

"You bet we are. But we might need to go to the toy store first."

Liv gave him a sideways glance. Like she was going to say something, but stopped herself. Instead she grabbed his butt. "Let's go find the van, sugar daddy."

"Eww." Maggie made a face. But there was the hint of that smile again.

It was two hours before the driver announced that they were in Tulum. The van blew past signs for the beach, and through the strip of tourist shops on the main road. It cut right onto a side street. The area had a grittier feel, run-down buildings painted in faded primary colors. Palm trees with brown leaves sagging over chain-link fences, a maze of power lines drooping overhead. The consequences of booking at the last minute during the busy season.

Liv looked at her husband.

He could read her mind. *Don't worry,* he said with his eyes. *It will be an adventure.*

The van took another sharp turn into a small lane carved into a thicket of jungle. At the end of the road was a complex, six rental properties, each separated by a tall privacy fence. The van dropped them at the front gate and waited for Evan to punch in the code and get inside before taking off. The sounds of the forest filled the air.

Evan entered another code for the front door and he was pleasantly surprised at the space. It had stone floors and an open floor plan with a modern kitchen overlooking a dining area and living room.

Tommy ran down the hall to find his room. When he returned, he fast-walked, twisting around the sofa and the rustic wood table, ultimately landing on one of the stools at the granite kitchen counter. He jumped down from the stool and raced to the sliding doors in the living room.

"Where's the beach?" he asked, staring out at the patio.

Liv knelt and looked into Tommy's eyes. "We've got something better than a beach."

He looked at her, his eyes wide.

"We have the jungle." Liv made her hands like a tiger and pawed at Tommy. She glanced up at Evan, offering a smile.

Maggie looked around. Evan couldn't quite tell what she was thinking. She peeked out the patio doors. "There're bikes out there. Maybe we can ride into town for dinner."

And by nightfall, they were on rickety old bikes, riding down the secluded road into town. Evan's bike had a child seat tethered to the back of it, one of the old models that had likely been recalled in the US years ago. Tommy rode in the lopsided seat, his arms in the air, Liv nervously behind them, calling out for him to hold on to his dad.

They found their way to the highway and waited for cars to rip by before they crossed. From there, it was a quick journey on a dirt road that had a wall painted with a mural of a Mayan god.

In a restaurant on the strip, they ate tacos and Evan and Liv drank too many margaritas. He and Liv laughed, flirted, and couldn't keep their hands off each other. Embarrassed, Maggie pretended not to notice and helped Tommy color the kids' menu, which doubled as a small coloring book.

After dinner they walked through the tourist shops, then made the perilous journey back to the rental property. Maggie insisted on riding the bike with the child seat with her little brother, saying Evan had downed too many cocktails.

Evan and Liv rode side by side. Her hair blew in the wind, and she looked lovely in the sundress and sandals Maggie had packed for her. At one point she challenged Evan to a race, and he pumped his legs with everything he had. The old bike jostled and Evan had a hard time maintaining control. The front tire skidded on some gravel. Evan careened in slow motion off the asphalt and into the small weed-filled ditch lining the road. Liv threw down her bike and ran to him, concerned, but when she approached, Evan pulled her to the ground and the two lay in the weeds, laughing hysterically, their daughter looking at them like they'd lost their shit.

It was, Evan thought, one of the greatest nights of his life.

CHAPTER 48

SARAH KELLER

Keller sat at the desk in the dreary Adair Motel, her investigation notes and files spread out in front of her.

"What's wrong?" her husband said through the speaker on her iPhone.

"I'm just so damn frustrated," Keller said. No, *fucked* was the word Louise Lester had used earlier that day, and Lester fought lost causes for a living. "This is going nowhere. And I'm supposed to give Stan a report in the morning. He's getting a lot of pressure from D.C."

"You'll figure it out," Bob said. She wished she could bottle his confidence in her, consume several gallons a week. She'd been gone only three days, but she missed his calming presence. Missed cuddling the twins. Missed sleeping in her own bed.

"I'm no closer to figuring this out than I was the day I first met Matt Pine. And get this, I just got a call from the lab. My big lead—the blood the filmmaker's investigator found at the scene—it wasn't even blood. They think it was marinara sauce."

Bob barked a laugh. "Spaghetti sauce?"

"It's not funny."

"Wait, you're telling me the blood sample wasn't genuine; it was an *impasta*."

"Really?" Keller grinned in spite of herself.

"Sorry," Bob said, "I'm around six-year-olds all day."

The situation was so ridiculous, you almost had to laugh. She didn't know what she dreaded more, telling Stan—who'd have to report the spaghetti sauce up the chain of command—or telling the Adlers.

The sound of Bob crunching on something, probably his favorite Ruffles potato chips, came through the tinny speaker. "Okay, so the DNA fizzled out and you've talked to everybody. But don't you always say that people are unreliable anyway?"

He was right about that.

More crunching. "So why don't you be you? Look at the documents, the records. They don't lie."

Keller smiled again. "You really do listen to me."

"Did you say something?" Bob said.

"Shut up." She laughed.

"So what do you have so far?"

It was against the rules to talk about an investigation with anyone outside the Bureau. Keller was usually not one to break the rules. But Bob was always her sounding board. The big lug not only calmed her nerves, he was a rare commodity in this world: a good listener. It was why she'd taken to Matt Pine, she thought. He wasn't your average twentysomething with delusional confidence, eager to tell you how things were. Like Bob, he listened. Sometimes just saying things out loud—working through her thoughts—helped Keller connect the dots.

"There's a video the daughter posted. A tip she'd received shortly before they left for Mexico. The timing alone suggests it may be connected."

"Okay. What's it show?"

"Just a few seconds of teenagers being teenagers. Danny Pine being egged on as he chugged a beer. He's down to an undershirt, surrounded by a bunch of football players. In the last second on the recording, someone's face comes into the frame. The armchair detectives think it's the Unknown Partygoer."

"What do you think?"

"I think it could be anyone. There's not enough for facial rec. And I think the video was sent for some other reason. But I've watched it over and over again, and I don't see anything."

"How'd Maggie Pine get it? I mean, who sent her the video?"

"It was an anonymous tip."

Bob blurted a laugh. "You're Big Brother. Get on that, G-woman. What's the use of all those NSA toys if you don't get to use them?"

"Trust me, I've been pushing the computer guys to track the sender. It just takes some time."

Bob was right, though. The source of the video was important. Whoever sent it did so for a reason.

"Okay, what else you got?" Bob asked.

"When they were in Mexico, Maggie sent her brother a photo. It was of their father. But I had it enhanced and Matt noticed something new today. In the background, a woman who'd tried to set Matt up."

"Noooo," Bob said. "She was in the photo the daughter took *before*?"

"I know, right?"

"Well, you gotta get on that."

"I am. I have my contact in Mexico trying to find the woman. But there's something bigger. The photo also has a partial view of a man who seems to fit the description of a guy who tried to mug Matt in New York, shoved him into the street."

"You're kidding me? The sister took a photo of two people, one who tries to set the kid up in Mexico, the other who pushes him into traffic? I mean . . ."

"Right?" Keller said.

"Why, though? What was the point?" Bob asked.

"The phone," Keller said. "I think they were trying to get Matt's phone because Maggie had sent him a photo of them. The rest of the family's phones and computers were wiped clean."

"So it's, what, a professional? Like a hired killer?" Bob was excited. He loved the FBI shows on TV, and for once Keller's work bore some resemblance.

"That's what I'm trying to figure out."

"You love a good paper trail," Bob said, "so what records aren't you thinking about? Where haven't you looked?"

Keller did a mental tally. She had a team going through the Marconi records scooped up in Chicago.

She had the computer forensics lab tracking who'd sent the party video to Maggie, the facial analysis unit analyzing the photo Maggie had sent to Matt, and an AV expert enhancing the video and photograph.

"Airline records," Keller said. "I still need to get flight reports. If the guy was in Mexico with the family, then was in New York, I might be able to identify him by cross-checking flights. But without a name, it's a needle in a haystack. Do you know how many people fly to Cancún every day?"

"No, but I also don't know how many bank wire transfers there are every day. I suspect that's way more than flights, yet somehow you catch the bad guys."

More with the unbridled confidence in her. And Bob was right. If the man with the cleft lip was in Mexico with the Pines, then flew to New York to go after Matt, then followed Matt back to Tulum, that could narrow the search. Maybe, just maybe, she'd get a hit.

Bob exhaled loudly into the phone.

"What?"

"Maggie Pine, I mean, she was *seventeen*. She gets admitted to MIT. She gets investigation tips, tracks bad guys to Mexico, gets their photo. She was the shit, you know? I watched the show. Even when she was in middle school, she was unstoppable. It's just a damn shame."

"I know."

"That's why she's lucky you're on the case."

"I'm not so sure about that."

"No, no, no. None of that. You're the shit too. I mean,

how else would you have this slice of beef waiting for you at home?"

"I've got to get to bed. I'll call you tomorrow after the funeral, you lunatic."

"Aight. You got this, Federale. I'm out."

CHAPTER 49

MATT PINE

Matt drove his grandfather's old station wagon into the Adair Motel parking lot. Tonight the lot was more crowded than before, jammed with news vans and cars with out-of-state plates. More troops to cover the funeral tomorrow, Matt supposed. He saw Kala standing in front of the door to her room. She wore jeans and a shirt knotted so you could see her midriff. The piercing on her flat tummy.

She walked around the long vehicle, eyeing the wood-paneled sides with an amused squint in her eyes.

"Nice wheels," Kala said, pulling the seat belt over her shoulder.

"My grandfather's. I think he's had it since my mom was a kid."

"How is he?" Kala asked.

"Not great. They say he has moments of lucidity. But I haven't seen any."

"I'm sorry." Kala put a hand on his shoulder, rubbed it.

"It's all right." Matt thought back to Cindy's remark. The only family he had left was a brother in prison, a curmudgeon aunt, and a grandfather who didn't recognize him.

"I'm starving," Kala said.

"I told you to go to Lincoln with everybody," Matt said.

Ganesh and company were getting cabin fever. He'd texted Matt that they needed to go to a *real* restaurant and a *real* bar, preferably one without tumbleweeds outside and inbred hicks trying to kill him. It was sweet of Kala to hang back. To make sure Matt wasn't alone. She was from rural Oklahoma, so he supposed she had a higher tolerance for small towns. Though even Kala was starting to get that cooped-up look about her. Once you lived in Greenwich Village, it was hard to go back. That was why every New Yorker comes across insufferably superior.

Kala said, "I needed a break from everyone. And I wanted to see you—you've been gone all day."

"There aren't many food options this late," Matt said.

"You'll think of something."

Matt drove the clunker out of the lot, not sure where to go. He could head to Lincoln like the rest of them, but it was already late. He was tired, though he wasn't sure why. He'd spent the day watching TV and visiting with his aunt.

Kala gazed out the window at nothing. The air was thick. It was already feeling like summer.

"Anything would be great," she said, still staring

outside like she was searching for something on the horizon. "Even that crap fast food you and Ganesh like."

"You're really slumming it," Matt said.

"When in Rome," Kala replied. It was something she always said, and Matt had picked up the habit of saying or thinking it himself. Funny how you acquire the verbal tics of your friends.

"We could go to Runza," Matt said. "I think it's open late."

"Go to what?"

"You've never had a runza?"

She shook her head.

"Oh, you don't know what you're missing."

Soon Matt was veering onto the interstate, keeping his distance from the semis barreling down every lane. He punched the gas, concerned the old tank wouldn't even hit fifty.

Kala gripped the plastic handle that hung over the passenger window as the station wagon rattled and finally picked up speed.

Ten minutes later Matt pointed out the window. "It's still there."

Kala glanced at the glowing green-and-yellow sign atop a long pole designed to be visible from the interstate. Matt took the exit loop and pulled into the lot.

"It looks like a McDonald's, but green," Kala said.

"I told you not to get excited. Eat here, or get it to go?"

Kala peered into the restaurant. Empty except for a kid in what undoubtedly was a polyester uniform pushing around a mop.

"Definitely let's get it to go," she said.

As Matt pulled up to the drive-through speaker, Kala said, "What exactly are they?"

Matt thought about how to describe them. "A runza is like a warm bun filled with beef, onions, and cabbage. It kind of looks like a Hot Pocket. I know it sounds horrible, but it's actually good."

A distorted voice came through the speaker. Matt ordered an original runza, fries, and a Coke.

Kala leaned over Matt and called out the window, "Make that two of everything."

Back on the road, Kala plucked out one of the fries and bit into it. "Is there, like, a park or somewhere we can eat? Anywhere but the motel."

"My old school isn't too far away. There used to be outdoor tables."

"Ooh, I get to see the institution that shaped Matthew Pine."

"I'll spare you the suspense: there was no Dead Poets Society."

Kala sipped through her straw, her eyes twinkling.

The benches were newer, but in the same place: across from the outdoor basketball court, next to the gym.

Kala examined her runza with curiosity, poking at it with a plastic fork.

Matt picked his up like a burrito and took a bite. The taste took him back in time. He had no specific memory, just a feeling.

Matt scanned the area. The cliché was true that everything looked smaller. The school was a two-story redbrick building. The front was barren, no trees or landscaping, an empty plain of concrete.

The dark sky lit up beyond the building, lightning in the distance. So far away, you couldn't hear any thunder.

"What grade were you in when you left?" Kala asked.

"Ninth," Matt said. "The school goes from seventh to twelfth grade. Not enough kids around here for a separate middle school."

"So your brother and sister went here with you?"

"Just Danny. Mags was in elementary school when we left. Mom was pregnant with Tommy."

"Why did you leave town? The documentary made it sound like townsfolk with pitchforks."

"It wasn't so dramatic. Just a lot of whispers and stares wherever we went. I actually got in a fight right over there about it." He nodded at the basketball court. He hadn't been defending Danny's honor. A kid had said that maybe someone would take Maggie down by the creek. It had scared him, how he'd lost control and whaled on the boy. And if he could lose it like that, he'd realized, so could his older brother. "And that was it. We packed up and moved."

"That was pretty selfless of your parents. I mean, your dad leaving his job, your mom giving up her hometown."

Matt had never really thought of it that way. But she was right. He liked that she didn't hesitate to talk about his family. He was learning that it was a topic people were finding uncomfortable. Matt liked talking about them. He didn't want them to vanish as if they'd never existed.

Kala picked up the half-eaten runza and put it and her wrappers in the bag. She cleaned up Matt's mess, too.

A heavy silence fell between them.

At last Kala said, "Ganesh said that girl at the bar, the one who broke up the fight—that you, like, met her at four in the morning?"

Matt told her about Jessica. How he'd met her at the Knoll the night Charlotte was murdered. He almost told her about seeing Danny in his letterman jacket, pushing the wheelbarrow. But tonight wasn't about Danny.

"She was your first love?"

"I wouldn't go that far."

"Okay, your first something else . . ." She cocked a brow.

Matt rolled his eyes. "I was fourteen."

She watched him, waiting for him to tell her more.

"It was just a kiss." One electrifying kiss.

"You've got unfinished business with her."

Matt shook his head again. "I was a kid."

"Unfinished business," she repeated with a clipped nod. "You'd better finish it."

Maybe Kala was right, maybe she wasn't. Either way, it would have to wait.

"Thank you," Matt said.

"For what?"

"For coming to Nebraska . . . For"—he paused—"for everything."

She looked at him for a long time. For a split second

he thought she was going to lean in, give him another kiss he wouldn't forget.

"Un. Finished. Business," Kala said, emphasizing each word with a poke of her index finger to his chest. She took his hand. "Let's get you back. You have a long day tomorrow."

It would undoubtedly be the longest day of his life.

CHAPTER 50

EVAN PINE

They spent their first full day in Tulum at the beach, dozing in rented cabanas, ordering cocktails and virgin daiquiris and watching Tommy splash in the blue ocean. Sun-drained and tired, they decided to pick up some groceries, eat in for dinner.

Evan sat at the kitchen counter, watching his family prepare the meal—Tommy's favorite, spaghetti. Not exactly in line with local cuisine, but it brought Evan back to when they would spend Sunday nights cooking together, telling stories and laughing at the table.

Tommy was cutting onions with a butter knife, Liv guiding his hand in between sips of wine. Maggie was in charge of the sauce, and she stirred a big pot with a wooden spoon.

"No, really, sit down, relax, the womenfolk have got this," Maggie said to Evan.

Evan sipped his beer, taking in the scene. He looked at his son. Tommy's face was tomato red, this after Liv applying sunscreen seemingly every two minutes. He was trying to pierce the onion with the dull blade, but it kept rolling off the cutting board.

"The water's boiling, sweetie," Evan said to Maggie, noticing the pot nearly bubbling over. He jumped off the stool and ran around to the stove to turn down the burner.

"You been sneaking my beer?" he said, noticing that Magpie seemed a little spaced-out, lost in thought.

"Gotta prepare for college," Maggie said.

Evan grabbed his heart, feigned a pain in his chest. "Don't say that, not my little girl." He hugged Maggie in an exaggerated embrace that she ordinarily would've fought off, but tonight she just stood, arms at her sides, until he released his hold.

With the meal finally ready, the four sat at the dining table. And for the first time Evan could remember in ages, they held hands, bowed heads, and Olivia said grace.

Liv's tradition was to give thanks and then say a blessing for each of the children. When she got to Danny, Evan noticed Maggie's eyes fixed on him, as if she were waiting to see his reaction. As if trying to discern whether the only thing on his mind was the case. He gave his best poker face, but his daughter knew him too well.

Later Evan sat at the edge of the bed, contemplating his wife in the faint light seeping in from the en suite. Liv was naked and had kicked off all the sheets and blankets, out cold from the sun and cocktails and wine at dinner. She was a stunningly beautiful woman.

Evan was still buzzed himself, and didn't want to

leave her. But he needed to get this out of his system. The plan was simple: He'd sneak over to the Moloko Bar, where the call had been made, check things out, confirm Charlotte wasn't there, and come home. The rational side of him knew it was crazy—understood that Charlotte was dead—but with Evan, reason often gave way to desperation.

He slipped into his shorts and T-shirt from earlier, and padded quietly out of the room. The map app on his phone said the bar was about a ten-minute bike ride away.

"Where are you going?"

Evan felt a thunderbolt rip through him at the voice. Maggie was sitting on the couch in the dark.

"Hey, what are you doing up?"

"You didn't answer my question."

Evan looked at her.

"You don't have to answer—I know where. I'm coming." She stood.

"No way."

Maggie looked at him. "I suppose we could wake up Mom and ask her."

Evan narrowed his eyes. Man, he loved this kid.

"Seriously, let me come."

"It could be dangerous."

"Well then, I should definitely wake Mom." Maggie headed toward the master bedroom.

"Wait," Evan said. He deliberated for a moment. But once his daughter grabbed onto something, she didn't let go. He knew where she'd acquired that trait.

"You'll wait outside."

Maggie nodded.

"And if I say you go home, you listen."

She nodded again.

"And—"

"I got it, Dad. It's only eleven thirty. Trust me, the place is gonna be packed. It's Tulum, not Naperville."

Evan let out an exasperated sigh. "I mean it. If I say you need to leave, then . . ."

Maggie smiled, already tying the laces on her sneakers.

They rode the bikes along the dark road, Evan wondering if this was a mistake. Maggie was in front of him, her hair in a thick braid swaying back and forth like the pendulum of a grandfather clock. For some reason he thought of the out-of-place clock in Dr. Silverstein's office. He saw lights up ahead.

When they reached the intersection, Maggie waited for Evan, eyeing the map on her phone. "Not too much farther," she said. "The place is just off the main drag."

They continued on the dark asphalt, music floating in the wind now, the lights in the distance brighter. Maggie led the charge as they pedaled around clusters of pedestrians and to the Moloko Bar, which was just around the bend from an outdoor cantina. Even this late, the area was bustling.

Maggie stopped across the street from Moloko. She looked conflicted, like she wanted to say something.

"Everything okay?" Evan asked.

"Just be careful, all right?"

Evan smiled, got off the bike, and crossed the street. The doorman looked at him wearily, as if Evan was the sad old guy at the club. But he waved Evan through.

Inside was what he'd expected: large crowd. Pulsing dance music. The smell of perfume and sweat. He scanned the faces, looking for her. It was at times like this, unexpected, unusual, that he had moments of clarity. Charlotte wasn't here. He was chasing a ghost. Wasting his final days before Magpie went to college. Squandering his life with Liv and Tommy. Ruining his relationship with Matt. He needed to let this go.

But he was here. Might as well . . .

He navigated through the crowd and made it to the bartender. The barman had tattoo sleeves and a hipster beard. He wasn't Mexican, but it wasn't clear he was American, either.

The music was loud. The guy shouted over the noise, "What can I get you, mate?" He had an Australian accent.

Evan laid a five-hundred-peso bill on the bar, if only because that was what they did in the movies and TV when they were trying to get information. He held out his phone, displaying a photo of Charlotte.

"I'm trying to find my daughter," he lied. He assumed the bartender might be more sympathetic to a father than if he thought Evan was a cop or a private investigator or a creepy old guy looking for a young woman.

Evan waited for him to say he'd never seen her before, that he was sorry he couldn't help.

The bartender smoothed a hand over his beard, then closed his fist around the money.

"Yeah, I've seen her."

CHAPTER 51

SARAH KELLER

Keller awoke to the buzz of her phone. She was disoriented for a moment, trying to comprehend why her nightstand was different, the window of her bedroom not where it should be, then she remembered. Nebraska. The motel. The old alarm clock said it was only 11:40 P.M., but she'd been in a deep sleep. She was going to ignore the call, but it might be Bob, an emergency with the twins.

The number was from Mexico. Keller sat up, switched on the lamp, swiped the device.

"It's Carlita Escobar."

Keller's thoughts were still fuzzy, and she blanked for a second. But then the fog lifted. Of course, the consular officer, Carlita "No Relation" Escobar.

"Hi, yes, thanks for getting back to me."

"I'm sorry, did I wake you? You said to call when I got news, no matter the time. I can call back tomorrow."

"No, please . . ."

"I've identified the girl."

"Hank?" Keller asked.

"Her real name is Joanna Grace. She went by Joey. It turns out she is from Oklahoma, but she's no hairdresser."

Keller felt a rush of adrenaline. The fake persona confirmed that her meeting with Matt was no accident, that she'd lured him off with her, likely to deliver him to someone, until she apparently had a change of heart.

"She's a party girl," Escobar continued. "Works for a company out of New York."

"You mean a prostitute?" Keller was on her feet now, pacing.

"Not quite. I checked into it, and her employer is basically like a leasing company. But instead of renting products, it's pretty girls. Nightclubs and resorts pay to have American girls hang out at their establishments; it's like a temp service."

"That's an actual thing, go figure."

"In my day, the clubs had ladies' night, but I guess that's not enough anymore," Escobar said. "I suspect some of the girls make money on the side doing more than looking pretty, but it's otherwise a legitimate business."

"Did you speak with her?"

There was a long beat of silence. "No. The reason we identified her so quickly was that some of the other girls in her troupe—they're all working out of a club called Moloko—they reported her missing."

Keller felt her stomach drop. She stopped pacing, opened the curtains, and looked outside for no reason. Several news satellite trucks were parked in the lot. "Let me guess: no one has seen her since the night with Matt Pine."

"That's right."

"I suppose she could've taken off. Matt said she got cold feet, so maybe she's hiding from whoever she was working with."

"She and the other girls stayed in rooms above the club. We searched her bunk and locker. She left her passport. And the rental car—she shared it with two other girls—was found abandoned in Chan Chemuyil, about fifteen minutes from Tulum." Escobar paused. "I'm sorry."

Keller let out a breath. "What else do we know about her? Any priors? Known associates?"

"She had a prior for cocaine possession in Oklahoma, but that's it. Nothing that identifies the man with her in the photo. She's had a tough run, Ms. Grace. Her father died in the Oklahoma City bombing when she was young, she spent her teenage years in foster care, then worked at a gentleman's club, which is where she probably got hooked up with the party girl company."

"Nothing on the man with the cleft lip scar?" Keller's blood pressure was rising, her jaw clenched. She shut the curtains and sat on the bed. She needed to calm down, think clearly.

"He's a ghost. It does look like he rented the place at the address you sent me."

The address tenacious Maggie Pine had found through a cell phone aggregation service. Keller had a random thought: Maybe Maggie would've become an FBI agent.

Escobar continued. "He gave the last name Smith, paid in cash. The owner never dealt with him in person—he sent the money by messenger—but the neighbor saw him a few times. And the rental property, it was scrubbed down with bleach. I don't think it has ever been so clean."

"Cleaning crews usually aren't that detailed. I can send a team and—"

"I don't think you're hearing me. The place was *clean*. And not by any maid service. More like a forensics expert."

"A professional," Keller said. It was consistent with the staged crime scene, the wiped phones.

Escobar said, "Makes sense."

"CCTV cameras in the area?" Keller knew the answer, but had to ask.

"I'm sorry. But this isn't Manhattan, Agent Keller."

"Is there anything—anything at all—that will help us ID the guy?" Keller knew the answer to this as well.

Escobar paused, then said, "I feel like Gutierrez knows something. It's a pretty corrupt force."

"The cop who gave us trouble releasing the bodies? The one who threatened Matt Pine."

"*Sí*."

"Did you talk to him?"

"I tried, but he refuses to speak with me."

Keller worked through this. She couldn't force a foreign municipal police officer to cooperate with them. And Carlita Escobar was the person the State Department said had the best chance of dealing with the Tulum force. Now even she was getting stonewalled. "I'm open to ideas," Keller said.

After another long silence, Escobar said, "There may be a way to get Gutierrez to tell us what he knows."

Keller wasn't sure what she meant by that. The way Escobar said it made Keller wary.

"What do you mean?"

"He won't answer my questions. He knows I'm constrained by American interview techniques. . . ."

Keller tried to digest where Escobar was going with this, and didn't like it.

"But I'm family friends with a state senator. He holds sway with the Mexican federal police. And I'm sure he could get them to question Gutierrez."

Keller was starting to wonder whether, despite her protests to the contrary, Escobar was in fact related to Pablo. She imagined the local cop in a basement that had a drain in the middle of the floor.

Escobar said, "Of course I would never ask them to do that. But if the senator knew Gutierrez was making the US State Department unhappy, he might take the matter into his own hands. . . ."

Keller wanted the man with the cleft lip. He was now linked to the disappearance of Joey Grace and death of the Pines. But she wouldn't break the law. "Let's call that Plan B," Keller said.

"Of course, I wasn't suggesting—"

"Did you find anything else?" Keller said, sparing Escobar the false denial.

"One more thing," Escobar said. "The bartender where the girl worked. He said he'd seen her with a man who fits the description. Just one time. But he remembered because Joey Grace made the bartender an unusual offer."

Keller felt a flutter of excitement again. "What was it?"

"She paid the bartender four thousand pesos to call a cell phone number if anyone came to the bar looking for an American girl."

"Did he ever make that call?

"*Sí*. He said a man, an American, showed up at the bar one night looking for a girl."

"Evan Pine," Keller said.

"*Sí*. I showed the bartender a photo, and he confirmed."

Keller played this out in her mind. The man with the cleft lip scar hired a local party girl to pose in a video as Charlotte to make a deepfake and lure Evan Pine to Tulum, perhaps making it easy for Evan to trace her to the particular club. Then he paid the bartender there to call him when Evan arrived and started asking questions.

This had to be a professional.

"Thank you for all your hard work on this," Keller said.

"My pleasure." Then, in a matter-of-fact tone that sent a chill down Keller's back, Escobar said, "I'll contact you when we find the girl's body."

CHAPTER 52

MAGGIE PINE

BEFORE

Maggie and her father walked side by side along the dirt pathway at the Mayan ruins in Tulum, the afternoon sun beating down on them. Mom was chasing after Tommy, who'd run ahead. The ruins were somewhat disappointing, Maggie thought. Too many tourists. Not so many ruins. There was even a Starbucks, for goodness' sake. It reminded Maggie of an ancient college campus made of crumbling stone. The centerpiece was a tall temple facing an open field, with smaller buildings at the perimeter. The area wasn't in a jungle, like in the old Indiana Jones movies Matt used to watch over and over, but atop a cliff overlooking the ocean.

"Dad, you know this isn't right. It's all too perfect. The caller ID leads us right there. The bartender at Moloko just happens to know Charlotte out of all the customers they get every night? Wants you back there tonight at midnight—by yourself?"

Her dad put up his hands, as if to quiet her down.

He looked out at Mom and Tommy again. "We'll talk about this later."

Maggie frowned. They hadn't had a chance to talk since last night. And she didn't like keeping this from Mom. She looked at her father and had the sinking feeling that nothing she could say would stop him. The never-ending loop of her life: Evan Pine fixating on a clue, running it into the ground, getting discouraged, swearing he was done with it all, then identifying a new clue and repeating the cycle. A drug addict in search of a fix. Now he was going to screw up this trip—put himself in danger!—walking into a trap. Was it a trap? Or a prank? Someone trying to shake him down? She didn't know. But she did know something was off. And that they'd been lured to the Moloko Bar.

"It's a scam," Maggie said.

"I know."

This surprised Maggie. Her father wasn't one to give up so easily. But something was different today.

"So you're not going back tonight?"

"I haven't decided."

"It could be dangerous, Dad."

He didn't respond, just waved to her mom, who was looking hot and exasperated as she wrangled Tommy back toward them.

Maggie decided she couldn't keep it from him anymore. She hoped it wasn't a mistake. But telling him about the cell phone report, the address where the phone that called him pinged, was the only way to get him to stay away from the bar. "I have something I need to tell you. A new lead. But only if you promise not to go to Moloko tonight."

He looked at her for a long moment.

"I uncovered something. It could answer who's behind this. Who really called you."

Her father looked at her intently in that way he would.

"What is it?" he said. "And why didn't you tell me before? What's—"

"I need a promise."

"Okay. I promise."

"I'm serious," Maggie said.

"I know, *so* serious," her dad said playfully.

Her mom and Tommy appeared. Mom gave them a skeptical look. "What are you two up to?"

"Maggie's decided to take a gap year. Or two. Live with us until she's thirty," her dad said.

"That would be totally fine with me." Liv gave her a side hug. They were so embarrassing.

"Actually," Maggie said, "Dad said he was taking me out to dinner tonight, just *me*."

"He is, is he? What are you two plotting?"

Tommy interrupted them. "What's a human sacrifice?" He pronounced it *sac-pre-price*.

"Where'd you hear that, sweetie?" Mom said.

"Those people over there were saying that's where they would make human sacrifices." He pointed to a stone platform in the center of the ruins.

Her parents looked at each other.

Dad said, "You want to take this one?"

"All yours, handsome," Mom said. "That's what happens when you ditch me for dinner."

CHAPTER 53

Maggie and her father had a quick dinner at a place called Burrito Amor, then turned to the plan. They didn't have all night to wait for someone to come out of the house identified in the cell phone report. So they'd have to be more proactive.

Maggie wrote a simple note:

> WE KNOW YOU MADE THE VIDEO PRETENDING
> TO BE CHARLOTTE AND WE'VE CALLED THE
> POLICE.

It took some doing, but she convinced her dad to give it a try. He'd be crazy to go to the bar tonight. That was where they wanted him. They needed to be the hunter, not the hunted. Maggie felt so cool right now.

They rode the bikes to the small run-down house in the twilight. Maggie waited at the corner under the cover of a stand of shrubs. She watched her father ride his bike to the broken sidewalk in front of the house. He looked around to see if anyone was watching, then pedaled to the front door. The place was a one-story ramshackle structure with bars protecting the windows. She'd googled the address and it popped up as a vacation rental property, so with luck the owner of the phone that pinged at the location was still there. Otherwise, the new tenant would likely be freaked out by the note.

Her dad's back was to her, but when he turned around, she saw that he'd taped the note to the front door. He positioned the bike away from the house, gave a hard knock, then rode for his life. Maggie's heart pounded as she watched him race away, praying he'd make it without being spotted. With only seconds to spare, he disappeared around the corner as the door opened a crack. The silhouette of a man emerged in the doorway and he removed the note.

It felt like an eternity, the man standing there a dark mass. Maggie's father had circled around and was next to her now.

"He's reading it," Maggie whispered.

The man's movements became quick, jerky. His head snapped back and forth, looking for whoever had left the note. Then he turned and went back inside, slamming the door behind him.

Maggie and her father looked at each other. Her dad was perspiring, out of breath. "Now what?" he said.

Maggie honestly hadn't thought that far ahead.

She didn't need to decide, because the door to the house flung open. The man was wearing a ball cap and sunglasses. He walked, head down. His gait suggested he was agitated. He said something into a cell phone.

They followed him to the main drag. It was easy to keep a safe distance. He was tall and skinny, and his hat drifted above the crowd on the main road. Sure enough, he went to the Moloko Bar, which looked different in the daylight. The place apparently didn't open until the evening.

He waited out front, as if he were expecting someone.

Out came a woman, pretty. She wore shorts and a bikini top.

The man said something to her. She shook her head repeatedly.

"Let's get a picture," Maggie said. She held up the camera. It was too far away to get a clear shot, even if she zoomed.

"We need to get closer." She got off the bike.

"No," her father said.

"Come with me, keep your back turned. They'll think we're tourists."

Her dad didn't have a chance to object. Maggie pushed his bicycle's handlebars, wheeling him backward so she could get the picture. She pretended to take a photo of her dad. His face was in the frame, but Maggie was really trying to get a clear shot of the couple.

They were in the shadows, the neon from the sign casting a glow over the woman. Just as Maggie was taking the shot, the man covered his face with his hand. The woman seemed to fix her eyes on Maggie.

"We need to go," Maggie said. She turned, climbed on the bike, and started to ride away, her father right behind her. She didn't look back.

CHAPTER 54

MATT PINE

Four coffins were stationed at the far end of the church, but it was the fourth one—the tiny wooden box—that caused each and every mourner to gasp as they entered First Presbyterian Church. The stained glass, the same windows Matt used to stare at bored out of his mind on the Sundays of his youth, dulled the light, fitting the gloomy occasion.

The place was packed, though Matt didn't recognize many of the bereaved. Several had the grooming of television news reporters, hair helmeted with too much hair spray. Faces too tan for the spring. His aunt said they were going to keep out the media and gawkers and grief junkies, but there was only so much they could do. Despite the Pines' persona non grata status, several townspeople filled the pews.

As Matt paced the long aisle, he could feel the eyes on him, hear the murmurs as he walked toward the four caskets. He just looked ahead, feeling distant, vaguely out-of-body.

When he reached the front, Aunt Cindy patted the open space on the pew. Next to her was his grandfather, with a faraway expression, his Jamaican nurse looking more grief-stricken than Charlie. Next to Grandpa was the governor, Mom's old friend. With the prison refusing to allow Danny to attend the ceremony, that was it, the Pine contingent.

After lowering himself to the pew, Matt felt hands on his shoulders. He turned and it was Kala. Next to her, the rest of the Misfit Toys. All were dressed conservatively, something he'd never seen before in all their time together. Even Ganesh was in a suit—an expensive one, by the looks of it—the contrast with his unruly hair and unshaven face giving him the look of a tech mogul. Curtis's head was bowed in prayer. Woojin looked like a giant next to Sofia, whose makeup was already streaked down her face. Matt gave them a nod and turned back.

He stared at the caskets again. They were simple, understated. Despite her beauty, Matt's mother had hated flash. When his aunt had emailed him the catalog of coffins, it had taken Matt only a moment to choose.

The old minister—the same one from all those years ago—approached the front of the church and waited for the crowd to settle. Then, in a weak voice that again brought Matt back to when he was a boy, the minister began his remarks.

Something else hadn't changed. Matt was able to tune out the guy instantly. Instead he focused on the caskets.

He swallowed at the smallest box. Matt said goodbye in his head. *Tommy, I'm sorry the world won't get more of you. You were loving, hilarious, and you came when we needed you most.* Tears rolled down his cheeks. *Goodbye, Little Man.*

His eyes slid to the next box. *Maggie.* Matt released a sob. *You were the heart of this family—the glue—and there won't be a day that goes by where I won't miss you. The world is a worse place without you. Even when I was away at school, you were with me—my conscience, my better angel, my proof in the fundamental goodness of people. Goodbye, Mags.*

He had a fist lodged in his throat now. There was movement in the church, and he saw a figure take the microphone. The governor.

Matt eyed his mother's casket, then his father's. He wanted to say goodbye before the politician started blathering on. The rituals, the remarks, didn't mean anything to him. He didn't need the show.

Before he said his goodbyes, a siren wailed outside.

The sound intensified, and the church filled with a low rumble of voices. Matt turned and looked at his friends. Ganesh was making a *what the fuck* expression at the others. They all looked dumbfounded at the noise. Except Kala, who was from Oklahoma.

Matt heard her whisper, "Tornado warning."

"All right, folks, I hate to do this," the governor was saying into the microphone. Next to him, the minister was giving him instructions. "We need everyone to get down to the basement."

The din of the crowd grew louder. "We've all been through this a million times and it's probably nothing, but better safe than sorry, so let's stay calm and make our way to the stairs."

Quickly, mourners moved one pew at a time and marched up the aisle. The minister was at the top now, directing traffic.

Matt caught Ganesh's eye. His friend gave him a sly smile and winked at him. It was an odd gesture, but somehow perfect.

It was an orderly exit. Aunt Cindy tried to usher Matt along with her, but he held back, said he wanted to make sure his friends got squared away. In truth, he wanted a moment alone to finish his goodbyes. Matt wasn't scared of the tornado. In his fourteen years in Adair there had been countless warnings, a twister or two touching down in cornfields, but he'd never even seen a funnel cloud. His aunt reluctantly agreed, mostly because she needed to tend to Matt's grandpa, who was riled up by the commotion.

With the church cleared out, Matt stood alone with the caskets. The wind was whistling outside, and there was a crack of lightning.

He touched a hand to his mother's coffin, then his father's.

There were no words, he decided.

Matt turned, and instead of heading to the basement, he loosened his tie and walked out into the storm.

CHAPTER 55

SARAH KELLER

Keller looked at herself in the motel room mirror. She wore her usual navy pantsuit and white blouse. It wasn't perfect funeral attire, but it would have to do. She considered skipping the ceremony, wondered about the optics—an FBI agent at the church—but she decided to risk it. Though she'd never met them, she felt like she knew the Pines. She'd been through their belongings, studied their internet searches, talked with their friends, spent time with their surviving son. Surviving *sons,* plural, she reminded herself. She wanted to pay her respects.

Her cell phone rang. She was already running behind, and was going to ignore it. She wanted to slip into the church with the flock rather than rush in late with a spotlight on her. But the call was from Fishkill Correctional.

"Agent Keller," she answered.

"Hi, this is Marge Boyle at Fishkill returning your call." The prison liaison sounded bored, lethargic.

"Thanks for getting back to me. I'm just closing my file, crossing my *t*'s and dotting my *i*'s, and I wondered if you could send me the visitor log for Daniel Pine for the last six months?"

There had been leaks about the investigation coming from different fronts and Keller wanted the liaison to think the request was routine.

"No problem. We keep electronic copies. If you give me a second, I can email the log to you right now. I have it somewhere, I'm sure, but can you give me your email address?"

Keller did, and waited, gathering her keys and handbag so she could race out the door to make the funeral. She heard keyboard clicking as the liaison worked, excruciatingly slow. The woman was on prison time.

"I'm actually running late to the funeral, so I need to—"

"It's really terrible about Dan," the liaison said, not taking the hint.

"Yes, it's disappointing the warden wouldn't let him attend the funeral, but I understand it's a drain on resources and—"

"Wait," the liaison said. "You don't know? No one notified you?"

"Notified me of what?" Keller said, not raising the obvious question of who the hell would notify her of something, other than the *liaison* she was on the line with.

"Oh, sweet Jesus." The woman paused. "Dan Pine was attacked yesterday. They're not sure he's gonna make it."

*   *   *

It was another half hour before Keller arrived at the church. She'd been delayed because she needed to tell Stan the news about Danny Pine before the media picked up the story.

The church was not picturesque. No old-time steeple with pristine grounds. Just a modern-looking structure that could've passed for a bank were it not for the stained-glass windows and sign out front. Lining the road were satellite trucks and makeshift tents made of tarps to protect equipment from the imminent rain. Reporters milled around, holding paper cups of coffee and primping in hand mirrors, waiting for the ceremony to end.

Keller pulled in next to several other vehicles parked illegally in the grass at the far end of the overflowing lot. She walked quickly, and the reporters paid her no mind. The air was strangely still, the sky an unusual shade of green. She felt an electric current in the atmosphere.

Inside, the front entryway of the church was quiet. She could hear voices coming from behind the two large doors that led into the nave of the church. She debated waiting it out, not wanting to interrupt the ceremony, but a man in a dark suit came out of one of the doors, and headed toward a sign for the men's restroom. Reaching to catch the door before it closed, Keller was startled by a piercing sound—a wailing siren—coming from outside.

What the hell?

Keller realized that it was a tornado siren. The Pine family just couldn't catch a break.

The doors opened and mourners started filing out. They headed to a stairwell near the restrooms. Keller found herself in the queue, pushed quietly along to the basement stairs. The old man in front of her grumbled as he made his way down one painful step after the other.

"Overreacting as always," the old man said. "It'll be gone by the time we get down there."

Keller imagined that this was how it was everywhere. If you lived in Manhattan, you were immune to terror warnings. If you lived in San Francisco, you didn't get jarred when the ground shook. If you lived in Florida, you took hurricane watches in stride. And if you lived here, you calmly shuffled to lower ground when funnels threatened to fall from the sky and destroy everything in their path.

She must've looked rattled, or maybe it was plain she was an out-of-towner, because once they reached the church's basement an elderly woman put a hand on Keller's arm. "Don't worry, dear. We get these all the time."

After a few minutes, mourners filled the entire basement. Keller stood near a bulletin board pinned with announcements—community bake sales, an AA meeting schedule, a poster for the Cub Scouts—and tried not to knock over the folded metal chairs leaning against the wall. Looking for Matt, she scanned the crowd.

In the far corner, a small group huddled around Matt's aunt. A black woman stood next to Cindy, and Keller could make out someone's head—the grandfather, probably—who was sitting down. She didn't see Matt.

In the other corner, she spotted a group of college-aged kids, an interesting ensemble. A drop-dead gorgeous blonde, a mischievous-looking Indian kid, a Korean guy who was so tall that he had to crouch to avoid his head hitting the ceiling, a black kid with kind eyes, and a tiny woman with mascara that had run down her face. Matt's friends from NYU, she assumed. Matt wasn't with them, either.

She needed to talk to him. It was the absolute worst time to tell him about his brother, but she didn't want him learning about the attack from the feed on his phone. She was becoming an expert at delivering bad news to Matt Pine.

She looked over to another small crowd. The governor was standing in the center, holding court. The only surprise was that there was no camera on him. No footage for the sequel to *A Violent Nature,* though Keller imagined the aunt had banned the Adlers from the ceremony. The minister was making his way through the mourners to speak to the governor.

"All right, folks," the governor said in a loud voice, slicing through the noise. The minister was standing next to him. "The warning has been lifted. If I can ask everyone to head back upstairs." He directed an arm to the stairwell. "Single file, please."

The crowd parted to let Matt's grandfather and aunt head up first. Led by a caregiver, the grandfather looked disoriented, confused.

Keller watched everyone else go as she looked for Matt, hoping she could pull him aside. No, she decided, she'd ask him to meet her after the services. Wait until then to tell him about his brother. She checked her phone to see if Danny's attack had made the news. Nothing yet.

Two emails, back-to-back, grabbed Keller's attention.

First, the liaison had sent the prison visitor log for Danny Pine. She could review that later. Second, the computer team had found who had sent the video of the party to the Free Danny Pine site—a local Adair woman whose name Keller didn't recognize.

Keller glanced toward the stairwell. The line up the stairs had stalled. Killing time, she dispatched a text to the field office to get background on the woman who'd sent the anonymous tip. Next, she clicked on Danny's visitor log. It was not extensive. Visits from his parents. Lawyers. But one name jumped out at her: Neal Flanagan. The name was so familiar, but Keller couldn't place it. Where had she heard it? She decided to use every cunning FBI agent's secret crime-fighting tool, and typed the name into Google.

Newspaper stories lit up her phone.

Flanagan was embroiled in the former governor's sex scandal. A fixer who'd arranged parties for the governor and his wealthy benefactors. Underage girls. Drugs. A grand jury had indicted Flanagan, and everyone expected him to turn on the former governor and others in his circle.

Why would this creep visit Danny Pine? Just two weeks before his parents were killed by a professional. She thought of her meeting with the filmmakers. They said Charlotte had a secret life, older men. Several of the newspapers quoted the lead prosecutor, an AUSA out of the Lincoln US Attorney's Office. Keller tapped out an email to Stan. She needed to talk to Flanagan pronto.

CHAPTER 56

MATT PINE

Matt walked along the road, the sky dark and green, a single raindrop splashing his face, the preamble of more to come. The sirens had stopped, at least, no funnel clouds forming, so the only thing Matt risked now was getting drenched. He should return to the church. He didn't want to look back and regret skipping the ceremony. But would he, really?

He sauntered along with no destination. Papillion Road was a slice of asphalt that led to nowhere. He'd cut across the church's playground for the Sunday school kids and through a side fence that bordered the grounds to avoid the reporters camped out front.

The shoulder was rocky. It reminded him of his death march in Tulum. Was that really only three days ago? Was that possible? His feet hurt in the tight dress shoes. He owned only one suit and one pair of nice shoes. Before leaving New York, Ganesh had plodded over to Matt's dorm and packed them for the funeral. It was a thoughtful gesture, and Matt would never take his friends for granted again. He'd taken too much for granted in his life, so no more.

From behind him, a car tapped two fast beeps of the horn. Matt turned and looked at the vehicle, which was trailing him. The windshield was speckled with rain, and he couldn't see who was driving. He was in no mood to talk to a reporter. The vehicle crawled up beside him, the window humming down.

"Um, you know there's a tornado warning, right?" Jessica Wheeler looked at him from inside the car, a tiny smile on her lips. She was dressed in black, her hair pulled up, a strand of pearls around her neck. She must've seen Matt slip out of the church and followed after him. "Where're you headed?"

"Nowhere."

"You and me both," she said. The car kept the slow pace of his walk.

Matt stopped and the car came to a halt as well. He looked inside.

Jessica pointed her chin at the passenger seat.

Matt really wanted to be alone—at least, he thought he did.

Jessica just sat quietly, waiting for him to decide.

His feet did hurt, he supposed. He climbed inside, and was met with the smell of Jessica's perfume, a pleasing, spicy fragrance.

She shoved the stick shift into gear and they drove.

The rain was still coming down in tiny drops, not yet a downpour. The windshield wipers wisped back and forth, an arc of brown from dirt and drizzle.

"Wanna talk about it?" Jessica finally asked.

"Not particularly."

"Okay. Wanna drink about it?"

"That sounds more enticing."

She nodded, looked in her rearview, then made a sharp U-turn right in the middle of the road.

It wasn't long before Jessica was unlocking the front door to Pipe Layers. The place didn't open for a few hours and it was dark, quiet. Jessica slapped on the lights, threw her keys on the bar, and went to the jukebox.

Matt took a seat on one of the stools and watched her in the reflection of the mirror behind the bar. With her conservative black dress she looked out of place bent over, peering into the jukebox. Music filled the room.

Jessica walked over and ducked behind the bar.

"Bon Jovi?" Matt said.

Jessica stood in front of Matt now. "My uncle hand-picked the jukebox selection thirty years ago, and I haven't had the heart to change it. And who doesn't love some Jon Bon Jovi?" She gestured to the liquor bottles lining the wall. "What'll you have?"

"A beer would be great."

"Ah, come on," she said, disappointed in him. "Wait, I know." She pulled out a glass, plopped an oversize single ice cube into it, and started mixing some concoction. She slid the glass to him.

He held the drink at eye level, the clear cube bathed in brown liquid with a citrus rind. "What is it?"

"An old-fashioned."

He raised an eyebrow. "Is this just some Don Draper fantasy of yours or—"

"Shut up. Try it!"

He took a sip. It was actually quite good. Smoky, with a hint of sweet. "I didn't peg myself as an old-fashioned guy, but it's good."

She nodded, then poured herself a beer—smiling as she did so, silently acknowledging that she'd just given him shit for wanting something as pedestrian as a beer. She took a sip, foam covering her top lip.

They didn't speak for some time. He'd finish a drink, she'd make him another. She'd finish hers and pour another, as if it were a competition.

It wasn't long until both were feeling the booze.

Matt's phone shivered repeatedly in his pocket, but he never checked it.

"The funeral was nice," Jessica said.

"You mean until the blaring sirens and the surviving son took off?"

She made a face. "Your grandpa looked well. I haven't seen him around town in forever."

Matt held the old-fashioned in his hand, contemplating it. "You don't know how much I appreciate this, but really, there's no need for small talk." He drained his glass.

"No?" she said. "All right." She leaned over the bar, grabbed Matt by the lapels of his suit, and pulled him into a kiss. He wasn't expecting it, which gave the adrenaline slamming through him even more of a kick. Not moving her mouth from his, Jessica scaled the bar, knocking over glasses and bar tools, until she was on the other side. When she finally pulled away, both were breathing heavily, Jessica's hair falling from the pins that held it in place.

"There's a room upstairs," she said.

He nodded, following her to a door in the back. She fumbled for her keys, kissing him again as she unlocked the door to a narrow stairwell. She took his hand.

His head was swimming. From the booze, from the hunger for her, from the surrealness of the day. Jessica walked unsteadily up the stairs.

Matt started to have second thoughts. He beat them back, but they kept leaping into his head. He'd thought of this girl for seven years, and was this how he wanted it to go? Sloppy, in a room above a bar—on the day of his family's funeral, no less? But he *did* want her, and he needed something to make him feel good right now. Finish the unfinished business, as Kala had said. But the thought of Kala only intensified his feeling that this was a mistake.

At the top of the stairs was a small room with a twin bed, a nightstand, and a television. Jessica tugged off Matt's suit jacket, pulled the loosened tie over his head, and unbuttoned his shirt, then his pants. Then she stopped and said, "Wait here, I'll be right back." She skipped to the bathroom connected to the room.

Matt sat on the bed, battling with himself. His phone started buzzing again. His aunt looking for him, probably. His friends. He pulled it from his pocket to put it on silent mode.

A text on the home screen caught his eye. The display showed only a few words of the text, but one of them was *urgent*.

He shouldn't check. *Don't check*. But his thumb didn't oblige, and up popped the full text message from Agent Keller.

Urgent. Please call me.

Simple and to the point, like Keller. She wasn't the kind of person to throw around the word *urgent*. He clicked on her number.

Right as Keller picked up, Jessica came out of the restroom wearing nothing but the string of pearls. Staring at her milky-white skin, he was speechless for a moment.

She looked stunning.

He was about to hang up when Keller's voice said, "Matt, thanks for getting back to me. I've got some terrible news." She waited a moment, then said, "It's about your brother."

CHAPTER 57

OLIVIA PINE

BEFORE

They spent another full day at the beach. Liv liked the beach as much as the next person, but it was hard going with a six-year-old. There was no relaxing. It was either worrying about drowning, incessant trips to the bathroom, or being forced into sandcastle-making hell. She shouldn't complain; they were only little once. But Liv was glad they were back at the rental.

She also had her eye on Holmes and Watson. Evan and Maggie were doing their best to pretend they weren't working on the case, but Liv knew better. You'd think she'd be annoyed, but it brought Maggie and her father together. Liv couldn't think of any father-daughters as close as Evan and Mags. The entire trip was somehow related to Danny's case, she knew. But right now she just didn't care.

Liv studied her husband. He was sitting at the kitchen counter tapping something on his laptop, Maggie looking over his shoulder. Her daughter seemed more melancholy than usual. For the entire trip, Liv had sensed that something was bothering Maggie, that she was always on the verge of telling Liv something, but stopped short. It was probably to confess they were working leads in Danny's case, but Liv decided they needed some mother-daughter time. After they all showered, she asked Maggie to go for a walk. "Dad got his dinner with you, so it's my turn."

A path to the woods lay just outside the property. Evan told them not to go too far. To bring their phones. Who knew what was in that jungle? He was nothing if not a worrier.

"Do I want to know what you and Dad have been up to?" Liv asked, walking along the footpath, surrounded on both sides by dense trees.

Maggie looked at her. She gave the blushing smile she displayed whenever she was caught in a fib. "I'll let him tell you. He said he was going to tonight."

Liv nodded. "I can't wait. . . ."

"He doesn't mean to let it consume him," Maggie said. "It's just that he can't accept what happened to Danny, and feels like if he gives up, everyone else will too, and—"

"You don't have to defend your father to me. It may not seem like it sometimes, but I love him for it. I've been too hard on him, worried about the rest of you—Matt—but I know Dad is just doing what he thinks is right. He'd do the same for any of you." Liv thought of the line, the one from the book Evan loved. *You have my whole heart. You always did.*

They walked for a long while, the sun lowering in the sky, partially hidden by the canopy of trees.

"Is there something else you wanted to talk about?"

Maggie stopped on the trail. Her eyes filled with tears, and then she threw her arms around her mother and started to cry.

"It's okay, my girl," Liv said, rubbing Maggie's back as her daughter's body shuddered. "You can tell me anything. I'm here. Tell me."

And she did.

CHAPTER 58

MATT PINE

Upstairs at Pipe Layers, Matt sat on the foot of the bed, his shirt open, the phone pressed to his ear.

"Do they think he's going to make it?" he asked Keller.

Jessica in all her naked glory had retreated to the bathroom, realizing the call was important, the mood killed.

"I don't know," Keller said. "I found out just before the funeral and haven't gotten to speak to the doctor."

Matt wasn't sure what he was feeling. The only sensation that came to mind was *numb*.

"Do you think it's related to what happened to my family?" he asked. "Or was it just prison violence?"

"I don't know. We can talk about this later. I just arrived at the US Attorney's Office in Lincoln. I'm about to have a meeting with someone who may have some answers."

"Who?"

"I'll fill you in afterward. I really need to go."

Matt didn't have the energy to push it.

"Are you okay?" Keller said. "When you left the church, everyone was worried."

"I'm fine, just spending some time with an old friend."

Jessica reappeared from the bathroom, dressed, a look of concern on her face.

"All right. I'll call you. Last thing," Keller said. Her voice was breathy, as if she were walking now. "We know who sent the video tip of the party to your sister."

Matt gave no reply.

"We tracked the IP address to a computer located at 15 Stone Creek Road. The Wheeler family. Your aunt said you know them."

Matt looked at Jessica, who was pulling her hair up, staring at him with those large eyes.

"Yeah," he said, "I do."

CHAPTER 59

Matt kept his eyes on Jessica. She was slightly disheveled, her face still flushed.

"What?" she said.

He needed to be smart about this. Compartmentalize. Put the funeral, Danny's attack, out of his mind. *One bite at a time.*

"That was the FBI." His tongue was still thick from the booze, but he was sobering up. The adrenaline was like a full pot of coffee. "My brother—he's been badly beaten."

"Oh my goodness," she said. "Is he going to be okay?"

"We're waiting to hear."

She sat next to him on the bed.

Matt stood. Buttoned his shirt. Gesturing to the bed with his chin, he said, "I'm sorry about . . ."

"Another time." Jessica blushed again.

Matt wasn't sure there would be another time. And for some reason he was okay with that. For now he needed answers from her. Straightening himself, he walked downstairs to the bar.

He picked up the glasses and napkins and tiny straws they'd knocked on the floor, piling the debris on the bar. He reached over and grabbed the neck of the bottle of bourbon.

Jessica watched him, confusion on her face. "Are you okay?"

Everyone kept asking him that. He tipped back the bottle. It stung his throat, then warmed his insides. "The FBI also figured something out."

Her eyes lifted to his. "Oh yeah?"

"They know who sent the video of the party to my sister."

Jessica's eyes didn't leave his. Eventually she looked away. Her expression, what was it? Guilt? Worry? No, resignation.

"Why?" Matt said.

The word hung there forever.

Finally: "You know how long I thought about you?" Jessica said.

"Why?" Matt said again, ignoring her question.

"Everything changed that night," she said. "My life was ruined."

He had no idea what she was talking about. And it was pretty rich saying that to Matt, of all people.

"Ricky was never the same. I knew something had happened with Charlotte. I *knew* it. Then he crashed his car into that tree, and I've been having to care for him ever since."

She'd previously made her brother's crash sound like an accident, but she was suggesting something else now.

"What are you saying?"

"I always had a feeling something had happened that night. After you walked me home from the Knoll, I saw Ricky. I told you that." Her voice quavered. "He was shit-faced, fighting with his date. After that night, Ricky became withdrawn, depressed. Then he tried to kill himself. I wanted to ask him, but he gets confused now."

Matt still wasn't following, but let her continue.

"Then, last month, Ricky was at the bar the night news broke about the Supreme Court denying your brother's case. People were giving toasts and buying rounds. After closing, he was trashed, and started crying uncontrollably. He wouldn't tell me why. He just kept saying *'they smashed her face, they smashed her face, they didn't need to smash her face.'*"

Matt's heart tripped at that.

"He was watching a video on his phone, mumbling," she said. "It was right before your eyes. Everyone's. And all anyone could focus on was Ricky's profile in the video as if he was the Unknown Partygoer, a person who doesn't even exist. They made him up."

The picture still wasn't coming together. She seemed to be suggesting that Ricky was involved in Charlotte's death. That there was something in that video everyone was missing.

Tears were spilling from Jessica's eyes. She was having a hard time catching her breath.

Matt went to her, rested his hands on her shoulders. "Deep breaths," he said, demonstrating by inhaling loudly through his nose, out through his mouth.

When she seemed to be breathing regularly again, she said, "Ricky gets confused, so I wasn't sure. He kept saying you didn't see what you thought you saw that night. And he kept watching the video on his phone. When he passed out later, I searched his phone and found the video."

"What are you saying, Jessica?" Matt said. "That I saw Ricky pushing the wheelbarrow that night, that he saw me? Is that what he told you?" Matt's mind jumped to seven years ago. The figure stopping, head turning right at Matt as if making eye contact. Ricky was on the football team and wore a letterman jacket, but Matt had seen the name PINE on the jacket. He was sure of it. But he'd never told anyone about seeing something that night, so Ricky had to have been there.

"You're not listening," Jessica said.

Either it was the alcohol—in Matt's system or Jessica's—but she wasn't making sense.

"Not Ricky," she said.

"Then who? *Who, Jessica?*" She said Ricky was with a date that night, but it wasn't making any sense.

Jessica had her phone in her hand. The first frame of the video of the party. "I didn't know if he was confused, if he was imagining it. I sent the video to the Free Danny Pine site, knowing you'd see it. If what Ricky was saying was true—if you really saw them that night—you'd understand the video."

She ran her finger across the phone and the scene of

the boys chugging beers popped up, Danny in his undershirt surrounded by boys in letterman jackets, the mystery man's profile—no, Ricky's profile—on the fringes of the frame.

That's when Matt saw it, and it nearly leveled him.

He turned and ran out the door.

CHAPTER 60

SARAH KELLER

Keller scrutinized the man in the conference room of the US Attorney's Office in Lincoln. Next to the man was a lawyer. She had curly hair and an air of confidence.

The lawyer looked at Keller, then at Trey Barnes, the prosecutor heading the case against Neal Flanagan, the former governor's henchman. "So *now* you want to hear what he has to say?" the lawyer asked. "What's changed?"

"I'm not sure anything has. But the FBI asked for a sit-down"—the prosecutor gestured to Keller—"so here we are."

"He's got plenty to say. But I need a commitment. Time served."

The prosecutor guffawed. "Sylvia, there'd be a lynch mob outside my office. Some of the girls were fourteen years old."

Flanagan chimed in: "I didn't know—"

"Shut up," the lawyer said to her client, not looking

at him. To the prosecutor, she said, "They'll understand that you did what you had to do. This'll be the biggest case of your career." She looked at Keller. "Both your careers."

"You keep saying that," the prosecutor said, "but I need more than the fairy tales you've been floating. I'm not going to ruin the reputation of good people without some corroboration."

"I'm sorry," Keller said. "I'm late to the party. I have no idea what either of you are talking about. How about we go off the record, a proffer, let me ask a few questions, and then you all can see if there's a deal to be made?"

Flanagan's lawyer crossed her arms, then nodded reluctantly. The prosecutor gestured for Keller to ask her questions.

Keller leaned in, looked at Flanagan. "I need to know why you visited Daniel Pine in prison."

Flanagan smirked.

The indictment said he'd cultivated a troupe of young girls—runaways, wannabe models, lost souls—and held parties for rich and powerful benefactors who funded his lavish lifestyle. He was, in short, a pimp for sycophants and pedophiles. One of his patrons had been the governor of Nebraska, who'd been forced to resign when one of the girls had the foresight to secretly videotape their encounters, then sold the tape and tales of debauchery to a tabloid. The Nebraska FBI field office soon uncovered the full sinister conspiracy. The hub of the wheel in the entire mess was Neal Flanagan.

The vile man finally spoke. "In addition to my, ah, parties, I used to do other work for the governor."

"What kind of work?"

"You know, special projects. Digging up dirt on political rivals, finding doctors with lax prescribing standards, keeping people quiet who needed to be quiet, stuff like that."

"You're a fixer," Keller said.

The man made a face, but he didn't deny it.

"So, anyhow, a reporter on Turner's payroll tipped him off that she heard someone had something on him—something big—but she didn't know what. And Turner, he'd been in office forever, so he had no idea what it might be." Flanagan chuckled. "I mean, he's so dirty, it could've been anything. But he had a bad feeling that the jig was up, that he needed to cash out, so he started looking for everything he had of value. And he decided to try to sell some pardons, so he had me make the rounds. Anybody who'd filed a pardon application who might have access to cash. Pine was on the list."

"You offered to get him a pardon for a payoff?"

Flanagan nodded.

"He's in prison. Why would you think he'd have any money?"

"He had the support of a lot of wealthy people, book offers, so it was worth a shot."

"What did he tell you?"

"He said the same thing you did: he ain't got the money."

Keller looked at him, waited for him to go on.

"I thought that was it, you know. We had other things in the fire, selling some legislative bills to lobbyists and whatnot, trying to get Turner his retirement fund."

"But . . ."

"Then I get a call. My encrypted business line I only give out to select people. You had to be in the know to get it." The guy sounded almost proud of all this.

Keller bit the inside of her cheek as he went on.

"So I get this call, and the guy—he won't tell me who he is, but I think I know—says he wants to be connected to someone who does wet work."

"A contract killer?" Keller asked.

"Yeah. I said I don't do that stuff. I'm a businessman. But for a fee I might be able to liaise. Friend-of-a-friend kind of thing."

The man was sleazy, but he made the job sound almost corporate. Keller was literally on the edge of her seat. She wanted to shake the guy to get to the point. But she had a sinking feeling she knew the trajectory of this story. That the person who called Flanagan hired a pro to kill Evan Pine. That Maggie had gotten a photo of the hitman, so he killed them all and staged the scene to look like an accidental gas leak. That he went after Matt to retrieve the photo.

"Let's get this straight," Keller said. "You get a call out of the blue asking you to connect someone with a contract killer and you just say, 'Okay, no problem'?"

Flanagan gave a one-shouldered shrug. "The caller knew things about my business."

"And you connected him with a contractor," the prosecutor chimed in, as if trying to speed things along. "A hitter no one seems to be able to verify even exists."

Keller was realizing why this story hadn't gone anywhere. The AUSA thought Flanagan was full of shit. And why wouldn't he? Flanagan was desperate, and the story crazy.

"I was just the go-between. I had no idea the man was gonna . . ."

The prosecutor waved him quiet. "We get it. You were a choirboy."

"So the contractor—I've never met him, just heard of him by rep—he doesn't talk directly with clients. He told me to get one hundred K and the name and photo."

"How did you reach him?" Keller asked. "And what do you mean you'd heard of him by rep? What had you heard?"

"If you're in my line of work, you hear stuff. The contractor, he had a rep as someone who did clean work, specialized in making things look like an accident."

"Did he have a name?"

"No, people just called him the Lip."

Keller felt goose bumps crawl up her arms. She thought of Maggie's photo of the man with the cleft lip scar.

"The caller drops the money, plus my cut, at a locker in the statehouse. And I take the cash and envelope to another drop for the Lip."

"Why not just wire funds or send encrypted files?"

"Because that's not how he wanted to do it," Flanagan said, as if it were the dumbest question he'd ever heard. Keller presumed that cash, paper, was the only way to ensure no digital footprints. The hit man was old-school.

"But, you know, I'm a curious type," Flanagan said.

Keller understood. The weasel not only hid to see who dropped off the envelope at the statehouse, he looked inside. No honor among thieves. "Who was the mark?"

"That guy on the news. From the TV show. Evan Pine."

"Who hired the Lip?" Keller said, tired of Flanagan holding her in suspense.

The lawyer put a hand on her client's arm, stopping him from responding. "He gets time served," she said to the AUSA.

Flanagan offered a greasy smile that Keller wanted to smash in with her fist. The prosecutor looked at Keller. He must've been able to tell from her demeanor that Flanagan had said something that resonated. *The Lip.* It corroborated his story, connecting the man with the cleft lip scar Maggie had photographed. It wasn't a coincidence. Flanagan was telling the truth.

"Make the deal," Keller said.

"This is above my pay grade," the prosecutor said. "I'll be back." He stepped out of the conference room.

When he returned fifteen minutes later, he looked at Flanagan's lawyer and nodded.

The lawyer looked at her disgusting client and said, "Tell her."

CHAPTER 61

EVAN PINE

BEFORE

"I'm tired, Daddy," Tommy said.

It was only six o'clock, but Evan supposed it had been a long day. The sun and heat—all the walking—took it out of you. Tommy looked flushed, and hadn't finished the dinner Evan had made him when Liv and Maggie went out for a long walk. It wasn't like him to leave any mac and cheese behind. Liv constantly forced bottled water on them all, so he didn't think Tommy was dehydrated. The half-empty bottle was next to Tommy's plate.

Evan put his hand on his son's forehead. A little warm. Probably nothing to worry about, but ever since the appendix scare, Evan never took routine symptoms for granted. Tonight, though, it seemed like simple fatigue. Hell, Evan could curl up and go to bed right now himself.

"Let's get you to bed, kiddo," Evan said. Tommy was already nodding off right at the table. Evan carried him to his room. He dug out Tommy's pj's from the suitcase, then lowered him to the bed.

"Arms up," Evan said.

His son lifted his arms, which were noodles. Evan tugged off Tommy's shirt. He gently slipped the pajama top over Tommy's head.

Tommy flopped on his back and Evan repeated the maneuver with the bottoms. Evan tucked him under the covers, positioned Sweet Bear next to him.

Evan gazed at his son. The rise and fall of his tiny chest. His handsome face. He kissed him on the head and clicked off the light.

Back in the living room, Liv and Maggie had returned from their walk. They seemed somber, subdued.

"Everything okay?"

Liv looked at Maggie. "Yeah. We're just tired—right, Mags?"

His daughter gave Liv an admiring look. Like they shared a secret and it was just for them. "Yeah, just tired," Maggie said.

"There's some mac and cheese or leftover spaghetti," Evan said. "Or I can make you something?"

"I'm not hungry," Liv said. "Too much food on this vacation." She retrieved a bottle of water from the refrigerator and took a drink.

"Maybe later," Maggie said. She also took a bottle of water, then went to the bedroom.

Alone with Liv, Evan said, "You sure everything's okay?"

Liv nodded. "We can talk about it more later, but she's okay, I promise."

Evan wondered if Maggie had told her about the reason for the trip. Their futile investigation. The couple who'd tricked Evan into coming to Tulum. That would explain the mood.

He needed to swallow his medicine and tell Liv himself. He needed to be honest with his wife, otherwise the magic of this trip wouldn't be real.

"I have something to tell you," he said.

Liv sat next to him at the dining table.

He took a long gulp of water, stalling, thinking how he'd explain. "I haven't been totally honest with you about the trip."

"When you said we could afford it? Yeah, I kinda figured."

"No, not that." He told her about the call from Charlotte, or at least the person pretending to be Charlotte. About Maggie tracking the phone. About the couple who had set him up. He felt foolish. He braced himself to tell her the rest—about his job, about their finances, about him taking the pills.

Before he could do so, Liv said, "Well, I have something to tell you too."

Evan tilted his head to the side.

His wife went to the bedroom and came out with a thin file folder. She handed it to him.

"Ron Sampson's wife gave this to me when I was in Nebraska. Her husband told her the file proved Danny was innocent."

"Why didn't you—" Evan stopped himself. It didn't matter.

"I knew we were here because of Danny," Liv said. "I didn't know what exactly you and Mags were up to, but I knew. And I'm sorry I didn't give you the file earlier.

We were having such a good time, you guys didn't seem completely consumed by the case, so I thought it could wait. Sampson's wife seemed out of her mind, and it looked like just random papers, and I thought there was nothing we could do here anyway, so I—"

"It's okay," Evan said softly. He opened the folder, which held three sheets of paper. Examining the first two pages, he said, "It's blood work. It looks like tests of samples of Charlotte's blood and Danny's." The file assigned numbers to the samples. Charlotte's 4215, Danny's 5094.

Evan inspected the third document, realizing it was a page from an evidence log. Why would Sampson have these in his files? Then it hit him. What if Charlotte's blood work had been switched out with someone else's? Because the murdered girl wasn't Charlotte. He caught himself. He was doing it again. And the separate log—a police chain of evidence record—didn't show anyone having access to Charlotte's sample. Then Evan realized that it did show someone—Ron Sampson—gaining access to sample 5094, Danny's blood.

Evan pointed to the log. "It looks like Sampson had access to Danny's blood sample for some reason. And he must've stolen the page in the log, not wanting anyone to know."

"So what's it mean?"

Evan shook his head, mad at himself. He'd spent thousands of hours combing through the files, pulling every thread, testing every theory. But he was drawing a blank. A complete and utter blank.

Liv said, "Why'd they test Danny's blood anyway?

His blood wasn't found at the crime scene. There was no DNA evidence against him."

"To prove he was the baby's father. His supposed motive," Evan said. Then it struck him like a bullet. "Holy shit. Holy *shit*!"

"What?" Liv said, not containing the excitement in her voice.

"Danny wasn't O negative blood type." He pointed a finger to sample 5094 on the report.

"You know Danny's blood type?"

"No," Evan said. "But I know he *couldn't be* O negative. Because I'm type AB."

Liv shook her head. She didn't understand.

"A parent with Type AB blood can't give birth to an O negative child."

"How do you know that? What—"

"Tommy's appendix," Evan said. His son's emergency surgery.

She was staring at him, confused.

"Tommy needed blood."

"Right, they got it from the blood bank when we were freaking out."

The terrible memory came back to him, that day in the ER. Evan rushing in late, the doctor explaining that Tommy's blood type was rare—type O negative—and he'd ordered some blood, but it would be faster if Evan could be the donor. Liv couldn't because she was type A positive.

"They asked me to give my blood," Evan said. "Tommy is O negative." He pointed at Danny's blood sample, which had the same blood type as Tommy.

Liv turned white.

"The doctor pulled me aside, said he didn't know how to tell me this, but I couldn't be a donor. A type AB cannot give blood or even be the parent of a type O negative."

Liv's eyes were wet. "You knew? All this time, and you knew?"

He nodded.

"But why?"

"Because he's still my son," Evan said. He'd long considered telling her that he knew Tommy wasn't his biological son, but he could never bring himself to do so.

Tears spilled from her eyes. "I'm sorry, I'm so, so—"

Evan put his hand on her shoulder, made a quiet *shh* sound, looking toward Maggie's room.

Liv didn't look well. She took a gulp of water. "I don't know what to—"

"Do you love me?" Evan said.

She looked at him.

"Olivia Pine, do you love me?"

"Yes." She searched his face, her own set in despair and confusion.

"Then there's nothing you need to say."

They sat in silence, Liv quietly trying to catch her breath, her hands shaking, her body quivering as if she were cold.

"I want us back," Evan whispered, not wanting Maggie to hear. "Like we were. I want our family back."

Liv sobbed, "That's all I ever wanted." She wiped her face with her hand.

They heard a noise from Maggie's room. Liv wiped

her face and Evan focused again on the computer, trying to act naturally.

Then Liv said it, the thing that caused the world to tilt: "If it wasn't Danny's blood—if he's not blood type O negative—then whose is it?"

Evan looked at her for what seemed like a really long time until her face drained of color again.

"Noah?" she said.

"No, his son. It explains why no one saw Charlotte after the party. It explains the rumors about another boy. It explains why Sampson would change the blood—he'd been friends with Noah. They switched Danny's blood for Kyle Brawn's."

"The baby wasn't Danny's," Liv said. "It was Kyle's."

Just then Maggie emerged from her bedroom. "What's wrong?" she said, looking at her parents. "What's going on?"

"We got him, Magpie," Evan said. "We got him."

CHAPTER 62

MAGGIE PINE

BEFORE

Maggie looked at her parents. "I can't believe it. Dad, you did it." Her voice broke; she was nearly vibrating with excitement.

Her father looked dazed. He squeezed Mom's hand, and said, "No, we all did it. And you get the most credit, Magpie. *You*."

Maggie felt a welling in her chest. "But Kyle Brawn. Why? I don't understand."

"I don't know why. Maybe he got her pregnant, and maybe he didn't want to let that get in the way of his life."

Her mom chimed in: "And maybe he had help covering it up."

"You think his dad . . ." Maggie didn't finish the words. Noah Brawn had been on their side, a Free Danny Pine warrior like them. She felt a wave of betrayal. He wasn't trying to help; he was creating a diversion. Kyle's friend Ricky was who'd identified the Unknown Party-goer. Noah Brawn was the one who got the filmmakers to focus on the Smasher.

"Who's the guy with the scar on his lip, and the lady?" Maggie asked.

"Maybe scam artists or weirdos. Or maybe some-one Noah hired to pull us off the trail when Detective Sampson's wife gave Mom the evidence."

Maggie still wasn't quite sure. Why would they lure them to Mexico? Why the elaborate ploy pretending Charlotte was alive? But those questions could wait. "I'm gonna go text Matt!"

Maggie was so excited, she felt almost light-headed. She darted into the bedroom and flew onto the bed. She pulled her phone from the charger and opened a text to send to Matt. Where to begin?

All at once, her thoughts were jumbled. The room was wobbling. She wasn't feeling well, and tried to sit up.

But she couldn't move.

What was happening?

Then she nearly leaped out of her skin.

A figure. A man stepping out of the closet! Maggie tried to jump up, tried to scream, but she was incapacitated. What the hell was going on? Her heart was banging in her chest, but it was as if she were paralyzed. Her body wouldn't listen to the commands of her brain. *Get up. Get up!* But she was motionless, petrified wood. The man moved in her line of sight.

Holy crap, it was him. *Help! Dad!* The words wouldn't come out. A terrible panic enveloped every part of her.

Maggie could still feel the phone in her hand. Her eyes could still move and they went to the glowing screen, the open text to Matt. Her thumb. She was having a hard time controlling it, but it moved. She managed to tap on the photo reel. Up popped all of her photographs. The last one, the couple. The man in her room! She tried to tap it, but her thumb wasn't listening.

She felt far away. She told her thumb to move again, and it bounced on the screen. The photo of the couple was attached to the text to Matt. She just needed to press send.

The man ran over to her. Just before he grabbed the device out of her hand, she thought she heard the swish of a departing text.

The man cursed to himself when he examined the phone.

She was drifting.

The man lifted her arm and then let it go. It fell like a rag doll. He crouched down, looked into her pupils. He had a plain face, forgettable except for a scar that went from his nostril to his lip.

Maggie's eyelids were heavy. She watched as the man took her water bottle and put it in a trash bag he was carrying. He was fiddling with her phone, connecting it to some type of handheld device. Then he wiped it down with a rag, positioned it back in her frozen hand.

The terror left her.

She felt warm and calm and loved and proud.

We did it, Daddy. We did it.

CHAPTER 63

OLIVIA PINE

BEFORE

The elation at uncovering the truth, that her son wasn't a murderer, the forgiveness from her husband for her infidelity, the pride in her daughter for never giving up, were overcome by a pain in Liv's chest.

"I feel strange," she said to Evan.

Evan examined her. His face turned to concern.

Her eyes closed. "I'm not—" When she opened them, she was on the floor. She tried to get up, but her limbs were frozen.

Her head fuzzy, she saw Evan stooped forward on the dining room table, his water bottle on its side, dripping onto the floor.

She didn't understand what was happening. She tried to speak, but her mouth wouldn't oblige.

Liv tried to reach out for her husband. But nothing would move. It was as if she were buried in sand.

Her thoughts were muddled. She started praying, but she didn't know why. A blessing for Evan and each of her children.

She felt a stabbing pain in her abdomen, then a jolt of fear when she saw a pair of feet. The shoes were covered in surgical booties.

She was a puppet with its strings cut.

More darkness, then spots before her eyes.

Her thoughts floated away in the blue ocean. She looked at Evan again. *Despite all of my mistakes, all of the grief, I would do it all over again.*

And then things went black.

CHAPTER 64

EVAN PINE

BEFORE

Evan was a pile of deadweight strewn across the table. He could feel water on his arm, dripping on his leg, but he couldn't move. He felt the wood from the tabletop on his cheek and watched in anger, in rage, as the man fiddled with his computer, his phone. Like he was running a program to wipe them clean. It was him, the man he and Maggie had tracked to the house. Evan tried to follow the man with his eyes, but even they wouldn't move. The man bent down, out of Evan's field of view.

When he rose, Liv was flung over his shoulder.

What are you doing? Let her go! The words were trapped inside him.

The man slowly lowered Liv to the couch, which was directly in Evan's line of sight. The man folded her hands, which were limp. Lifeless.

No. No!

The man grabbed a book on the end table and positioned it on her chest.

Evan needed to find the strength, the will, to overcome whatever drug, whatever poison he'd ingested. He felt dampness on his legs. Then he understood. The water bottles. The man had drugged them all. He remembered Tommy's sudden fatigue, Liv collapsing. His own blackout. His arm was spread out in front of him. He saw his fingers move. He realized that if he concentrated, put every bit of thought into it, he could move his hand. But he also knew he was fading fast. A pen was near his right hand. He watched his hand twitch. He needed to focus. His brain told his hand to grab the pen. He closed his eyes, visualized it. When he opened them, the pen was in his grasp.

The man was gathering the file Detective Sampson's wife had given Liv. He put the file and water bottles in a trash bag. He wore latex gloves.

Evan's vision blurred.

The man disappeared down the hallway, then returned.

Evan felt a wave of remorse. A wave of panic. A wave of consciousness fading.

He felt a poke on his shoulder. Evan's body had no reaction, no reflexes. He was hoisted over the man's shoulder.

Staring at the floor, the blood rushing to his head, he could see his dangling arm, the pen still clasped in his hand. Everything was far away, and for a surreal moment he wondered if the whole scene was a terrible nightmare.

Evan was feeling the pull of darkness. The world was

a Pink Floyd video. He focused every cell in his brain on his right hand.

Then he told his body to do it, use every remaining muscle under his control. And he stabbed the pen into the man's side. He heard a yell—"goddammit"—and the man dropped Evan to the floor.

The man's face twisted in anger. He kicked Evan in the head. Evan saw stars. Blood was dripping into his eyes. The world was fading.

The man staggered out of Evan's view again. When he returned, he had a kitchen towel pressed to his side, a large knife in his other hand.

He held the knife to Evan's neck, the cold blade under his Adam's apple. Terrified, Evan couldn't even close his eyes now to brace himself for what was next. But then the man moved away from him, and Evan no longer felt the steel on his neck.

The man seemed to be examining the mark he'd left on Evan's head from his boot.

He stood, hands on hips, studying Evan and the blood trail.

Then he seemed to make a decision. He carried Evan outside and dropped his limp body on the patio.

On his side, Evan could see everything. The man looked around, as if surveying whether Evan was visible from outside the property. He was gone again, but returned with what looked like food from the refrigerator. He poured leftover spaghetti meat sauce all over Evan. Dumped mac and cheese and bread near the gate. With his latex gloves covered in red from the spaghetti, he unlatched the gate for some reason, opened it a crack.

"I'll give you that," the man said to Evan. "You've got a lot of fight in you. We'll see how you do with the dogs."

Evan didn't know what he meant by that.

At that moment, he was in the football bleachers holding Liv's hand on a cold Friday night in October, the kids—Matt, Magpie, and somehow even Tommy—sitting beside them cheering at the spiral that had just connected and won the game. The quarterback tore off his helmet, his eyes searching the stands until he found them, pointing at Evan and his family, as if it were all for them.

And it was.

CHAPTER 65

MATT PINE

The front door was open. Matt walked from the foyer to the living room. Well decorated with crown molding and wainscoting, the room was filled with flowers and wreaths on stands.

Matt went into the kitchen and saw dishes in the sink, half-eaten slices of cake, finger food on plates, the remnants of the wake for his family.

Kyle Brawn walked into the kitchen, carrying more dishes.

"Matt! Oh crap, you scared me," he said. "We were just cleaning up. We had so many people wanting to pay their respects, your family was so loved, it was just so—"

Matt charged him.

Kyle Brawn flew backward, his arms flailing, the dishes flying, crashing to the floor. Kyle's back slammed against the large stainless-steel refrigerator. Matt's forearm jammed against Kyle's neck. Kyle's eyes bulged, wild with fear.

Matt screamed, *"You thought you got away with it!"*

Kyle clawed at Matt's forearm, trying to wedge his fingers in, relieve the pressure, allow himself to breathe. He looked Matt in the eyes and shook his head.

Matt felt hot tears on his cheeks. He told himself to calm down, get ahold of his emotions. If he pressed any harder, he'd crush Kyle's windpipe. But why shouldn't he?

Kyle's eyes were wet too, his hands still tugging at Matt's arm. He tried to speak, his voice little more than a rasp.

And then Kyle did something unexpected.

He gave up.

Kyle's arms fell to his sides, any fight in him gone. As if he were awaiting—welcoming—Matt to snap his esophagus.

Just a little more pressure, and Kyle would get what he wanted. But if he died, so many answers would die with him. Matt yanked his arm away.

Kyle raised his hands to his neck, then bent over, coughing. A sickening barking cough. He finally stood, his back still against the refrigerator door, and he slid to the floor.

For a moment Matt thought he'd exerted too much force and that Kyle's windpipe was destroyed. That Kyle was dying. But sitting amid the broken dishes and left-over food on the floor, Kyle started weeping.

It seemed like a long time, but it probably lasted only a few seconds. Matt still had an electrical charge tearing through him. He waited for Kyle to say something, but Kyle just sat there, his whole body trembling.

Matt recognized broken when he saw it.

"It was an accident," Kyle said at last.

"Liar," Matt said it calmly, but his voice was full of menace. "You killed her, then you wheeled her to the creek and framed my brother."

Kyle took a deep, juddering breath. Not saying anything, but he was shaking his head violently.

"It's over," Matt said. "The video. At the party. Danny was wearing only a tank top. *You* were wearing his jacket. It was *you* I saw that night. And you saw me, and all these years you let me think—"

"It was an accident," Kyle said again. "After everyone cleared out, she stayed behind. She was angry, and she said things that weren't true, and when I told her to get out of my house, she came at me, and I just pushed her away, and she fell and bumped her head. It was an accident." He was gulping for air.

Matt felt a slash of rage again. For a riotous moment he considered shoving Kyle's face to the floor, smashing it into the broken shards.

"What did Danny—or my family—ever do to you?"

"We weren't trying to hurt Danny. We tried to make it look like the Smasher."

It explained why Charlotte's head was caved in, the differences from the Smasher slayings Matt's dad was always talking about.

"All these years I thought my brother . . . But it was *you*. . . ." Matt felt a crushing remorse in his chest. He'd hated his brother. Resented his father. He'd been such a fool, such a stubborn fool. *"You!"* Matt screamed.

"Not him," a voice said from the kitchen doorway.

Noah Brawn stood holding a handgun. "Get up, Kyle," he said to his son.

Kyle just looked up at him, didn't move.

"Get up!" his father yelled.

Kyle rose slowly to his feet.

"Turn around," Noah Brawn said to Matt.

Matt turned and felt a gun barrel jabbed into his back. Noah marched Matt out of the kitchen and into the great room. Bookshelves lined the walls, high-end furniture, expensive art. Noah told Matt to turn around, put his hands on his head.

Kyle came in after them. Noah seemed to be debating what to do. He gazed out the large glass window to the backyard, which was illuminated by party lights strung along the patio.

Then he seemed to make a decision.

Matt didn't like the look on his face. "You covered for him? Framed my brother," Matt said.

"I never meant Danny to get the blame. I wouldn't do that to your mother. The state police had given the governor's office a heads-up about a serial killer in Kansas that they thought may have ventured into Nebraska. I called in tips to the prosecutor and Danny's defense lawyer linking Charlotte's murder to the Smasher."

Kyle chimed in: "That's why I got Ricky to report the Unknown Partygoer. We thought they would think he was the Smasher. We didn't know Danny would confess. It just all got out of hand."

Maybe it was the truth. It explained Charlotte's head. Explained why Ricky was the only kid who saw the Unknown Partygoer—creating a monster other than

Danny to blame things on. Explained why Ricky raced his car into a tree, from the guilt.

"Dad, put the gun down," Kyle said. "It's over. I'll tell them it was an accident. We can tell them I moved the body, that you and Ricky had nothing to—"

"Shut up," Noah said.

Images of that night were forming in Matt's mind, the pixels coming together: Charlotte finding a place to hide in the house when the police broke up the party. Finding Kyle in a bedroom. Kyle shit-faced, putting his hands on her, Charlotte pushing him away. Then she was on the floor, blood seeping from her head. Kyle called Ricky to help, and they brought her body to the creek. Kyle was still wearing Danny's jacket from the drunken party shenanigans. He saw Matt on the trail, panicked, called his father for help.

Maybe Kyle and Ricky were disagreeing over calling Noah—the fight Jessica saw the night Charlotte was killed. But Jessica had referred to the person as Ricky's date.

Then it came to him. Maybe Kyle wasn't interested in Charlotte. Maybe she stumbled upon something she shouldn't have. The class president and the school's star running back in a compromising position.

"She found out you and Ricky were *together*. Caught you. And you killed her to keep your secret." It was so unnecessary. Adair wasn't the most progressive place, but being gay wasn't exactly something to kill over.

Kyle shook his head. "Dad," he said again, "put the gun down."

Noah kept his aim trained on Matt.

Matt understood then that Noah had no intention of letting him walk out of there.

"You won't get away with it," Matt said. "The video shows Kyle in my brother's jacket. The FBI knows." A lie, but he had to try.

"The video proves nothing."

"Then why?" Matt said, his voice pleading. "Why kill them?" His voice broke. "Why kill my family?" Matt was taking a leap. But everything had happened after that video had appeared. And the only person who had the resources to kill his family, hire a professional, as Keller had speculated, was Noah Brawn. Kyle was a law student who relied on his father for support, and Ricky was disabled.

"It wasn't supposed to go that way. I loved your mother," Noah said.

The words hit Matt like a two-by-four in the head. He was right.

"What does he mean, Dad?" Kyle asked. "What's he talking about?"

Matt shouted again, "He's talking about how he paid someone to kill my family! To protect *you* for killing Charlotte. And her baby."

Kyle Brawn looked confused, then gut-punched.

"You *wouldn't*." Kyle spit the words at his father. He looked at his dad, his eyes filling with tears. "You *didn't*!"

Noah ignored him. "Let's go," he said to Matt. He gestured to the sliding back doors.

"Oh my god," Kyle said. "That's why you were acting so weird about that cop's wife giving Mrs. Pine evidence. The blood work she was talking about. It was *you*. Charlotte wasn't lying." Kyle started breathing heavily, like he was hyperventilating.

"We'll talk about this later, son."

"*No! We'll talk about this now!* I told you it was an accident. I told you we should tell the police what happened. She was saying all those things about you, and I just pushed her to get her out of there. But you . . ."

"What? Saved your ass. It would have ruined your life."

"And yours," Kyle said. "She said you forced her."

Matt felt the wind knocked out of him.

"She was lying," Noah said.

"She said she had proof." Kyle took in a ragged gasp of air. "Said the baby was yours!"

Noah turned to his son, the gun momentarily not pointed at Matt's chest. "It wasn't like that."

"When I took you to see her at the creek. I thought she was still breathing. That she'd moved. I thought—" Kyle and his father faced each other. "But you—you took that rock and—"

Matt lunged for the weapon in Noah Brawn's hand, thinking it was his last chance. He felt the cold metal in his grip as he tugged to get the gun away from him.

Noah kneed Matt in the gut. Matt held on, the air stolen from his lungs.

But Noah managed to release Matt's hold.

The gun fired.

Matt was on the ground. His shoulder burned white-hot. He touched it, and his hand came away covered in deep red blood.

Noah stood a few feet away, standing over Matt, the gun pointed at his face. Matt lunged for the weapon, violently heaving Noah's arm, running on only adrenaline and rage. The world was a blur, and then the gun discharged again.

When Matt reopened his eyes, Kyle was on the floor. *"No!"* Noah Brawn ran to his son. Red seeped through Kyle's shirt, his eyes distant.

"Noooo!" Noah wailed, cradling his son now.

Matt was still on the ground, the blood loss and pain making him light-headed. He needed to get out of there. Matt reached to pull himself up, when Noah's head snapped over to him.

"You and your fucking family. You just couldn't let it go." Noah picked up the gun from the floor next to his dead son.

"So you killed them? A six-year-old boy? A teenage girl? The woman you claimed to love?" Matt clutched the bookshelf and pulled himself to his feet. His head was spinning, his shirt soaked in red.

"None of that was supposed to happen. When the video appeared, I just wanted your father to let things go. Then your sister found *him,* saw his face, took a picture of him in Mexico. He said he had no choice. I would've never hurt your mom. I just wanted your father to . . ." He let the words die.

Noah wanted Dad out of the picture. Maybe Mom would come back to him. Or maybe he wanted to end the Pine investigation once and for all by killing the driving force behind it.

Sirens wailed in the distance.

Noah looked at his lifeless son, still cradled in his lap. His eyes turned dark. He gently lowered Kyle's body to the floor with one hand, pointing the gun at Matt with the other. He rose to his feet.

It was over. Matt could see it in the man's face.

Noah said, "I want you to die knowing that your brother will rot in prison for the rest of his life. And that the world will know you confessed to hiring someone to kill your parents for the insurance. That you killed my son."

He was going to get away with it all—again. Say that Matt and Danny hired the killer for the insurance money. Say that Matt broke in and attacked Kyle, and that Noah killed Matt in self-defense.

Fuck that. Not today.

Matt channeled every football move he'd ever seen his brother perform and barreled at Noah, ducking under the gun and flinging his arms around Noah's waist as they both flew onto the floor. Matt scrambled on top of him and began punching, pummeling his face, as Noah clawed at him, blood everywhere. When Noah stopped moving, Matt staggered to his feet.

Noah said something unintelligible through the snot and blood.

Matt reached above to the bookshelf, removing a marble bookend. He thought of Charlotte on the bank of that creek. Still alive, fighting for her life like Danny was right now. He thought of his father and mother and little brother and sister. And he raised the heavy bookend over his head.

"Matt, no!" a voice yelled from behind him.

He turned and saw Agent Keller, a group of local officers behind her, one of them with his gun drawn.

"You don't want to do this, Matthew."

"He took everything," Matt sobbed.

"We know, Matt. We have the proof," Keller said. "But don't let him take you, too."

Matt looked down at Noah Brawn, who was shielding his face with a hand.

Matt raised the marble bookend as high as he could and with every ounce of strength he had left, he hurled it toward the floor.

Excerpt from
A Violent Nature

Season 1/Season Finale

EXT. STONE CREEK - DAY

A beautiful day. The sun shining. The sound of water flowing down the creek.

C.U. on bank where Charlotte's body was found.

> EVAN PINE (V.O)
> People think I'm obsessed, that I'm crazy. That I'm selfish and a fool. But what would you do if your son was convicted for a crime he didn't commit? If he was locked up for the rest of his life and you knew in your bones he was innocent? If your family was broken?
>
> You have two choices when you're confronted with your every last fear:
>
> Give up or fight like hell.
>
> And I'm going to fight until my last breath for Danny, for Liv, for Matt, for Maggie, for Tommy—for Charlotte—to uncover the truth.

FADE TO BLACK

EPILOGUE

MATT PINE

AFTER

"This your brother, Affleck?"

"That's what I said, Reggie. Now, don't look at the camera. Just play the game like always." Matt aimed the Blackmagic camera at the two men playing chess in Washington Square Park, the sun lowering in the sky. Danny had arrived early, before Matt finished the shoot for his short film, and Reggie seemed fascinated with him.

"You was the one who was inside?" Reggie said.

"I am," Danny said. "Fishkill."

"Shoot, how'd a pretty boy like you survive the Fish Killer?" Reggie looked at the chess opponent sitting across from him for affirmation.

Matt's brother smiled. "Kept my head down, I guess."

"And ass to the wall," Reggie cackled.

Danny didn't mention that he almost didn't survive prison. That he'd been hospitalized for nearly a month.

"I heard your bro got you out?" Reggie said.

Matt lowered the camera, defeated. "No," he said.

"My family got him out." Matt pictured Maggie and his father poring over mountains of evidence piled on the desk in their home office, his mother plodding off to Nebraska to plead with the governor about a pardon.

Danny rested a hand on Matt's shoulder. "I wouldn't be here without this guy." It was partially true, but credit went to the new governor, whose first act in office was to push the board to pardon Danny. The governor's predecessor, Noah Brawn, would be spending the rest of his days in a cell at the very prison where Danny was first incarcerated.

"Damn, Affleck. Maybe there's hope for you after all."

Matt raised the camera. "Seriously. I'm losing light. And we have someplace to go before sundown."

Reggie made a noise of annoyance and turned back to the chessboard. Mumbling to himself, he said, "Who's gonna watch a movie about two old men playing chess anyway?"

An hour later, Matt and Danny sat at an outdoor café on Fourteenth Street. Matt had a tall mug of beer in front of him, the glass sweating, the brew cold and perfect on a hot summer evening. Danny sipped a glass of water. He'd given up alcohol.

"How long until it happens?" Danny asked.

Matt checked the time on his phone. "They say at eight twenty."

The sun was starting to appear between the gap in the street grid. They'd know it was time when crowds took to the streets with their phones.

"Remember our first Manhattanhenge?" Matt asked.

Danny looked up, trying to conjure the memory. "How old were you? Five? Maybe six?"

"Six."

"Like Tommy," Danny said.

Matt felt a rush of emotion.

"What was he like? I mean, Dad and Mom talked a lot about him, but I never got to . . ." Danny let the thought trail off.

"He was funny, a mama's boy."

"Like you at that age."

Matt smiled.

"I remember now," Danny said. "That was the trip when you had the allergy attack when we visited Mom's friend who had a cat. You were wheezing and you scared the shit out of everyone."

Matt had an image of himself in an unfamiliar bathroom, his mother filling the room with steam to try to open up his lungs. Her soothing voice. Keeping him calm. Making him feel safe.

"You were a real drain on the family. Everything was about you," Danny said, tongue in cheek. A recognition of what they'd given up for him. Then Danny's face turned serious. "Matty, I want you to know that—"

Matt held up a hand. "Don't."

Danny swallowed, stared at his brother, mist in his eyes.

"Interrupting something, ladies?" a voice said.

Matt turned and saw Ganesh squinting at the sun. Behind him, Kala, looking exquisite, her skin bathed in golden sunlight. They pulled up two chairs at the small table, Kala wedging herself close to Matt.

Matt looked over at his brother, who gave him a small nod of approval.

"Where is everybody?" Matt asked. He'd invited the entire gang from Rubin Hall.

Ganesh shrugged. "Curtis is probably at a meeting for his cult, and watching the sunset is probably too symbolic of toxic masculinity in the patriarchy for Sofia. And we don't want Woo-jin here; he'll block the sun."

"Remind me," Matt said, "why are we friends with this guy?"

Kala shook her head like she hadn't the foggiest. "They're on their way," she said.

Ganesh disappeared into the bar. Danny then stood, put some money on the table.

"Where are you going?" Matt said. "You're gonna miss it."

People were making their way into the street, smartphones in the air, twisting around to catch themselves in photos of the sun as it centered between the buildings.

"I just love to walk out here in the open," Danny said. "I'll catch up with you later."

Matt watched Danny make his way down the street, his back to the sun, still that cocksure strut. He had a limp now, a remnant from the prison attack, but otherwise it was still the stride of a confident man. Two girls stopped Danny, said something, like they recognized him from all the coverage of his release from prison. Danny took a selfie with them, then kept moving.

Matt had only one regret: that his father wasn't there to see the sight.

Kala reached for his hand.

A car pulled next to their table. The street was jammed with pedestrians filling their Instagram feeds with photos of the sun slowly dipping below the horizon. The car's windows were down, music blaring.

"Numb" by Linkin Park.

"Everything okay?" Kala asked.

Matt looked her in the eyes.

Those eyes.

"It is now."

SARAH KELLER

AFTER

"I'm scared," Keller said quietly into her satellite phone.

"No shit, I'm scared too, and I'm three thousand miles away, not in some hut in Colombia," Bob said.

He never tried to tell her how to feel, always validated her emotions, which was weirdly comforting. Keller never used to be afraid of anything. But that was before she had so much to lose.

"Is the Texan there?" Bob asked.

Keller looked over at Cal Buchanan, the Chicago field office SAC who'd helped her raid Marconi LLP. Cal stood next to several hard-looking men holding large guns and wearing tactical gear. As a result of the Pine case, Keller had been promoted to head of the New York office when her boss Stan Webb was elevated to D.C. It paid to make the president's daughter happy. With the new position, Keller could pull together the teams she wanted. Some jobs required finesse, some needed a BSD.

Cal was stealing looks at her like he was getting anxious that they'd miss their chance.

"I want to talk to the twins," Keller said, still feeling the nerves.

"You talk to them *after*."

Bob was right. *Think positive.*

"I'll talk to you later," Bob said. No hesitation there.

"I love you," she said.

"You more. And, hey, you got this, G-woman."

Keller severed the connection, collected herself. She went over to the group huddled near the only window of the run-down shack.

"We've got someone coming up to the place," the spotter said from the window.

"Tough business staying off the grid," Cal Buchanan said. "How in the hell'd you find him?"

"Airline records," Keller said without elaboration. She went over to the spotter, took his binoculars, peered through a crack in the blinds.

A man carrying a plastic jug of water approached the doorway to a shack even smaller than the one they were in. He was tall, thin, had what looked like a freshly shaved head. He wore a mustache. But the 'stache didn't fully cover the scar—from a cleft palate—that cut from his right nostril to his lip.

The man went inside the shack and Keller handed the agent the binoculars. "It's him."

The team stood at attention, the sound of the men locking and loading filling the room.

"You can stay in here," Cal said. "We've got this. I've got the best breach men in the business."

Keller thought of a fearless young woman named Maggie who always charged in. She got in the stacked position with the rest of the team. Cal gave her an admiring look.

Then she and the men charged out the door.

ACKNOWLEDGMENTS

This novel came about in the most old-fashioned of ways—a writer and an editor sitting in a grim New York City watering hole talking about books and life—and an idea I had for a story about a family torn apart and ultimately brought together by tragedy. Joseph Brosnan, you're a genius, and I'd be lucky to spend the rest of my career benefiting from your sage guidance and vicious pen.

I'm blessed to be represented by the best literary agent in the business, Lisa Erbach Vance. I'd walk through fire for you, Lisa, which is fitting because you've already done so for me.

I also extend my deepest gratitude to the talented and dedicated team at St. Martin's Press, including Kelley Ragland, who threw her considerable force behind this book; Martin Quinn, Steve Erickson, and Kayla Janas, who expertly made sure the world knew about it; and Kaitlin Severini, who fixed all of my mistakes.

Special thanks to friends who read early drafts or

helped with the medical, State Department, and technology research, including Reeves A., Lou B., Mara B., Deborah C., Kimberley H., Brian H., Dawn I., Stanton J., Robert K., Barry L., Doug L., Tony M., Sheila S., Carmen V., and "the Squad" from Recanati, Italy (Stephanie G., Jennifer R., Lynn S., and Charlie S.).

I must also recognize the Center on Wrongful Convictions for its harrowing work, and the exonerees who spent years of their lives in prison for crimes they did not commit. I drew inspiration from some of their stories in the exceptional *Anatomy of Innocence: Testimonies of the Wrongfully Convicted* (Liveright, 2017).

Of course, I must thank my family. In creating the Pines, I borrowed from my children: Jacob's tales of life, friendship, and chess at NYU; Emma's tenacious ways and our hours binge-watching Netflix true-crime dramas; and Aiden's love of movies and travel—and his admiration of a rogue country club caddie master. Kids: *You have my whole heart. You always did.*

And none of this would be possible without my wife, Trace. Like everything else, *Every Last Fear* is for you.

Read on for an excerpt from

THE NIGHT SHIFT –

the next exciting novel from Alex Finlay,
available soon in hardcover from Minotaur Books!

PROLOGUE

NEW YEAR'S EVE 1999

The night was expected to bring tragedy.

Planes falling from the sky. Elevators plunging to earth. World markets collapsing.

A digital apocalypse.

But Y2K was an otherwise typical Friday night at the Blockbuster Video in Linden, New Jersey. Steve had been store manager for six months now, and it was sure as shit a step up from his last job at the Taco Bell. Where his clothes always smelled of cooked meat and grease, and where cadres of drunken teens arrived loudly around eleven until he kicked them out at 2 A.M.

Here, they closed at ten, sharp. The customers were polite. Tonight, mostly couples looking for a rom-com or "something scary."

They didn't call Steve "pizza face," on account of his acne; didn't mock his uniform or leave smashed enchiritos all over the floor. His employees were better here too, more or less. The night shift included four sweet, albeit mischievous, teenage girls. All juniors or seniors, like the Taco Bell hooligans. Hell, like Steve himself only a few years ago, but somehow the girls treated him like he was their embarrassing dad. After only a few months on the job, he truly felt for their real fathers.

"Can I go on break?" Mandy said, shoving a VHS cartridge into the store's machine. It was the bane of the job, proof that nobody read the BE KIND, PLEASE REWIND stickers on the tapes.

Steve studied the long checkout line, the new girl, Ella, fumbling at the register next to him. "We close in half an hour," he said, exasperated. "Can't you wait? I need you to take register three."

"But *Steeevie,*" Mandy said, lowering her voice to a whisper, "I have *girl* issues."

Steve blew out a loud breath. Unless he'd missed something in Sex Ed, it was impossible to have *girl* issues every single weekend, but what could he do?

"I can cover for her," Katie said, coming in from the cold, snowflakes in her hair, a pile of videos stacked in her arms from emptying the metal return receptacle stationed in the parking lot. She was the most responsible of the group, a Catholic school kid, a rule-follower. But even she was a pain in the neck. Just an hour ago, he'd had to remind all the girls not to venture out to the parking lot alone. The buddy system—was that so friggin' hard to grasp?

"Make it fast," Steve said to Mandy. "And where's Candy?"

Candy O'Shaughnessy was Mandy's partner in

crime, the other perpetr... ...

Inc. Employee Handbook call... ...

Though the store was four thousa... ...

open space, Candy always managed to d... ...

constantly gave him attitude, and once smuggl... ...

coolers into the break room. And Steve remained co...

vinced that *she* was the one who put *Friday the 13th*

inside the box for *101 Dalmatians*. Those parents had

given him an earful. Said their kid would need therapy.

Join the club.

"I think she was in the kids' section," Mandy said

with a smirk as she sauntered off to the break room.

Steve shook his head as he reached around the theft

censors at the door and handed the customer the small

plastic bag full of movies.

By closing time, neither Candy nor Mandy had emerged.

They'd be hearing about this. For sure. Not cool.

Steve instructed Ella to work the door, unlocking and

locking the dead bolt to let customers out but ensuring no

one got in. She could handle that much, he thought. He

told Katie to close out the registers. He'd go deal with the

other two. Always something. He just wanted to get out

of there, stop by Dad's house for a Pabst to celebrate sur-

viving another year before the old man fell asleep. Then

maybe catch more beers at Corky's Tavern, watch the

ball drop on the TV behind the bar, see if there'd been

any real chaos from the computer bug the news wouldn't

shut up about. Not exactly "party like it's 1999"—if he

never heard that song again it would be too soon—but it

beat being alone at his crap apartment.

pes, past the
k room. It was

dy, as he noticed
owling. If they were
od . . . He'd told them
they weren't supposed
could get in big trouble

with —

He froze two sets of legs on the floor jutting out from be ne break room table.

As fear shredded through him, Steve felt someone grab a fistful of his hair and yank his head back. Then a strange coldness at his throat.

He was on the floor now, an ugly gurgle emanating from his neck. He watched as the figure turned out the break room lights. It felt like a small eternity before the door flew open, a burst of light filling the room. The sound of teenage chatter abruptly dying.

Steve wanted to call out, to warn them. But he felt his body convulsing and the world turning dark.

The last thing he heard was the screams.

DAY 1

FIFTEEN YEARS LATER

CHAPTER 1

ELLA

APRIL 2015

Ella pops a Xanax as she waits for the valet to take her keys. Driving into Manhattan always stresses her out. The frenetic confluence of cabbies rage-driving, cops jetting by with sirens blaring, pedestrians all but challenging you to run them over as they step defiantly into the street.

What the fuck is she doing here?

Last time, she'd promised herself that it would be the *last time*.

A young guy in a bellhop uniform stands at her window now. She hums down the glass.

"Checking in?" he asks. He's in his twenties and gives her the once-over.

"No, just meeting a friend."

He nods as if enjoying the euphemism. Sure, in that outfit, *a friend*.

Ella slips out of the car and palms the kid a five. She catches him stealing a look at the bill, unimpressed.

Give her a break. She's a therapist making $30K a

year, for fuck's sake, not some businessman on an expense account.

Inside the marble lobby of the Carlyle hotel, she makes a beeline for the bar. Against all sound medical judgment—she'd taken a pharmacology class at Wellesley—she pops another tiny blue pill.

She feels eyes on her as she enters the mahogany room. Faux old-money decor and the din of Franz Liszt from the gray-haired pianist trying not to look defeated at the culmination of his music career.

Ella should talk. She's barely making her half of the rent, coming into the city so she won't bump into one of her fiancé's friends. Or a client from her fledgling practice. She thinks about sixteen-year-old Layla from their session that morning. She's cutting herself again. Layla didn't need to explain why. Ella understands.

Surveying the bar, Ella snags the look of a man in an expensive suit holding a tumbler of Scotch. They always drink Scotch. And love to talk about it. The special barrels this, the unique region that. Beyond the Scotch prattle, most tend to have a pale band of skin on their left ring finger. Ella doesn't bother to take off her engagement ring. The Scotch guys don't care.

The man smiles at her.

He'll do.

Ella is always surprised how easy it is. She doesn't need Tinder when she has this black dress.

So she goes to meet her new friend.

A few hours later, her phone chimes. She's in a hotel room now, the only light from under the door. On these frolics, she always sets the alarm for 5 A.M. It avoids awkward morning-after talk.

But it isn't the sound of the alarm. It's an incoming call. She extracts herself from under Rick's hairy arm. She wonders if that's his real name. He looks like a Rick. Though he probably thought she looks like a Candy. Something sweet but bad for you. Much like her old friend, whose name she borrowed. She always uses their names. Candy, Mandy, Katie. She has no idea why.

"Hello," she whispers into the phone. She scuttles quietly to the bathroom, scooping up the black dress off the floor. The marble is cool under her feet.

"Ella, I'm sorry to call this late. It's Dale."

"Mr. Steadman?" After all these years she can't bring herself to call him by his first name. You're always a kid to the teachers in your life. She hasn't spoken to him in a year, not since her former teacher and now principal at her old high school had her meet with students in the wake of a school shooting in a neighboring township. "Is everything okay?" She feels drumbeats in her chest. *Why would he be calling at this hour? Could it be? Could they finally have caught him? No, good news rarely arrives in a wee-hours call.*

"Something awful has happened. I know it's asking a lot. But can you come to RWJ?"

Come to the hospital? Now?

Before she can ask, Mr. Steadman says, "There's been a—one of my students needs your help."

She wants to protest. Wants to make an excuse. But she can't. Not after everything Mr. Steadman has done for her.

"Sure, of course," she says. "I'm visiting a friend in the city. I can get there in about an hour."

"I wouldn't drag you out here if I thought there was someone else who could . . ." He trails off.

Ella's head is swirling. She's exhausted. Still tipsy. Confused. She composes herself. "Can you tell me what this is about?"

Mr. Steadman's voice catches. "Four girls were attacked at an ice cream shop in Linden. Only one survived. She needs someone who understands, who can—"

"I'm on my way," Ella says killing the line, knowing she's uniquely qualified to help this girl.

Knowing what it's like to be the only one who made it out alive.

CHAPTER 2

The parking lot of the Robert Wood Johnson University Hospital is covered in a spring fog. The lot is nearly empty save for a gathering of police cars. A woman in scrubs paces outside the front doors, talking on a cell phone.

Ella grips the steering wheel even though she's parked, and looks down at her bare legs. She debates going home to change into something more professional. But Mr. Steadman sounded uncharacteristically rattled. He's usually a rock.

She takes a look at herself in the visor mirror, thumbs her smearing eye makeup. Climbing out of the car, she decides the fuck-me heels are a bit much. She reaches back for her gym bag, pulls out her sneakers.

The woman in scrubs is still pacing out front. Ella sees her discreetly put a fist to her mouth, suck in a deep breath, followed by a plume of vape mist.

We all have our secrets.

The receptionist inside barely gives her a second

look. The woman has probably seen it all working the ER night shift. Ella once dated a med student who'd done an ER residency rotation, and he regaled her with tales of the guy with a Barbie stuck up his ass, the PCP fiend who'd eaten two of his own fingers during a bad trip, the construction worker with a nail deep in his brain yet still conscious and talking. A therapist in nightclub attire probably didn't make the Top 10 for weird.

The receptionist says something into the phone, then waves Ella inside the treatment area. The door makes a jarring buzz and Ella walks into a large room bathed in fluorescent light, beeping and voices echoing from behind beds surrounded by blue curtains. At the far end, she sees Mr. Steadman talking to a group of men. Three uniformed police officers and a stern-looking man with a mustache whose polo shirt is tucked tight into his jeans. He and Mr. Steadman seem to be having a disagreement.

For a split second, Ella feels a flight instinct. A memory slithers into her head, the procession of cops, doctors, and social workers asking the same questions. *Did you get a look at him? What do you remember? Did he touch you?* She looks at the floor for a moment, trying to collect herself, then catches a glimpse of her bare thighs again and is transported back to the exam room, her legs in stirrups.

Ella had been nonresponsive after the attack. The hospital's psych team was unsuccessful, and Ella's parents were at a loss. The school sent over Mr. Steadman. He wasn't trained in trauma response, he was merely the fill-in for a guidance counselor out on maternity leave. The cool teacher. Young, good-looking. The one the moms fawned over. At the same time, he was capable, no-nonsense, the kind of person who you wanted in charge, which is probably why they later made him the school's principal.

Mr. Steadman sees her and gives a small wave. He doesn't react to the muffled screams coming from a curtained room near the huddle of men. A doctor emerges from the room, grimacing. He says something to the group gathered with Mr. Steadman, shaking his head. Mr. Steadman puts a reassuring hand on the doctor's shoulder, then walks over to Ella.

"Thanks for coming. I'm sorry to interrupt your night," Steadman says, the only acknowledgement of her getup.

He fills her in. After midnight, the teenage employees of the Dairy Creamery were found murdered in the back room of the ice cream shop. The mother of two of the girls, sisters, got worried when they didn't return home from their shift and didn't respond to texts. The mother is sedated now.

"There was a survivor?" Ella knows the answer. It's why she's here.

Mr. Steadman nods. "A student at my school. She didn't work there. We think she was just a customer. Maybe interrupted him." Mr. Steadman takes a cleansing breath. "I was hoping you could talk to her. The doctors and detectives aren't getting anywhere. She's— well, you'll see. The Union County prosecutor called me, since . . ."

He didn't need to complete the sentence, the reason clear: because it worked for Ella after Blockbuster.

"But she won't talk with me or anyone else or let the doctors examine her. I hoped you could try before they're forced to sedate her."

"I'm not sure I have the—"

"You're our best hope. And I won't be able to hold them off for much longer." Mr. Steadman directs his gaze to the man in the polo and jeans, a detective, she presumes, who undoubtedly is itching to interview the girl. A killer's on the loose.

"What's her name?"

"Jessica Duvall, but she goes by Jesse."

"Where are her parents? Won't she talk to them?"

"She's in foster care. I'm not sure why. She's new to my school, and they don't give us much information."

The murmuring from the huddle of cops grows louder. They're looking at Ella.

She takes a deep breath and steps into the room.

CHAPTER 3

KELLER

Sarah Keller reaches for her phone, which is pinging on the nightstand. Three texts at 5:30 a.m. She's been lying awake for an hour anyway. Feeling the two sets of feet inside her belly kicking wildly, fallout from the Thai food last night. She spent those sixty minutes listening to Bob snore. Worrying about keeping up with her job and money when the twins arrive. In their five-year marriage, she's never known Bob to lie awake about anything. Not a worrier, her husband.

She reads the texts from her boss.

LOCALS NEED ASSISTANCE.
UNION COUNTY.

That's unusual. The FBI usually doesn't get involved with local law enforcement unless it's something big— terrorism, kidnapping, or the like—and Keller's still a relatively junior agent.

Another text pings. A link to a news story. She feels a flutter in her chest as she reads the details, which are still sketchy. A mass killing at an ice cream store in Linden, three dead. A possible survivor.

She taps out a return text.

SURE, NEED ME THERE RIGHT NOW?

There's a long delay as the dots pulse while he types. He likely thumbed out an annoyed response—*of course, now*—then erased it. A good boss deletes annoyed messages before sending them. And despite his cold, Swiss-banker demeanor, Stan Webb is a good boss.

As she struggles to get her giant, eight-and-a-half-month-pregnant body out of the bed, the text finally arrives.

YES.

Always an economy of words with Stan. She'll call him from the car.

After showering—a precarious endeavor of stepping into the tub without crashing to the floor—Keller puts on her maternity suit, one of two that still fits. She smells something coming from the kitchen. She's not one to buy into old wives' tales about pregnancy, but her senses really are heightened.

Bob's out of bed now and washing a pan in the sink. On the small kitchen table, he's set a plate with scrambled eggs and grilled tomatoes on a bagel. All month he's been preparing recipes from a website catering to pregnant women.

"You didn't have to get up," she says.

"When Clarice Starling gets a text at five in the morning, I know I'd better cook or my bambinos will only get a PowerBar to keep 'em going." He pulls back the chair for her to sit.

"I've gotta run. Stan needs me to—"

"Ah, ah, ah, when Stan has two humans in his belly he can tell you to hurry up." Bob sits across from her. He has bags under his eyes and looks ragged.

"What time did you get home last night?" she asks. He's a soundman at a recording studio, his schedule at the whim of the artists.

"Three or so," he says. "A rowdy polka band," he adds, as if that explains the late night. She doesn't know if he's kidding. It's hard to tell sometimes.

"You shouldn't have gotten up, I can get my own—"

"I almost forgot, I made you something." He jumps out of his chair and retrieves a Thermos from the counter.

"Please, not the pregnancy smoothie you've been going on about?"

He raises his eyebrows up and down.

When she finishes the bagel, Bob helps her out of the chair.

"I'm pregnant, not incapacitated, you know."

Bob doesn't reply. He kneels so he's facing her belly. Looking down at his bald head—the dome surrounded by the donut of hair that is ironic without him intending it to be—Keller feels a surge of warmth run through her.

"Take care of your mama, little Feebies," Bob tells her tummy.

Keller has never discharged her firearm in the line of duty, yet her husband treats her like she's a serial-killer hunter.

Today, though, maybe she is.